REDEMPTION

REDEMPTION

A FALLEN EMPIRE NOVEL

JEN FINELLI

Cannon Publishing
https://www.cannonpublishing.us/

CHAPTER ONE

Ken Kamakura

HE NEVER KNEW what he didn't know.

Former Specialist Ken Kamakura squeezed his narrow shoulders past the heavy bodies in the crowded bar, wrinkling his nose against the tangy scent of urine and—stale pasta? Parmesan? Armpit? He envied the slender Lachan who pushed ahead of him, tail flickering as its four hind legs carried it scuttling across the cement floor around the other patrons until, like a ghost—or perhaps, more like a snake—it was gone. Ken himself was thin, but not that thin.

He rehearsed his spiel to himself as he scanned the crowd for the fabled corner booth. He'd heard his contact was an Illyrian, and he'd spent the morning scouring the internet for cultural tips, since he'd never actually—well—it wasn't like he hadn't seen the occasional Trader's ship docked back home on Alpha Prime, but they weren't as common there at the heart of the Terran Union as out here on its fringe planets. He didn't have any experience negotiating with them, or anyone, really: because he'd enlisted in the Terran military almost the moment he was eligible as an adolescent, this was literally his first time being interviewed for a job.

That was one of the things he probably shouldn't mention—Illyrians didn't seem to like military folks much. He wouldn't lie about where he cut his teeth as a medic, but it was probably best not to appear too hooah.

At least, that's what the anonymous strangers on the city's cobbled-together computerized information network said. Ken would have to stop relying on intranet searches like these at some point: while the planet he'd grown up on had various interconnected private and public networks, and most inhabited worlds with basic computer technology had *something*, no one had real access to the interplanetary Ansible FTL comms network his parents' generation had been used to, not after the Secession Wars. Many war-torn worlds didn't even have the luxury of planet-based internet anymore—and where he was hoping to go, they'd probably never had the luxury at all.

Where was this guy? So far Ken saw no sign of any red-faced, sharp-toothed, horned people that matched the interviewer's description. Ken craned his neck as someone's sweat-slick back slid past his chest. If the music and shouting weren't enough noise already, the rhythmic thunk of ancient-tech heloship blades blared from the wall screen. *Some kind of educational long-form news feature.* Onscreen, the airborne vehicle's open door showed a teeming mass of life forms fleeing from something below as a gray, hook-nosed mammalian reporter with a thick Grausian accent shouted into the camera: "Here on Eden Crescent, familial clans of iridescent, bipedal Edenians war for technological supremacy on a world with no indigenous space travel. A former Imperial territory, Eden Crescent was deserted by its rulers when Loyalists were ordered to migrate to the New Empire. Claimed alternately by Terran and Charee factions in the Secession Wars, the declaration of the Demilitarized Zone saw the planet returned to its native inhabitants, but at the cost of peace as—"

"Turn on the game!" someone roared. "No one wants to hear those poor bastards squeal anymore!"

The light changed as the wall screen changed, and finally Ken caught sight of the corner booth. *Huh.* It seemed occupied with Terran women out for a night on the town. He leaned up against the bar and hunched his shoulders so it didn't look like he was looking—but this seemed like such an unlikely, nasty place to take a silk dress like that. Trying not to stare was like trying not to smell the piss in the air.

"'Name your price, I shall hear, and then we will negotiate'," he rehearsed, distracting himself. He'd had trouble telling if that was just something Traders said to each other, or something you should always say at the beginning of a business dealing with an Illyrian, but he'd decided to play it safe and have it ready…

"Hey kid, drink something, or get out," grunted the bartender, a rotund, multi-armed Charee primate with more jelly-rolls than a donut shop.

Ken almost laughed. Back on Alpha Prime he still wasn't old enough to drink—ever since that clerical error in his demobilization orders stranded him here it'd seemed like there was nothing to do *but* drink. He forked over a New Empire credit bill, creasing it over his middle finger out of habit. "Whatever's cheapest," he said.

"I hate people like you," the bartender muttered.

"I know. I mean, if you feel like giving me something nice from Uri Nara, I'll take it, but this is what I've got, so." Ken had a taste for liquors from his heritage world, even though he'd never been there. "Something cheap."

The bartender grabbed a can and a glass with two hands while scrubbing down the faux-cedar countertop with another—he even had an extra hand available to scratch his hairy back. Leaning over, Ken could see the floor on the Charee's side of the bar was more than half a meter higher than the floor on Ken's side. *Smart.* This way the height-challenged bar-tender could comfortably serve his mixed—but generally taller—patronage without resorting to scrambling around on stools.

"I like your set-up," Ken smiled.

The bartender grunted, holding out his palm. Ken paid, and cracked open the can of whatever-it-was with a sigh. "Nice hiss," he said. "Thanks."

"'Nice hiss?' What are you on?" The bartender leaned over as if to check if he'd accidentally given Ken something good. "You're too young and happy to be a soldier," he huffed.

"And you're just the right mix of grumpy to be a bartender," Ken laughed, drinking straight from the can instead of pouring into the glass he'd been given. *Give the guy less washing up to do.* "Been in the game long?"

"Since before you were born, that's for sure. Even started in a shitty neighborhood with the Sons of Terra fucking up my clientele for a while." The Charee's grin revealed missing teeth, and Ken wondered if he meant to imply the human-centric extremists had taken them. "I outlasted 'em. That's a ritzy strip now, and my bar back there's the center of everything. This is my second establishment—everyone says these outer worlds aren't worth the flight out, but I see the money in you stranded putzes. Figure if I could gentrify that hell-hole I can gentrify anything."

Ken tilted his head and pursed his lips.

"How'd I know you're stranded?" the bartender asked for Ken, handing someone else a drink without so much as looking at them, that third arm still wiping down the clear plastic on the countertop like it had OCD all on its own. "Maybe other civilians don't recognize the undershirt you're wearing like a tee, but I do. That goes under your uniform jacket. And I figure you wouldn't be wearing it out if you had other clothes—you Terrans make a point not to wear your uniforms off-duty—and it's faded as fuck, but you're way too peppy to have seen any real action, so it's seen all its wear and tear here pretending to be a real shirt."

Ken smiled at the accidentally-accurate leap in logic, more amused than embarrassed. "You got me. I only have the three shirts and I wouldn't be wearing this one if I hadn't got bumped down the laundry queue this week." There'd been a family of seven—refugees from somewhere—that desperately needed his spot.

"Shows off your biceps, though," the Charee nodded, as if to console Ken. "Bet those girls over there don't see what I see." He jerked his round head towards the corner booth Ken had noticed earlier. "They'll just see a ripped young ex-military hunk if you want them to."

"Eh…" Ken shifted. That *did* make him uncomfortable.

"What? No stolen valor? Fuck, you *are* innocent," the Charee laughed. "Half the idiots here won Silver Novas, the way they tell it when some cute thing walks in." He snorted, but his "Good for you, kiddo" didn't have a trace of sarcasm. He hopped to the other end of the bar to serve up an order, and slid back, still wiping the counter while two hands entered numbers into the digital payment pad he slipped out of his apron. As if he'd never left, he added: "So you're here to meet…"

"Job interview," Ken said, sipping the beer now. "Trying to go to Eden Crescent."

For the first time the Charee actually stopped moving. "Cheeze-us," he fake-swore—funny and almost jarring, given all his real swearing up til now. "Are you stupid?"

"Like you said, I didn't get to contribute anything when the war was going on," Ken shrugged. "I've got all this training—and yeah, like you can see, I'm healthy, and okay in a fight—so I've got to find a combat zone or something to make use of it all. Seems like I can be useful there."

"Whoa kid, I said you were too peppy to have seen a lot of

action—that's not the same thing as being useless," the Charee said.

"I know," Ken said. "And it wasn't by choice. But I was useless." He stared down at the glint of light at the top of the can of beer. It glittered like the neighbor's lawn-lights back home. "If people want to sit back and put their feet up while fellow sapients suffer somewhere else, that's fine for them. I've seen that life. I come from Columbia on Alpha Prime," he referenced the government seat of the Terran Union. "Neighborhood so rich they called Crash-Down poor *before* the crash. Top league diplomas and high-priced retirement plans, homeowner's associations and historically-accurate picket fences, senators' spouses with glowing tans talking like they know anything while others fight and die to keep them safe. Even the bunkers that got built in my neighborhood—they're like underground pent-houses. Everyone wears those smiles, but it's all empty like their eyes. Meaningless. Everyone dies in the end anyway without ever actually living for anything." Ken made hard eye contact with the bartender now. "I enlisted as soon as I could get my parents to sign an age-exemption."

"You're afraid of an empty life," the Charee summed up.

"I'm not afraid, because it's not going to happen," Ken said.

The bartender stared at him for a moment as if far away—then cash in some patron's outstretched hand brought him back to the present, and all four limbs flickered back into action-mode, and he dashed off to work.

Ken thought the bartender might return, but as his eyes absently followed the Charee's smooth, efficient movements—spin a glass here, more cleaning, serve two people there—

He caught sight of a slight scuffle at the other end of the room. An older, straw-haired Terran with skin like rust and leather—not that old, but at least twice Ken's age—leaned up against the wall, balancing on two legs of her bar stool. The top half of a Terran military uniform hung lopsided off her shoulders; her bottom half wore some kind of—Old Empire-looking Grausian toga-skirt thing he'd never seen on a human. Both halves were covered in freshly-spilled beer.

A bulky woman closer to Ken's age laughed and shoved the old drunk again, trying to unseat her from the leaning stool. The drunk's eye gleamed. Ken couldn't hear what she said from across the room—

But it made Ms. Pushy furious. She swung a punch. The drunk ducked; there was a clattering of smashed glass—and suddenly Ms. Pushy was screaming with a broken bottle embedded in her palm. Her scream ended abruptly when the drunk reached both hands behind herself, ripped the wooden placard off the wall without breaking eye contact with her opponent, and smashed Ms. Pushy across the face. Twice. Oh, three times.

Ken had already started moving across the room almost unconsciously when he first saw the two women—by the time Ms. Pushy spun around and thudded to the ground, he was there to check a quick pulse before putting himself between the drunk and the three men now closing in. They roared about girlfriends and sisters—

"Oh yeah? Well you can tell your girlfriend—whenna she wakesh up, because sleeping beauty's gotta 'pointment with the floor—that bramshabala…" The rest of the sentence was unintelligible—still apparently intelligible enough to the men that they wanted a fight.

"Gentlemen, wait!" Ken roared. He completely expected to take a fist to the face if he couldn't get his words out—fortunately he'd always had what people called a *command voice*. "Your family member has a medical emergency!"

Three people spoke at once.

"No she don't, you numbshkull," said the drunk.

"*You'll* have an emergency if you don't move, man," said a brother.

"Oh my gosh she's bleeding," said the boyfriend.

Ken used both hands to direct the angriest brother's vision towards the woman on the floor. "She needs someone strong to carry her to a hospital right away. She needs you." He snatched the bartender's towel and shoved it in the boyfriend's hand. "Wrap *around* the glass, and don't take it out—let a surgeon do that." *And the third guy?* "Uh—you sir—you need to get some hot water."

"Hot water?"

"Yes, you'll need hot water," Ken said. It was a trick his favorite physician had taught him, half-joking, to keep extra family members busy during childbirths that somehow happened without the luxury of a hospital. There wasn't a baby to wash up here, but, eh…? "It's essential." He yanked his cheap stethoscope out of the side pocket of his cargo pants. "I'm a doctor. I'm off-duty, but I know emergencies."

"Yer notta doctor, yer a combat medic," murmured the soup-sandwich-looking woman behind him, but Ken's confidence sold it just long enough to guide her off her chair and out the side door while everyone else considered the jobs they'd just been given.

The fresh air in the alleyway hit Ken like the door that slammed behind him as he stumbled forward with his charge. He was so grateful Captain Wimmer hadn't felt like fighting him, too—for that was who this violent drunk was. It'd taken him a second, but here, dripping and draped over his arm, he definitely had his former unit physician. She'd only worked with him for three months in his first unit before he was reassigned, but she was the doc who'd left the biggest impact on him.

What the hell had happened to her in the last year?

"She'll be fine," Wimmer grumbled.

"I wasn't aware you had a CT scanner on you, ma'am," Ken smiled.

"Sure, sure, every unconscious blablabla gets a cognitive

score and a concussion rule-out, brain bleed blabla, but I'm telling you, she'll be fine," Wimmer slurred. "I've seen that same broad twice'n had the same interaction, twice. Mebbe this time'll learn."

"Are *you* alright, ma'am?" Ken asked, eyes darting over her from head to toe as he tried to stand her up on her own.

"Shouldn't'chyou be in with your patient you," Wimmer said.

"You're my patient at the moment, ma'am," Ken said. "Your friend in there probably needs a hand surgeon, and as you established, ma'am, I'm not one."

"See, if they listenna you and she goesa hospital she'll-be fine," Wimmer said. "Man, fucking—Kamakura. That's you, the fresh outta AIT guy." She referenced the specialized schools soldiers went to in order to learn particular trades after basic training. "Lucky you, war ended right as you got in."

Ken frowned—he was less enthused about that. He'd literally left Wimmer's unit and deployed to a field hospital *months* before treaty negotiations began. It wasn't like he wanted war to happen, but he sure hadn't signed up to play pretend for six months and then get stuck on a fringe world for a year angling for a ride home.

"If we'were in the field I'd show you howta take the glass out myself, but yeah prolly not like this," Wimmer pushed him, attempting to stand on her own. She swayed. "Oh… shit."

He caught the woman just as she blacked out.

Ken was an easy-going guy with a decent sense of humor, but seeing his former officer sprawled in a dirty alley with blood splattered on the white skirt riding up her knees, half-sewn unit patch dangling off her uniform top, as drunk, dumb, and senseless as his idiot bunk-mate from basic… well, he knew enough to know bold leaders with path-forging clinical tricks and steady scalpel hands didn't become *this* for no reason. Wimmer could say what she wanted about her—self-defense—incident, but there was rage in those blows that her target hadn't caused. He usually found dealing with drunks kind of funny, but… not this time.

Ken was rolling the unconscious Captain onto her side when he heard his name behind him. He looked up to see one of the women in silk from the corner booth had come out to—watch?

"Who's this?" she asked.

"My—former boss," he said. "I'm trying to keep her from choking while I figure out how to get a ride back to where I'm staying."

"Aren't you a dedicated employee," the woman crooned. She offered him a hand—a very firm hand—and pulled him to his feet. This close he could see the outline of a pistol under her blouse. "I'm Stacey Howard. Staff Sergeant Retired, if that matters—and you're Ken Kamakura."

"How—do you know that?"

"Well, the authoritative-sounding guy with a stethoscope and bright smile probably didn't come to the world's ugliest dive bar to ask for the cheapest drink and leave without it."

"Oh shit, my dri—wait, I thought I was meeting someone else," Ken pursed his lips. "Are you with FXRS?" He'd planned to negotiate for a position with the mercenary group most known —at least to him—for search-and-rescue type operations. "The guy I contacted said a humanitarian organization in Eden Crescent was working with FXRS to contract medics trained in combat care."

"Gamma Pavonis took over the contract with Galaxy Aid, actually," said Howard. "Galaxy Aid's the actual client. But between FXRS and Gamma Pavonis Special Services, I figure you don't care as long as someone's paying."

Ken narrowed his eyes. "Why do you say that?"

"Oh no, you're one of those," she laughed. "You're really going to go save the world, huh? Well, no one actually employed with either group wants to go to that backwater edge of nowhere, so they're lucky to have you, I guess." She gave him a small hand-held computer with an olive-green screen. "Congratulations, you're officially an independent contractor with GPSS. The only FTL transport out there for a while is chartered to a media crew who's agreed to take you on—they leave planetside for their jump-ship tomorrow evening. They're waiving deep space life support fees—food, air, everything else—since you're with Galaxy Aid, but you still have to pay basic fare. Your packing list—"

Ken stepped back, his mind reeling. "Wait, just like that? I'm, what—pre-hired?"

Howard shrugged. "Just like that. Even if Galaxy Aid could afford to be picky, I don't think they'll complain after I tell them what I saw today," she said. "You seem to know your stuff."

"I could've been—" Ken shut his mouth before he could accuse himself of the capability for bluffing. Gift horses, and all that. "Never mind. When do I meet the rest of the squad?"

"Squad?" Howard laughed. "Oh, there is no squad. Galaxy Aid only sprang for two medics, so it's just you and whatever other poor soul I'm able to round up in the next day or so."

"So, your own people aren't going? At all," Ken asked.

"That depends entirely on whether or not I have personnel free after we close out another more urgent contract. If I do, they'll meet you at Eden Crescent."

Ken narrowed his eyes. "So medical is what's wanted, and you're not that. Why wouldn't I just negotiate with Galaxy Aid directly, then?"

"They couldn't find medical professionals willing to go—we did," Howard said. She didn't have to add that realistically, the charity probably needed someone ex-military anyway for such a tumultuous planet. "Finder's fee. And for you, it's worth it for the equipment and fare we're gifting you."

Ken tilted his head. "Is that how you usually do things?"

"No. But it's for charity, so it's a write-off." She smoothed down the front of her dress and clasped her hands together, apparently quite satisfied with herself. "Well, if you have any questions for the next forty-eight hours, you'll be able to contact me. You'll find your equipment on board—except for the packing list, of course. That's your responsibility. Don't be an idiot and run off. We always take a small portion of our fee up front—your cut bought your gear—but you don't really get paid until you arrive at the outpost. I'm sending you tickets for all the transfer points you'll need until you actually get to the planetary system. Once there, some leftover Grausian anti-transport defense grid tech keeps us from being able to mount a dropship directly down to the charity compound, but you'll break atmosphere just a few hours away by helo. Now, if you wait just a moment, I can probably drop you and—your 'boss' here—off at your place, if you're not far."

Ken gave her the address almost mutely, writing it on a bit of paper for her before she waltzed off to get her driver. He was quiet in the vehicle, mostly focused on making sure Dr. Wimmer was still breathing. He'd rehearsed at least ten different scenarios for this job interview. It was wild that he could be so prepared and still completely caught off guard.

The merc company seemed to have everything figured out, which was as reassuring as it was unnerving. Ken didn't ask what was to stop him from selling his gear and disappearing—he supposed that was probably why he wouldn't receive it until he was already onboard the transport. But even with his major payment inaccessible before arrival, there was no guarantee he'd—actually—arrive at all. "Galaxy Aid's rather—trusting—huh?" he said as he pulled his Captain out of the car.

"They don't have a choice," Howard said. She lifted a finger into the air as if something had just occurred to her: "And once you're on board the transport… neither will you."

CHAPTER TWO

Jocelyn Wimmer

THE STAFF SERGEANT hunching over in the sick call office, clutching her lower abdomen with bitterness in her eyes looked like my mom.

Fucking—

Fucking damn headache—

The blood running down my soldier's forehead looked like jam, thick with brain. He was still smiling. He didn't even know he was dead.

Nauseated as a Scrit underwater—getting old sucks.

The premature baby was red, his fingers still squeezed together, wet, his forearm no bigger than my thumb; he opened his mouth like he was begging for air, but there was no sound, not with those unbaked lungs.

His mother screamed for him.

Damn light, would somebody cut the light stabbing into my eyes—

My "superior's" face.

Your fucking fault. If you'd listened to me. But you wouldn't listen—

I took a swing.

My fist hit cement wall, and I woke up from my alcohol-laced slumber. I swore, shaking out my hand, but it was fine except for a slight abrasion not worth the time it takes to say "abrasion"—hard to break anything when you don't cock your elbow to fire straight on. I was more swearing because I had no idea how I'd come to wake up in this dingy apartment. I clutched the side of my head, blinking hard as I tried to get my bearings. In my dizziness the past still hung over my hangover, and for a moment all I could think about was how small this room looked. *No bigger than the extra-shitty excuse for a "medical bay" I slept in when our STOAR got stranded…* that'd been a few years ago. Like their acronym implied, those Surface To Orbit And Return 'rocket-ships' weren't designed for long-term living, just for up and down, space and back, and when Charee forces took out the intersystem transport ship that was supposed to carry us to our next jump—well, we had nowhere to dock. We shut off everything but minimal life support and played dead for days, just floating in debris with almost literally no breathing room. I did a lot of sleeping in my chair with a metal wall centimeters from my face back then.

This apartment now was just as small as that medical bay—but it was a cement box, not a durasteel one, and it smelled a hell of a lot better. I wouldn't've been able to find a speck of dust even with a microscope, and part of what made the place look so meager was the total lack of clutter. Just a small assault pack by the door next to neatly-placed boots. I was in a bed, with clean sheets, and even the luxury of a pillow. I wasn't mad at the accommodations—I was pissed because this was the fifth time in two weeks I didn't recognize where I'd woken up and Sylvie was nowhere to be seen.

Instead, curled up on the floor where I was used to seeing my full-grown Scrit, lay a not-fully-grown human I *kind of* recognized from a Role II I'd aided for about three months on my way to what would end up being my final war-time destination. I stared for a second—well, several seconds. Took me a while to understand whether or not the ghosts were playing tricks on me. *Pretty sure this kid didn't die. Pretty sure we didn't see action there.*

At any rate, he wasn't dead now. Slow, even breaths blossomed from the sleeping kid's chest, and the long black forelock that'd fallen over his face fluttered with the movement of his dreaming lips. *Hot damn, to actually rest like that again...* I caught my mind before it could grumble about his "out of regs" haircut—there wasn't a war anymore. Hair could be as long as it wanted to. Mine just didn't want to grow.

I looked down at myself. The hell was I wearing? I recognized the Grausian tunic—that was mine, from 479, when we Terrans begrudgingly fought alongside the Old Empire against Callan the Usurper. I'd won it in a combatives tournament I entered for fun. *Fuck, there's blood on it.* The uniform top was from the Seccession, first against the Grausians and then the Charee. In what world did my drunk mind think this combo worked? Oh—I'd probably gotten myself skipped in the laundry queue again. There was some family or some shit that needed diaper washing or something, I kind of remembered that. I could feel I'd apparently misplaced my underwear somewhere along the way, and even dizzy and dazed I could tell I reeked of what I wished I could call vinegar but was probably just piss.

The splitting headache demanded attention. I needed to get my sorry ass out of here—I was a disgusting stain on this pretty room and far too sober. I didn't need to be noticing myself.

I didn't need to be noticing anything at all.

I started to slide down to the edge of the bed to creep out—

The kid stretched, fluttering his eyelids as sleep lifted off him like a magical cloak. *Shit, he's waking up.* I decided against stepping over him to flee—no one needed to be subjected to *that* under-tunic vision first thing in the morning—and squirmed back under the covers before he sat up. Maybe if I looked asleep, he'd leave to get something, and then I could sneak out without having to talk to him. Above all, I wanted to avoid talking to anyone. At least until I could get something fermented in my gut. I shut my eyes and let my jaw droop just a bit, waiting as I heard him walking around the apartment. The clink of ceramic… the hiss and pour of warm liquid…

I almost jumped when I suddenly heard him by the bed again. "Ma'am, I'm sorry to bother you, but I'm going to need to help you leave." The firm voice surprised me. It was clear, and confident without bravado. "I don't mean to be an awful host—I'm shipping out for a job today and need to check out of here for good. Do you have any family around I can drop you off with?"

I turned to him with a grunt. The kid was standing by the bed now with a cup of a dark liquid and a little red and blue capsule I recognized as the old-fashioned migraine combo I still taught my medics after centuries of history almost erased it: aspirin, acetaminophen, and caffeine.

"Kamakura," I suddenly remembered his name. Fuck, my voice was dry. I sounded like I'd deep-throated a sand dune.

"That's me, ma'am." He tilted his head. "I guess that was a stupid question, huh, about family."

I sat up on the edge of the bed now to take the mug—it was warm—and pop the pill. "Not a stupid question. I could be the traditional alcoholic with some poor husband at home, cowering in fear right now, hoping I *don't* come home to beat his ass over the laundry."

"No offense, ma'am, but if you had someone doing the laundry…" The grin was friendly, not mocking. He didn't need to call me ma'am anymore, but it did feel right.

I smirked. "I just said I beat him for *not* doing it. Clearly he's a bad homemaker. Unlike you—" I sipped. "This is *jola.* It's fucking fantastic. How the hell you get jola out here?" I'd had the creamy, thick natural stimulant often during my time with the Legion—Grausians shipped the various savory bean-juice varieties from plantations back in the New Empire with all the same pride we Terrans held for our various beers and coffees. It'd been a year or so since I'd last had it. The stuff kept well enough for interstellar travel, but this city was basically just a huge demobilization colony—not exactly a haven for culture.

"Is that what it's called? I've been calling it 'not-coffee,'" Kamakura chuckled. "It was all I could find at the nearby trading post. A bunch of merchants have kind of popped up in the last six months—I think they realized the demobilization thing's kind of an admin nightmare in some sectors and this place's actually a more permanent business opportunity than it looks. But that's just a guess."

"Huh." That was fair enough—I hadn't exactly been anywhere but the bar lately. Probably why I couldn't find fancy things like jola.

"I do need to head out, though," Kamakura said. Where did this kid work? Maybe a civilian hospital now? No, not actively wearing his military uniform. He saw me scrutinizing him and added, "I'm traveling to Eden Crescent. I've been invited, by Galaxy Aid, to work as a field medic in one of their rural centers." My eyebrow threatened to raise; I held it still, but come on—did the kid not watch the news? My stare seemed to bother the kid, and he added again: "It's a decent chance to use my military training—active conflict zone and all, between all the local warlords trying to gain control of the planet after the Grausian satrap fled." He made it sound like a simple resume match, not a life-threatening drop into a world that didn't even really have space travel yet.

"You ever had a patient try to shoot you?" I asked suddenly.

"No, but I've gone through AIT and basic—I know the protocol," Kamakura said.

Now the eyebrow did raise, and with it, my leg shot out, hooked behind his knee, and dropped him to the ground. I slid down after him, dug my knee into his stomach—the pistol at his hip had a locking holster, too hard at this angle to open myself. My right hand slammed down against it to keep him from drawing—

With the other hand I smashed the mug on the floor and held a jagged shard to his throat.

"Sschwick," I made the sound of flesh cutting. "You're dead."

The kid breathed hard, but no fear—or even surprise—registered on his face. He looked up at me with brow furrowed, lips pursed. "That was my only mug."

"I'm serious," I said, ceramic still pressed against his carotid. "You're dead, and now you can't help anyone, and all that 'training,' all your idealism—it's all wasted, gone. Look, I don't know you, but I know you're a good person. The Universe needs good people. As someone who's *not* good, let me give you some advice." I pressed my knee a little harder into his solar plexus to make the point. "Find a nice hospital on a civilized planet with a good retirement plan, get you a sweet girl, and just—you know. Just be. You're still not broken yet. Why throw everything away?"

His voice remained clear with just the hint of exertion. *Huh. Decent core strength.* "Because people there need help, and no one's helping. It's that simple for me, ma'am. The indigenous people don't even have space travel yet—maybe there's medical science they're missing, too. I may need to brush up on combatives and watch my back," his eyes flickered downward towards my hand, "but if no one better than me is willing to go help them then at least I can send them *me*."

I searched his face. His jaw tightened, but the determination didn't seem willful or rebellious like some cowboy out for a joyride. *Hm.* I let him up with a grunt.

"Thank you, ma'am," he said, stepping back for his boots as soon as he escaped the floor.

I watched him lace up, my lips pursed. I couldn't stop remembering, and he looked so much like—I shook my head, letting the dizziness of the motion rock away the unwanted thoughts, but death hung over me. Over him. In my mind's eye he and *they* juxtaposed against each other, and he needed to not die. I still didn't know if I should knock him out to keep him from running off and killing himself—sometimes people like this tried to 'help' but only got in the way, made things worse, or died before they could lift a single idealistic finger. "Now I need to figure out how to clean up this mess without a broom…" he was saying.

"Someone's taken fire from a needler pistol," I interrupted to grill him. "That's all you know, you arrive on scene, what do you do first?"

"I secure the scene first," he recited, tilting his head. "Sometimes the best medicine's a bullet, as they say. I scan for hemorrhage, but with all those little flechettes shredded into my patient's flesh I'm probably looking for death by pneumo or hemothorax, not massive blood loss. I pop a needle-D into his chest—both sides, if I don't have a silencing stethoscope to block out the sounds of the skirmish, since I want to make sure I didn't treat the wrong side. If it's really obvious what side I'm working with and the needle-D's not enough, I've got an auto-tube in my bag." Needle-D was short for a needle decompression—literally a small, sharp needle we used to insert a catheter to vent air out of a chest cavity in the case of what people called a "sucking chest wound." Those injuries killed because with air or blood filling your thorax, you'd crush your lungs every time you took a breath, and the worst ones needed a chest tube inserted to drain off blood. In ancient times chest tubes were mostly inserted by surgeons, but modern auto-tubes had battery-powered homing sensors that repelled the undersides of ribs, protecting nerves and blood vessels, and a really easy-to-work mechanical latchkey that even the weakest fingers could turn to push the tube in place. Three twists, usually, and you were good—it'd mechanically lock up when placed, too, so you couldn't push too far.

"How do you know his lung's collapsed in the first place?" I snapped. "No stethoscope."

"I ask his name the moment I walk up. If he can't say it, we're in respiratory distress. I check his airway with my ear and then get my hands on both sides of his chest to see if one side rises further than the other." Kamakura mimed this as he spoke. "It's the elevated side, the one that really doesn't move, that I know's filling with blood or air. This should all take seconds."

"His face is red and swollen. His neck's bulging, and his blood pressure's suddenly dropping when taken on the left side," I said. I could see the patient in my mind's eye, and Kamakura standing over him as shots rang out in the distance…

"So now I'm thinking cardiac tamponade. If I can't get him to a surgeon soon, I'm pulling out my targeter for pericardiocentesis." The medic knelt for his bag now, zipping it open to show me a series of metal measuring rods that folded out to a square—in the center of the targeter lay a huge syringe. Kamakura held the targeter with one hand across his chest to show me alignment with the apex of his heart, and in the other hand a small, portable, solar-powered ultrasound. "I've got him trauma-shirtless by now, so now I'm lining up the edges of the measuring line with his ribs. I sterilize the area as best I can first, and when I'm set I use the twisting key to puncture the syringe through his thorax."

These twisting keys were great for folks with weak fingers like mine… this invention, too, made a life-saving surgery quick and accessible as long as you had basic medical training. "I'm careful to avoid the bottom edge of the relevant ribs, guiding the needle via ultrasound, and I drain the liquid compressing his heart. If he doesn't improve, I swap out the syringe with a wire-blade." The syringe came off now in his hands as he knelt for this other attachment—a reverse-cutting, scissors-like pair of blades on a wire for pericardectomy. "I use the wire-blade through the same entrance, but guide it further, more superior and anterior, towards the chest wall, and then click this to resect a piece of pericardium when the ultrasound's machine learning model lets me know I'm good."

I crossed my arms now, nodding, still watching Kamakura's face as he tested the mechanism in front of me without opening its sterile tip. He hadn't tried to walk out the door or avoid the questions—seemed like he knew he needed to be sure of himself, for himself, and a little pop quiz didn't hurt. There was a certain humility in that. A confident humility. And glancing at his open gear-bag, it seemed organized. Familiar. He knew his shit.

Yeah—maybe he could do this. My woozy brain overlaid him into a memory of my long-term medics triaging patient after patient, gloves tinged with blood—their commanding young voices through the transmitters as they stood in the wind in the shadows of the old hovering helos when we couldn't get real space-capable ambulance support, loading the stretchers on rope—the chief medics I chose, the ones I trained, always spoke like NCOs even as privates, and they learned how to keep our team organized so I could focus on tough cases and nasty decisions.

But I saw the blood running down my medic's forehead again, thick like jam…

Sure, the kid could save a bunch of people. And then he'd get killed.

"Even if I can help just one person everyone else ignores," Kamakura said, closing his pack now and stepping towards the door. "That's worth it to me, ma'am."

Worth it?

My guys didn't need to die. It was a pointless fight triggered by a miscalculation. But I couldn't help but remember the way the soldiers on the stretchers looked at my chief medics—my organized, capable medics… I saw my guys and gals give up their sleeping systems or their MREs for those soldiers, and if I had to count how many lives we'd saved…

Numerically it was worth it, right?

My throat stuck. I didn't like that. "Hm," I grunted, trying to eye Kamakura's physique—couldn't tell through the uniform if he'd been keeping up PT, but I vaguely remembered now he had probably mostly carried me here, and, looking out the window, we were at least four stories up. "S'pose you can lift more weight than I can, too," I grumbled. So all he really needed was a body guard, honestly.

And if I kept him alive, said my time-trapped mind, it'd be like keeping them alive.

"Okay," I said. "You can come."

"What! I'm the one with the ticket, you're the one who—"

I guess my grey eyes suddenly remind him of hours spent in formation.

"You know what, yes—ma'am." I could see him calculating as he pulled out his phone to show me the address for take-off. I would bet credits to cookies he planned to get the crew to ditch me when he got the chance. "We're taking off here. I was on my way to pick up—"

"You get your supplies. I'll meet you there at nineteen-hundred hours," I said, smiling now for the first time since waking up. I finally had a good reason to put pants on. "Tell them I'm coming."

CHAPTER THREE

Ken Kamakura

WIND HOWLED over the landing platform as the doors of the private security checkpoint closed behind Ken; he found himself outside in the shadow of a huge, multi-story aerodyne rocket pointed at the sky. The setting sun glinted off the shimmering glass of the cockpit near the rocket's tip, illuminating it like a transparent jewel; the rest of the STOAR's body seemed grey and dull, as if someone colorblind had once tried to paint it camo for fun and given up halfway through.

"Guess it's an older model," Ken remarked to himself, scanning the structure up and down for some sort of Gamma Pavonis emblem or something to reassure him he'd found the right place. Of course he had—he'd checked in with Gamma Pavonis personnel at the gate. Still.

Ken pulled the straps of his assault pack tighter against his shoulder and stepped forward with a deep inhale. He didn't mind the excitement racing in his chest, but the twisting in his stomach seemed unnecessary. Nervous? Why? A deep breath into his belly stifled the feelings for a moment—this was just something that needed to be done. Too much emotion made this about him, and it wasn't supposed to be about him.

Deep breath, and move. Don't overthink.

Still the churning uncertainty lingered. Two small figures standing beneath the STOAR caught Ken's attention as he neared. He recognized the long, waving blond hair of Staff Sergeant-Retired Howard, the Gamma Pavonis operative who'd hired him. Even from here her shapely form stood out against the ship's dusky underside in that slim white dress—she almost glowed in the shadows of the four thick jet engines that, like limbs, held the STOAR's center tube of a body upright.

The other woman didn't seem familiar. Definitely ex-military, and more obviously ex-military than the elegant Stacey Howard—even from here Ken could make out a Terran uniform undershirt like his worn over civilian cargo pants. A Mark XV shortsword hung from her hip and a large procyonine translator Scrit folded itself around the new woman's shins, its round ears and eight legs flicking here and there as it purred and chittered, pointed black nose sniffing the air as its black and gold fur rubbed against her legs. The animal's spine seemed as flexible as fluid—but the woman's stance was rigid. Professional. With purpose. Familiar, but—

"You're late," shouted Captain Wimmer.

"Holy crap," Ken breathed, breaking into a jog. "She actually looks like an officer now." It was like this morning's hung-over wastrel never existed.

Howard laughed as Ken crossed the cement. "He's not late," she protested. "He's literally a minute early. 'Early is on time…'" she quoted the old drill sergeant saying.

"'Early is on time, on time is late, and late is unacceptable,'" Captain Wimmer chuckled, finishing the quote. "But it's a meaningless sentence. If p=q, and q=r, then p=r and by the law of equivalence early is late." She gave a cheeky little grin, amused by this for some reason, then nodded for Howard to step aside as she heaved a large duffle bag into the air—an elevator lift was descending from the STOAR's central tube now, creaking as it touched down between the four jet engines. The Gamma Pavonis merc obliged, and the older doctor grunted as the momentum of her own swing almost knocked her forward into the elevator.

Ken darted over to take the small woman's bag. "You'd get along with my dad," he remarked. "That was his sense of humor, too."

There was a brief pause before Wimmer released her hold on her duffel and allowed Ken to carry it for her—almost a struggle, Ken thought. But it was a small moment, something only he noticed, and it ended as the physician gave a stern nod and followed Ken into the narrow cylinder of the elevator. She held her hand over the sliding door slot to keep the door from closing as the Gamma Pavonis operative spoke:

"You both have your itinerary now, I hope," Howard said. "You'll take our STOAR to a civilian interrange corporation ship out in orbit, and from there I've arranged a small packet ship to take you to the nearest jump point—about ten days out from atmosphere. A passenger liner there will jump you to the gate nearest Eden Crescent, and from there you'll take a packet to the news company's explorer, which will send a dropship planetside. It's a Grausian media corporation, so you'll be comfortable there, given your background," she nodded to Captain Wimmer.

Comfortable in Grausian company... enjoys Grausian food... "Were you in the Legion?" Ken asked, eyebrows raised. "I didn't realize you were packing that many years in, ma'am."

"Only during the feuds against Callan the Usurper—just at the end of the civil war. After the Massacre we were one of the first units to turn on the Grausians," Wimmer said. There was a hardness in her voice that made Ken wonder if she'd seen action against the very Loyalists she'd previously protected: Grausian… 'friends', even. Her lips twisted into something of a sardonic smile. "But it's bold of you to assume I'm comfortable anywhere, sergeant."

There was an awkward pause—the Gamma Pavonis operative didn't seem to know what to say to that. The comment felt unnecessary. Extra. For a moment the only sound was the purring of the psychic translator beast at Wimmer's feet. Then Howard cleared her throat, and after coughing through a few more quick logistics points, she waved them off. Wimmer allowed the elevator door to close, and Ken's sigh of relief was echoed by a soft hydraulic hiss as the cylinder creaked into motion. *No more conversations like that, hopefully.*

But his stomach hadn't settled. He pulled out his mobile data screen and stared at the complicated itinerary. Literally two ships just to get to the jump point. And how many packets did the first interrange ship have? It sounded like a merchant vessel used as a transfer point for a lot of different businesses. So they'd have to find the right docking bay just to get the actual journey started, and then even after the jump they had yet another ride to hunt down. So very many transfers… so many places to mess up and get stranded somewhere before even starting the mission.

"It's easier in the service," Wimmer nodded. Ken looked up—she glanced at his itinerary, and then stared out at her muddled reflection in the moving durasteel around them, folding her hands behind her as if at parade rest. "It's nice when someone literally takes you where you need to go, every time, and you don't have to think."

"Eh, I shouldn't be so overwhelmed. I wasn't really in long enough to make civilian travel seem alien to me, ma'am," Ken said. "I don't know what my problem is."

"In a little, in a long time, doesn't matter," said Wimmer. "You sign on the dotted line, and something changes."

Ken didn't know if he agreed. He didn't feel changed. And that, he thought, was precisely his problem.

ONCE THE STOAR docked with the interrange transport, Ken and Wimmer had no trouble finding the packet they were supposed to ride to the passenger jump ship. Pushing their way through the bustling crowds of merchants, travelers, and miners was easy with Wimmer's resting bitch face, and the pair's joint sense of direction was decent enough that all the flashing gate lights and somewhat illogical lay-out choices didn't slow them down.

Getting *on* the packet presented a bit of an issue, though—someone back at Gamma Pavonis had fumbled the purchase of their last-minute ticket registration, and it took some convincing to prove the pair really had tickets on the cruiser at all. By the time Ken and Captain Wimmer tossed their bags into the packet's tight little sleeping pods for the ten-day journey to the jump point, it was about 2300 hours back on the planet, and Ken's body wanted to sleep.

Ken flopped back onto the rough mattress and dropped his arm over his face. "Man, why is talking to customer service so much more draining than actual work?"

It was a rhetorical question, but Wimmer answered anyway. "Customer service, bureaucrats, admin, logistics—they're all the same like that. You're using so much energy trying to get someone to help you when their entire *job* is supposed to be to help you," she said. "The sheer confusion and uncertainty messes with your cortisol levels—and there's nothing any amount of adrenaline can do to help you, so your body's just flailing while your brain works. It's a special kind of helplessness." She didn't sit down. "Get up. We need to brush up on your 'hands-on' skills."

"Combatives. Now?" Ken sat up. He narrowed his eyes for a second at the older woman's tone—he hadn't exactly planned on creating a supervisor when he agreed to let Wimmer in on his assignment. But he did need to practice, and he was too psyched up to sleep just yet anyway… "Alright. Sure."

Ken had barely risen to his feet when Wimmer's leg swept towards his ankle to take him down.

This time he stepped forward, into her, over the sweep, to keep from falling—and his hand darted towards her side to snatch and unclip her pistol from her waist. Wimmer shut her arm over his like a spring-trap, squeezing his elbow against her side—

And her other arm snaked over that trapped elbow into an improvised joint-breaking arm-bar—

Pressure became pain. Ken started to tap out, but something hard in the Captain's face stopped him.

"Say I don't let you tap out," she suggested, eyes on his arm, and not his face. "Then what?"

"Anything goes?" Ken tilted his head.

"Well I mean, if someone doesn't let you tap out, are you gonna just let 'em destroy your dominant arm? How you gonna help all your patients then?"

The pain was becoming decidedly more real. Well—Ken could deck her with his other free hand, using shock to loosen her grip. Should he, though—? No, no way, right?

The crazy woman really wasn't letting go.

Thought disappeared. Ken kneed his former boss in the stomach and shot his palm towards her forehead—in a real fight he would have sent a fist to her philtrum, but even now he had his limits—

Wimmer tucked in her head to avoid the blow, but her midsection folded just a bit and she wheezed, just jarred enough for the grip on his elbow to loosen. Ken tried to yank his arm free, still clutching the Captain's pistol. She gnashed her teeth and managed to clamp down again—caught his wrist with her elbow, still pinching his hand against her side—

Suddenly she yanked his arm back and her shoulder punched in his chest. There was a weird twist of her body weight, an ankle wrapped around his, her shoulder pushed forward—it was too fast to really catch the exact movement and before Ken could blink, he'd lost his balance and a smashing impact blasted through his back.

They'd fallen on the floor by his assault pack. She was on top. He just had time to hear the bag unzipping before her hand darted to his neck—

His hand reached hers far too late. He could feel her fist against his neck, and the plastic edge sheathing the scalpel blade pressed to his carotid.

"Now you've died. Again," she said.

Ken didn't move. *Dang it.* He now regretted unbuckling his own pistol from his belt and leaving it in the assault pack—Wimmer could easily have stolen that, too, if she were just a little closer to the bag, just close enough to reach more than the front pocket. But shot at point blank, or opened across the throat—it made precious little difference.

Wimmer waited.

"Alright, I'll bite," Ken grunted, straining not to pant. She was basically on top of him, and not light, despite her small frame—she had what his sergeant once called 'good weight'. "What could I have done to avoid this?"

"You're just too gentle," Wimmer said. "You should've followed up that knee with more. It's hard to hold someone's arm when they're pummeling your stomach and face nonstop."

"Roger," Ken sighed. "And the take-down?"

"Oh, you let me control your upper body weight too much with the grip on your elbow," Wimmer said. "You're stronger than me. If you just planted your feet wider, you would have been able to pull back, but your stance broke when your foot came back down after you kneed me—your ankles? Too close to mine. Huge fuck-up." Wimmer reached across Ken's face to return the scalpel to the bag, and let him up. "You know if you were a bit more aggressive you could probably have pushed forward when you first kneed me—followed the movement through—and gotten my back leg off balance. Could've maybe gotten me on my back—maybe you'd even be in mount right now."

Ken eyed her for a moment as he handed back her pistol. "Physicians aren't usually known for their combatives skills," he said. He nodded towards the vibroblade shortsword laying across her assault pack. "What's the story behind that?"

It was as if he'd thrown a match in her hair, and this woman was explosive. Captain Wimmer didn't answer the question with words—she lunged at him. When he sidestepped, she doubled around to his back—an arm wrapped around his neck—he just managed to tuck in his chin and shove his palm between her forearm and himself, breaking the attempted chokehold. As the pistol in her right hand came up all Ken's internal alarms about firearm safety went off—even if the gun was empty, she was flagging him on purpose like she was going to point the muzzle at his temples, a huge absolutely *no-no-do-not* just asking for an accident to happen—*what the hell?!*—

In something of a panic Ken gave her wrist a sharp knife-hand strike, knocking the weapon to the ground—he whirled—there was no technique in his push as he shoved her backwards.

He practically threw her against the wall—she hit it with a ringing thud and a laugh. Ken crouched on the balls of his feet to snatch the pistol off the floor just as Wimmer bounced back off the wall and dove at him—

"I shouldn't have flagged you," Wimmer coughed as she knocked him off-balance again, managing to land her torso atop his, perpendicular, in something of a messy side-mount. The gun was pinned in Ken's hand under her leg. "But you're better scared."

"Don't do that again," Ken warned, shrimping out from under her and steadying his grip on the weapon. He didn't aim it at her, but rather at the ground underneath her—following the rules but making his point. "Please."

It was too hot in the room now. The older veteran nodded. Her bangs clung to her forehead as she eyed the weapon—she seemed to be calculating a way to pin him again. She didn't acknowledge his win. "We'll use some other prop," she said. "'Train as you fight,' they used to say."

"I'm hoping I'm a good enough marksman that I don't need much close quarters combat, ma'am," Ken said, backing up. He was just a little bit done with this. "I qual'd expert on everything they handed me. We had plenty of time for target practice with so few real injuries on our FOB."

She laughed and shook her head. "It's not good that someone as weak, old, and shitty as me can kick your ass. It's always exactly the skill you think you don't need that you end up needing most."

Ken doubted that very much—he'd learned in Evidence-Based Resilience Training "always" was generally a sign of a thought distortion.

Maybe they didn't have EBRT when Wimmer took basic. She was obviously cognitively all here, but the glint in her eyes was like light reflecting off the butcher's knives in the Crash Down slums back home. Ken had volunteered with relief efforts there not just after the disaster, when aid was socially acceptable and patriotic, but long after the cameras moved on and the undesirables moved in. Each knife at the fly-infested local butcher's had a specific purpose honed by friction and steel, and if Ken's posh neighbors were to be believed, every blade in Crash Down's shanty-town had been used to kill more than just today's steak-heavy Bovies. Even his usually-practical mother believed that: *"I get the point—the soup kitchen's volunteer program matters to you. Fine! But Ken, too long in Crash Down and you might just get one of those 'points' right between the ribs—and then who'll you help?"* she'd begged. *"Every blade there has a story, kiddo."*

But Ken wasn't afraid of stories.

"I'll keep my distance," he said, nodding again to the pistol in his hands.

"Not if you're rendering aid, you won't." Wimmer stood now, wiping her forehead on her sleeve. She sat on her bunk with another little wheeze and dug through her duffel—Ken didn't relax until what she brought out turned out to be a water bottle. "It's easy to say you'll shoot first and save lives later. But who do you shoot? What if your patient turns on you? These clan feuds don't generally have really cut-and-dry good guys and bad guys. I hear there's a healthy kidnapping economy, too, so not everyone's a willing combatant. I saw that pretty little Mark X you were carrying earlier—"

Wimmer nodded towards Ken's pack, referencing the rather expensive pistol now stowed there: a gift from his mother, the definitely-not-standard-issue personal item had been an incredible administrative hassle for Ken to transport on active duty and spent most of its time in a high-security gun locker. "—so I know you've got access to stun rounds, but kid, child soldiers exist. They don't tolerate the electrical doses adults do. And when you run out of those it's a lot easier to nonlethally grapple someone into submission than to nonlethally shoot someone and still have stopping power." Wimmer slipped something from her sleeve into her water and took a fierce swig. "You're going into a brand-new combat zone without a real army to tell you what side you're on—right time, right place, right uniform ain't enough out there. Maybe you're thinking you'll just shoot and run triple-C like it's AIT again—" she referenced the military's Tactical Combat Casualty Care algorithm. "But you're not a soldier anymore, you're an asset being delivered by a merc unit to a nonprofit. You're just supposed to be a medic for Galaxy Aid, remember?" She took another large gulp, and wiped her cheek on her sleeve. "So who are you even shooting?"

Ken pursed his lips. "There's a pretty famous warlord in the territory where I'm headed. Yako Bisraya—sounds like he's probably *the enemy*. Most of the news reports attribute a lot of the violence, in the region, to his imperialism. Galaxy Aid's specifically trying to bring food and medicine to the families of his victims." He handed the Captain's pistol back to her. "But you're right—I don't know. I can't know, really, not when I didn't grow up there and I haven't gone through what those people deal with every day. I'm just there to help whatever people I can with whatever misery I can see."

"Noble as shit." Wimmer clearly wasn't that tired or dehydrated, but she practically inhaled her water, gulping like she literally wouldn't be able to breathe without it. She almost gave herself a coughing fit. "Just be sure you don't wake up one day and realize you're someone else's tool for something you don't actually believe in."

"I have a moral code, ma'am."

"That's nice. How many stun rounds does it come with?"

Ken sat down across from her on his own bunk—apparently, they were both going to leave top bunks for other passengers. Wimmer seemed to be referencing something *so* specific it tickled the edges of Ken's imagination as if he was already supposed to know. He scratched the back of his neck for a moment, searching for a way to word his query that would fall somewhere between compassionate and casual…

Best to be direct. "Ma'am, did your command make you do something you didn't believe in?" he asked.

"It's not that simple." Wimmer shook her head. "Nothing really is. Bad leaders don't actually go around cracking their knuckles and cackling that they want all the insert-race-here to die today. But I will say this." She leaned in. Her voice remained even, but her pupils seemed slightly dilated to Ken. "I've treated plenty of sexual assaults and beat-downs *on* my guys caused *by* my guys. We have a military tribunal for a reason. Even in the best command—with the best leadership in the Universe—you have traitors and bastards." She tugged at the laces on her boots, and kicked them off with something of a satisfied sigh. "You need close quarters combat where you're going."

CHAPTER FOUR

Jocelyn Wimmer

TEN DAYS, thirty days, twelve days, and then we were surrounded by fire in a crashing media explorer ship. The familiar smell of roasting flesh reminded me of my surgery rotation, and it was like I was right there again—and for some sick reason that calmed me amidst the chaos.

Time is a funny thing.

Ten.

It was ten days from the transfer ship to the jump point. Uneventful. Lots of sparring. Mostly trying to get the kid to turn on that inner desperation at will—I thought if he could get used to small spikes of adrenaline maybe he'd fare better when that inevitable ocean of it met him later. Real emergencies always left my muscles feeling like they were melting in acid. Maybe he was young enough to avoid some of that.

Thirty.

Thirty days from the jump point to the zone just outside Eden Crescent's Roberts Limit. Kamakura had pretty bad Jump Disorientation Sickness but took it like a champ. I treated him with some basic antimuscarinic patches and some oral antiemetics. There's an old Grausian dessert that incorporates a lot of a plant that's chemically similar to Old Earth ginger, and the passenger cruiser actually had the shit on board—that helped him almost more than the antiemetic.

Staff Sergeant-Retired Stacey Howard met us when we arrived at the Eden Crescent jump zone. She'd had other business to attend to—Gamma Pavonis was a small merc unit of only two permanent companies, so time was more expensive to them than money. Sounded like she'd taken the detour to a neighboring system to coordinate a quicker, more important job—and riding in a light assault-transport literally owned by GPSS and capable of generating its own wormhole vortex meant she wasted a lot less time transferring ships like we did. The GPSS ship moved on to a different contract, leaving Howard and two other mercs with our jump ship; they planned to escort us for just the time it took to collect evidence that we arrived at Galaxy Aid's delivery point. I didn't pay much attention to any of them—Howard seemed to hold Kamakura's attention pretty well, though. Girl had hips.

Twelve.

Twelve days in the packet from the passenger cruiser to the news crew's explorer. Interthought Media was the name of the Grausian conglomerate that owned the odd ovoid transport—most of the reporters and camera folk seemed to wish they were on any assignment other than this one, but a few had that same eager adventure-lust Ken had: the crests on their heads flashed bright yellow with excitement as they traded stories about the stories they'd captured and planned to see.

Only Ken didn't want to tell a story about what he saw. He wanted to fix it.

Twelve. Yeah. It was day twelve when the missile hit our hull.

We'd already broken atmosphere—actually almost landed.

The pilot must have been a damn good one because despite the sudden jolt that yanked my restraints against my shoulders—*shit, that's going to leave a nice rug-burn*—I don't think we ever really rocked. Except for the breach alarm that went off, you might have thought we'd just had a small landing gear malfunction.

We bumped. Weapons went up. The reporters clutched their writing tablets to their chests; cameramen raised their cameras, the GPSS mercs their rifles. Kamakura instinctively reached for his seatbelt.

"Stand fast," Howard ordered, tapping the comms mic by her ear listening in on the ship's radio chatter.

"If we haven't really landed yet," I muttered in Ken's ear to explain, "you're more likely to get injured getting thrown across the room."

"Aren't we under attack?" he asked in that low voice of someone trying to question without looking like they're questioning.

"Wait," I said.

Wait. Hardest thing to do, with your chest shrinking inside you, your breaths shallower and shallower as your limbs itch to run, to fight, to *something*. The ache of uncertainty, the tension in your fingertips, the total lack of information forcing you to trust someone else's decision against your body's every screaming instinct—I'd have bet my Scrit's tail the kid beside me was surging with healthy adrenaline. I was surging with bitter memory myself.

If I hadn't felt like I needed to set an example for Kamakura I probably wouldn't have been able to keep my mouth shut—wouldn't've have been able to keep from peppering Howard with questions while she tried to contact the pilot. Was she sure we shouldn't move now? What'd the pilot said? I mean, she looked so young—did she know what she was doing, really?

Was this just more career vainglory, another higher-up

looking for a pretty deployment award soaked in someone else's blood?

The sudden, unmistakable, sweet, almost *creamy* scent of burning flesh ironically kept me from flashing back to my dead people. I was as cool as the surgery ward. I'd been happy back then. The acrid chemical smell of melting wires hit me next—from my seat closest to the door between the cockpit and the passenger bay, I was the first to catch it.

"We're on fire, sergeant," I announced. "Probably from the front."

"Where are the main fuel tanks on this thing?" Howard snapped to the reporter by her side—it wasn't rude snapping, just a matter-of-fact bark of someone who doesn't have time to waste modulating their tones. The reporter didn't seem to know, and the sergeant didn't seem to have contact with the ship's captain anymore—

"Up front's just the cockpit—the fuel tanks should be back behind us, with the engines just under us," Ken piped up. "Chatted with engineering earlier."

"That's good. Even if the alarm system's busted the extinguishing system should kick in any second now," Howard nodded. We weren't going to blow up, she meant—*hurry up and wait*, as my commander always said—

But the second jolt was a lot harder than the first one, and it came with the roaring screech of bending metal and shattering modified fiberglass. Heat surged through the passenger compartment. We'd probably dropped onto the planet surface.

"Eh—*now* it's time to go," Howard said with a cheeky nod toward Ken.

Kamakura was on his feet and at the sliding door to the cockpit almost before I could take off my safety restraints. I didn't need to tell him the door was hot. His open palm hovered over it first to check—the automatic sensor didn't open—he ripped a kerchief out of his pocket to try to grab the emergency handle without burning himself—

“Exit’s this way,” called Howard as she and her mercs dashed to the door on the other side of the room.

“The pilot’s trapped,” Ken shouted back, pointing to the floor. It angled down toward him: the front of the ship had probably smashed shut over the cockpit. “He might still be alive!”

I snatched his wrist. “Backdraft!” I barked. I wasn’t a firefighter, but we all took enough evac classes to know what that meant: opening a hot door into a closed space risked causing a massive explosion back towards us.

Ken’s hands clenched and unclenched by the door handle in hesitant desperation. “There might not be a backdraft, though!” he argued. “If we were hit the fire might be venting out the impact side, ma’am!”

Yeah, I felt him—shit, I was too sober for this, because I felt him. Someone was dying. Were we just going to let it happen? I softened my voice. “Do you *know* it’s venting?” I asked. “I can’t see smoke coming out under the door crack.” If air was flowing *into* the sucking cockpit instead of out, that meant a hungry fire just waiting for a rush of oxygen to unleash it.

Kamakura groaned, pressing the heel of his fist to his forehead. Kid knew I was right.

“It’s risking ten lives for one,” I said.

Ken’s eyes jumped to the mercs at the other end of the room struggling with a jammed back door. It was hot enough in here now that the fire safety system had sealed us in to protect the rest of the ship. An emergency trap door to the outside popped open in the floor instead—

“Suits sealed!” I ordered. I wasn’t in charge, but they wanted me to be a doctor, right? “We’ll go through IDCP once we’ve established a safe point.” You normally ran Interplanetary Decontamination Protocol *before* you stepped out on any new planet with little to no intersolar travel—we could be carrying any number of diseases the new population wasn't immune to, and vice versa—but, at the moment, well, we couldn't exactly set up test tubes and spit samples, could we?

"I'm less worried about germs than bullets right now," one of the GPSS mercs muttered—under his breath, but I heard it.

"Then we better get out there and do something about the bullets," I said.

Suits clicked and hissed as everyone's helmets sealed. The two lower-ranking mercs went first, weapons raised to protect the reporters. I gave Ken's wrist a gentle tug—we needed to go, too.

"If it's any consolation, I don't hear screams," I said. "If impact didn't kill him, smoke's put him out."

Ken clenched his teeth.

"I'm sorry," I said.

You always want the campfire story to end with "and then I ignored the officer and saved the day." It never feels right when it goes "and then I obeyed, and someone died."

Ken Kamakura

Ken gave in to Captain Wimmer because of the math. She couldn't have physically stopped him, screamed the pounding in his temples—combat skills aside, no force in the world *could* have.

That made abandoning the pilot of his own free will feel even worse.

The old doctor stepped between Ken and the cockpit door at his first sign of surrender—and she stayed behind him, blocking that door, until he reached the emergency exit. Howard's two mercs went first, with the civilians; Ken and Wimmer brought up the rear with Howard herself herding them like the payload they were.

Vibrant pink sand wafted beneath the open trapdoor. They were maybe half a meter off the ground even with the ship's back end angled up into the air. Ken could swear he now *heard* the flames crackling in the cockpit. *Maybe we made the wrong call…?* But it was math, and too late now. Even if there hadn't been an explosion, there was no guarantee Ken could get the pilot out without disengaging the fire control system's seals—no guarantee he'd even make it through the fire itself. Toxic fumes, too… he was willing to die, but to kill everyone else?

What if he waited until everyone else got some distance from the ship, and then tried it?

And that thought was probably why Wimmer was behind him like flies around a Bovie's backside.

He's already dead. She knows what she's talking about. Already dead. I'd risk an explosion for nothing. If we evac fast, the extinguishing system might be able to halt the fire, save the ship, and we can use the ship's resources to help people—

Blablabla. No one even tried to save the guy! What if we create a vertical breach from the other side to vent the air once we get out—then come back in and try again?

Okay. Okay, that's a possibility.

Ken's boots hit the ground with a surprising firm softness. It took a moment for his eyes to adjust to the brilliant hues in the sunlight, but he could hear the peppering rattle of gunfire punctuated by screams in a language he didn't know. Wimmer's well-trained Scrit prowled between her ankles, calm, its psionic field actively translating between everyone's neural networks like a biological EEG interpreter as its golden eyes blinked behind the bandit-mask markings of its black face fur. But the combatants were still mostly too distant to really understand—or maybe the accents registered strangely in Ken's head, or the sounds and lights were too disorienting as Ken's brain tried to wrap itself around what little he could see peeking out from under the metal protection of the ship's bulk looming over and behind him like an artificial cave.

Orders, Ken's brain did understand. And training: in a firefight the guy who knew how to use cover would beat the guy with better aim. The former Terran soldiers surrounded their Grausian civilian charges, crouching or laying in the shadow of the ship with weapons drawn. Wimmer was the only one short enough to stand hunched, pointing her borrowed GPSS pistol at the ground with both hands and elbows locked as she pressed her back against the metal of the downed ship, grey eyes scanning first her team, then the horizon.

Colorful robes dashed from boulder to boulder amid swirling salmon-blush sands. The people were like painted blurs—Ken only caught glimpses of iridescent skin that almost seemed to reflect the landscape. Howard was radioing contacts and trying to get a handle on the politics of the moment. *Are we actually a target? Did someone hit us by accident?* Always kind of important in combat to know who was trying to kill who.

"If the engine's anywhere below where we were sitting, we can't stay here much longer," said the bigger merc on Howard's left, a muscle-bound monster Ken had heard went by Bone. "Fire's spreading."

"Extinguishing system must have been damaged in the crash," said the other, Tack, a guy whose face was so pale beside the darker skin of his compatriot you'd think he was translucent, a ghost possessing a space-suit. A friend of some Interthought Media lead, Tack was apparently the man who'd scored them the ride with the reporters in the first place. "I told Stafford this model was a bullshit buy."

"What'd you expect? He's a fucking CEO, you're just some guy. It's not like a former Loyalist wants to listen to an ex-lapdog Terran anyway," Bone laughed.

"You don't know him, man. Anyway, he was smarter back in my Legion days."

The men sounded so calm between bites of whatever psychotropic plant-chew they gnashed between their teeth—like it was just another day at the range. Ken glared at both of them. How could they be so—*distracted*—talking about used ship sales and politics *now*. A guy just died. They all might die. *Focus up!*

"They're paying attention." Wimmer lowed over Ken's shoulder. "Watch the body language. His kneel, his crouch, the coordination as their sights and aim shift back and forth. Rifles cocked, heads on a swivel. They know who to cover. Next maneuver. All that. When Howard gives the okay to move, they'll shut up."

Ken looked at her for a second. It was weird how the woman's voice could alternate so easily between that hard rasp and this soothing rumble that almost reminded Ken of the peaceful mooing of the Bovies grazing his uncle's estate greens during those summers away… he'd heard this voice a few times during the short time she spent at his Role II, and just once in the past month when Jump Sickness had him vomiting up everything but his large intestines. *This is her patient care voice. I wonder if I've got a separate medical voice myself.*

A loud clap—the first shot from Ken's team came from Tack. "Triangle-shirt fucker behind that rock," he said.

Bone nodded and fired, too. There was an Edenian peeking around the edge of a boulder with his weapon aimed at the group. "The hell do they want?" Bone asked.

"Nobody knows shit," Howard said, finally ending her transmission. "We can't just run out into a field of fire without knowing where to go."

"Well, I know those robes seem to be of the Third clan," squeaked the shortest Grausian reporter with them, the one with the slightest greenish hue to his microscopic gray scales. *Ham, I think he was named.* About Wimmer's height, Ham was *very* short for a Grausian, almost juvenile size. *Maybe he's got a growth hormone disorder. He's making up for it in moxy, though:* even the gently-angled crest on his head only flashed a dim emerald color—he was pretty calm, despite the excitement. His large eyes twitched, nictitating membrane blinking against the harsh light as he nodded towards the field: "See the triangles embroidered in the hem."

"We're about to explode here," Howard said. "Is this a fashion lesson, or are you going to tell me who's trying to kill who?"

"The Third are more of a 'scorch the past to return to our ancestors'—they're probably not happy about a big outsider ship bringing potential new technology to further corrupt their world?" Ham asked. "I saw a few Sevella hems. They're supposed to be our contacts—more liberal, more likely to want to take advantage of any technology we have available, but with Quasar Day today—"

"I'm gonna need you to bottom line this," Howard said.

"The triangle-shirt guys might be trying to kill us, the circle shirt guys kind of invited us to land here," stammered the flustered Grausian. "We showed up on an important religious holiday that our contact didn't think it'd be such a big deal, but apparently it is."

"Great," snapped Howard. "So now it looks like we were called in as backup for iconoclasts."

"Could we maybe save the ship and take refuge inside again if we vent the front to support the fire-fighting system?" Ken interrupted. He couldn't get his mind off that cockpit. He *needed* to see inside.

"Nope. We have artillery incoming." Tack pointed off to the distance—Ken poked his head out from the shadow of the ship just for a second, just for a glimpse, before ducking back into cover. *What was that?* It was almost too far away to make out, but Ken recognized the huge surface-to-air missile—literally a freaking rocket—very inappropriately lowered directly at the downed ship.

Even Ken knew it was like dropping an anvil just to kill an ant.

"That is not what that is for," Bone laughed.

"Are they fucking insane?" Howard grunted. "The backfire's likely to destroy the whole launching mechanism aimed low like that—maybe kill them, too."

"They are probably not worried about destroying something their hated Grausian overlords left behind?" Ham's thin voice carried over the gunfire. 'Hated' sounded almost sarcastic coming from a Grausian himself, but there was empathy in his voice. "They probably want to eliminate the ship and punish the Sevellan heretics for bringing it, more than kill us. Ruining the abandoned technology is most likely a bonus."

"Okay, well, we need distance, now." Everyone followed Howard's gaze towards a cluster of pinkish mud-brick buildings off to the right, beyond the field of stones. "Rendezvous at the settlement on our three o'clock. Bone, you lead, take three Media crew with you. Everyone who's armed will do the same." She nodded to Wimmer and Ken. "Tack, you cover us and take the rear. You all," she turned to the gaggle of huddled reporters and cameramen. "Run low and fast like we do. Stay close to your escort—*behind* your escort so you don't get shot. You're lucky we're here: no extra charge for protection today since it's a holiday." The half-joke almost got lost in the speed of her rapid-fire orders, but she flashed a smile Ken could only see as beautiful—heck, with all the adrenaline pounding in his temples, she could've said anything and still sounded charming. "Let's all try to stay alive long enough to get to Galaxy Aid so we can get paid."

CHAPTER FIVE

Jocelyn Wimmer

WE DUCKED out from under the cover of our downed ship; the landscape spread around us with aggressive barrenness. Clumps of short bushes and ragged low mountain peaks broke up the blinding vibrance of the colorful sand with grays and dull green; except for a cluster of small red and pale-pink mud-brick houses in the far distance, our ship was definitely the biggest cover around

In that distance, gunfire smattered over the wails of what were probably children.

Kamakura's eyes lit up like a hunter's at the first audible cry. I could see him ducking behind a boulder to my right, ready to run. He had his own two reporters to protect, and I had mine, but I was already calculating how many medpacks he could spare for how many injured civilians.

Once we've cleared a safe-ish building for a mini-Command Point and Howard establishes comms we can start triage.

Our medical resources were paid for by GPSS, but *they* were being paid by Galaxy Aid—as long as we had what we needed to keep the mercs alive I'd be able to argue we were complying with the client's stated mission if anyone complained about 'wasting' bandages on Edenians.

"There!" shouted both Kamakara and Howard at the same time—probably for very different reasons—as we got close enough to just make out a squat building surrounded by circle-shirt Edenians tending to wounded.

Getting 'there' did not look like an easy trip. We were almost smack in the middle of what was clearly now no-man's land. It was easier to see the combatants now—at least every time one of them managed to leave cover and get shot. They were bipedal humanoids with sharp pointed ears and iridescent skin that I imagined had evolved to blend well into the incredibly colorful geology of their landscape. Alive, they were mostly shifting shades of pink stripes right now—at least the ones I could see—with a sheen of rainbow tint. They went full-on oil-spill rainbow when they died, though—at least I was fairly sure that guy was dead. He seemed to have taken a bullet through the head.

My little group were pretty badly pinned down. Even if no one actually wanted to kill us, with shots ricocheting everywhere, anyone could hit us by accident. And that guy behind the bush on my left definitely wanted to kill us. My aim was shit, and we couldn't cross from this rocky crevasse to the next boulder with him spraying the open space like that.

Suddenly one of the reporters with me screamed. "Behind us!"

"Wait!" I yelled too late as he jumped to his feet to run. I heard the bullet zip into his chest as bush-guy got him; I was firing rapidly on the Edenian dashing at us from behind with two thick cleaver-looking swords. The attacker bared his black teeth in a crazed grin—he didn't seem to care about my pistol.

Cleaver-freak got close enough for me to see the Legion-class armored vest under his robe. I shot his upper thigh, then his shoulder—he stumbled, and hurled a blade. I was lucky to duck; it bounced off the stone behind me, knocked against my back—

With him grounded I finally got his head.

"Can you shoot?" I asked the calmest camerawoman beside me.

"I am shooting!" she said, nodding to the porta-cam on her wrist.

"A gun. A gun!" I shoved my pistol into her hands—"Cover our backside, this whole thing's too open. Just point and pull this trigger if anything moves at us." The reporter who'd stood up to get himself shot wheezed on the ground by my knees; bright orange blood ringed a small hole in his atmosuit. I tore open the IFAK individual first aid kit at my hip—*need a needle-d, now*. "Idiot giving me more work," I grumbled. "The hell we're going to drag your ass across no-man's land now. Say your name!"

"Salan," he whispered.

"Okay Salan, sounds like your airway's clear." But his chest heaved as he gasped for oxygen, sucking at the air. The crest on his head flopped flat against his skull—he was already exhausted with the effort it took to breathe.

I rolled him over to see if the bullet had come out his back, tearing open his suit with my pocket-knife as I went. Gah, my hands were weak—took me so much damn effort to rip the material. His skin was cold through the conductive material of my gloves' sensory fingertips—not too cold for a Grausian, though.

I found the exit wound. Sweet. No massive hemorrhage, just some sunset-colored trickles. Laid both hands across his chest to confirm what I already knew: rise and fall uneven, probably left side pneumothorax. Needle-d first, then patch the two holes with a sticky plastic pad, leaving one side un-glued so air could burp out—

"Keep your eyes behind us, lady," I reminded the camerawoman. "Weapon pointed out. Stop trying to film me." I'd never had kids, but I had those 'mom-eyes' in the back of my head everyone always talks about.

Salan squealed as I held the needle-D above his chest to stab him. "What the hell are you doing?"

"Opening your chest so your lung doesn't collapse and kill you. If you prefer to die that's fine, too." I stabbed him before he could state his preference. I'd already broken the sterile seal and wasn't going to waste the medical supplies.

Grausians have bigger spaces between their ribs than Terrans do—my fingers still remembered exactly where to go. But my thin arm *almost* didn't generate enough force to plunge the needle through his chest wall. Shit I was so weak. The malnutritive alcoholic life was getting to me. "That didn't hurt," I assured him before he could whimper. "Not like getting shot, right?"

"Are you sure you got the right intercostal space?" panted my third charge, an overweight Grausian with a heavy pack that I suddenly realized was probably full of medical supplies. "You're a Terran doctor, our anatomy's decidedly different, and—"

"Son, are you Interthought's medic for this group?" I asked, rolling my reporter again to apply my chest seal to his back.

"Yes I am, and as a Grausian myself—"

"Get to work then," I said. "What the hell you so slow for? I was shooting knife-boy for a good thirty seconds while your guy was dying in the sand."

I guess he'd expected me to get territorial—maybe to argue about all my time in the Legion and all the Grausians I'd served and saved before their people massacred our commanders. I didn't have time for ego mid-fire-fight. And I didn't give a shit, actually, as long as the patient got fixed. I hated medicine anyway. And I could kill—Chubs here couldn't. Let him work for his pay and I'd keep them alive.

"'Ey." I patted the camerawoman's shoulder to take back my pistol. *Now to get bush-guy gone.* I couldn't help one last annoyed bark at the Interthought medic, though—not because I was insulted, but because I was annoyed at the fucking waste of my time.

"You should say something sooner next time, *Thal*," I dropped the honorific with a half-mocking tone. "I could've been shooting this other bastard in the meantime."

Granted, if I wasn't so reclusive during the twelve days it took the explorer to get us here from the Eden Crescent jump point, I'd probably know *Chubs was their medic already…*

A bush isn't as good cover as a rock, turns out. If I'd been a better shot, I wouldn't've had so much trouble—he just kept pinging the boulder right next to my face every time I peeped around it to aim at him. I was basically lying on the ground, trying to see if I could inch my weapon around the edge at a point he hadn't seen yet—*damn these shaky-ass hands.*

Wind behind me, whistling around the edge of my atmosphere helmet.

Jam. Jam on foreheads. Little red baby-mouth gasping for air.

Wind behind me…

Shut the fuck up.

Couldn't focus to aim. Too weak, too shaky. *Nope. No time for this bullshit right now.*

Back on the ship before suiting up—before we'd even strapped into our seats for landing—I'd dissolved my crushed amphetamines in the water in the hydration system hooked into my facemask. Now I just needed to squeeze the pouch by my hip to increase the water pressure, and the drinking tube straightened to reach my lips. One heavy swig and I was good to go. Relief flooded me long before the drug could kick in. I was going to function. Nothing else mattered. I'd long ago stopped feeling guilty about the hypocrisy of a physician poisoning herself without a legitimate diagnosis. I'd be dosing myself with benzos tonight to prevent alcohol withdrawal, too.

I inched around the other side of the boulder from where the Edenian had seen me last. Just the comfort of knowing comfort was coming tightened my vision. *He's behind a bush, for shit's sake, this is easy. Just aim!*

My problem at the range had always been overthinking and catching the wrong details—it was like despite 20/20 vision I couldn't actually *see* my sight picture. I wasn't autistic, but when a friend of mine on the spectrum once told me he couldn't hear me on board transport vessels because he kept hearing all the engine noises, it sounded like what I felt like with a gun in my hand. I'd never had that trouble during my time in the Legion—it was during the Secession some time that this'd started. I didn't know when. I didn't care.

"Got him." Center mass. The Edenian slumped to the ground —no dramatic falls, no grunts, no yells, just that simple cessation of movement. "See that purple-ish fallen column over there?"

"The petrified log?" asked the camerawoman.

"I think it's actually something from Gaussian construction," suggested Shorty.

"Follow me there. You got your boy here?" I asked the Interthought medic. "Loop your hands around his chest and drag running backwards." I tensed to rise—we still had a lull in the gunfire just here—

"It'd be faster if someone helped and got his feet!" the medic protested.

"If you need help, sure," I said, nodding to the camerawoman: "Cross your arms under his knees like this." The one-man drag was faster to explain and got more people to cover faster, but I wasn't going to waste the opening I'd created trying to argue with someone else's medic. "Now. Go!"

I dashed forward, hunched low, weapon held out in front of me. Where I looked, it pointed—left, right, forward—I saw movement on the right and gave a warning shout *"Stay back!"* before popping off a warning shot at the ground—*trying not to kill anyone I shouldn't here, but hot damn is it hard to tell these 'uniforms' apart—*

It was all familiar. There was ritual to it, almost. It wasn't that it felt good. Even with the drug nothing really felt good, anyway, and right now my body and mind roared with the pulsatile rhythm of those familiar stress hormones that, once the adrenaline died down again, would leave me sore and hopeless and hating the world. I was here on this planet—in this Universe, really—not because I *wanted* to be here, but because I felt something worse would happen to more people if I wasn't. But in these emergency moments the instructions drilled into me over the thousands of patients and dozens of combat skirmishes and hundreds of training exercises provided an order, a beat, a time stamp marking the difference between noise and notes. Algorithms and protocols turned mess into music, and even though I hated the song that was playing, at least I knew how to dance along.

Ken Kamakura

It was well past 2300 hours in the small port village. The night sky still rattled with gunfire, and Ken was in a dream.

Not a sleeping one. His body was moving almost on autopilot as his mouth gave orders—some his own, some Captain Wimmer's—and his brain and eyes saw nothing else but problem, solution, problem, solution, problem, solution, over and over in quick succession, with lulls and peaks in activity washing through him like breaths. Here an Edenian soldier with circles on his robe's hem vomited blood, crimson seething through his ebony teeth; there a child screamed, clutching an iridescent arm that'd blown off at the elbow.

"This one's immediate evacuation, another immediate, this

one's delayed—this one's minimal, you, you're minimal, can you help carry water? Thanks." Ken triaged and stabilized the patients he could while Wimmer came behind him for the worst cases, her translator Scrit bounding by her ankles with a jaunty pep that now seemed almost sinister. "This one's… expectant," Ken said to Thessalucia, the elegant Grausian reporter from his makeshift 'squad' who'd stayed around to help him while the others filmed their stories. She nodded, her thin lips pursed hard under her slender beak-like nose: Ken said "expectant" in a low voice, looking over a female civilian with clear fluid leaking from a blown-open spine—he would ask the reporter to keep the female comfortable with the others like her. The others whose care would take an entire medical team on their own—whose care would allow no one else to be saved—who even then with every available resource allocated to them would still have had an almost zero chance of surviving.

They were 'expectant' because they were expected to die.

Ken was in a dream because this was what he'd waited all his life to do—something he'd only heard about in stories, something he'd trained for but almost didn't believe could be real. It was also a dream because it was so much like a living nightmare. Not for him. He was fine. This was a normal day at work, the first of the rest of his life. But for every person his gloves touched, his normal day at work was one of the worst days of their entire lives.

As the hours marched on his helmet grew dead heavy. His boots kicked deep green gashes in the pink sand with each leaden step of his slowed shuffle; through the humid, sweaty sting under his eyelashes and the fog creeping along the edges of the anti-fog space-mask he could feel his gaze dimming, blurring—fixing itself at random points in space without looking at anything at all. *Stay here!* He shook himself, spoke to himself, ground and loosened his jaw, squeezed and released his fists, anything through the fugue to keep his mind awake. *Stop it. It's not even that late!* He'd dosed his camel-back with caffeine before they'd landed, and every few seconds found him squeezing the bag by his hip for a sip.

"Stop chewing on your drink-tube." Wimmer's gravelly voice didn't sound unpleasant as she passed him—just a bit annoyed. "You're going to break it. Do you not know how to suck?"

"No ma'am, I do not know how to suck," he quipped back. "Only excellence here."

He caught her chuckle as she rounded the corner away from him to talk again with the Edenian Sevilla-clan leader. There wasn't any way to evacuate people off-world for advanced medical care right now—next known space-flight left from a city almost on the other side of the planet—but there was supposedly an old Grausian medical cache only about thirty kilometers from here and Wimmer was suggesting she and Ken take the 'immediate' patients out there as soon as the fighting died down somewhat. The Interthought Media medic had protested about being left behind, but Wimmer very *very* quickly pointed out how badly his team of *Grausian* reporters would need *him*—she emphasized Grausian for some reason—and the reporters would be heading literally in the opposite direction from the cache now that they'd filmed all the gore they needed here. *Meanwhile we might find Galaxy Aid workers at the cache,* Ken understood from her, *to take us on to our actual mission.*

But Ken was already at his actual mission, as far as he was concerned. The jog across the sands from the damaged ship to the makeshift 'spaceport' hadn't been that difficult—almost exactly like a training simulation he'd loved in basic, actually. But like the rest of the journey, every step up through the sand had been just a means to an end.

Interesting? Sure.

Meaningful? Maybe, maybe not.

But this. This was the end. This was the goal. Holding still the delirious guy vomiting blood so he wouldn't drown in his own fluids before Wimmer could inject him with a tranquilizer; placing a handful of opioid candies in Thessalucia's thin palm so she could calm the dying in their last moments; tightening a soldier's tourniquet and teaching him to show his buddies, fast, so they could save their own lives while he tended others; and actually delivering a baby because nature never chose the most convenient days for new life. Edenians were apparently pretty similar to humans and Ilyrians in this area of their lives. Easing the placenta out after the baby with that slow, slightly rotating tension on the cord; the thick, almost crunchy wet resistance of that cord under his scissors as he cut it; the heartwarming, tearful panting joy of the mother as her travail ended; the baby's brilliant flush of color after he rubbed it with a towel and wiped gunk off its face—all pretty similar, except that this baby flushed from grey to rainbow, and its little pointed ears looked like something out of an old fairytale.

That'd been a good moment.

It was all good in its own way—all moments of beauty made brighter by the terror contrasting them. But he was so damn tired. Lifting this suit now felt like carrying a prison. It was so hot. When would they have time to go through IDCP so he could take it off? Never. Everyone was so injured. How could they spare even a minute for something so slow, so—subacute, nonemergency, as prevention protocol?

He was glad for the feeding tube in the helmet. He'd almost forgotten about it before Wimmer punched him in the shoulder—again in passing—and reminded him of some ancient study about firefighters performing better with carbohydrates in their systems. Gunky, gritty wet sweet mash—old Terra 'apfel' flavor—seemed in those moments richer than the food of the gods.

God, he found his delirium asking. *Do your creations conquer hell by laughing through it?*

A thought that seemed random, trivial, inane. Maybe it

occurred because Wimmer cracked some comment in the distance, and Tack and Bone both laughed from their defensive positions at the makeshift perimeter—the row of burnt-out vehicles they'd pushed in front of the two mud-brick buildings where they'd established CP. Time seemed to lag in the twilight—"*when will this be over?*" his weary cells begged as his will dragged them forward—and at some point Ken came outside of the lit building again to realize the silhouettes at the perimeter were no longer Tack's and Bone's, and the thin lady following around the 'minimals' and comforting the 'expectants' was no longer Thessalucia. Sevellan Edenians had taken their posts—was he alone? He didn't have time to pay attention—not with his supplies freshly exhausted and him scrambling for something cloth-like to stop this bleed—but his brain worked the question in the back of his head as he ran—slouched, actually—to the other building to grab the last IV-antibiotic baggie. The Interthought medic was asleep in there, curled up clutching his aid bag with a small scratch still bright on his cheek. Ken fought back the disdain that surged from his belly to his throat like bile—it didn't matter what some other guy did. *Stay in your lane.*

He trotted back and knelt to insert his IV. This was for an Edenian whose abdomen had been blasted open—you could see his intestines—but who'd otherwise managed to maintain stable vitals. The wet towel on his belly plus strong antibacterials might keep him alive long enough to get to the medical cache where hopefully they'd find tissue growth injecta-grafts that would close him back up again. With any luck there'd be an AI-powered camera to highlight damaged areas that needed injection, and a tissue sampling kit that would let them grow him custom tissue for his genetics instead of just hoping the standard biological 'glue' held without causing an autoimmune reaction. If they didn't have any of that stuff, hopefully at least the Edenians had a manual surgeon. *They've at least got to be at the level of pre-conquest Terra, right?*

He was explaining this whole plan aloud to the Edenian, even though he knew his ability to be understood went in and out every time Wimmer's Scrit stepped too far away from him. Thessalucia had studied most Edenian languages as an anthropologist before becoming a reporter—she'd once lived on Eden Crescent, she mentioned at some point—and for a bit she'd translated for him when something was just too urgent to leave to chance. But she was—somewhere?

"Alright Kamakura, you're up," Wimmer croaked. He felt her hand on his shoulder—a firm quick pat, like a dad afraid to show too much affection. "Go sleep."

"Sleep?" Ken almost laughed. His aching, sagging limbs cried. "I'm good, ma'am."

"No, you're not good, kid. I don't want someone who's been on for over twenty-four hours making medical decisions unless it's absolutely combat necessary. Get you six hours—eight if you need them—and start back up again with triage and first aid. I'll wake you up if we're able to transport before then. I hope to high heaven—" She shook her head, hands on her hips as she stared out the door at the tiny flashes of light on the dark horizon. "We're probably looking at a death or two every hour if we can't get out of here soon."

"That's why I don't think I can take off, ma'am, I—"

"The Interthought guy's subbing in for you. He slept, he's fresh. Every team's rotating to maximize effectiveness." She nodded, and he realized one of the bodies in the corner was Tack, sleeping against the wall with arms crossed over his pecs and head tilted down to his chest, while Bone sat by the doorway eating an MRE, weapon down by his side. They both seemed somehow alert in their rest.

Wait, eating? Bone's space helmet lay in the dirt, and his suit was peeled down to his waist—he was just sitting there out in the open air with only a sweaty white tanktop between him and the new planet. *So, he did IDCP? He's safe to be suitless?* IDCP was mostly an automated process with minimal medical intervention, but still—when was there *time?*

"We had to make the time for the GPSS guys. They were doing the brunt of the active defense work. No good if they get heat stroke in their suits and become two more casualties to take care of," Wimmer said, following Ken's gaze.

"I guess not ma'am." Ken's eyes returned to his fingers. Had he still not inserted this IV? He thought he'd done this already. He stared for a second at the needle—it seemed to have two points—

"I said get the fuck to sleep," Wimmer suddenly snarled, almost pouncing to take the liquid antibiotic pouch from him. "Give me your report on this patient. Now. Then you either go to sleep, or you clean that pretty little pistol your mama gave you so it doesn't misfire on someone. Which do you prefer?"

Ken blinked. What was wrong with her? What the hell did his weapon have to do with—

She elbowed him to the side. "Wasting my fucking time and we've got people dying here," she spat, slipping the needle into the patient's vein and securing the catheter.

"Hey, don't disrespect my young doctor like that," the abdominal patient groaned, giving a little hiss as the needle entered—still cognizant despite the heavy dose of ketamine Ken had given him for pain management. "Mr. Kamakura's been nothing but excellent and kind to me. I don't know how you outworlders do things, but here we treat good people good."

"Good for you," Wimmer said, spreading her teeth in a strained smile. The faux-grin dropped as quickly as it'd appeared: "I once had a medic die because his battle-buddy's weapon jammed just when he needed it to defend them both. Idiot hadn't cleaned the rifle in days, and it took its revenge like all broken things do." She turned harsh grey eyes to Ken; in the dim lamplight the shadow under her helmet hid almost every feature of her face except for the reflection in those eyes. "Your body's your rifle. Your mind's your rifle. Fail to keep 'em sharp… someone dies. When I was with your unit, I cut down the Role II set up time from twelve hours to two by getting my sergeants to rotate shifts instead of keeping my guys up for thirty-six hours straight like fucking lobotomized Grats. You wanna help people or just feel like you're helping people because you're suffering so nobly?"

The patient shut his mouth—his ketamine-ridden brain probably couldn't come up with a response to that, even if he could process it. Ken answered with what she wanted—the patient details—but found himself stumbling through the steps… damn, he really was tired. His face burned as he rose. He would have appreciated the concern for his well-being if she didn't manage to make it into an insult somehow.

"You know, ma'am, I'm not trying to argue with you," he said at the doorway. "I just don't want to be one of these shitbags who wake up only to collect their paycheck."

"If you were a shitbag, I woulda knocked your ass out, robbed your fare, and shipped you to Alpha Prime with a cute little postcard that said 'in need of babysitter.' I didn't do that, so clearly, you're not a shitbag. Shut up and go the fuck to sleep."

Ken paused once more by the door as if to say something—but his brain forgot what. He got the feeling the rifle story wasn't the memory that made Wimmer freak out at him, but he got the point, nevertheless.

Sleep was his job now. So he slept.

CHAPTER SIX

Jocelyn Wimmer

IT WAS ABOUT 0500 by my watch when we realized we were hostages.

The Sevellan in charge can't have been much older than Kamakura. He stood by the pile of scrapped Grausian leftovers that ringed our perimeter with both hands on his rifle, his frayed scarf dancing in the wind. A pale beige headband hid his pointed ears, and when he closed his mouth you couldn't see the characteristic black teeth and gums, so if it weren't for his skin changing color every time a different hue of sand blew past him, you'd almost think he looked like some underprivileged Terran youth from one of the fringe worlds, or maybe an Alpha Prime kid playing dress-up. The cynicism and authority in the deep voice seemed fully out of place coming from that fresh face.

"You've been here long enough to see the situation we're in," he said. "We need medical supplies and food. Our Third brethren blame the offworlders for our ravaged planet—and, as you've seen, they'd like to wipe us out for touching the unholy leftovers—but the truth is that rapid Grausian withdrawal ruined our local economies." *Huh.* More perceptive and on the nose than I expected for someone so young and—poor. "We need resources, and your home worlds have them."

"Your planet's full of natural ores, though," protested Ham—the know-it-all reporter I'd nicknamed Shorty in my head. The crest on his head stood straight up in fear. "Surely you're underestimating yourselves. You don't need to resort to—"

"Not that I need to explain myself to you, Grausian, but where mines haven't been absolutely drained by your representatives they've been sacked by Terrans and Charee repurposing equipment for warfare," the Sevellan interrupted. "We shouldn't have to rebuild on our own. Your peoples owe us. And you're going to help get us what we're owed." He motioned with his rifle, and one of the taller, more built Edenians placed a chair before him and waved to the reporter to sit.

Ham's eyes flew from person to person in panic, nictating membranes blinking wildly. "When you said we could land here you assured us safety!"

"And that assurance remains as long as you cooperate."

Tension itched at my stomach muscles—just one or two wrong moves, one or two misplaced sentences, separated *hostage video* from *execution* in my mind. I was here because Sergeant Howard needed my Scrit—I'd expected just a quick ten-minute pause from patient care, not a potential interplanetary incident—so I stood behind her now with my hands on my hips close to my borrowed pistol.

"Have a seat, Mr. Ham," Howard suggested, her voice clear and even, blue eyes wide, alert, her intense gaze fixed on the Sevellan leader. "Let's hear our hosts out. They don't have any reason to harm us—not after all the help our medical crew's given them. As I understand it, his sister is currently dying, and if anything happens to us, she might not make it, either."

"That's exactly right. Can you call over your camera crew, please?" The Sevellan returned Howard's locked-on eye contact.

Whether he took the sergeant's statement as a warning or a threat, I didn't know, but I didn't love her putting that bargaining chip fully in the lap of my tiny three-man team. I didn't know which patient was this guy's sister—if she was an 'expectant', this was a terrible move. Was I supposed to suddenly let a bunch of other people die to try to save an impossible case?

This was familiar ground—medical manipulated in service of some leader's miracle without consulting us first. I'd seen it a hundred times if I'd seen it once—usually for admin purposes, though, and deployment ramp-ups, not for… this. I cleared my throat under my breath near Howard's ear while the Sevellan instructed Ham on what to broadcast back via Interthought's media system. "Mind telling me which patient you're talking about, Sergeant?" I asked.

"Kamakura's with her now. Sibila's her name—our enterprising negotiator here is called Sereno."

"Lotta s-names. That's gonna get confusing fast," I smirked. "Look, you need to tell this guy he stands to lose about ten people if I can't get transport to the cache within the hour. I'm wasting my time standing around here with you all and we've got people, as you said, dying."

"Kamakura told me everyone's stable for now?"

"'Stable' isn't 'safe.' Just because no one's bleeding out right now doesn't mean their limbs aren't going to start dropping off from tissue necrosis under those tourniquets." I pointed with my chin to a row of drugged-out Edenians leaning against the medical hut, bloody arms and legs losing color beneath the blinding sun. "I can only keep an open abdominal wound wet for so long, and I've got no TXA or fluids left for the folks who've got slow internal bleeds. Our respiratory collapse guys can't just hang out here with makeshift vents in chests, either. These are temporary fixes for permanent problems, Sergeant."

Howard nodded and cleared her throat. "Captain Sereno," she said. "Speaking of your limited medical supplies—"

"I heard the doctor," Sereno interrupted. He seemed to not even know I'd been whispering. *Looks like the big ears aren't just for show.* "I'll arrange transport for the medical team. The reporters stay here and live off our supplies, with us, until aid arrives for them. If we starve, they starve. If we're slaughtered by the Third, they join us in the afterlife." He didn't smile, and his voice didn't hiss with the bitter spit of hatred, either—he was simply stating facts, like "children who play in the road might take a tank tread to the face." *Kid's a professional.*

"Well, Captain, before you commit to starving—maybe before you turn on that camera—" Howard stepped towards Ham and the chair. A larger Edenian stepped in her way.

Howard raised both hands in quiet understanding. "We have a contract with Galaxy Aid. If you let me escort my medical to them, we can probably convince them to divert resources this way." She flashed a charming grin. "We don't even have to mention the coercion."

"Coercion?" Now it was Sereno's turn to smile. "If I remember correctly, Interthought Media wanted to capture the reality of Sevellan life, and share it with the world. This is that reality. And now, at great cost to ourselves, we've protected them from the radical fundamentalists who destroyed their ship." He waved to the crater where the ill-used land-to-air missile had struck. "It's simply too dangerous to transport civilians like them out of our clan's territory—not without outside support and aid, of course." He tilted his head in a soft bow.

The double-speak made me wonder if he was the one who'd actually tipped off the Third to our arrival—I didn't know if Howard had guessed the same thing, but she returned his smile with a knowing glint in her eye. "We thank you for your hospitality. So, in return, I'll escort your wounded to the old Grausian medical cache with my medical crew and my two combatants, and then escort your representative to Galaxy Aid to secure supplies. What vehicles are available to us?"

"Mm, not so fast." Sereno's smile remained unchanged. "I'm well aware you're two separate outfits in one ship—what's to keep your mercenary band from simply abandoning these poor journalists in order to go fulfill your contract?"

"Greed," Howard said so quickly it was almost scary. "Greed's to keep us from abandoning them. I'd personally like Interthought Media to pay an upcharge for our protective services—especially after this messy little exercise cost us a heap of supplies. So I'm invested in the reporters living."

"'Even a land-lord will go homeless for the price of his life,'" Sereno quoted back. The corner of his mouth twitched—he was amused by Howard. "Greed isn't always quite as powerful as fear. Or family and unit bonds. I want to keep one of your group back as collateral as well."

"You can have our Grausian medic," I piped up—*shit, too eager.* Sereno raised an eyebrow. I was making it terribly obvious Chubs wasn't actually ours.

Howard saved me with an annoyed grumble. "We might need him—don't you have a Grausian patient with a chest wound you'll need to take to the cache?"

"No, no!" Ham protested, falling right into her play. "He stays with us. We need him in case the rest of us are injured!"

"That seems fair," Sereno declared, and that was that—preparations to load out began with a clap of his hands. I waited until I turned my back to breathe a sigh of relief. Talky talky shit was the worst.

Ken Kamakura

The rumbling transport truck lurched to a start; Ken pressed another augmented cis-scopolamine patch to the back of his ear, wishing he didn't have such a motion-sensitive stomach. It didn't help to not have windows—the only light in the vehicle filtered through the cracks in the door, or blipped from the medical instrumentation monitoring the various patients. He took a deep breath and closed his eyes, leaning back against the hot metal wall, choosing to shift his focus away from the waves of nausea and towards how freaking cool this vehicle was instead.

Cool because of age, not because of beauty: the military truck currently taking them to the medical cache was Terran-make from perhaps a hundred years ago—boxy, chunky, clunky and old, but in great shape for a historical piece. Ken had only ever seen anything like it in films and school projects. On the outside, of course, the eight-wheeled monstrosity wasn't exactly an accurate period representation: its current owners had flecked it with bright spots of pink, orange, and neon-green paint to help it blend better into their technicolor landscape. Inside, canvas stretchers were stacked on each wall like bookshelves, each holding a patient strapped in place with metal and cloth belts much like the material currently holding up Ken's pants.

Ken and Wimmer sat in the narrow alley between the canvas shelves so they could easily access each patient without moving much. The boots of the GPSS mercs and Edenian soldiers thunked every now and then on the roof above. Howard had firmly insisted she see where they were going, and Sereno hadn't objected: so far, she and Tack and Bone had proved formidable in a firefight, and out here without a global positioning system or a supply drop for days they were incentivized to help keep their would-be captors alive—at least until better resources presented themselves.

"Captivity" seemed like a strong word for it. If anything, this felt like an arranged marriage of convenience: GPSS needed to get Ken and Wimmer closer to the Galaxy Aid checkpoint, the Sevellans needed medical supplies—and Wimmer needed to get as far away as humanly possible from the Interthought medic who annoyed her. She hadn't openly showed any disdain for the older medical professional—whose advanced training actually probably ranked more along the lines of nurse practitioner than medic—but Ken had watched with great amusement how every time 'Chubs' entered the room Wimmer somehow managed to find somewhere else to be very, very quickly.

He felt bad he couldn't remember the guy's actual name after Wimmer's description…

Ken blinked to take in the compartment again, eyes flitting across the various monitors and IV bags they'd hooked up. Chest rise and fall here… movement there… so far all seemed well. He closed his eyes again. Gah, he was tired.

Nurse practitioner. Ken sighed. During his time stranded, post-demobillization, he'd thought a lot about finding a civilian apprenticeship that'd let him rank up like that. Ken had always been a history buff, and there'd never been a better time in human history to study medicine than now. *Bio-technological* improvements had blossomed over the hundreds of years of Grausian occupation, and major historical improvements in medical *access* had developed pre-conquest when Terrans abolished corporate medical boards' government-sponsored licensing monopolies. Crushing the power of costly associations like the North American ABMS and AMA on Old Terra in favor of evidence-based competition sent costs of medical training plummeting. Ken could increase his scope any time he wanted without leaving the workforce.

Career planning all seemed so far away now. He couldn't even imagine what his parents would say—he hadn't really bothered to tell them anything. For all they knew he was still waiting on transport papers to return to Alpha Prime.

Squeaks and whirs from an old-fashioned radio on the wall interrupted Ken's thoughts with the cooing purrs of some Edenian tongue. Wimmer's Scrit translated via psionics—the radio didn't have a brain, and its broadcasters were well outside the beast's hundred-meter range, so while two sapient speakers in the same room could understand each other across languages the Scrit did nothing to translate transmissions over old tech like this.

Ken looked around instinctively for Thessalucia's slender shadow—she'd been such a helpful translator over the past two days—before remembering she'd remained back with the other hostages at the drop site.

He felt bad for her.

"You want to know what they're saying?" asked a soft, hoarse voice by his side. "Your raccoon-spider isn't working right now, eh?"

Ken looked down at the Edenian on the stretcher to his right. Sibila was the sister of the troop leader—she'd taken a shot to the inner thigh that would've bled out and killed her without Ken's quick action and still might cost her the leg if they didn't get her a surgical solution soon. Even with the heavy dose of ketamine and the fentanyl lollipop, Sibila's voice masked severe pain: the temporary tourniquet Ken had snapped 'high and tight' over her femoral artery cut off all blood flow to her entire leg—that had to have her nerves *screeching* for oxygen.

"What's a raccoon?" Ken asked her, returning his attention to her description of the Scrit.

"An extinct animal from your homeworld," Sibila said. "You're not familiar?"

"I don't think so," Ken shrugged. "I'm from Alpha Prime. Do you mean Old Terra?"

"Yes. That is your homeworld. Your homeworld is always where your ancestors were born," she said with a finality that implied this was very important to her for some reason. "That is where you actually belong."

"Probably kind of hard to belong on Old Terra," Ken smiled. "It's absolutely destroyed. Mostly a museum now."

"Well, if you ever go to a museum there, you can learn about the raccoon." Sibila gritted her teeth and closed her eyes, whistling into her nose through probably another wave of pain. Or nausea. Some people couldn't handle the ketamine.

"Are you dizzy?" Ken asked, already running his mind through possible solutions.

"It is easier if I do not think about myself," she said with a deep breath. She opened clear eyes that seemed lilac in the shadows. "The radio broadcast is about supply line interruptions. The scattered warfare makes trade difficult and we are having widespread epidemics in city centers. It is strange to me, because you would think the industrial areas should have the most modern medicine. But the areas cut off from modern medicine are having less disease. What do you think about that?"

Was she testing him, or challenging the concept of modern medicine altogether? "Maybe crowded populations are spreading more disease. Or there's more biowarfare in city centers," Ken suggested.

"I don't think there's more biowarfare in the city centers. The Bantai control most of the cities, and they tend to spread chemicals in the countryside," she said. "Like where our clans live—the Third, and the Sevella. That's why the Third hate us—since we welcome outside technology, they see us as no better than the Bantai. 'Cursed fools toying with the weapons of the gods.'" She turned to look at him with piercing eyes. "Metaphorically, of course. No one believes outsiders are gods."

"I would never assume that." Ken tilted his head. "But I thought the Bantai's primary enemy was the Yada."

"The Yada are the enemy of us all," Sibila grumbled. "You have heard, I am sure, how the Grausians helped them steal our best land, leaving the rest of our clans to fight over scraps. We have a unified front against them most of the time. But they have so many spies and diplomats always working to sow discord among us." She sighed, then changed the subject abruptly: "Did you have many die in your spaceship crash? It seems strange to save so few people, from a craft so large."

Ken shook his head. "Just the pilot. Explorer-class ships have to be large to sustain even small crews—they take really long flights and land in all kinds of environments, hostile and otherwise. That mass is mostly engines and life support. It's more than just a vehicle—it's your food store, your farm, your hospital, all in one."

"Like a small floating village," Sibila nodded. "That makes good sense."

She shifted with a small groan, and a little pang shot through Ken's chest—just a little one, not enough to distract or distress him. Just enough to remind him other peoples' pain twisted that imaginary blade deep in his core if he couldn't do anything about it. He despised suffering. *And we're all out of meds...* He glanced at the chronometer on his wrist. They probably had less than an hour before most everyone's pain treatments would wear off. This truck would become a little metal box of hell then.

He took a deep breath. They'd solve that problem when it arose.

Another deep breath...

Ken suddenly felt that warmth on his cheek he would get when he was being watched. He turned—Sibila was staring at his face, lips pursed and eyes narrowed. "What?" he asked.

"You seem to actually care," she said.

"Yeah, well, I do," he said. "I don't know you, but I know when one person suffers we all suffer, even if that's from lightyears away. All sentience is connected to one common thread beyond space and time."

He heard Wimmer cough—or scoff. He'd almost forgotten she was there, in the darkness, at the other end of the room. He ignored her.

"It is a pretty thought," Sibila chuckled. "How much are they paying you to think it?"

Ken tilted his head again, chewing his lip. "I actually don't remember," he said. "And I forgot to leave my solar pocket-pad in the sun to charge, so I can't pull up the contract right now." He grinned, and looked down at the pretty rainbow-shadow-person studying him. Her eyes were almost as big as Grausian eyes, and to him, twice as bright. "How much should they pay me, you think?"

"Mm, well, let's see," she tapped her lip mirthfully. "I think maybe you saved twenty lives yesterday, including mine, and made perhaps thirty other people feel better. Oh, and plus the organizing—I know poor organization wastes time, and wasting time kills…"

"Triage, you mean," Ken said. "Any idiot can triage, though."

"I disagree," she said. "I would find it hard not to try to save every single person, I think."

Ken's jaw tightened. "Was it that obvious?"

"Not obvious. You were kind to the ones you could not help," she said. "But we all learned fairly quickly that if you said 'expectant' it meant we were going to the death room."

"I'm sorry," Ken said. His voice seemed small and soft to him suddenly.

Her hand found his forearm in the dusky shade—her palm seemed cold, and rough, almost gritty like the sand itself. She said nothing for a moment as her thumb stroked a little pattern on his skin. He said nothing either, taking in the soft sensation radiating up his arm into his chest and core, little waves of comfort punctuated by an alertness that almost made him pull away. *Uh oh,* said part of him.

Shut up and relax, said another part. *You're just tired and she's just grateful. Maybe it means something, maybe it doesn't. Don't be a creep. Just be in the moment.*

He closed his eyes and let the weight of her little hand just be. What was it like, for these people—for this person, this *being* attached to these rough, gentle fingers, day by day? What kinds of touch did she feel, day in and day out in her constant fight for survival? He didn't know much about Edenian culture, and what he did know came from an entire planet of stereotypes created by foreign news broadcasts. The meaning sapients attributed to touch often depended on religion and historical violence as much as it depended on biology and individual trauma. What was the story of this palm, and its leathery creases and grooves?

Her fingertips rasped against his wrist as she pulled away again. His forearm felt naked, suddenly, with her hand's absence —he folded his arms across his chest to cover up the sensation.

The cot rustled as Sibila shifted again, stifling another little groan. *Distract her from her pain, you idiot.*

"What's it like here when things are—good?" Ken asked. "Like what's your favorite food, or ceremony, or Sevellan— memory—you have?"

"Like Sevellan culture, you mean," Sibila said. "What do I like about my culture?"

"Yes," he said.

"Strange that you would care to ask," she laughed. "You have your own culture, and all the guns and drugs."

"It's not strange," Ken said. "You seem—interesting to me." *Great, now you're making her sound like a science project.* "I mean, I don't know you, but I know you're empathetic, and good at reading people, probably, from what I can tell, and of all the experiences that make up you, some of them must be beautiful."

"Beautiful like me, you mean?" she teased. "Specialist Kamakura, are you flirting with me?"

"I mean, if you don't want to tell me about yourself you don't have to." He sidestepped the question. "I just find when I'm in pain it helps to think about things I enjoy that also have some meaning to me."

"And what do you enjoy, Ken Kamakura?"

"Hmm, I think I asked first," he grinned.

"Fair, fair." She sighed. "Alright, I'll tell you about my

people if you'll tell me why your doctor carries a shortsword she never uses."

"Because I was in the Legion," Wimmer grumbled. "Now shut up and leave me alone."

Sibila chuckled. "Alright."

She took a deep breath, and began to share until she finally passed out, and Ken was left alone with images of swirling sand-dance ceremonies, and soft flutish music in the setting sun, and rich spices that could make the worst meat safe, and birthdays with hundreds of siblings. Ken himself had never had a birthday—it wasn't something his family really did—and the noise and sweets and lights sounded lovely to him.

Jocelyn Wimmer

My chest was tight as fuck when we finally pulled into the city. Light slapped me in the face as the double doors in the back of the truck slammed open, and a violent blast of putrid air peppered with a spicy chemical scent punched my nostrils. Ken coughed; I laughed a little to cover up my own reaction.

The sky was grey, and the ground a dull burnt ash that might have once been green speckled with pink. Huge bombed-out skyscrapers towered around us; felt nomad tents huddled around their bases, and here and there people clustered around fires cooking various greasy animals I didn't recognize.

Well, I recognized that one. That was probably someone's very expensive Scrit. Silvie hissed and scrambled behind my ankles, her eight legs stretched as she arched on her tiptoes.

"I hear you, girl," I said, rubbing her leg with the side of my boot. "I hear you. You just stay close to me and you'll be good."

She did stay close to me—very close—the rest of that day, and into the night, as we unloaded patients and sorted medical equipment. The old Grausian medical 'cache' turned out to be thirty or so metal containers in the back of a yellow abandoned hospital—finding the damn goods in the mess of expired packages turned out to be a bigger challenge than the actual medical treatment. Here a container filled almost to the top with plastic bags of no-longer-sterile vaginal speculums met us with a swarm of tiny arachnids that fled for cover when we let in the light; over there three of us shoved through a rusty door into a room of broken robotic parts and blades interspersed with pristine boxes of unopened surgical automatons and graft growth kits.

I immediately waded in past the knee-deep tangle of metal parts, my boots and shins picking their way gingerly past sharp edges and poking bits. I'd just tug free the brand I was most familiar with *and—be—on—my—way—*

I grunted with exertion. I'd been hoping to find perhaps an actual supervisory surgeon here in the city, but a robotic neural network with myself at the helm would have to do today. Eventually I'd just make a list of what I needed and send the mercs 'shopping' through the medical wasteland, but for now I just wanted to get treatment started and move on.

Fucking thing was heavy. I took another laced water-sip to silence my stupid back. I could still feel it—I just cared less.

There are moments during a day of medical care where the day seems never-ending—where the next person, and then the next, and the next, keep coming while your brain begins to run out of glucose and the fog begins to close over, and your neck and shoulders ache from nodding and bending over, and it seems like this will be eternity. There's an old legend about rolling a stone up a hill forever in hell, and that's medicine—because everyone will eventually die no matter what you do, in the end, and doctors only exist to buy people time. That's very, very clear some days.

There are other days—especially during emergencies—when everything's moving so quickly you can barely breathe, and one patient takes three hours to stabilize, and you're racing against time itself and wondering how the hell something as simple as "get this guy from this hospital to the other one" can take so fucking long.

That day was a bit of both—a rash of moments that piled on me one after another without rest, sprinkled with little logistical emergencies that slowed everything down. I barely noticed that the sun was setting—all I could think about was trying to target this surgical bot into this leg wound, and get the right size mouth-tube to get *this* tissue-accelerating bonding spray into *this* set of lungs on the verge of respiratory collapse…

And shit, my camel-back was empty. I glanced around the transport truck, palms tapping the little crate I was using as a medical table, then my pockets, the stretcher, for a water source —I thought for sure they'd brought me water about an hour ago. Oh—yeah, I'd given it to a patient. Okay. I actually only wanted the water to wash down the pills. It seemed so much less obvious to just drop a few tablets into my camel-back than to pop them down my throat raw, but—

I glanced at the patient on the stretcher—they were busy trying to understand how to time their breaths to the tissue growth inhaler without coughing on the awful thick sensation that shit always created on the way down. I turned my back for a second to slip the little envelope from my sleeve—

"I think it's time for you to turn in now, right, ma'am?"

My throat spasmed shut as I jumped; I coughed and swore as two little tablets rolled out from my envelope and onto the metal floor. I planted my boot over them— "The fuck you creeping up on me for, Kamakura?" I snapped, shoving my hands into my pockets.

"I seem to recall you said something about lobotomized Grats and making medical decisions after thirty-six hours on duty." Kamakura raised an eyebrow. The normal jolly sparkle in his eye was missing—was he staring at my boot?

"I'm plenty awake," I said. *Impossible not to be with all the catecholamines I've been pumping into my system,* I didn't say. This last little batch that was just starting to wear off was closer to old-school cocaine than anything else. "It's different for me."

"Is that how that works, ma'am?" Kamakura asked, shoving his hands into his pockets now. I instinctively wanted to tell him to take them out—it looked unmilitary, unprofessional—but caught myself, and took my hands out of my pockets first.

He mimicked my action—well—was it mimicking, or just mirror neurons acting subconsciously?

A growling grumble rose in my throat. Even if that particular movement just then hadn't been that most sincere form of flattery, the kid was sharp. He probably would copy what I did more than what I said. If I wanted the kid to sleep like he should—and therefore be more useful in the long term—I probably needed to sleep, too.

And he should definitely not catch me using uppers as an excuse for productivity.

"Is there anything that only you can do that needs wrapping up before you turn in, ma'am?" Kamakura asked.

"Mmm," I repeated my grumbling sound. There wasn't actually anything anymore that *only* needed me. There was still work to do, but none of it was above his ability. Still, I didn't want to leave him in charge.

Why not? The kid had done absolutely nothing that wasn't exemplary in the past couple days. *A lot better medic than I am a doctor.* I'd had to catch myself several times already… granted, the decisions I had to make and the manual techniques I had to perform were harder, but I was pretty sure if he'd had my training, he'd be calling the shots right now, not me. *Fucker's brain still works.*

I didn't want to let go, though. I needed to control every outcome—even more so because I didn't trust myself. I needed to try *harder* because I couldn't try *smarter.* Kid hadn't made a mistake yet, but that didn't mean he wasn't due for one.

"Also," he asked. "If I need to wake you, how do you want me to do it—and for what?"

That gave me an emotional out. I wasn't slacking, I was still supervising, I was just stepping back.

"Wake me up for vital sign abnormalities," I said. "And anything you've not seen before. Or don't know about. Or think maybe you don't know about. Don't be cocky. I'd rather be sleepy and mad than well-rested and someone's dead."

"Roger that, ma'am." Ken waved me towards the makeshift wooden ramp we'd pushed up against the back of the truck, and stepped in behind me to take my seat on the crate by the patient's side. "The sergeant's put our whole GPSS team in one tent. You can even see everything from there."

I shuffled off with another wordless grumble, eyeing the yellowed patch of light flickering from the open hospital room door where we'd stowed our other patients, and then back over my shoulder at the few still in the hospital truck, and then to the sad little square tent backed up against the courtyard corner. Yeah, you could see everything from there, including the vehicles of the rest of the convoy gathered in a circle around us, and the distant campfire where Sereno sat alone with one of my patients who had just started to walk again—a purple-eyed Edenian who looked a lot like him. *That must be his sister.* The flames threw brilliant shadows on the brick walls; Sereno looked up, through them, at me for a second, as if assessing a threat.

His eyes flickered with recognition and glazed with disinterest—*I'm not a threat.* I stepped further into the shadows, pretending to mess with the meds in my sleeve, and the Sevellan turned back to his heated debate.

"The pleasure guard should seek out nearby Bantai *now*—we're already late," the sister was arguing. "If they catch us—"

"We'll be gone tomorrow," Sereno interrupted. "They won't

even know we were here. It's not as if they know how to use half these materials anyway."

"Sereno, please, you are taking an enormous risk! They could argue—"

"Risk?" he snapped. "We have four of you and three are severely wounded. The risk is that those carpet-lickers *kill* you in the act of 'resealing the alliance'."

"Will you let me finish talking?" she hissed "Grandfather decreed—"

"I'll let you finish if you voice your thoughts, not *hers*." Sereno's cold voice didn't confuse me, but the pronoun change did. *Must've misheard.*

The sister didn't answer for a second—she stared at the young man as if he'd slapped her. *Oh, guess I didn't mishear. That was intentional.* "You should be more cautious around whom you throw insults," she said.

"If it's an insult, why do you wear it?" Sereno answered, looking away from her. "You would make a finer battle guard than Grandfather yourself, you know."

"I—that is unjust." The girl's voice shook with rage. "I've already told you I don't want to undergo the change."

"There must be some way to mimic it without actually doing it." His voice lowered now—he sounded uncertain, and his sister pounced on his weakness.

"You think that because you know nothing of what goes on in our guard," she laughed. "I'm telling you, they check." She stood now. "Anyway, if one or two of us die so everyone else can live, I see that as an acceptable trade. Especially if the sacrifice was weak already." She motioned down her thigh. *That's right—this was a femoral bleed one. Tissue factors seem to be taking well, but she sure as fuck shouldn't be walking yet...*

"There's no guarantee keeping the trade would help the rest of our wounded live. The Bantai are struggling with medical supplies themselves, which means we get only the scraps—I doubt they care about some offworlder's idea of triage." He looked back up at me; I pretended not to see. *What an interesting sleeve I have*... The sister still hadn't noticed me. "What matters to me is that you die either way. Would you rather die free here, with us, or on your back under one of them?"

I raised my eyebrows at my sleeve; I didn't have to see the girl's expression to know that was cruel. Personal. "You hateful thing," she spat. "Have you no respect?"

"Such is the price of princehood." He chose now to shift his tone and announce my presence, signaling to her that the conversation was over. "Captain Wimmer, good evening! How are our brothers and sisters?"

"Better," I grunted. This was a signal to me as much as it was to her—I didn't want small talk, and he knew it. I took one last look at the old rifle lying by his side, and then slouched to bed.

CHAPTER SEVEN

Ken Kamakura

KEN DIDN'T NEED to wake Captain Wimmer. The gunshot did that for him.

It rang out across the courtyard with an unsettling echo—Ken didn't need a Scrit to know the Sevellans and mercs alike were scrambling to figure out what direction it'd come from. From the open back of the truck Ken saw his comrades in the tent dash for cover in the hospital, hugging the wall. Sereno's soldiers dove under vehicles and behind piles of rubble.

"Don't get up!" Ken pressed his nearest patient's chest to stop the sit-up, and quick-stepped to shut the rear door.

"We're in the middle of the courtyard! We're going to be killed!" The warrior groaned.

"If they have armor-piercing rounds or tank explosives, maybe," Ken said. "Will you lie down and let me close the door. Please? I will knock you out if you fight me."

"Harsh words from a soft voice," grumbled the Edenian, his green eyes glowing—but he was still wheezing from healing lungs, and did nothing as Ken eased the two back doors shut and drew his Mark X. Peeking through the crack, he could see the body of the gunshot victim, straight ahead. No sign of the shooter. The gleam of blood began to shimmer in a soft smear on the cracked pavement…

The body twitched. Arms stretched out and clawed the ground in pain. "Oh no," Ken breathed. "She's not dead."

"What?" asked Sibila from her cot behind him. "Wait, why would you say that as 'oh no,' who's not—"

The Sevellan princess was well enough post-surgery to drag herself out of her stretcher before Ken could stop her—but he planted his body between her and cracked door before she could see. He'd learned about this trick in training—

Oh, and sure enough someone had just fallen for it. Another shot rang out over a screeching moan. Sibila tried to push past Ken. He pressed his weight against her, gritting his teeth—his chest tensed as she started to squirm and cry out— "Stop!" he shouted. "It's a trap!" He shook her shoulder hard with his free hand, trying to keep his pistol as far away from her with the other and *also* trying not to knock her over and hurt her— "You injure someone as bait to get their friends out of hiding—then you can pick off the best one by one. It's a trap, Sibila!"

"What is the point of the best if they do not save their kin?" she hissed. Her purple eyes seemed to flash red in the dim light. Ken's grip on her shoulder didn't loosen. He stepped forward, firm pressure guiding her back to her stretcher—

"Lay down, please," he said to the chest wound victim who'd started to reach towards the crate-table between the stretchers. Damn it, how was he going to keep these people alive if they didn't listen? "Please. Look, the best medicine right now is a bullet, okay? We can save your companion if we can kill your sniper."

Sibila and the other Sevellan looked at each other; Sibila sat, her nostrils flared, tense fingers gripping her tunic as if trying to choke it to death.

Soft groaning. Footsteps slapping across pavement. Another shot. The rustling plop of another body falling.

"Are they shooting over the far wall?" Sibila asked.

"I don't know. I can look." *But now I don't exactly want to turn my back to you two.*

"The courtyard gate is shut, but if we drive the truck over there you can park so I'm shielded, and I can get out and open the gate," she said. "We can drive around outside and find them."

Ken gnawed his lip as his brain chewed the idea. *Damn it, the silence between the gunfire's worse than the gunfire itself.*

He couldn't help jumping when another shot rang out. It was just a tiny jolt—just a twitch—but the chest wound victim called it out.

"Are you afraid, outsider?" he sneered.

"Silence," Sibila snapped. "Help think or silence the yammering that stops others from thinking."

"Have you forgotten the difference between battle guard and pleasure guard?" the other shot back. "You give me no orders, whore."

"Why do you say there's more than one shooter?" Ken shouted his interruption, waving his hands in a firm, fast movement like the cutting of a cord. His Mark X glittered in the sliver of light from the door—and the other Sevellan closed his mouth.

"This hospital changes hands several times a month," Sibila answered, also eyeing the weapon. "You do not take out a clan force with only one shooter."

"So the target's not your brother—not political," Ken said, not at all convinced. "The target's the supplies."

"Yes."

Ken bit his lip, chest tightening. Every second seemed wasted and eternal. "Well, if you know how to drive, I'll gladly cover you," he said finally. "I was never rated for a vehicle like this."

"You weren't?" the chest wound survivor laughed. "All our warriors know how to drive."

Ken ignored him; Sibila crouched to climb through the hatch at the front of the vehicle, into the driver's pit. Ken followed to kneel behind her in the space between the front seats. His hand hovered instinctively over her back, as if at any moment to press her down to the seat or the ground, clear of the small windows—

Another gunshot. Ken could now hear Wimmer cursing and yelling—something like "how fucking stupid are you; will you all just stop feeding them—"

Ken met Sibila's eyes, just for a split second. Her thin, pursed lips seemed so grim, but there was a flicker of delight in her eyes somehow as she reached up for the ignition key. She was desperate—this close he could actually see her pulse pounding like punches in her carotids through the translucent oil-spill skin on her neck—but this wasn't her worst day, by far.

The engine thrummed to life with a sputtering rumble. The metal floor buzzed against Ken's knees—the walls began to vibrate with pings of gunfire as Sibila shifted the controls to arc the truck in a slow circle, her eyes just above the edge of the dash—

"At least we're drawing fire away from the victim," Ken encouraged. His body pressed against the navigator's seat; he leaned his pistol on the window's open edge. He still couldn't see the sniper…

Sibila nodded, cheeks puffed in concentration. One hand trembled on the wheel as the other fought with the accelerator on the floor, little steady taps urging the truck forward with tiny spurts of gas—it was so slow. Ken could feel the impatience in the heat radiating off her skin. Yes. Yes, this was so frustrating. Taking fire with no real return, inching along at a snail's pace for the gate—

A huge bump rattled them, knocking Ken's forehead against the door. "Ow!" The chest wound patient cursed behind them. "Be careful!"

"Sorry," Sibila hissed. "I cannot see potholes!"

"No idea what *he's* complaining about," Ken grumbled, rubbing his head.

Just at that moment he caught movement over the wall behind the tent. He fired without thinking—someone yelped as dust and stone splashed on them from his bullet's impact site—

"They're definitely over the wall in front of us!" Ken shouted out the window, peppering said wall with fire now. "Not on the roof!"

"Then we can shield the injured." Sibila sped up, daring to straighten with Ken's fire covering her. The truck roared over to block the growing pile of shot Sevellans. More bullets smattered against the cement—Sereno's troops rushed the yard behind the new cover. Ken scrambled to the back of the truck to throw open the doors for the wounded—almost hitting Captain Wimmer, who met him with a bleeding man draped over her shoulder. "Tourniquet, left arm!" she shouted, practically shoving the guy at Ken. He knelt with a grunt to grab the soldier around the torso and heave him backwards into the truck—snatched a tourniquet from the bag on the wall—Tack hopped in to help drag warm bodies in to safety—

"Watch the gate!" Someone roared. "It's Bantai artillery!"

Ken didn't have time to feel the panic. His fingers were tightening a rough tourniquet winch as fast as they could. If the truck exploded in two seconds, he would explode with an excellent job done. It wasn't like he was better off jumping out the back screaming like his first chest wound patient did.

Out the corner of his eye he could see the man crash into both Wimmer and Tack, basically trampling them as they tried to load patients—*idiot!* Heat surged up Ken's neck. It was fine to be scared, but to endanger others with your fear?

No.

Ken yanked back the slide on his Mark X, shifted the setting button sideways with a tap of his index finger, and fired a stun shot into the crazed patient's back. The man crumpled like crushed paper. Various people shouted at Ken at the same time, but his hands were already busy dragging someone else back towards a stretcher. *Need to make room for more people loaded on the floor.* They could punish him later. Right now, this selfish bastard needed to not hurt people. *And not undo all the hard work we did on his damn lungs!*

An explosion went off at the gate, rocking the truck. The engine shut off. *Are we hit?*

No—Sibila's voice made it clear she'd silenced the truck on purpose. "I have a pleasure guard pact sign!" she was shouting. "Do not reload that cannon!"

The popping gunfire slowed to a stop like the last kernels in a popcorn fryer. "We require proof!" called a new accent Ken hadn't yet heard here—this one more staccato, with sharper sibilance and 't's.

"The fuck are they talking about?" Wimmer snapped, looking up at Ken.

He didn't know. He couldn't see, and he was busy.

Jocelyn Wimmer

I could see.

I could see because I was lucky enough to be facing away from the front gate when the blinding blast of the plasma blower took it out. I was standing just off the back of the truck, so I saw when the driver's door creaked open. A Sevellan we'd saved from a femoral bleed hobbled out, jumping the tall step to the ground on her good leg. She held her head high like a queen—I was pretty sure she was Sereno's sister—and a medallion hung from her upraised hand.

"If you are Bantai, you must heed," she said.

The gaggle of attackers at the gate split; three emissaries stepped through the smoke, rifles poised as they stepped around the cannon. Bright red cloth covered their entire faces, except for their eyes and mouths, and multiple glittering emerald-colored gems dangled from each pointy ear and ridged eyebrow.

The commander in the center squinted at the medallion. She was a thick woman about twice the size and bulk of any Edenian I'd seen so far; they'd bound her ample breasts to mimic masculine pecs, but I could still make out her vague hiply shape under light robes.

"The pact sign is real," she declared to her entourage, straining her voice to a growl obviously lower than her natural timbre.

Sibila bowed low—keeping defiant eye contact with the commander the whole way down, medallion still raised. "We are entitled to a portion of supplies and your mercy," she said.

"Entitled? We're in the middle of an epidemic, and you've already broken your side of the pact," the Bantai commander spat. "Am I insane, or were you here all night robbing our sick instead of on your knees in my camp where you should have been the moment you entered our city? I know your kind. You're squeamish. You thought you could sneak in here without paying the flesh-price while the sand-rat Third kept us busy to the north."

"I did try locating your mobile headquarters," Sibila said. It was a lie—as far as I could tell she'd spent the last two days *trying* to not bleed out, not hunting rival clans. "Now that I know your location, I can rectify mine immediately."

The Bantai commander snorted. Her eyes traveled up and

down Sibila's form as she elbowed her male companions. She chuckled something I didn't catch, then added: "Immediately is still too late. I will take *you* either way, but I wonder whether I should even bother returning you or just roast your bones afterwards instead. Would that teach your people to ask permission first before touching what's not yours?"

I doubted the hospital stores had ever formally belonged to the Bantai—pretty sure everything I'd seen here that wasn't Grausian was Terran—but Sibila didn't argue. Instead, she asked: "Do you prefer to eat for a day, or eat for a year, my lord? No one kills a milk heifer before the teat runs dry."

"I'll be the judge of the heifer's production, thank you," the commander grunted, eyes still locked on Sibila's hips.

My abdomen clenched. I was beginning to get an idea of what they were talking about. "You know, maybe we don't negotiate with these guys," I muttered to Howard. She was kneeling beside me, huddled against the open door with her rifle sight trained on the Bantai speaking. Her blonde hair clung to her face, slick with sweat and blood—not her own.

"You'd rather die?" she asked in a tone that said she was seriously considering that herself.

"That's my plan, anyway. Life's already fucked me enough."

I caught Ken looking out at me from where he still crouched in the truck, fingers on someone's carotid pulse. "This one's gone," he said. His eyes darted to the side as if motioning outside. "Is there something cultural I'm missing?"

I shook my head—no point explaining shit I was just guessing from body language he couldn't see. "Help me with this one, she's heavy," I said. I wanted to get as many casualties loaded as we could before the fighting started up again. I could only solve one problem at a time. Even if we were seconds from everything going to shit, the next second's problem was next-second-me's job.

Ken Kamakura

Seconds became minutes and minutes hours as Ken and his accidental boss stabilized the remaining three casualties—he kept expecting the shooting to start up again at any moment.

It didn't.

There was some cryptic talking outside he didn't really have time to pay attention to; at some point he hopped out the back of the truck in time to see Sibila and several other women throw shawls over their heads and trail out through the gate after a group of soldiers. The soldiers must have been Bantai—at least, their flashy headgear and jeweled piercings seemed nothing like the muted robes of the Third and Sevella, and they seemed to have slightly broader noses, and maybe less colorful skin. *Kinda hard to generalize after seeing only a few of them.* The tassels on the fringe of Sibila's cloak waved behind her in the smoke and sand-like fingers clawing at the wind, stretching towards her kin, but she didn't look back. Ken blinked against sweat, and the women were gone.

After about midday Wimmer no longer needed Ken's help with anything—none of the soldiers they'd brought along in their evacuation efforts had died, and none were well enough to return to duty, for the most part what everyone needed now was simply time and continued access to the medication stores. The major work was done—at least, inside the compound. As the afternoon shadows began to lengthen at the foot of the walls, Ken decided to occupy himself with something else useful: prevention.

He found Sereno heaving wooden crates of something that smelled like sardines into a small Old Empire hovercraft that'd been outfitted with rust-colored tank treads. The original lift repulsors still glowed orange under the vehicle as it tried to stabilize itself, compensating for the increased weight. Clearly, without the hacked-together support of the old-fashioned wheels the whole thing would collapse to the ground. The hovercraft's occupants looked as cobbled and mishmashed as it did: both of the Sevellans loading boxes wore many-pocketed Terran uniform pants under the Edenian cloaks they'd hiked up and tied around their chests, and Grausian vibro-blade naval dirks hung at their belts.

Ken hadn't had a chance to wander the hospital's darkened halls yet—they were apparently heavily booby-trapped and rife with random diseased corpses and hives of rodents—but looking at the dinged obsidian edges on the daggers and the tears in the pants it seemed he hadn't missed much interesting equipment anyway.

Ken stepped up to the former hovercraft with a gentle clearing of his throat.

"Sereno—or, er, captain? Are you the equivalent of a captain?" he asked.

The Edenian seemed in a much fouler mood than Ken had seen thus far, and for a moment only glared straight ahead, still tossing boxes to the soldier on the sputtering hovercraft. Beads of translucent aquamarine sweat glistened on his brow over a clenched jaw, and the red cloth tied around his thin bicep seemed like a flag of war as it followed his sharp, explosive movements.

"Apologies," Ken corrected, folding his hands behind him in something like parade rest out of habit. "Stupid question. I was just looking for an honorific. I actually wanted to ask if—" he paused, correcting himself: *never give anyone who outranks you an easy way to say no.* Asking "if" was asking for permission. "I wanted to ask *when* would be a good moment to share some basic combat life support techniques with your team."

The wiry Sevellan didn't show any sign that he'd heard—although Ken knew those long ears definitely had. Not a problem. Ken wanted to include him, but was totally fine teaching whatever Sevellan underlings actually wanted to learn.

"I'll let you be, then," Ken said, stepping back to leave.

"If you help us finish loading we'll all be able to attend," Sereno grunted. "My other kin are on guard duty or finishing up a brief logistics recon run. I'm not angry with you. Just thinking."

Ken squatted for another box—this one with bandages, and no fishy smell. "Makes sense you'd have a lot on your mind."

Now Sereno gave him a look. "What do you mean by that, plainskin?"

"Is that a slur?" Ken made the briefest of eye contact before shoving another box across the lowered hatch of the vehicle's loading bed.

"I call him green-eyes," Sereno nodded to the soldier up in the hovercraft, who flashed a black-toothed smile. "Is that a slur?"

"Not if he says it's not, I guess," Ken shrugged. He decided not to dig further into what he'd meant by his attempt at encouraging the young leader. *Not in this mood.* Wherever Sibila had gone, Sereno didn't seem to have much control right now, and the guy clearly needed control to survive.

"I know our way of resolving conflicts must seem barbaric to you—as it did to the Grausians," Sereno heaved presently. "Although our negotiation tactics seem to be on par with yours." He nodded over towards where Sergeant Howard was arguing something with her two men. "I've a strong suspicion she'd sell my whole people group to the Bantai if it meant arriving at your destination sooner. Our trades operate on smaller scales."

Ken's stomach twisted. "Is that what happened?" He didn't look over his shoulder to where Sibila and the other women had gone; the emptiness of the gate loomed in his mind's eye as his boots scuffled through pale cream-colored sand. The weight of the crate pressed against his shoulder kept his eyes fixed forward. “A sale, I mean. Did you…?”

“I didn’t sell my sister, no,” Sereno said. He glanced up at the other Sevellan again; the smooth motion of his heaving and lifting didn’t stop. “But more to the immediate point about your sergeant—your medical team has proved so useful I’m not sure we can allow you to continue on to your destination until and unless Galaxy Aid actually provides replacements. I’m not sure Howard is happy with that. You might warn her that despite your better weaponry your squad is still outnumbered, hm?”

Ken’s eyebrows raised. The manipulation was next-level. A threat shrouded in an open confidant moment, twisted into a third-party-messenger bid targeting the sergeant—the man knew emotional tactics. Ken almost laughed: it reminded him of the Neighborhood Wealth Management dinner parties back home, only here instead of the glorified homeowners’ association conspiring about who could and couldn’t paint their house orange… *oof.* Ken shuddered. He was actually very glad to be here. The sweat dripping down his spine, the sand grit in the seams where his uniform met his neck, the slow but powerful pumping in his chest that flooded his head with this new ‘tired but alert’ high he was starting to get used to—this was actual real life.

The memory of Sibila’s hand on his forearm…

Hm. His jaw tightened a bit, and he felt the muscles in his lower back stiffen. “I’m not really worried about where I work as long as I’m not shipped back to Alpha Prime,” he grunted, side-stepping Sereno’s tactics altogether. “You and Howard can figure that out. I'm more worried about Si—about your companions who left with the Bantai. I couldn’t really understand what was going on—I was kind of busy—but—”

“Sibila will be back tomorrow evening,” Sereno interrupted, straightening suddenly himself. He dropped his box into the loading bed and gave a sharp jerk of his head to the other soldier, who hopped out and dashed off like he had a sandstorm chasing him. Ken thought about mirroring Sereno's stance—a subtle sign of respect—but decided to double down on "I don't care as long as I'm working" and continue loading crates.

The Sevellan leaned against the vehicle with his arms crossed. It was clearly a practiced nonchalance—forearms flexed, chin tucked, shoulders wide and neck just a bit bared on the side, as the Sevellan's huge indigo eyes tracked Ken with hunger for movement. This wasn't a man who was comfortable standing by while others worked; the pause was learned, and feigned.

"No one's pawn or captive because you're not at war at all—or perhaps a war of your own," Sereno mused. "I see you, Kenta Kamakura."

He's well-read. Most Terrans didn't even know the full Uri Naran pronunciation of Ken's first name. Ken smiled, opening his palms wide to grip the edges of two medical crates now and swing them up in front of the leader. It was as close as he'd get to showing off. "This is what I prioritize," he said aloud. "What do you prioritize?"

"I prioritize technological development," Sereno said without missing a beat. "And resource acquisition."

Now Ken did pause, crouched by a large bandage crate. He blinked up at Sereno through his bangs. "To what end?" he asked.

"So that we no longer have to grovel and play games with every other thug and colonist that rides in with a bigger gun," Sereno said. His jaw clenched as he stared over at the compound gate. "My sister, like our clan leader, only accepts things as they are, now. The Third only accept things as they were, from an era none of us even saw. *I* refuse to accept anything but the future." He pushed away from his lean on the hovercraft and crouched beside Ken almost conspiratorially. "If the dominant forces like the Bantai and the Yada are to come to heel, I need a bigger gun."

"I'm not sure I can help you there." Ken's head tilted. He didn't step back, but the Sevellan was so close now he could see that tell-tale translucent pulse pounding in his neck.

"You will. Better utilization of medical resources will already give us an edge. There's a violent epidemic among the Bantai right now—which is strange, because they have access to all the medical points. Meanwhile the Third don't get sick—they just get shot." Sereno laid a hand on Ken's shoulder. "If I take your doctor around the city tomorrow to some of the Grausian medical points, can you help me understand why?"

Ken pursed his lips. "If we wait until Sibila gets back from the Bantai camp I may be able to get more information from her about what they're dealing with—or we could even go see their ill there, where she is?"

Sereno's eyes glinted with something like hunger or anger for a split second—or perhaps Ken only imagined it. He blinked, and a pacific smile spread across the Sevellan warrior's face.

"Battle guard is forbidden from interfering with pleasure guard business," he said. "Our presence could overturn the trade agreement and endanger her squad."

"We wouldn't interfere, just—"

"I can't," Sereno snapped, almost choking on—rage? Helplessness? He snatched the box between them and almost hurled it into hovercraft. *There's glass in there!* Ken instinctively rose to catch the crate—

But Sereno caught himself at the last second, and laid down his load with firm but controlled finality, punctuating the end of the conversation with a smile. "I need to speak to your sergeant," he said. "But first, I believe it's time for our combat life support class."

"Roger," Ken dropped a curt nod, and turned to leave.

"Oh, and Kamakura—"

"Hm?"

"Our language doesn't naturally have an honorific," Sereno said. "As far as our historians can tell we always used family terms. The honorific we use for military operations is the Grausian one for nobility."

"Understood, *Thal*," Ken smiled. He was getting somewhere with this guy.

Not sure where—but somewhere.

CHAPTER EIGHT

Jocelyn Wimmer

IT WAS NEVER QUITE silent downrange on Eden Crescent. Even without distant gunfire or people pestering me with medical questions—even in the dead of the night, or the peak of a weary hot mid-afternoon when the whole world seemed to nap—random squeaking howls of what Sereno called *death-rats* punctuated the air over rumbling wheels or arguing voices beyond the walls.

It was finally quiet enough, today, that we were able to leave the hospital compound and set out through the city streets. It was Ken and me, Howard and her mercs, and six Sevellans for our 'protection'. Howard had managed to convince their leaders to let us look for a Galaxy Aid outpost—every large city with Bantai presence had one—and Sereno had apparently tasked us with understanding the Bantai epidemic.

"Out of the goodness of his heart, no doubt," Howard muttered under her breath, eyes on the map on her finally-working GPS wristband as we picked our way past piles of rotting meats and burnt plastics; rivulets of some foul-smelling brownish liquid trailed through the dust by our feet. "That's our destination." Howard pointed towards the horizon where a golden minaret—Grausian Old Empire construction—rose above the layers of fallen skyscrapers and felt tents crowding around us in all directions. Smoke drifted around it, and the bulk of the noise of the city seemed to come from that direction. "I'm behind schedule for another job—if I can't find a Galaxy Aid rep to drop you off with today, we might need to actually treat this like a prisoner situation and break you loose by force. Not a fan of Mr. Conniving."

"He's kind of required to be conniving to keep his people alive, as he sees it," Ken shrugged. "Besides, you wouldn't really leave all those reporters back at the landing zone without a ticket home."

"You mean I wouldn't really leave all that Interthought Media money on the table," Howard smirked. "This negotiation for the freedom of their personnel should pay double what your contract's netting us. I've already managed to secure a contact back at their headquarters—can you see the credit signs in my eyes?"

Ken returned her sardonic grin with a bright smile of his own. "Come on, Stacey, I don't believe you're as cold as you make yourself out to be," he said. "You actually care about people. If this was all about the money for you, you'd have complained a lot more about all of the supplies we used when we first landed."

"They were Galaxy Aid supplies anyway," Howard said. "And I don't have to be cold to care more about the paycheck that supports the people I love than I do about people who've already dug their own graves."

Ken's smile vanished. "Alright, joking aside, the Edenians don't all deserve to suffer just because their leaders make poor choices. They have centuries of oppression holding back their mindsets and their resources."

"So did we!" Howard scoffed. "We were Grausian-ruled, too. You don't see me resorting to kidnapping and prostitution to feed my family. They're people, not social experiments—and that means they're responsible for their own messes. Anyway, I was talking about the drama-hunting reporters, not the Edenians." She shot him a glare. "Your hero complex really blinds you, you know that?"

"I don't have a *hero complex*," he snapped. "I feel sick when I know people are in trouble, and I have to do something to stop the feeling or I'll—I don't know. Die, I guess." He tore open a caffeine pill packet with his teeth and dropped the goods into his camel-back without slowing his walking pace. *Hm.* He already looked kind of jittery to me. "I've never claimed to be better than anyone else."

It was a little too familiar—a little too much like looking into an old mirror from another dimension. "How many is that today?" I asked, nodding at the cloudy water.

"The study you had me read during downtime back at our Role II said energy drinks decrease fine motor skills but improve athletic ability," Ken answered without answering. "I'm calibrating my dose accordingly, ma'am, in case we run into combat issues."

"But how many, though?" I asked.

"The same number you've had," he said, not looking up as he sealed his camel-back and took a swig. Was that meant to be a dig? Did he know? I hadn't actually had any caffeine today, but it wouldn't be impossible for someone as innocent as Ken Kamakura to mistake my little pills for something more innocuous. On the other hand, it wouldn't be impossible for someone as clever as Ken Kamakura to be punishing me for drug abuse by subtle proxy—this could mean *"the more you have, the more I'll have, until you stop."*

I could feel my face flushing; I changed the subject. "Where were you from noon to fourteen-hundred hours?" I challenged. I wasn't really thinking, just grasping for a way to punch back.

"Teaching CLS, ma'am," he gave me an odd side-eye now through that too-long nonmilitary forelock. "I only went because you told me you had things under control without me."

"I did say that," I grunted. *What are you doing, Wimmer? Trying to catch Ken Kamakura slacking? Are you crazy?* "But your time would've been better spent resting up," I added. "They've been at war how long? And they still fall for 'wound the soldier to kill the medic'—I'm not saying they're stupid or backwards, either." I really meant that—I didn't give a shit who was listening. "I'm willing to bet credits to cookies the Sevellans have a different honor system than the Bantai and that's probably putting them at a disadvantage. If they really wanted to change their combat life support tactics, they probably could have already—but it makes no difference if they're literally out here trying to defend an honorable warfare system that just doesn't exist anymore." The logical flaws were bitter on my tongue but my mouth kept working anyway. "Besides, you really want some offworlders coming into your neighborhood telling you how to drive?"

"Sereno seemed pleased with the CLS class." Kamakura's shoulders shrugged, but his eyes glinted as he watched my face—he was trying to figure something out. He didn't understand why I was suddenly jumping down his throat, and—I kind of didn't, either.

Come on, you know why. It's guilt. You're feeling guilty, and taking it out on him.

Shut up.

"I don't know about all that, but I do know we need to focus on finding Galaxy Aid," Howard put in. "I don't mind your big heart or whatever, but we have a job to do."

That was helpful. "Yeah, kid—if you put half that energy

you've got into getting your ass to your actual contract at—Sector—Bazilda—" I looked at Howard.

"Ben-haba," she said.

"That place," I breathed—it was a kind of relief, actually, to be able to find something wrong with the kid. "You could have spent those two hours helping Howard. Or recon."

Ken narrowed his eyes. "Is recon not what we're supposed to be doing now?"

"For who, though?" Howard pointed out. Sis was good. She looked at the Sevellans trailing us, and then back at Ken. "I know what I'm out here looking for. What are your eyes on?"

Now his shoulders rounded—not quite like a Caleb warfighter canine backed into a corner, but definitely bristling. Pissed. When he stepped away from us to suddenly dash over to the random Edenian kid vomiting into a sewage ditch by the side of the road, the look he gave us was almost—not spite, I guess, but definitely rebellion.

A *let's see you try to stop me* kind of look.

"Fucking kid's going to get himself a counseling statement," I found myself muttering under my breath as I dragged my feet through the mud-orange dust after him—forgetting again that this wasn't that military anymore. The Sevellans ambled ahead of me, multiple necks craned towards Ken to steal an intent peek at some learning. *Guess he won some rapport with his CLS class,* I admitted begrudgingly.

I caught a slight motion blur in my periphery: Howard jerked her head towards Bones, pointing with her eyes for him to follow Ken—and then she took this opportunity to duck away with Tack down a side alleyway almost faster than I could see—

A tall crimson-eyed Sevellan stepped in her way, his skin flashing brick-red with the color of the nearby walls.

"Good idea, Sergeant Howard." He spread his lips to show bright ebony teeth. "We should split up—you and I will take a small contingent to continue looking for Galaxy Aid while our medical squad sees what they can learn here."

Howard's curt smile mimicked the Sevellan's—broad, and fake. "Unless you have your own Scrit, Commander Lachish, I don't think we can both leave the doctor and still communicate with each other. On second thought, I'll stay here."

"As you wish," Lachish soothed. I was impressed that he managed to minimize the smugness on his face as he bowed. He got her… but was trying not to show it.

Ken's voice drew me away from the micro-politics: "Captain Wimmer, can you look at this?"

I pushed past Sevellans crowded around him—their bodies gave off so much heat, more than Terrans did, and their sense of personal space was nonexistent—*like pressing into a wall of warm flesh,* my weird brain announced as I grimaced. Patient privacy? Half the time the concept didn't exist downrange.

Ken was seated on a cement ruin with a blue-grey Edenian adolescent beside him clutching her stomach. She wore torn Terran cargo pants, but an elaborate pattern of interlocking circles framed her simple robe—she was Third. Ken's left hand rested on the kid's shoulder; the other turned a brown bottle over and over before handing it to me.

"She says this is her medicine for diarrhea," Kamakura said.

My fingers folded around the smooth, warm glass—most of the letters were in a language I couldn't read, but there was a Terran translation in the tiniest font in the back. "Shit, is this mercury?" I asked. *Figures these anti-technology people would be feeding their kids poison—*

"We call it the crawling silver," said the adolescent. I could see bluish stains now on her gums. *Yup. Mercury poisoning.* "The Bantai hoard all the stores, and with the limited supply lines to the city lately it's almost impossible to get if you aren't Bantai yourself."

My forehead creased. "Wait. This isn't Third medicine? You saying this is what the *Bantai* doctors are prescribing?"

The girl's hands flew up, palm out, as if to physically defend herself from the question. "I know, I know! A good Third woman shouldn't be skulking around Bantai settlements even if they have better supplies, but I have a Bantai love partner, and—"

"Don't care," I interrupted. "Don't care even the slightest bit. But I doubt this is 'better' for the Bantai, either." I handed it back to her. "This is what I'd give someone if I want to poison them. It's making you sicker, not better."

"But they say it will kill the microbes making me sick," she said.

"Oh, it'll kill the microbes alright." I watched the thick metal inside the bottle ooze from one side to the other as it tilted in her grip. "And you with it." To Ken: "Did you see any chelating agents in the storage bins? She's going to need that for the heavy metal poisoning now, in addition to a possible antibiotic if we think she had bacterial diarrhea before, or if she's got intestinal necrosis. It's hard to know, now, because ingesting mercury literally creates bloody diarrhea—that's why her excretions look like ground black *jola* over there. Mucosal bleeding. In an ideal world she could probably benefit from some carafate in addition to an anti-emetic, some probiotics—all just to give that inner lining a rest to heal. But the chelating agent's a must."

Ken nodded, lifting his hand to pat her shoulder again before withdrawing. "Can you come back to our camp with us for a bit?" he asked.

"Wait, no, I just—I can't believe this would be making me sicker," the girl shook her head even as she stifled a pained groan. "This is what the Bantai use for everything. And not just the Bantai—everyone, especially machine-lovers, at least ever since they recovered the medical texts from the satrap's palace library. I can't believe offworlders would be against modern medicine."

"Have you considered perhaps the Bantai physician gave you poison on purpose because you are Third?" Lachish piped up now, wiping a smear of colorful dust from his hands, onto his tunic.

The Third girl shook her head again emphatically. "No. No! I know they're not poisoning me. I saw them drinking the same—I thought of that, so I literally made sure to take the same bottle the nurses were using in the healing wards." She reached into her tunic. "I even took this medical book to make sure."

Ken's gloved fingertips pitter-pattered against the cover of the little pocket-tome, tracing its title—again, something I couldn't understand. Man, I missed that skinny Grausian reporter girl who knew so much about languages. I hadn't seen a physical book in years. They were mostly only in museums, or rich people's libraries, but here with more limited electricity they were actually a pretty practical way to preserve information. The yellowed pages crinkled as Ken turned them—

The diagrams I recognized. Amputations and "how to suture" were interspersed with random pictures of what was clearly a Grausian egg-selection technique for genetic engineering, and then something I'd seen before in a Charee e-text about how to inject quick tissue grafts into a wound with accelerated healing boosters. And in the table of medications, I could see the same pattern of letters as the bottle in the girl's hand: "See?" she pointed. "For consumption, dysentery diarrhea, cholera… and this is the dose I'm taking."

Ken flipped back to the first pages— "Is this a publishing date?" he asked.

"Yes—this was released just two years ago," the Third girl nodded. "As you can see, it's a complete collection of updated medical techniques from all the invaders and largest Bantai clans." She twisted her lips into a little half-scowl as she looked up at us all. "I know you people think we Third are all backwards savages, but only a very few of our most extreme brethren reject modern medicine. In that way we're very similar to all of you."

"Well, in this particular case those Third brethren would be right," I shrugged. "You keep eating this 'modern medicine,' you'll die."

"That's crazy!" Her aquamarine eyes glowed with suspicion now, as if maybe I wanted to keep the 'crawling silver' for myself, or play some other trick on her. "Why would you lie to me about this?"

Ken laid his hand out, palm up—he didn't reach across her for the bottle she was clutching, just offered her the opportunity to give it up. "That's a good question," he said. "Why would we? Let's try changing your medication for a few days, and if you don't see any improvement by a week, you can have this back."

"You won't be here a week from now, Kamakura," Howard interjected.

"I have to find an outpost for Galaxy Aid," Ken nodded, talking to the girl and not the sergeant. "But if you don't have anywhere to stay, maybe you could come with us. You're a runaway, right?"

"We have no space in our camp," Lachish interrupted.

Ken kept his eyes fixed on the girl still. "If I could find you a different medication, would you be willing to try it for a week?" he asked her.

The Third girl pursed her lips, blinking giant ruby eyes as she broke Ken's gaze to look around at the rest of us, and then back at him. Ironically, I was pretty sure everyone's naysaying worked to his advantage—and maybe he knew that. The backdrop of their coldness made his warmth seem warmer. More trustworthy. "Or if you don't want me taking this, maybe I could try the medicine of my elders for a week," the girl mused. "I won't return to their tents—I'm committed to my love—but I know where to find rock fungus."

Rock fungus? I struggled not to roll my eyes. *More back-*

wards nonsense—but it looked like we couldn't promise the kid any real antimicrobials anyway—and who knew if we even should? Meds were in short supply. Saving her could be killing someone else. Maybe let her eat rock fungus. At least it wasn't mercury.

No. We could definitely get just a little something out for her; the medication stores were stolen! So maybe we couldn't take anything the Sevellans had already claimed, but no one had yet ventured into the old hospital pharmacy—just the big storage containers outside—because of the death-rats and the strangle vines. I could probably…

"Can you show me where to find this fungus?" Ken asked. "We have a belief that certain fungus can kill bacteria, and I'm wondering if that's maybe why the Bantai are all dying while the Third have a reputation for surviving dysentery."

"It's not just a *belief*," I smirked. "It's a fact. 'Certain fungus' is where the first antibiotics came from."

"The Bantai are worse off than the Third?" the girl's eyes widened. "That can't be right. They have the crawling silver!"

"The Third don't listen to the radio," Lachish spoke over her head to Ken. "She doesn't know what's going on."

"Well, the radio could be propaganda, too," Ken said, his tone more annoyed now and eyes still on the patient as he tried to retake control of the disjointed conversation: "How long since you've last been to a Third camp?"

"It has been a year," the girl admitted. "I still keep to the ways of my people, but I've been living in the city to stay close to my love." She sighed. "So it could be true…"

I prodded the edge of Ken's boot with mine—*time to move on.* We didn't have anything more to offer the girl right now, nor she us. And if I had to hear her say *my love* one more time, I was going to drink mercury myself.

Ken nodded. "So, you can find me rock fungus?" he asked her, slapping his knees and standing to signal the end of the encounter. "And maybe once I find Galaxy Aid, they can give me more data on the death toll per population to check the rumors I've heard. For now, you need to hydrate, and I'll see what else I can scrounge up for you. Your blood pressure's good so I don't think the bleeding in your gut needs emergency treatment right this minute but you probably won't make it without further evaluation." He gave her a sleeve of water-purifying tablets and another of multivitamins, looking to me as he did so—I nodded back. He was doing fine, and these were all decent ideas given the limiting circumstances. "Can you meet us outside the old hospital before tomorrow evening?"

"If they don't shoot me when I show up," she motioned towards the Sevellans with bitter eyes.

"We don't shoot first. That's your people," Lachish smiled.

"Screw you and your whore Grandmother," she spat on the ground by his feet.

Whoa! Alarms screeched in my muscles—I'd seen deadly fights break out over much less. Ken and I bumped shoulders stepping between the Third girl and the Sevellan commander—

But Lachish laughed. "A storm does not waste lightning on an ant," he said. "She's not quite tall enough to draw my wrath, friends." He had his own arms outspread to hold back the other Sevellans beside him, his thick forearms blocking hands on hilts and holsters.

But the commander's bored, half-lidded gaze down at the adolescent simmered with a weaponized nonchalance that kept my tendons taut. He wasn't preventing the fight out of mercy. His sparing her was meant as an insult. "Search her for weapons and send her on her way."

KAMAKURA WAS INCENSED as we rounded the next corner away from the sick Third case. I didn't know exactly which thing he was mad about. I knew he wasn't pleased with any of us at the moment; I suspected the rough way the two battle guards patted down the screaming girl and took her kitchen knife didn't help. Ken didn't say anything, though. Probably even he knew that if they let an obvious hostile go without a search, and she threw that knife into Lachish's back, the whole thing would've been Ken's fault for starting the encounter in the first place. I did my best to talk the girl through the pat-down to minimize trauma— "they're just checking your arm here, your stomach, I swear if anyone tries anything I'll bite them myself, okay, so you just hold still"—in the end, even if she calmed down, she lost the only weapon she had to protect or feed herself.

And maybe that was why he was mad, I figured as I took another energizing sip of my spiked water. If he'd left well enough alone and let the girl vomit her guts out on the street without asking a lot of questions, she'd still have that knife. It wasn't like he'd been able to give her a lot in return, and now who knew if she'd trust him enough to actually show up for whatever meds we managed to get her later?

It sucked. I'd be mad, too, if I was a better person, and hadn't dosed myself with benzos just a few hours earlier.

So Kamakura walked far ahead of all of us, alone, breaking into a jog to keep his distance every time we almost caught up. Howard's lips got tighter and tighter every time he pulled away from us, until finally she barked:

"Do we need to march in formation, or can you muster some kind of situational awareness, here?"

"Isn't the protocol in a hostile area to stagger formation up and down the street, weapons up and each person at enough distance to get each other's backs without grouping up so tightly we'll all go out with the first grenade?" Ken retorted, with no attempt at decorum now. "Frankly, ma'am, I'd prefer that."

"Ma'am?" she snapped. "You know full well it's 'sergeant,'

not 'ma'am'. I worked for a living." Howard turned back toward me. "No offense, ma'am."

"None taken," I grumbled—actually, I was pretty sure Ken had slipped the wrong honorific on purpose literally to imply Howard *didn't* work. It was petty and Howard probably hadn't caught him, but I was quick to change the subject to protect him anyway. No reason for the star medic to somehow torpedo a job he excelled at just because he couldn't bury his morals like the rest of us could. "Frankly, Howard, I'm just glad to be away from that whole mess," I jerked my head back towards the street we'd come from. "I was gonna vomit if she brought up her forbidden love one more time."

"Yes, you can have your intertribal romance but don't wave it in our faces," Lachish agreed with me—and suddenly I didn't want him agreeing with me. He must have read my disgust, because he laughed: "I jest, Captain. It's a very Third way of thinking, segregation. Most of our peoples *survive* on flesh exchanges between clans."

"Not in love with you calling it a *flesh exchange*." Howard grimaced.

"Really? It is the technical term, for us," he said. "Although I suppose I could call it what the Grausians called it—genetic alliances."

"Oh shit—the pleasure guard trades aren't just sex," I suddenly realized. "You're all literally crossbreeding for certain traits?"

"When the encounters in question involve unmodified battle guards, yes," Lachish said. I thought back to the female Bantai at the gate—*the body mods are a common thing, then, not just her*. "Trades are selected based on the desirable talents each clan wants in their population."

So... literally baby factories. Oof. I didn't know if that was worse than what I'd originally thought or not. From a medical perspective, if we were going to be here long, I needed to know,

"How much of their lives do pleasure guards spend pregnant, then?" I asked.

"What? Pregnant? Oh no, we have incubation pods," Lachish laughed. "Allowing extended pregnancy would be a complete waste of time. They cannot spawn fast enough if they spend nine months out of the year bloated and slow. And it would be barbaric to put our pleasure guards through repeated births over and over for the sake of a political agreement. Many of them would die."

"So that's barbaric to you, but questionable consent isn't," I noted out loud before I could stop myself.

Lachish stopped in the road to turn towards me with his arms crossed. "Excuse me?" he asked.

"Never mind." Any physical intimacy initiated under financial duress didn't count as consensual to me—not to mention the disease transmission risk posed to all parties—but it'd be a waste of time to argue that with this guy, now. "If you've got incubators, why sell the sex at all? Couldn't you just harvest eggs and sell those?"

"There's a much higher rate of embryo deaths if fertilization occurs in vitro. You're killing five or six babies to create one." Lachish tilted his head. "I'm surprised you don't know this, doctor. Besides, what if a pleasure guard wants to have children of her own one day, with the partner she's chosen? If she's sold her eggs, she can't do that."

"Hm." I knew all about embryo transplantation procedures—invented just before the Grausian conquest, they'd essentially rendered the abortion debates moot by allowing any baby at any gestational age to escape his or her mother's body with a simple camera-assisted transcervical procedure that was almost as easy as a dilatation and curettage. Older children would still have to be removed by cesarean, but in general, the creation of the artificial portable placenta allowed any little one to move from the uterine wall to a new tissue pad with less than ten seconds of interruption in blood flow. If you didn't want to carry a pregnancy to term, you didn't have to—and no one had to die, either. It was pretty standard technology—and, contrary to what multiple Imperial textbooks taught, it was Terran-invented, not Grausian.

Which was why I was surprised the tech had made it out here. The Terran presence on this planet had predominantly been military, not colonist, during the Secession Wars—there wasn't much reason to bring along more than one or two incubator pods, at least not if you had a solid birth control regimen for your troops. Soldiers had always been and would always be terribly horny, so it was the job of every good battalion surgeon to make sure their STD and pregnancy prevention protocols were on point. That included but absolutely definitely needed to *not be limited to* explaining over and over to every soldier that no method except abstinence would ever be one hundred percent—*shit,* I chuckled, *I still remember the fight to keep chlamydia down when I deployed with the First Cav...*

Come to think of it, the use of mercury to treat diarrhea had once been Terran, too. Back when I cared to read things I'd studied an ancient civil war in the Americas on the old Terran homeworld, where the majority of casualties died due to poor medical treatment, not battle. The winning side—the more industrial side—used mercury to treat diarrhea, and for a while, broken supply lines actually worked to the benefit of the "backwards" enemy, because those who couldn't get 'modern medicine' ended up relying on plant medicine that either really worked or at least wouldn't kill you faster than mercury would.

Ooh, I'd bet credits to cookies that's what's happening here with the Bantai and the Third.

But that still begged the question: how did mercury make it into a textbook that also had accurate tissue transplantation rituals? Had the Grausians distributed medical misinformation on purpose to deal with undesirables covertly? That'd been something that'd happened on the old Terran homeworld at one point, too.

Although glancing at the book... its formatting had looked like a history book. Maybe the original hadn't even been intended as a medical text, just a compendium of 'foreign cures', and the Bantai translators had taken it out of context. It wouldn't have been the first time a few words mistranslated screwed over a whole people group. That'd happened on Old Terra, too, when one word changed an ancient religious text from saying a man had to provide for a woman he'd played, to saying in translation that women had to marry their rapists. The original word in question had been "take"—and the first time it ever appeared in the text, it'd been used of musical instruments, as in "take up the lyre," so the word "rape" didn't make consistent sense. But hey, maybe those old translator guys played the lyre with different body parts than the rest of us did.

My thoughts distracted me, and I'd become engrossed in the rhythmic swishing of my uniform pants and the scratch-shuffle of my boots. I was now walking mostly alone with Lachish while the others walked ahead, or behind, our small pairs staggered now on opposite sides of the street more or less like Ken had suggested. Lachish interrupted my thoughts: "No further questions, doctor?"

"Eh? No, it's all—kind of awful to me, honestly," I said. "Mostly the sex. The biological part I can understand."

"Well, I would be lying if I pretended the sex itself wasn't a selling point," Lachish said. "For the Bantai, there is some dominance symbolism over us, and of course as you know intercourse offers many cardiovascular and oncological health benefits."

"And psychological, too, if it's with the same person long-term, and you've developed trust, and the freedom to consent, with them. But that's not what's happening here."

"No, it's not. Pleasure guard is not easy, physically or psychologically," Lachish agreed, and again, I wished he would not agree with me like this. "It is a noble calling. Without it I'm not sure how our little clan would survive. Our genetics are in high demand among other Edenians—we were favorites for Grausian clinical trials, too. You know our planet was one of the farming sites for Grats? A few of their minor stabilization genomes came from Sevellans." He straightened his back with pride. "But Sereno would do away with the flesh trade altogether if he could."

"Does he have any actual power to do that?" I asked.

Lachish hesitated. I saw him swivel as if to get a head count —or maybe to see which Sevellans were standing closest to him. But we'd strayed some distance from the rest of the group. Howard's mercs were chatting away with the rest of the Sevellans behind us; Ken and Howard herself sped ahead of us, weaving through the scattered clusters of Edenian families ducking in and out of their homes. We'd reached a fairly quiet residential street, but the conversations bouncing off the scattered adobe structures were noisy enough that we could speak freely without anyone else hearing.

Satisfied with this, Lachish said: "Sereno is what is called a hidden heir. Our people always keep a public decoy and a few private distractors—of which I am one—but our commanders' panel knows the true heir. If something were to happen to the Grandfather, Sereno would have the authority to realign our public policy."

I fought to keep my body language relaxed, but my lips pursed and an eyebrow couldn't help but raise. "Why would you tell me this?"

"Because you may be with us longer than your sergeant expects." The tall Sevellan commander shortened his stride to stay closer to me. "We like you, to be blunt. Galaxy Aid predominantly works with the Bantai, and there's a strong argument to be made that a pair of medics is a fair exchange from the Bantai for our higher-quality pleasure guards. We can even point out that you'll be difficult for the Bantai to work with because you don't use their medical techniques."

I flinched. "Eh—maybe Kamakura and I can just put in a request with Galaxy Aid directly that they station us with you. You know, keep the flesh trade out of it."

"Either way," he said. "You will likely be entrusted with the medical care of some of our most premium assets, so you need certain information. We know whose side you're on." He lowered his voice with an almost wicked grin, elbowing me like a co-conspirator. "After all, when you first landed, you had no reason to spend yourselves into exhaustion saving our kin. The rest of the Terrans with you only helped us because they needed to shield *you*. We see you."

"Mm, in a hostile zone it's generally good practice to keep alive the people who know what they're doing and don't want you dead," I shrugged. "Don't take it personally."

"Mm, in a hostile zone I choose to believe my eyes," he mimicked me, broad smile unchanged. "The mouth always lies. Which is why even if you did choose to reveal Sereno's importance, no Sevellan will believe you. I wouldn't even need to kill you."

With that and a curt nod, he dropped back to walk with his squad.

CHAPTER NINE

Ken Kamakura

KEN WAS FAR ENOUGH AHEAD of everyone else that he had time to kneel and clean an older beggar lady's amputated knee stub without really slowing anyone else down. Wounds took on such strange colors in Edenian skin—except for black tissue here and there among the oranges and browns and greens it was hard to tell what was actually necrotic, and what was good flesh.

Thankfully they at least bleed red, not orange like Grausians, he thought.

That gave him some idea what he was working with. He had iodine and gauze in his assault pack, and a cheap antibiotic cream laced with healing acceleration factors. He glanced at the label, pointing out details from the ingredients to explain to the woman what he was doing as he did it—Wimmer's Scrit was still close enough for them to understand each other.

"Is this medicine from your world, then, kind alien?" the lady wanted to ask.

"Kind of. Terran scientists had never managed to develop acceleration factors without causing cancers—rapid tissue growth isn't always a good thing," Ken explained. "The tissue acceleration factors we use today were actually developed from an Old Terran plant called aloe, but it was Grausians who figured that out."

"Sometimes, unfortunately, it takes an outsider to see that what you've got at home is valuable," the lady smiled with a knowing eyebrow raised over her aquamarine eye.

Edenian eyes, Ken thought, had to be perhaps the most beautiful living artwork ever devised by God. Each person's iris wasn't merely unique in the way Terran eyes were—it was as if each person was born with their own new color. Ken didn't know how that worked—Terran hereditary traits for eyes generally followed dominant and recessive patterns that were relatively simple, with blue eyes, for example, generally a predictable recessive trait that required two blue-eyed grandparents. Edenian eyes seemed more like the flowers that hybridize to create new variations, with no two even remotely similar, and some with wild stripes and swirls.

"Kamakura," Wimmer barked behind him.

Ken zipped up his assault pack. "I'm going to get in trouble for getting caught up in your eyes, grandmother!" he told the elderly lady with a parting smile, remembering what Sereno had said about family terms as honorifics. "Best wishes to you. Goodbye."

She giggled, and that, he thought, was enough to absolutely make his year. She'd been weeping when he rolled up.

Kamakura's boots skidded a bit on the pink-dusted concrete as he dashed after the rest of the group. "I'll run on ahead so I can work without slowing anyone down," he said as he reached Wimmer.

"Stop." Her bony fingers snatched his arm like a claw—he shortened his stride with a quizzical look. What was her problem now?

"Okay, soldier, we all know you're very smart and very good

at your job," Wimmer hissed with a furtive glance at the group ahead of them—she seemed to want this conversation to be private. "But you're never going to get to your contract alive if you stop to patch up every injured squirrel and Kranal and bent blade of grass you see."

"I haven't seen a single squirrel, Kranal, or blade of grass here yet, ma'am," Ken quipped.

Wimmer released him with a frustrated, clench-jawed growl; her fist closed around the tube to the almost-empty camel-back hanging off her assault pack. "You've been really difficult today, but I'm going to try to get this through your head," she said. "I know there are a lot of people who need help. But life isn't first-come-first-serve. The other people who need your help are most likely just as deserving, and you will get to those people *faster* if you keep your head focused on getting to your mission."

Ken took a deep breath, eyes on his steps. "But I'm already *at* my mission, ma'am," he said. His tone was firm, and even, but for some reason he didn't want to meet her eyes—they were blazing pinpricks of gray chaos, a storm cloud he didn't understand. "The contract was only a means to my end. Just a way to get here and get supplies."

"Well, you're not going to keep having access *to* supplies if you can't play nice with the people who buy them for you," Wimmer said. "I don't think Sergeant Howard's too pissed, but if you pull too much of this 'holier-than-thou' attitude with whatever Galaxy Aid supervisor she hands us off to you could end up losing your contract altogether. The correct answer when someone tells you to stay with the group isn't a veiled *I'm more warfighter ready than you* unless what they want is actually going to get someone killed. We're not running maneuvers right now. It was totally reasonable for her to ask you to slow down."

Ken glanced up only to check if the doctor's hand was shaking on the tube—she was still chewing on it even though the waterbag was empty. Her grip was steady. Whatever addictive medication she was taking probably didn't affect her cognition, either, and she probably had good reasons for taking it. Just as she probably had good reasons for getting on his case all day. Trauma taught people all kinds of lessons—

But not all of those lessons were right.

"Respectfully, I already finished the mission where I went where I was told, filled out paperwork, and helped no one," he said.

Wimmer scowled. "You fucking—"

"Excuse me?"

"Drop it!"

It took Ken a second to realize she had her pistol trained on a *random guy behind him in the middle of the street.* It was a young man about Ken's age—maybe nineteen years by Terran development. Giant topaz eyes—blue laced with yellow—stared at the humans in unblinking terror. The hem of his Third-patterned robe shivered with his trembling.

And with good reason. Wimmer's snarl could have made the dead shake. "You don't get two shots at my team," she growled.

"Whoa whoa whoa," Ken threw out his hands, trying to take a step closer to the Captain. She had to be having a flashback or something. The guy didn't have anything. He hadn't *done* anything. But no one taught you in AIT how to talk down a PTSD survivor with a *gun.*

"Step the fuck out the way, Kamaku—"

The gunshot that followed didn't come from Wimmer's pistol.

Jocelyn Wimmer

I was not fucking having a flashback.

Well—I was a little bit. Just that tiny bit of time traveling where Skinner's head would transpose itself over Kamakura's, and I'd imagine the scarlet jelly sliding down his forehead. But I'd learned already to ignore that. It wasn't ever vivid enough to be a hallucination—just a memory that would stick its grubby paws into the stream of my present and fog up my vision a little.

That was why I sounded like I cared when I "snarled" at Ken.

No, I pulled my pistol on Golden-Eyes McGee because I saw him fire a silenced round in the middle of the street and miss. I didn't know who the shot was for. Nor did I care. It went in our general direction and *thwicked* into the corner of a little adobe house just before Ken and I passed it. The rest of our group had already rounded that corner—it was just me and this cub medic who didn't know that *scared* doesn't mean *not dangerous.* And I was feeling mama bear.

But mama bear took a shot to the shoulder pretty quick. It was a much better shot than the other one—almost center mass, dammit. I stumbled backwards, trying to maintain my grip on my weapon—dammit dammit dammit—

Either Ken was quick to recover from shell-shock or the shooter was slow to reload or it was just a fucking old gun—no idea which because to me it was all in slow motion anyway. But Kamakura sidestepped into the guy before he could take another shot. Ken's elbow locked down like a clamp over Golden-Eyes' arm—the blade of his other hand chopped violently at Golden-Eyes' forearm as he twisted around the joint—*good job, kid, attacking the wrist, not the gun! But—*

"Be careful, your back's to him!" I heard myself wheezing in warning. If the guy drew a knife right now it was game over—!

Oh shit, I was about to fall down. Okay then. I stepped forward to fall forward. *Roll and control.* I saw the offending weapon fall, too—oh, and then Ken and his new boyfriend, tussling to grab at it. "Yay, now we're all on the ground," I coughed. *Fucking aces my shoulder hurts! What'd I get hit with?*

Must be something plasma because it fucking burns! Wet red syrup spattered into the greenish-gray dust under me—*oops, that's blood. Hold pressure. Not plasma.*

Hold pressure, or help Kamakura?

You apply the tourniquet real quick, and then return fire, if you're the victim. That's the rule. But that's if you can be quick. There is no 'quick' about a shoulder. Or any junctional injury, for that matter. And I didn't have a junctional tourniquet in my pack.

The best medicine is often a bullet. I could reach the gun. I did. I aimed it. Golden-Eyes spun around on top of Ken like he was a floor-dancer and Ken was—well, the floor—to kick it out of my hand. Shit. *The fuck happened to my own pistol?* Oh, it was way over there, too.

I reached for the shortsword on my hip, my hands shaking—

Shit, if I passed out, I was about to be useless. I tore myself out of my uniform blouse and ripped the top of my shirt. There's a pretty huge artery that flows under the collarbone, and I was gushing more than oozing. I balled up my shirt and pressed it against the wound—my fingers were sticky and warm—*still breathing, though! Didn't drop a lung*—my other hand dug into my pocket for the sealant syringe. The fast-drying "blood sponge cream-puff" would be hell to remove later but it was better than dying now. I tore off the plastic end with my teeth, shoved the open end into the wound with a groan, and squeezed.

"Fuuuuck my cat and call it your dog," I cursed through wincing teeth. It felt like what it was—a poisonous mass that speed-hardened in my wound, puffed up twice the size, and wanted to keep puffing, if it could. The pressure throbbed. I let go of my shirt, opening my hand like a claw to unstick my fingers from each other—noticed my sweet new iron-painted tie-dye patterned top—also—*tap tap tap*—I wasn't bleeding anymore. The two wrestling men had rolled too far away from me again now. I scrambled on my hands and knees for the two firearms—

Ken Kamakura

The terror in the Edenian's eyes could not be calmed, only caught. He railed above Ken, palm bleeding around a huge broken shard of glass he was stabbing down towards the young combat medic like a knife.

"I saw you aliens grab that girl, I know you implanted something into her, I know you're here to experiment on us, I know we'll be conquered again if we don't kill every last one of you, I know—" The Third guy's voice was hoarse, almost a whisper of fear, squeaking on every other breath as he urged himself on. This was the bravest thing he'd ever done. Ken could feel that.

"We didn't do what you—agh!" But Ken's panting attempt at an explanation choked around a gasp of pain. To keep the glass from going into his eye he'd blocked with his hand. He heard a crunch—felt the resistance—closed his fingers, wrapping them around his attacker's to keep the faux-knife—from—pulling—out—again—*give me give me*—the only thing that existed in the world was that glass blade. No time to go for his gun. He gripped the young man's wrist with his other hand, squirmed his knee outside the man's leg, planted his foot, thrashed—flipped them over. Now he was on top. Pain flashed through his face as the man's free fist found his eye again and again—he pulled back—blocked with his forearm, fell back—fell off—

"Back up!" he heard Wimmer shout.

He obeyed.

A pistol zinged. *Wait, wait, let me get my stun shot!* he thought too late, reaching for his Mark X—

He blinked. He could see now. His head pounded. He was kind of dizzy.

The Edenian was dead.

Wounds took on such strange colors in Edenian skin, and as

the young man's skin faded to a shimmering oil spill, the pinks and greens seemed to flow across his temples in rivulets and waves, flowing, flowing, and leaking like a painted stream to meet the red oozing from the gunshot wound in the back of the man's head. The brilliant one-of-a-kind eyes dulled, and rolled upward.

Ken wanted suddenly to undo something. What, he didn't know. But his training told him, loud and clear: this one was expectant.

This one could not be saved.

CHAPTER TEN

Ken Kamakura

SERGEANT HOWARD and Commander Sereno agreed on one thing: Ken Kamakura was not allowed to leave the hospital compound anymore.

"It wasn't his fault," he could hear Captain Wimmer's grunted defense through the wall of the truck where he now 'slept'. She and the two leaders were huddled around a trash fire just around the corner from the entrance to the old 'emergency room' where most of their patients now lived, catty-corner to the merc tent; foul-smelling smoke still managed to sift its way into the sealed vehicle parked in front of it, where Ken lay on a taut canvas stretcher staring at the dark ceiling centimeters from his nose.

It wasn't his fault, Ken wanted to say of the jewel-eyed guy she'd shot. It was centuries of other people's actions. It was their inability to really communicate. It was the starvation in the man's cheekbones sucking power out of his frontal cortex; the brainwashing of his tribe; the oppression of the colonists; personal trauma, mental illness, *stupidity—*

What good was a tourniquet? It didn't fix the things that caused people to self-destruct their lives. You could save someone's life and they could still ruin it. Even saving that Third girl today, outside the wall, when they'd returned—stealing her the chelating agent, the antibiotic, the carafate in exchange for the rock fungus, and then convincing the Sevellan guard that was a reasonable trade—her ruby eyes sizzled with bitterness. What would the rest of her life be, in a world where she might just end up as a pawn in a trade? She was younger than he was. How old was the Bantai *love* who was running her life—the *love* who wasn't there when she needed help?

He flexed his injured hand, allowing the pain to wake him up. *These are just thoughts. They're not reality. Stay the course.*

"I'm going to transfer the both of you back to the tents of my Grandfather." Sereno's declaration interrupted Ken's inner monologue.

"Both of who now?" Howard protested.

"The two medical personnel. Captain Wimmer, you told me today most of our patients are improved—some of them can even return to duty in a few days, yes? So you're not strictly needed *here.*"

The Captain grunted something under her breath Ken couldn't hear. He could hear Howard, though.

"Hold on, before you make a huge mistake, let me get you better medical supplies, more medics, more resources, food—I couldn't get *into* the Galaxy Aid compound today because of this little emergency, but with Kamakura *here* I should be able to make it across the city tomorrow. It's a huge city, and the roads are—well, if your hovercraft could be repaired to actually fly, that would be ideal," Howard rattled off her solution *fast.* What was she afraid of?

"You're welcome to do that, Sergeant Howard. In fact, I'd say that's the only way you'll secure transportation for the reporters and your medic back at Welcome Village." Sereno's tone as he said the name made it sound like a joke—when he spoke to Wimmer, however, he spoke seriously. "Captain, you overheard my conversation with my sister the other day."

"Uh… yeah. Yes, commander, I did."

"Would you say she's safe to engage in high-contact activities?"

Ken knit his brow. The hell was Sereno… wow. His stomach churned.

Wimmer's voice was clear, and severe. "No. I would say if she stays there too long, with repeated friction someone's bound to break open that femoral wound and bleed her to death. If she's able to convince them to stay behind her, and not between her legs—"

Howard must have made a face—or perhaps Sereno had, because the doctor's matter-of-fact answer interrupted itself. "It's just the reality of the situation. I can't make it nice for you."

Ken's mind flailed. The images the doctor painted now made Sibila's exit so much more horrific. He'd known, in the back of his mind, of course, but the clear language out in the open—it made this real. What could be done? They couldn't mount an attack: the much larger Bantai forces would crush the Sevella. Could they sneak her out? Trade something else for her? Was that the idea?

"There will be a small summit called, not far from here, where our Grandfather and the Bantai Grandfather will meet," Sereno was saying. "Our pleasure guard contingent who left yesterday will be there, and I'd like you to take care of any medical problems that may have arisen as a result of their heavy duties."

Ken's heart thrashed against his sternum—yes, absolutely. Gah, he felt so sick. Someone needed to go see those girls and end the nausea pulsing in waves from his stomach to his throat.

Howard was saying something—Sereno interrupted. "Galaxy Aid predominantly works with Bantai populations, and I'm not really interested in giving the Bantai more medical information," he said. "I'm fairly certain our two medics—or, sorry, our medic and our doctor, I'm still learning the difference—" Ken almost gasped a little—or laughed. Ooh, it was a good thing Captain Wimmer didn't have *too* much of an ego. "Yes, Sergeant Howard, they are ours. Here on Eden Crescent, we have a saying, across all people groups: if my ancestors had this land, it is mine."

"First come, first serve," Wimmer grunted.

"Yes. You're mine—even if you're helpful to everyone. I am well aware the same doctor who shot a Third fanatic today might heal a Third fanatic tomorrow. That's part of my concern: if the Bantai are really killing themselves with false medical cures, I'm not sure I want to simply *hand* them truth-tellers to turn their epidemic around." There was no hatred in Sereno's voice—it was cold. Friendly. Clean. *Kinda messed up to let civilians die of ignorance, but it's impossible to blame him.* "And who knows. Perhaps Galaxy Aid has been arguing with them for months already. Either way I see no reason to simply hand them two valuable assets without additional compensation."

"I may be jumping ahead," a deeper voice interrupted—a slightly older, but still powerful voice, from the commander Ken had heard through the grapevine was the next regent if the current one died. *Lachish, I think his name was.* "But I fear if you hope to convince Grandfather to trade information instead of flesh, you're destined for disappointment, brother. Grandfather's policy has consistently been that of appeasement. If these assets belong to the Bantai via some foreign nonprofit, he's going to want to deliver them to keep our *neighbors* happy."

"I'm aware of that," Sereno said. "But Grandfather is in poor health. He may not feel well enough to negotiate in the summit."

"Where did you hear that?" Lachish's suspicion was tinged with confusion. "He seemed fine last I saw him."

"I'm not sure," Sereno mused. Something in his voice

sounded—fake—to Ken. Louder than it needed to be. Like Lachish wasn't his intended audience. "But since we have an amazing new medical team, perhaps we should have them pay him a visit. A thought I just had." Somehow Ken was sure it was *not* a thought he *just* had. *What does he want?*

The speech shifted to a volume Ken could no longer hear, but despite his uncertainty about Sereno's wishes Ken didn't actually need to hear more anyway. He knew enough: he knew where he needed to be. He didn't know exactly what he'd need to do there, but he knew the time, place, and uniform.

Hm. That was a very old military expression, and Ken was beginning to realize he was kind of a shit soldier.

Maybe he was just in the wrong fight.

KEN AWOKE in the middle of the night to a *body* squirming into the cot beside him.

"Hey!" he shout-whispered, pushing away, then "Ow!" as he accidentally touched whoever it was with his injured hand.

The body pushed back, shoving him against the wall. "Shh!" Howard's voice pleaded. "You'll wake people up!"

"Sergeant? What the hell?" Ken's instinct was to feel for his holster—why was that his instinct? Did he not trust her? *Be cool.* He squirmed as far into the wall as he could and lay still.

"I wanted to tell you the plan personally—not over radio and not in front of people," Howard whispered. "Since there's no one in here with you, I figured this was my best chance."

Ken tensed. "What plan?"

"We're leaving tonight. In about an hour Tack and Bones will escort Wimmer into this vehicle, and we'll take off."

"What?" *No!* Ken's balking resistance came out as confused stupidity. "What about the Sevellans? They need this vehicle, and they'd probably fight us for it."

Howard's warm body shifted as she laughed; hot, fast breath tickled past Ken's cheek in the dark. "What about the Sevellans? They're literally holding you here against your will. I'm still not a hundred percent sure they're not responsible for the Third crashing our ship. Remember the pilot who burned to death?" Stacey prodded—it was cruel manipulation, and Ken found it didn't work. He couldn't do anything about the dead, only about the living, the now. "Even if we end up shooting our way out, I think you're entitled to a few casualties. What, do you have Hostage Attachment Syndrome, now?"

"No, it's not Hostage Attachment Syndrome, I'm not *loyal* to Sereno," Ken insisted. "I just want to do things right. We can get to Galaxy Aid without killing anyone. You're an excellent negotiator. You can have them come to the camp where we go, where the Grandfather is, with supplies, and—you know, set something up. Isn't their whole thing to help people? Well, we're helping people."

Howard groaned. For a moment there was no sound but her frustrated breathing. Ken pressed harder against the wall.

"Look, if you want to help people, help me," she said finally. "I'm a single mom with two kids. I'm away all the time, so maybe I'm a shitty mom. But honestly? This is the only job I know how to do to put food on the table. At the big civilian career fair during our demobilization, I walked right up to the first booth and had a panic attack. I don't know what to do if I'm not in something kind of like a military." She paused, and Ken listened. He felt her hand grip his good one—was this more manipulation, or was she actually pleading here? "We solve problems, and I'm usually pretty good at solving problems. But now I've been away from my daughters for two months, and I promised them I'd be there in time for their birthday."

"You celebrate birthdays, too?" Ken found himself asking. He was sleepy, his head ached, and he didn't want to argue right now. He wanted to think about parties. So he did. "What are they like in your culture?"

"What, you've never had a birthday, you weirdo?" Stacey laughed. The breath that filtered over to his chin had a hint of sweetness on it, like Old Terran medicinal menthol laced with Uri Naran man-eating honeysuckle.

"It's just not a thing my family does. We're very—reserved. We celebrate earned accomplishments," Ken shrugged. He was starting to see a little better in the near-complete darkness, and he could now make out the outline of the face centimeters from his. The shadows complemented her round cheeks, button-nose, and sweet little tiny potato chin. She was altogether too adorable to be as much of a badass as she was—although he would never say that to her. "My classmates had them. I'd say we almost had something religious against them—not that other people couldn't celebrate them, but like—it was safer to give thanks to others on that day, or to thank God for another year of life, than it was to make a big fuss of oneself. What about you?"

"God? You didn't strike me as particularly religious," Howard chuckled.

"And you don't strike me as someone who evades questions," Ken shot back. "Oh wait, yeah you do. Answer the question. What are birthdays like for you?"

"But I don't want to talk about birthdays," Howard whispered.

"Then why try to use them to win sympathy with me?" Ken asked.

Howard said nothing for a moment. She withdrew her hand, and Ken realized suddenly he'd been holding it. This was weird —this whole thing. "Do you have a problem with me, Ken Kamakura?" Howard asked finally.

"A little, I guess," Ken said. "But you're just doing your job."

"You know, even if I say things to get something out of someone, that doesn't make the things I say less true," Howard said.

"I know. And I do care about fulfilling the contract. I just think I can maybe have both—help both." Ken was the one pleading now. "Like—running ahead but staying in sight, so I can help someone without inconveniencing you all."

"How did that work out?" Howard patted around the cot, and suddenly her cold palm found his injured hand and squeezed. He bit his lip to stifle the shout, and grabbed her wrist. Tight. A surge of throbbing energy shot up his arm, and he could feel his heart beat harder.

"It worked out fine," he said. "My Bantai amputee had nothing to do with my Third attacker."

She released him… but her fingers lingered by the wound, just barely touching the bandage. "You just always have to be right, don't you," Howard's voice smirked.

"I'm not even that opinionated, and that expression always bothered me." Ken sat up on his elbow. His heart kept up the steady, overpowered pounding. He felt hungry, suddenly, leaning over her. "Yes, I want to be right. I don't see the problem with striving for *correctness*. What, do you want to be wrong?"

"If it gets my daughters fed, yes," Howard said. "So you're not coming?"

"I can't fight you, Sergeant Howard," Ken said. "Please don't undo all the progress we've made, by shooting your way out of here. Please be patient."

Another long pause. He could hear her soft breathing in the dark; his began to match it. Something stirred in his gut. She was so *close*. If he just extended left elbow, his injured hand would find her waist.

"It's kind of infuriating how hot you are," she said suddenly.

"Really? That's a surprise. I've gotten *zero* signals from

you," he said. Literally. He saw her as a kind of boss. A boss with an *excellent* derriere and shapely hips, but those features were like—like a display at an art museum. Something you admire, but don't touch. "Sergeant."

"Soldier." She sighed. "We'd be a terrible match, too."

Her fingers tapped on the bandage absently. It brought his attention to it—made him realize how sore his palm was. Something ached deep beneath his gut… the urge to catch her hand, yank her close, and wrap himself around her suddenly surged from his belly to his chest in a racing wave of desperate heat.

"You had better go, then," he said. He steadied his breathing —it had become more ragged, hadn't it? She was gorgeous, but he was on this planet on a mission, and she wasn't part of it. Full stop.

"I'm sorry, I shouldn't have—" The body warmth disappeared with a flutter of moving air; boots *thonked* softly on the floor of the truck.

He sat up as far as he could without bumping his head. "Shouldn't have what, Sergeant? Nothing happened. You came in here to give me a message, we talked about it, and now you're leaving. We talked about your family and touched on how different we are. *Terrible match*. That's it. That's the play by play." He lowered his voice again—it softened for some reason. "We're professionals."

He heard her chuckle as her boots carried her a few steps towards the back of the truck. "Professionals? You're not a professional, you're a paladin. You're lucky you weren't in the military long."

"Why?"

She paused. He could see the silhouette of her turning back against the dim light of the cracks in the door. "Paladins look like good soldiers at the beginning," she said. "They learn the algorithms, develop their war-craft with excellence—yes sir, yes ma'am, perfect salutes, kill themselves in physical fitness—they believe in the mission so they'll mold themselves into exactly the thing the mission demands." Her voice smiled now. "But you know, they almost always forget to clean their weapons."

Ken narrowed his eyes. "Literally or figuratively?"

"They just have a tendency of deciding what's important, and when you want them to do something that's against what they've decided is important, they'll die on that hill. It's all about the cause, to them, their own code. They're almost *hunting* for a hill to die on."

"I'm not that," Ken said right away. "I'm pretty obedient, all things considered, and I'm not looking for martyrdom."

"Sure, at first. But there's always that thing inside of you looking for that hill. And unfortunately for me, I think you've found it." She sighed. "This contract is important to me—I need to keep my organization happy. I need this job, I need to keep my girls fed. But you're right. There's still a little time. After that I've got a freighter that needs a merc escort."

"I can still make it to Ben-haba even if you have to leave," Ken offered.

"If you don't die on some side-quest first. I need you to arrive intact and useful, not handicapped."

Ken flexed his fingers, ruminating on the ache. He'd been lucky—the glass had gone straight through the gap between his third and fourth metacarpals at a pretty narrow angle, missing the major tendons even if it did tear up some of the smaller muscles. But—yeah. "I'll arrive intact," he said. "Just—I know it sounds cliché, but maybe let's remember these people have little girls, too."

"That's kind of why I'm disgusted," Howard said. "A people group that can't get basic human rights straight just isn't one I'm interested in wasting time on. They don't want help, they want handouts, and they definitely don't want change. The victims empower the perpetrators—I don't know if you've been seeing the same shit I have, with all your medical work, but that's what

I'm seeing. This is one of the worst places I've ever been and I don't want to be here a second longer than I have to. I wanna go home, hug my kids, and punch something."

"There's more to the Edenians than that, though. They have—"

"Don't start with me on art or architecture or some shit like that. Stability, or paintings? I'd burn every museum in existence to make sure no one's selling me to anyone else." She swung open the door; a swatch of light from the street and the moon illuminated half her form, throwing the rest of her body in shadow. "Goodnight, Ken Kamakura."

"Goodnight, Sergeant."

He lay awake for a while after the door creaked shut. Howard was right. They did have really miserable lives, these people. He found himself clinging to images Sibila had sold him—her mother and aunts dancing around a bubbling cauldron that steamed with rich, meaty, creamy scents; her brothers throwing colorful sand in the air over sparklers into creative patterns against the setting sun… she'd told him her family kept a portable library of books from all over their planet, and even some off-world ones, redolent with the rich, iron-laced scent of pages fashioned not from the pulp of precious plants but from a plastic-like paper developed from sand. She used to curl up with her father and read for hours in the shadow of their felt tent. They carted that library to every home they fled to, first on the back of a hovercraft, and then, when that wore out, and no one knew how to repair it, on literal carts. She used to run her fingers across the pages, a warm milk bun in the other hand, and close her eyes, imagining as she chewed, while the simple but rich taste of the toasted seed-bread and its sweet filling reminded her of her mother.

It was, in Ken's mind, like he'd been there with her.

Were those oasis moments between the battles enough to fight for? Was that what he was keeping people alive for? It all seemed a bit pale—empty, even—compared to the vivid eyes of the dying Edenian, whose greatest act of bravery was against a monster that never existed.

Am I like that? Fighting something that doesn't need to be fought, something natural, merciful, even, only to get myself killed for nothing?

CHAPTER ELEVEN

Jocelyn Wimmer

It was evening already by the time the rattling hovercraft brought us to the Sevella wilderness camp. Large tents huddled in the lengthening shadows of tall rock formations twisting towards the sky in curlicues of bronze green streaked with rusted red. It wasn't a canyon or anything like that—not a good ambush site—more like a forest of dancing stone.

Howard had been unusually cheery when we said goodbye in the morning.

"After what you said last night, I thought you'd be pissed," I noted, swinging my dufflebag up into the vehicle. Hot *damn* that hurt my back. And my chest now—the little surgical bot had had no trouble getting the sealant out of my artery, but the patchwork tissue regrowth had me feeling like a stuffed rag doll.

"Pissed? Why would I be pissed?" Howard teased: "I finally get to ditch you."

"Same, same," I grinned. "Getting so tired of your pretty face making me look twice as old."

"Pretty?" she laughed. "Aw, thanks, Captain. I'll miss you, too."

"Psh, you better miss me. I didn't even know you'd been trying to hit me!" I chuckled; I liked Dad jokes like that.

Howard groaned, and rolled her eyes.

That had been this morning; she'd set off right away to find a contact for Galaxy Aid, and we'd loaded into this sad buggy playing dress-up as a former hovercraft and set out into the desert. We'd gotten to work immediately upon arrival—mostly gynecological first aid and some infectious disease testing on the pleasure guard. It was grim shit that I'd like to forget, so I won't go into detail. But there were injuries.

Now we sat on an embroidered brown rug—so many shades of brown—waiting for Sibila. She was our last patient of the evening, and Sereno had said something about dinner.

Ken fidgeted beside me, looking around the room. "Mostly Sevellan furniture," he remarked. "Even though it's a Bantai tent. I'm starting to be able to tell the difference in the designs—the arabesques and so on. Bantai patterns are more rigid and angled, I think. They might have a circle and a square and a triangle, but they'll all be separate and discrete and simple, not like the elaborate Sevellan trinity triangles or the flowing interconnected circles of the Third. It's almost like the less technological the group the more flowy their art or something here."

I followed his gaze. Thick pillows lay everywhere—*everywhere*—and small mahogany-colored lacquered tables lined the tent walls, bearing intricate glass vases holding various spirits. The color scheme was crazy drab to Terran eyes: as much brown and dull gold as possible, with some soft gray and black here and there. "I guess with how colorful the world outside is, they use their private spaces as sensory escapes," I mused.

"At least in the pleasure guard quarters." Ken's mouth said words but his brain wasn't really talking to me, I didn't think—I could see his eyes straying over and over to the entrance that led into the neighboring tent. “If color is seen as a battle sign, the battle guard quarters might be more colorful.”

“Boys are like peafowl,” I grinned. Ken had told me about how his wealthy uncle bred exotic birds descended from Old Terran stock, and I hoped to distract him by turning the conversation that direction—I just needed to come up with a question about his past to get him talking—

He spoke first—actually paying attention now. “I’m confused about that. ‘Boys’—maleness, gender, here, I mean. Is—”

“Oh, you better not be confused about maleness, Kamakura. I’m not about to give my star medic the birds and the bees talk. I avoided parenthood for a reason,” I tried to interrupt with a limp joke to avoid the uncomfortable conversation I could feel coming as Sibila slipped through the sheer tent curtain with a burst of shimmering color.

Kamakura ignored my teasing. “I know it should be obvious to me, but just to clarify, is battle guard actually a synonym for male?” he asked. “Is that why all the female warriors have body mods?”

Sibila was limping, and probably more pale than I’d seen her last. Vibrant purple skin faded to soft tans and browns as she gingerly lowered herself to the nearest pillow and her body adjusted to match it.

“Yes. You are either pleasure guard or battle guard,” she said. “If you are born battle guard, like my brother or yourself, you need no modification. If you are born pleasure guard, like myself, or your Captain here, all normal Edenians will expect you to alter your shape and voice to match the natural battle body.”

“Like my Captain? We don’t have a pleasure guard.” Ken squinted. It kind of seemed like he didn’t *want* to get it. “Doctor Wimmer’s a soldier.”

“She means female, straight up,” I interjected, getting up to settle beside her. I’d take her pulse and oxysat while we talked, and as she saw me open my assault pack, she automatically bared her inner thigh to let me inspect the femoral wound we'd worked so hard on. She didn't have to remove a lot of clothing for me to get to it—like the rest of the pleasure guards we'd seen today she was only wearing a silky robe emblazoned with stark Bantai shapes. "She means female bodies are assumed to be for sex, so if you identify as something other than a bargaining chip you need to mod your gender to match."

"Indelicately put, but yes," Sibila assented.

"Well, shit." Ken swore for the first time since I'd met him. He folded his arms across his knees, and looked down at the floor. "So you really are a socially deterministic society, instead of biologically deterministic. I was hoping I was misunderstanding. So a person literally has to change from female to male to have the job they want?"

"Womb to seed—yes. Yes, that's correct." Sibila's tone was so matter-of-fact and light—yet my medic seemed to deflate under its weight. Every death crowded into the span of less than a week—everything we've seen—hadn't been heavy enough to crush the Bovie's back, but this little feather was? *What?* "Or the other way around—there are born battle guards who fear combat, and undergo surgery to qualify for pleasure guard," Sibila added, scowling—I couldn't tell if that face was because I was peeling back the bandage she'd glued to her leg, or because of some personal disgust for modded males. I hoped it was the former. *Poor guys.* "The modded pleasure guard are generally considered cowards, and often discover very quickly ours is not in fact an easier role."

"Why can't—" Ken licked his lips and took a big breath. "Okay, but do *you* want this? This role, I mean."

"What I want doesn't matter. I've been given the equipment I was given—and it's decent equipment, no?" Sibila waved down at her half-naked self with a little grin. The grin faded: "If I'm to suffer either way, I would rather suffer in my original body."

"But why can't you just be a warrior *and* keep your original body? Why do you have to change?" Ken's query sounded more like a plea—and he caught himself, as if some political correctness training from his childhood or some over-educated anthropology shit popped up in the back of his head. The shift was almost humorous to me. "Forgive my ignorance, I mean—I know I'm just an outsider, and I'm not knocking your culture, I'm just—confused."

He clearly wasn't, though. *Come on, kid, stand your ground.*

"Well, you'll meet our Grandfather tonight, so perhaps it's best to un-confuse you now—please do not ask him stupid questions," Sibila sighed. "It is actually quite simple. People like Grandfather feel like battle guard, so they know they are battle guard. I don't feel like my body is wrong, so I must be pleasure guard. What you are is in your spirit."

"Okay, but how does battle guard *feel*? What does it *feel like* to be battle guard?" Ken asked.

"Like you, I suppose."

"How do you know I *feel* any differently than you do?" Ken threw up his hands. "I mean, really, what do you enjoy doing? Didn't you—I mean, I saw you light up when you were driving the truck to protect your kin. You enjoyed that."

"Of course I did," Sibila said. "It would have been nice to have been born like you. But I can't have both your life, and my intact body."

"But why not?" Ken protested. "Why can't you just do what you want?"

Sibila smacked the pillow beside her with a stiff, sharp jolt, her spine rigid and chin high. "Because Grandfather decrees it. You can't just come in here with your questions, outworlder, and pretend you're not trying to change us. I see what you're doing, and it's not appreciated."

Her movement almost whacked my syringe hand. "Hey, whoa

—maybe warn me if you're going to move, okay?" I laid a firm palm on her knee and gave Kamakura a look. "You know, maybe this actually isn't a good conversation to have right now at this moment while I'm working. It's great that you're doing deep cultural inquiry or whatever the fuck you're doing, but if you two can just—maybe argue later." The femoral wound hadn't re-opened down to the blood vessel, but it was starting to tear and ooze, and I needed to hold the needle steady to inject the liquid graft in the right tissue layer. *I'll probably need to throw in a stitch in a second, too...*

"I'm sorry. I will hold still," Sibila said—and then ignored the rest of what I'd said. "Kenta, the Grausians tried to change us too. Their schools and hospitals and corporations pushed this sexist supremacy of the pleasure guard body as the ruling body, as is their way, and they had almost a hundred years of rule over us." *Only a hundred, huh.* Eden Crescent had been conquered kind of late, if I remembered correctly—it was literally the edge of the empire. "They may have succeeded on other continents, but on this one, only the Yada accepted their ways—and those land-thieves have always been a knife in the rest of our backs anyway. We used Grausian medical technology to *improve* our transformation process, and in the end, they gave in. We are a strong culture."

She wasn't moving, but her whole body was tense—I could feel her quad tighten under my palm, and she had fight in her purple eyes. I made sure she could see my gray ones as I patted her shoulder. "Hey, hon?" I said. "I'm not in charge of you, so I'm not telling you to shut up like I'm about to tell Kamakura here. But if this is an uncomfortable conversation to be having when you're kind of vulnerable and exposed, you really don't have to feel like you need to explain yourself. When I'm touching you, I want you to feel safe."

"Yeah, sorry—I—" Ken got the message. He sighed hard, rubbing the back of his head, and looked away from us at his assault pack lying half-open beside him. "I guess as long as you're happy."

"Happy, I am not." Sibila gave a curt nod. "I just spent two days—ech. It is a sacrifice. It is a real sacrifice." She blinked, hard, and then tightened her jaw, lifting her chin as if in defiance. "But we all make sacrifices for our country. My brother sells his body on the battlefield as I sell mine in bed. My happiness is beside the point."

Ken ground his jaw. He didn't look at me, and he was so miserable—and she was so—I mean, the tearing femoral wound was staring me right in the face, and I could see new bruises on her neck and inner thighs, and I didn't know if she'd let me even examine the area I was kind of suspecting took the most damage. I had to ask the question, for both of their sakes. But I asked so gently and casually it was almost thought or a feeling more than speech. "But if it weren't?" I asked. "If your happiness mattered?"

"If my happiness mattered…" Sibila thought for a moment. "Then I would be happier if my brother were Grandfather—First Leader, you might call it. Our current Grandfather sees us as weak for not undergoing the change as he did, and this is why he trades us out so—I don't know—so easily." Her voice wavered, and sounded a little hoarse—I reminded myself I needed to check her oral cavity for injuries, too. "Our treaties have protections embedded about our treatment, but they're almost impossible to enforce. Those who rent us generally have certain preferences they cannot enact on willing romantic partners, or they wouldn't need us. In reality, the aggression is impossible to remove from the equation. We are evidence of their triumph and supremacy more than we are the fulfillment of their needs, and it is impossible to really press for our own rights without endangering others. Even in times of peace, when the trades are purely financial, if you complain, you run the risk of rejection, and your family starving. There is no such thing as egalitarian flesh trade."

She winced as I threw in that stitch to reinforce the wound sealant, but her voice held steady—she was accustomed to pain. "In some ways, it would be difficult for my brother to limit the trade's abuse without eliminating the treaties completely. But I do know he would protect us somehow."

"It's a tough gig. How do you usually prevent disease transmission?" I asked casually as I affixed a waterproof wound seal over my work. I nudged her leg to let her know to move a bit so I could wrap the other bandage around it. "I've noticed your culture has a working germ theory."

"Every battle guard is required to bring proof of cleanness from infection before touching us," Sibila said, shifting her thigh to follow the movement of my hand. She was easy to work on because of how physically responsive she was. "But on days when we must service a multitude, it is sometimes even difficult to ensure every battle guard's papers are real. And even if someone could guarantee our protection for every encounter, the body still physically does not tolerate that volume of—well, you know. You're a doctor. There is wear, and exhaustion, and—" She interrupted herself, and suddenly looked me full on in the face. "You know sometimes the things they say during the act are worse than the things they do?"

"That doesn't surprise me," I said. "I've never had to live through what you're living through, but I've seen enough death and misery and been beaten around enough to know I prefer a silent ass-kicking to one with too much talking."

"I can imagine you do a lot of the talking in a fight, though," she grinned. "I saw you on the airfield the first day, Captain. You don't kill quietly."

"I'm just a mouthy old bitch, is all," I smiled back. I tucked in the end of my bandage and gave it one last soft pat. "All done. Am I good to check your pelvic area?"

She shook her head. It was strange how they did that like my race of Terrans did—not all people groups used the same universal body language, and Edenians seemed simultaneously weirdly alien and eerily similar to me. Their movement was more of a one-off jerk than our repeat-shake, so it seemed doppleganger-ish, or like she was knocking away a fly. "No, I'd rather not," she said. "I can handle that myself."

"He can leave," I nodded backwards at Ken without looking in his direction. "Some people prefer a chaperone and it's nice to have a helper, but he can go."

"No, I'm not shy," she chuckled.

"Just proud," I said.

"Yes." She rose now. "And I have much to be proud of. Come. You will sit with me as we watch the dinner ceremonies, and then we will return here, and wait for Grandfather."

"Grub sounds good." I stood too, gripping her arm to steady her. To my medic: "You good, Kamakura?"

He looked from me to her with lines of pain on his young face. To me he seemed a bit pale—kind of like he'd looked when he got Jump Disorientation Sickness on our way out here. He swallowed, and in the silence the brave face he struggled to put on reminded me of when he'd held back retching then. Gah, he'd really handled that JDS well. I'd actually kind of loved patting down the kid's forehead with the cold washcloth, snatching the vomit mask to get its suction tube over his face to prevent a low-gravity mess, pressing the cis-scop patch to the back of his ear with firm but kind fingers—little shit like that, where no one was gonna die, and I just kinda made someone feel better—it was menial shit that became a total honor when I was taking care of my soldiers. Or in this case, a former soldier with a durasteel soul. Even when I was taking glass out of his hand, he'd been more worried about the dead guy than himself: I knew he wasn't nauseous now because of a weak constitution.

No, he was nauseous now because he was *mad* and didn't know what to do with it. Shit, kid probably didn't even know he was mad. Probably thought it was just a thing that happened to him when people suffered.

"Yeah," he said. "I'm good."

Ken Kamakura

The huge bonfire sent sparks to the heavens that rivaled the winking stars. Silhouettes of families clustered here and there in its light as the Sevellen and Bantai Edenians cooked and danced in its heat. Each little cluster mostly kept to themselves; every now and then, someone from one cluster would rise to pass a utensil or a bottle of some fermented white substance to another cluster, or to approach the flames with a pot made of some discarded bent-up piece of metal that had probably been part of a space-capable vehicle once. Some of the clusters—usually ones with the brownest, plainest robes—used stone pots with intricate patterns carved into their surfaces. Ken was beginning to realign his idea of status symbols: on this neon-bright world, it was the wealthy who wore soft browns, and the poor carried the stains of color on their rags.

He had a lot to realign, he thought. To what standard, he didn't know. He almost felt too embarrassed to apologize—he *did* know when the patient was half-naked was not the moment to be challenging her about her occupation. He'd been more than useless in there; he'd been a hindrance. "I'm an idiot," he said aloud.

"No, you're not," Wimmer said, leaning back on her palms beside him. They were seated together on a woven brown carpet off on their own. The entrance to the pleasure guard room where they'd tended patients was barely open behind them, and it threw a soft yellow light through the doctor's platinum hair like a halo. She was probably younger than all the stress-related gray made her look, and flames nearby cast little shadows that alternately hid and highlighted her wrinkles, making her look almost caught in time. "Your timing was just off and you've got to learn to come in from an angle of curiosity and affirmation—when you're helping someone who's fucked up by shit they're not ready to fight yet, you can't show any emotion except safe acceptance 'til just the right moment. It's totally fine to have strong feelings, but you sounded like you were interrogating her. Which—I mean, no one likes that naked. Or almost no one." She grinned, taking a swig of the white bottle Sibila had left with her before tip-toeing off to cook. "I don't know what your naked preferences are, of course."

The teasing almost didn't register. Ken found himself watching for Sibila's shape by the fire. She was technically still at work, and not allowed to put on normal clothes—just that robe that marked her as Bantai pleasure property for the night. Firelight glistened on the bare leg that slipped out of it as she stood, pot on her out-thrust hip, speaking with confidence to a battle guard who looked Bantai from his square red earrings and nose piercings. Her body language seemed to shift depending on which battle guard she spoke to—with this one, she lifted her chin and let the robe fall free, while with another, she'd ducked down her head, lips only answering "yes" with utter submission pressing her shoulders into a hunched bow. Which one's fingers matched the bruises on her neck, Ken wondered?

He tried to come back to the conversation. He had to. These thoughts were making his whole stomach want to climb up his esophagus and hang itself with it.

"I should have been more helpful," he said.

Captain Wimmer had even managed to make Sibila smile in there, to open up—it was wild that someone so rough and rude could become such a social savant during patient care. If even the merc with a mouth could put on her nice girl words, he should have been able to do so much better himself.

"If even"? He looked at the doctor now. As if reading his mind, she said, "You know, I do know what the fuck I'm doing. My personal life may be a nuclear fall-out zone, but the shit that ended my career wasn't incompetence."

"I didn't even know your career had—ended," Ken said. "You weren't just demobilized like the rest of us?"

"Fuck no," she smirked. "The military likes to hold on to doctors even in times of peace. Especially ones with perfect patient scores." She took a swig of the bottle and chased it with a sip of her water. Ken found himself wishing she'd stick just to the weird white substance.

"You sure those are okay to mix?" he ventured.

"Did I not just say I know what I'm doing?" she scowled.

"Sorry—yeah. I really shouldn't be—" He sighed.

"This is why you got stabbed and I got shot, you know," she said.

"I know! I know. Like I said, I'm an idiot." He hunched his shoulders. "It's just you—I mean, I did find you utterly trashed in a bar, fighting someone twice your size in what I suspect wasn't entirely an unprovoked conflict." He tried to add the tone of a joke to it, but only managed a weak smile that probably looked more nervous than anything. "But you clearly have the social graces to… you know, *not*. And during sparring sometimes—" Ugh, how did you call out someone who knew more than you did without sounding like a little snot? "I don't know, ma'am. I worry sometimes you're—not okay."

"Not okay as in, I'm insane and you don't trust me?" Another swig. "You can speak plainly, soldier. I'm too fucking tired right now to kick your ass."

"Ha *ha*." Ken *said* the sardonic laugh instead of laughing. "No, I'd never say that, Captain. People can suffer mental illness and not be insane. Gah, I'm—uncomfortable even saying the phrase 'mental illness' around you, for some reason."

"You shouldn't be. It's just clinical shit like everything else.

I'm not, though—ill, I mean." She took another sip and chased it again. "I'm just an asshole." She turned her eyes away from the fire now to look at him. "You know I actually don't know if I provoked that fight or not? I don't know how to—how to *people*. When I'm with a patient—when I'm fingers-to-skin with someone—I—I know things. It's not woo-woo shit, I mean—I know what to say because there's an algorithm to follow, and their body language, their blinks, their heartbeat, their little sighs or micro-expressions, their temperature against my fingertips, it all guides me down that algorithm. Written or no, spoken or no, taught or no, there's an order to healing, even if you're healing something you've never seen before—in some way, you're marching together to the rhythm of the divine, towards a—I don't know. There's just a definite answer to that shit." She set the bottle down for a moment and tipped her head back towards the stars. For a second her eyes gleamed, and then closed, and something like peace flickered over her hard face. "God," she muttered—it was difficult to tell if it was a swear, or a prayer, or the answer she was looking for. Or perhaps all three.

Her peace couldn't even last two seconds. Someone shrieked—Ken and Wimmer both stiffened, and he was on his feet before he realized it was a shriek of laughter, and the woman at the far edge of the shadows was doubled over giggling. Wimmer huffed, looked back at the world around her, and picked up the bottle again. "There's no definite answer to *this* shit, meanwhile," she said, nodding to the fire as Ken sat back down. "Politics sucks. You were saying you already did the mission where you filled out paperwork—well, I wish one or two of my guys could've stayed back somewhere filling out paperwork. I sure as fuck didn't know how." The drink found her lips again and hovered there as she muttered into it: "Maybe if we had the right people filling out paperwork to begin with, we'd have more people come home."

Ken didn't quite understand what she meant by that—or what

forms had to do with politics exactly—so he said nothing. He'd interrogated her enough. That miserable look she gave the world after looking up at the sky comforted him somewhat—not because he enjoyed her misery, but because it let him know that he wasn't alone in his, and maybe he wasn't wrong.

———

Jocelyn Wimmer

Dinner for us was roasted little giblets or fritters of some savory, beef-like meat with a nice char to it—the spiced crust was just firm enough to give the outside a little crunch while the soft inside melted on my tongue. Fatty. Buttery. The crunchy, fried cactus-like plant that accompanied it under a sprinkling of rock salt made the whole thing feel like an elevated stir fry. It was simple in a confident way, as if to say it didn't need a bunch of sauces because its ingredients had nothing to hide.

Couldn't say that about all the people. Sereno sat on a nearby mat to our right with a young woman about Sibila's age and three kids. *Are those—his kids?* He didn't have much peace. Every now and then someone would come over, and he'd get up and walk around the fire with them, his head bowed and eyes burning, before returning to his cluster. Every time he returned, he would grip the hand of the little girl who sat there, and his jaw would clench before he took his seat and held her to his chest. I found myself wondering: if you were a dad, and your daughter's future was Sibila's, did you pressure her instead to 'undergo the change' to protect her? And what if she didn't want to?

He caught me watching him, and raised his bottle to me. I raised mine back.

An elderly Bantai woman from a cluster a few mats over hobbled over to us with a shy but determined look on her face—I steeled myself for that *dinnertime consult* I'd grown to hate as a physician, where you couldn't even eat in peace without someone bringing you one more problem to fix. People really don't understand how wearying that gets. They think it's just a casual scientific question when they bring you their newest wart or stomachache on your off-hours, but what they're actually bringing you is the weight of possibly missing a cancer at worst and at best, you're now teaching a whole impromptu class on lab results where the teacher's failure can get the student killed. What they're actually bringing you is another face of the spectre of death you already carry with you everywhere you go.

But this lady wasn't a patient. "This—for you." Her wrinkled lips spat clear, loud syllables like we probably wouldn't understand her otherwise. "Guests." She pushed a colorful blown glass dish into Ken's hands without warning—it was heavy, and my hand shot out to catch the side where his injured hand was. It was hot, too—we both let out little hisses of pain, and then laughed as we put it down between us.

"Thank you," Ken said to her immediately. "I hurt my hand the other day, that's why I'm a little baby."

"I'm just Terran, that's my excuse," I said, bowing my head a little and gripping the older woman's hand with both of mine. I'd seen folks do that to Sereno and it looked like a sign of respect.

"Here, this is how you do," she said, still talking to us like we were toddlers. She grabbed the spoon from the metal hubcap-pot between us, and pushed the food inside it to one side. Then she tilted the glass dish she'd bought and emptied half its contents into our pot, and took half our pot's contents into hers. "Food trade."

"Ooh, I can get behind trading food," Ken said. He hovered his chopsticks over the pot—she'd brought some kind of round tuber that glowed red in the firelight. It smelled like roasted nuts with honey—definitely enticing—but I put my wrist next to his before he could commit. "Oh, right—" he said. "Is there anything else I should know? Like you don't mean an actual, legal, political trade or anything—I'm not signing up for your army or something am I?"

"What?" her wrinkly face wrinkled more, and her eyes danced. "Is that how you sign up for the military in your world? Someone offers you food and then you fight?"

"In my case it wasn't far off," I grinned, satisfied and digging in now myself. "Three square meals and a roof. Shit, that's good." I turned to Ken, chewing on squishy sweetness that tasted just as nutty as it smelled. "Sorry if that destroys your noble image of me."

"Ma'am, I—I don't think noble is the image I have of you," he said. "Wow—that is good." His eyes brightened at the old lady, and she nodded.

"It is. Let's try yours." She dipped two fingers into the glass dish and grabbed a morsel of meat. Music had started to play in the background, and she closed her eyes and hummed with it as she chewed. "Hmm. Death rat is hard to prepare right. It is close. Next time, less salt, more citrus juice to soften the meat. Good fat, though."

And with that, she picked up her dish, and hobbled off.

"Death rat?" Ken and I looked at each other.

"She's got to be joking," Ken said.

"No—I did poke my head into the pharmacy wing at one point and there were definitely some Sevellans bagging up rodents. I thought it was for sanitation reasons, but, ah, now I know why they were picking ones with the weird fat pads over their rumps."

"Don't they emit toxins?" Ken narrowed his eyes.

"Yeah, well, I guess that's why they're hard to prepare right," I said. "I did see Sibila cook this, *and* take a bite, so unless we all have some murder-suicide pact I didn't know about I think we're good." I grinned. "They've got those little tiny hooves and I'm pretty sure they chew their food twice, if you're worried about kosher," I teased.

"That is not what crossed my mind!" Ken laughed. "It's got a rat's face and a rat's tail, it's a rodent to me." He tilted his head. "Do you keep food laws, ma'am?"

"When I'm in charge, yeah," I shrugged. "I don't ask what's in food if someone gives it to me, though. Especially not at a political summit where I don't know shit about what table rules get people mad enough to kill."

"You don't strike me as—huh."

"Not noble *or* religious, eh?" I took another chug of the *makka* Sibila had left me—fermented milk alcohol that kind of tasted like a beer that'd somehow gotten cream in it. It was good shit. "What am I?"

"Okay, I didn't mean you're *ignoble*, just that *noble* isn't what comes to mind," Ken protested, but he didn't seem stressed about it. Food seemed to have calmed him down a lot. "You're a badass, Captain. That's the word I'd use."

"If you swore."

"If I swore."

I leaned back again, enjoying the warm glow of the drink in my gut and the literal glow of the food on my sticks. The music wasn't too loud, the dancing wasn't too annoying, and people flowed from mat to mat, cluster to cluster, without all the crowding and stress that'd made me avoid shindigs back in the service. It was as if an extrovert had designed the whole system with introverts in mind because every Edenian knew each person mattered to the whole.

Various people came over to trade bits of food or alcohol with us, and at one point Ken even ventured over to try the same thing with the neighboring mat, at which point several Sevellan women twice his age whisked him off to teach him to dance. I grinned. If you looked past the pleasure guard slave robes and battle guards lording over them as conspiring leaders made hushed rounds around the fire—if you overlooked the fact that beneath the wholesome veneer of comradery and community lay the threat of half of these people eliminating the other half if their daughters failed to perform—

All kind of hard to overlook, but if you could—

The party was actually pretty sweet, in both senses of the word. I didn't think I'd ever seen any people group so affectionate with their kids. There wasn't a single raised voice or tantrum—everyone seemed to know that they didn't necessarily have tomorrow together, and so parents cuddled and pet and laid soft palms on little round faces with eyes full of kindness, and children ran back and forth with spoons and pots and brands of fire, eager to help in any way they could.

"Huge safety violation," noted my Alpha Prime medic when he returned with brown paint streaked in elaborate Sevellan patterns across his left cheek and right forearm. "You'd get in trouble for child neglect in my neighborhood—letting a toddler carry a lit log like that."

"Oh, come on—" I began.

"I like this better," he said, taking my drink from me with a smile. "I always felt so watched there." With that he took the *biggest* gulp from my bottle and kept going.

"Whoa, hey now!" I tried to grab it back from him. He laughed and held on to it. I gave a tiny tap to the knuckles of his other hand—the cut hand—and he let go with a chuckling "ow."

"Cheater," he said.

"Are you even old enough to drink?" I cradled the bottle like a stolen child. He laughed again. It was good to see him cut loose a little. I was almost sad when Sibila came over—her existence would bring him down, I thought.

But he seemed to forget her troubles when she smiled at his face paint. "My friend!" she cried. "I see you've meet Leena."

"I have!" he laughed, looking with Sibila now in the direction of an unmodified woman about my age wearing normal Sevellan garb, laughing and cracking jokes in the distance with a group of men as she painted them. *Maybe you get lucky enough to age out of the pleasure trade,* I thought. *If you survive.* "She's very friendly!"

"Her mammaries are getting heavy," Sibila remarked.

I almost spat out my drink. "E—excuse me?" I laughed. "Her mammaries are *what*?"

"It's a cultural expression," Ken explained. "A joke or idiom for 'she's wanting a child'. To, you know." He made a motion with his hand that to him must have looked like some kind of sign language for emptying a bag, but to me looked like a very bad time. "Drain them."

"To *drain* them?" I coughed and wrapped my arms around my chest as my drink tried to murder me. "Medic, I'm going to need surgical removal of my fucking ocular nerves STAT after what you just did there. What the hell was that move?" I replicated it to tease him. "Is she a Bovie now?"

"Man, I don't know, ma'am!" Ken protested, reddening a little. "I'm tired, okay, I defaulted to my uncle's farm for a second."

Sibila shifted, probably uncomfortable with our boisterous Terran noises. "We're not backwards, you know," she muttered. "We know that's not how mammals—we know there's no production until after pregnancy. It's just an expression."

"Oh honey, I'm not laughing at you." I dropped a palm onto her thin shoulder. "I'm laughing at Mr. Farmer over here. You're fine." I leaned in. "You'll have to forgive my ignorance, too—I'm a bit of an asshole. And this is damn good makgal."

"Makka."

"That." I paused. I was close enough to her ear now that the green bruises around her neck seemed to taunt me, and as I lifted my hand off her shoulder, I realized she was wincing. I glanced down and let my fingers brush her collarbone as I backed off. *I think there was an old break here. Is it even with the other one?* "Not an asshole like the ones you've been dealing with, though."

"I have had pleasant encounters, too," she said quickly. "And it's not forever. I can be bought back as long as there is a battle guard who will partner with me permanently."

"You can't buy yourself back?" I asked.

"No—if I have no permanent partner, I merely return to the pool of potential trades. After all, if I'm not using my body's best years for my family there is no excuse to keep them from the common good."

So you're screwed and screwing either way I managed to translate to something more sensitive: "So if you're not traded or married while you're young..."

"Then I must transition to battle guard. I must be useful."

"Shit. Literally use it or lose it, then," I whistled and let the soothing bottle kiss me again. "Did Leena age out, or find a partner?" I asked.

"Oh, you never age out. She simply was not selected this time. You are less likely to be selected after—you know." She blushed purple, looking at me. "Time—passes. It is not that older women are less attractive universally, just battle guards—prefer—"

Ken snickered, but wisely kept his mouth shut. I raised my trademark eyebrow now in amusement. "Girl, I'm not that old. I'm barely past forty-five. And I'm certainly not vain enough to get offended that I wouldn't make the cut for slavery."

"Oh, you might, though," she said. My eyebrow stretched so hard it almost hurt my forehead. "With some wrinkle treatments and smile practice, you are similar enough to us—not like the Grausians—that you seem like an exotic fairy-tale. A plainskin seems—honest, and calming. And the battle guards who've seen you fight would have questions about your physical ability in other areas."

"Well, I'd like you to stop talking now," I said, sloshing makka into my mouth and joke-miming chugging: "And I'm going to get as drunk as I can as fast as I can so I don't remember what you just said."

Ken laughed out loud finally and rescued both of us with a bow, extending his hand to Sibila. "Let's leave Captain Wimmer alone to forget," he smiled. "Can I show you what I just learned?" His motion as he reached for her was so gracious, and his soft grin so suave, I had to hide my face so no one would see me looking proud of him. *What am I, his mom?*

"I can't dance with any Sevellans tonight," Sibila said, stepping back.

"Good thing I'm not Sevellan," he retorted.

"Better wipe that off your face, then," she smirked. "You're wearing our coming-of-age pattern for battle guard."

"Oh shoot," he raised a hand to wipe it off. She caught his wrist— "Oh right, I wouldn't want to offend them either." He looked a little panicked, and now it was my turn to chuckle. "Man, I was worried about treaties in the food and didn't even think about the paint!"

"Treaties in the food?" Sibila laughed. "Kenta, you're fine. You haven't signed up for anything. You're just—very clearly ours right now." She leaned forward, and lifted his hand to her lips for just the briefest instant. "We'll dance later, when I'm free to go home."

"When will that be?" he asked.

"When Wimmer lets me borrow her shortsword!"

Ken turned to me with a questioning grin and arms open.

"Tough, buddy," I said. The comfortable weight tugged at my hip as it always did, and that wasn't about to change. "She's gone."

"What?" He whirled, but Sibila had already flitted away, her robe swirling around her like a cape in a storm as she spun into the arms of the nearest watching Bantai warrior. The way Ken watched her leave I would normally have teased him, but under the circumstances that just seemed cruel.

She came back to us one more time before the fire died down —when Sereno came over. He and his family had walked over to our mat with a stone pot in hand under the pretense of sharing a soft stewed cactus. I say pretense because it seemed like nothing he ever did lacked an agenda, and this time his practiced smile seemed strained.

"Everything alright?" I asked him. I could see Sibila hovering—she'd danced her partner nearer, and kept tucking his hungry head into her neck so she could keep worried eyes on her brother without her partner noticing.

"I see you've been learning the art of the food trade," Sereno smiled, kneeling on our mat besides the three little girls who crowded around him. "Girls, oh, do you see the doctor's short-sword? Hers is different than mine, isn't it?"

They nodded with wide-eyed shyness; thankfully no one asked to touch it.

"Oh and look," he went on. "They have all kinds of different trades here. What haven't you tried yet?"

The girls leaned over our pot. There was a lot they apparently hadn't tried yet: turned out part of the trick of this whole thing was you could spend one on one time with people if you wanted to—it was rude to go to a mat while someone else was trading—but you could also avoid talking to people you didn't want to while still trying what they'd made. Sereno's partner seemed shy, and hung back behind him, almost literally ducking between his shoulder blades when I tried to make eye contact, so in all likelihood she'd avoided meeting too many people tonight herself.

"See which things they've eaten," he pointed with his chopsticks at the food that looked more disturbed, and then—as relaxed if he wasn't telling children about *death*: "That's a sign that's *probably* not poisoned, at a big event like this, and it's probably pretty tasty. But you kind of have to look at the two people to really see. Do they look poisoned to you?"

Ken gave Sereno a mischievous look, then put his wrist to his forehead and pretended to stumble and fall backwards—which made the girls squeal in delight. "He's not poisoned! He's pretending!"

"I'm dying..." he said on his back beside me. "Must... have..." He snatched the bottle out from under my arm and rolled away. "Your drink!"

"Hey!" I reached after him too late as the little girls clapped and giggled. He jumped to his feet and took a swig.

"Wow, he's fast, Father."

"Look how pretty his eyes are. I've never seen anyone with brown eyes."

"A lot of Terrans have brown eyes," Sereno said, standing himself now.

"His ears are weird though. Hers, too."

"That's true," he said. "They don't hear very well, either." He looked at Ken as he said this for some reason; Ken seemed to pick up on something, and replied:

"Or sometimes they hear, but don't really understand because people aren't very clear about what they want," Ken said. "I'm assuming you want us to do a check-up for your Grandfather, though—right? Is that what you're talking about?"

"More or less," Sereno said.

"Oh, really?" Ken lit up. "Shit, I was really firing in the dark there, I wasn't at all sure you knew I was listening the other—yeah. Anyway. It's getting late, right?"

"There's still time," Sereno said.

I was starting to put a few pieces together myself—and starting to wonder how much of what the young leader had said the night before was actually intended for Ken for some reason. That wasn't a good thing. It meant he thought he could manipulate the kid. "Sereno," I asked. "Lachish was talking to me in the hovercraft on the way over here. Is it true Sevellan law requires a leader to submit himself and his family to the same conditions his people suffer?"

Sereno raised an eyebrow, much like mine. "As a whole, yes.

If they go to battle, he goes to battle. When the Grausians required ore, the Grandfathers went to the mines. Leadership is forfeited otherwise."

I stood so I could lower my voice without the children hearing. "So his daughters couldn't escape flesh trade, for example," I pointed out.

"No, doctor, they couldn't," he said. He spread his cheeks over black teeth in a wide, horrific smile with dead eyes, and for the first time since meeting him I heard hatred in his voice. It was calm, and laced with the venomous promise of violence if what I was about to say next was a threat.

"So you know Lachish told me, then," I murmured. He wouldn't react this way if he didn't know I knew he was the hidden heir. I stepped a little closer to him. "Young man, if you want something from us, ask. Don't play games with my medic and don't puppet your people around us until no one knows what's going on. People shooting blind tend to cause friendly fire. I know you want to make a bid for change sooner rather than later. I know you want to protect those you love. Help me help you."

He stared at me for a second as if truly confused. In the firelight the indigo eyes were almost black except for little jagged lines of a deep red I hadn't noticed in the daylight, and those little jagged lines pulsed around the reflection of a thousand stars as he thought. His cheeks softened for a moment, and for just a split second I saw pain, *honesty*, and he opened his mouth to answer—

The look faded. He shook his head. "I'm sorry, doctor. I'm already on this path." He stepped away from me, still looking directly at me as he answered loud enough for both Ken and Sibila to hear: "I don't know what you mean, Captain." I raised my own critical eyebrow now.

"What? Mean about what, Father?" asked one of the girls—a quieter one who hadn't spoken yet, who was probably about tall enough to be creeping up on puberty now. If Sevellans started young—because Sereno himself was pretty young to have a kid this age—that meant she might just be a few years off from becoming pleasure guard.

He put a hand on her shoulder. "Can you send your sisters away with your mother for a second? Captain Wimmer here's asking something I'd like you to answer."

Why did that feel sinister? The woman gave a firm nod and took the little ones away, and they went playing and dancing. The quiet older girl blinked up at me with vibrant blue eyes—not blue like Howard's were blue, but blue like a boron-laced diamond is blue: deep, dark, rich navy-violet with a million facets behind the pupils.

Sibila looked frightened. She managed to untangle herself from her current target and dart over to us, wrapping her robe tight around herself and hugging her breasts with her arms.

"You know, actually Sereno, I think never mind," I said, eyes on Sibila. "I think I'd like to go wait for the Grandfather in our patient room."

She nodded, fast and hard. "I think that's a good idea. Let me set you up—"

"Well just a minute," Sereno held up his hand—performing. "Just because you've found out I'm the hidden heir doesn't mean you have to be nervous around me, Captain."

Sibila froze. Her eyes darted around us to see who else might have heard. "Why would you tell them that?" she asked under her breath through clenched teeth.

Ken's eyes widened. He stepped closer.

"Would you like to tell the nice medic here what that means, Serena?" Sereno asked his oldest.

"It means you're the next Grandfather, Dad," she said. "So you eat the same royal jelly that Grandfather eats that lets him not get old—so you'll be around long after we grow up and die, and when something happens to Grandfather you'll be around to help our people."

"Grandfather and I eat the jelly together, don't we?" Sereno nodded.

"So you don't poison each other, of course," she said. "And you're *only* allowed together when you're eating the royal jelly. With witnesses, like Uncle Lachish." She turned to us. "The jelly recipe was the secret that the Grausians came to our planet for. They wanted it for their genetic engineering, but we made them believe it was a myth in the end. If someone tells anyone where it is, or what it looks like, we have to kill that someone. People can know it exists. We don't have to kill *them*." She blinked up at her father again. "Anything else, Dad?"

"No. We should go join the Lady of our Lives," he said, eyes still on the girl's as he jerked his head towards the rest of their family. "I'm sure you've given our new friends a lot to think about."

And with one last look in our direction, he guided the little girl away, leaving Sibila panicking and Ken with a pensive expression that I couldn't figure out how to read.

And for some reason, suddenly I couldn't stop thinking about the night before my last battle in the service. I saw the officers lounging around the lit table, its silvery top shimmering with notes and battle-model holograms as the spacecraft engines hummed around us, and I couldn't stop remembering their eyes as I held back what really wanted to be a scream. *"My guys aren't fit for duty! It's literally going to be a massacre!"* I was struggling not to shake. But their eyes were so—dead. Not in a dramatic, frightening way, like an animal or a ghost. In a boring way. Like what had once been a soul was now just a readout from hours of board room meetings where men turn into models and lives into lucre. They said something noble about sacrifices while the guy next to me spent half the meeting sketching out his OER, the resume-boosting paperwork he'd write once this attack made his whole career. When I tried to point it out, they pointed out I had patient notes open. *"We're all getting work done,"* they said. *"Stay in your lane. If you wanted to be a commander you should've put in for it, 'doctor'."* But that wasn't the point. They didn't get the point. I couldn't come up with the thing to say, the game to play, the right person to twist or pull, to stop them from trading my guys for bullet-points, and they could lecture me about sacrifice all they wanted, but there was another way.

I just didn't know until the next day what it was.

"Well, that was interesting," Ken said as he took his seat on a cushion beside Sevella back in the pleasure guard room we'd taken over. The sounds of festivities dimmed almost to nil as she closed the curtain behind us. *Pretty impressive sound-blocking technology. Wonder what that material is.*

"My brother trusts you far too much," Sibila grumbled. "He's a fount of good ideas but his recklessness is worse and worse these days."

"Probably because his little girl's getting too old," I said. "He's running out of time."

Sibila's eyebrows knit. "Running out of time for what?"

I wasn't about to accuse the next heir of plotting assassination—not directly to his sister whose loyalties I didn't quite understand. "If he's taking some hyper-effective antioxidant biologic that makes him outlive his kids," I said instead. "He knows he's going to watch all three of them go into the trades. If I were him, I'd be scrambling for a way out, too."

"I'm not sure what you're implying, but Sereno would never break our laws," she said. "We all need him, as a people, and I've watched him all his life—he may be a bit of a modern reformer but he would never—he would sacrifice everything for us."

"So he can't just leave." Ken's head tilted and he again wore that inscrutable expression from earlier. "To protect his daughters."

"And abandon everyone else? Without him there would be no voice for us in the councils," Sibila gave that Edenian head-shake. "And his family would die. The wastelands are too difficult to work for sustenance with just five people. No," Sibila straightened her back. "As I said before, this is our purpose from birth. It would jeopardize our relationship with the Bantai if I fought back, too. It's better a few of us be slaves than all of us… dead."

"You really believe those are your only options, then?" Ken asked.

"Yes," she said.

"Hmm." Ken furrowed his brow, his lips pursing. He seemed to be calculating something he didn't care to share. His arms crossed as he leaned back on a firm double-tiered cushion that was pressed against a ring around the thick tent-pole. "We all saw how Sereno handled the reporters," he said. "Whether he gets Interthought Media to fall for his hostage ploy, or Howard to get Galaxy Aid involved, he's at least trying whatever tricks he can to avoid playing the pleasure card for resources. Shouldn't it work the same way with military threats? Why can't the current Grandfather enlist other groups against the Bantai if he wants your freedom?"

"Enlist who?" Sibila scoffed, pouring a small shot of makka for herself now. "The largest other military force is the Yada."

Ken closed his mouth and looked away, deflating again. I was starting to see the Yada were almost a kind of boogeyman to him, built up by Interthought Media to an overwhelming unstoppable imperialist force—the Edenian trump card. And for some reason, seeing him shut up now sent my blood pumping and my chest puffing. Sure, when we were doing patient care, I wanted him to shut up, but right now? Kid had been fucking on point tonight, with the old ladies and the face paint and the laughing little girls, and his grim eagerness to play Sereno's game, or even in the patient room how he'd changed his tone for Sibila when I called it out—kid was *trying,* he was calculating, he was putting together the variables in that smart young brain to solve the mess that was this unsolvable world and who knew what he might come up with, so just fucking *let him do his fucking math.*

"Question. And again, forgive my ignorance here, Sibila." I raised my new bottle to her and took another sip. "The Yada want land, right?"

"They don't just want land, they have ours," Sibila said. "Until they're removed from the region there will be no peace."

"A little genocide-y, but I hear you," I said. It was nice not to be sober with all this. "Would, maybe, a little land be a reasonable exchange for your personal freedom? Diplomacy's give and take like that. Are you less important to the Grandfather than grazing space?"

"They shouldn't have to make that choice," Ken muttered. "Between national and personal autonomy."

"Yeah, and what choice are they making now?" I shrugged. "Look, Sibila, like I said, I'm an asshole. And I don't really give a shit either way. Just personally, if I've got to throw away tomorrow's sausages to a tiger to stop a bear from mauling me *now*, I'll toss the sausages. Even if they're all the fucking sausages I own."

"I do not understand the metaphor," Sibila said. "But I understand, as I said, we all make sacrifices for our country."

"For your *country*, or for your commanders?" Uh-oh. There was venom in my tone. I heard it, but couldn't stop it. *Huh. Guess I do care, for some reason. Shit, did Sereno get to me?* There was a table covered in papers flickering in the back of my head, and I heard engines hum, and smelled that smokey-spicy burnt-plastic-like after-waft of plasma guns going off…

I should've put down the makka, but found myself tilting it

back all the way down my throat instead. "And are they ever going to sacrifice for you?" I snapped. "Or do they sit back and collect the Silver Nova while you—" I sputtered to a stop as Ken grabbed my hand and rose.

"Excuse you," I said.

"Ma'am, don't you think it's getting late?" he asked. The dark brown in his eyes glittered black in the torchlight—concern. It was concern. The fuck was he worried about? Poor kid. I let him pull me to my feet mostly because the bruise over his left temple and the bandage on his palm made me feel like I shouldn't thrash him. He was a good kid, trying to save a world that didn't want to be saved.

"Don't let reality win, ever," I found myself saying as he walked me through the cool of the unlit tent corridor towards my bedroll. "You've gotta live in it with the rest of us, but don't let it beat you. Don't give a fuck what it's called. Yada, demons, gods, impossible choices—just—don't lose—this." I stumbled back and waved a hand over him, at him. "Don't lose this." I didn't have clearer words for him. I just didn't want to see him shut his mouth like that again. "Die a fool if you have to. It's way better than living like this." I waved a hand at myself. "As reality's sage and reality's bitch."

"A sage now, are we, ma'am?" Ken teased.

"And a bitch."

"I'll see you in the morning, ma'am."

I thought he'd gotten the message. I was too dizzy now, suddenly, for it to matter.

CHAPTER TWELVE

Ken Kamakura

KEN HAD GOTTEN THE MESSAGE.

From Sereno, from Wimmer, from the people themselves. He knew what Sereno wanted him to do, and he didn't see it as manipulation so much as communication from a gagged man with tied hands. If anything, Sereno was the only person who'd been halfway direct with a possible solution. Everyone else didn't dare even hint at what Sereno came centimeters from asking; Ken's mind itself didn't dare put the request into thought or plan. The young Terran simply put himself into a flow state and acted.

The pleasure guard quarters they'd used as a patient room had several corridors branching off of it. Originally the two medical partners had planned to sleep in the patient room—but now instead Ken placed Wimmer and her bedroll in the darkened corridor just beyond it, furthest from the battle guard tunnel. He'd seen the doc drunk before and knew she'd remain conked out through pretty much any sound. He made sure Wimmer's bedroll was close enough to the tent wall that when her Scrit curled up beside her its psionics would still translate for him, and he coaxed it to eat a quarter of a caffeine pill he'd tucked into some leftover death rat so it'd stay awake—he didn't know much about Scrit biology beyond what they'd taught him about keeping them alive in battlefield scenarios, and he wanted to keep it awake in case its psychic abilities didn't work unconscious. With that done he returned to Sibila, ready with an easy lie about Captain Wimmer leaving him in charge, and settled in to wait for the Grandfather. He would normally never take command of a medical situation completely on his own like this —even inebriated, the doc had over a decade of education and multiple decades of experience on him—but the doctor had conveniently forgotten to remind him to come get her when the leader showed, so he technically wasn't disobeying orders.

And the Grandfather wasn't a real patient.

Sibila shifted uneasily as Ken sat back down. She'd said nothing since he returned from escorting off his medical partner. He almost offered to leave—was she uncomfortable alone with him?

They'd been alone together a lot during her medical treatment, though—he was the one who'd twisted that painful tourniquet around her leg, pinning her down with his teeth gritting, his voice as soft as he could manage while she held back a scream. He'd had to hurt her, to save her life, so he didn't feel guilty. But —still. He hated her pain.

"You know," Sibila said finally. "If your goal was to remind me of my discontent you've both succeeded. I do not appreciate it."

"I'm sor—" Ken started to apologize, and then caught sight of that fateful femoral bandage again as she shifted positions in her sheer robe. "You know what, actually, I'm not sorry," he said, bringing his eyes up to hers. "I recognize that I can't possibly really know what it's really like to be you. But I do know you deserve better. And I stand by that."

"Why would I *deserve better* than everyone who came before me?" She pleaded now. Her eyes were tired.

"I don't know everyone who came before you," he said. "But I know you're smart enough to be anything you want to be, and you're right—your body is great. You shouldn't have to change it."

"Guard Sibila's physique is mid-range at best, and on what do you base your evaluation of her intelligence?" asked a raspy tenor behind him. "You've known her less than a week."

Ken startled, but Sibila *darted* away from the voice and prostrated herself on the floor, trembling. Ken stood and turned—he hadn't even heard anyone come in behind them, but a sizable Sevellan battle guard smirked in the center of the room, arms crossed. Long, rich chestnut robes trailed on the ground behind the figure; cloud-gray cloth bands with embroidered triangle patterns cut out wrapped muscular limbs that now took on the soft tan hues of the room. Without the distraction of too much color the elaborate shapes draped across the form took center stage, highlighting delicate needlework against a powerful physique, and in the brown-toned room the speaker's dark aquamarine eyes almost seemed to glow and dance with flame above a chiseled jaw laced with scars.

"Well?"

Ken blinked. "Excuse me?" he stammered.

"Here we are accustomed to bowing to our betters," said the battle guard. "And to answer when questioned by the Grandfather."

For a split second upon hearing the name, and seeing Sibila's terror, rebellion flared up in Ken's stomach and for the first time since landing on this planet he wanted to violate a local custom—and he wanted to violate it completely, brazenly, violently. Bow? *Bow* to the traitor who sold his own people?

Stop. You don't know everything yet. Do this right.

Ken bowed—all the way to the floor, on hands and knees like Sibila, and responded: "Forgive me, Grandfather. I was taken aback by your glory and unable to answer for a moment. I was expecting someone more touched by age." He made a Sevellan triangle with his hands flat on the floor, and lifted his head just a few centimeters to be sure the Grandfather saw it, keeping his own eyes on the carpet. "To answer your question, I observed Guard Sibila display strategic intelligence when she plotted ways to shield your soldiers while under fire from the Bantai; practical intelligence when she drove a complex war machine while huddled under its seat; and emotional intelligence when interacting with and predicting the feelings of her caretakers and fellow patients during her convalescence on our journey from your Welcome Village to the city. She displayed valor under fire with no concern for her own safety and I can't imagine a soldier who wouldn't be glad to have her work alongside them." He kept his head on the floor but dared to flick his eyes to the side to meet hers with a soft smile. "She's pretty fun to be around, too," he dared to add.

Ken heard bare feet pad around him under the swish of robes. His every hair stood on end as he watched his periphery. He was acutely aware of the emptiness of the holster on his hip—they'd had to lock up their weapons in the squat, heavy safe in the corner and Sibila had the key.

"Rise," the Grandfather said. "I'd like to inspect the outsider so bold as to lie to my pleasure guard after knowing her so little time."

Ken pushed up and stood, snapping to attention. "I don't recall lying, Thal," he said.

"You do her a disservice offering glimpses of a reality that can never be hers." The Grandfather stepped back, looking Ken up and down with a distinctly unimpressed scowl. "Are you really the medic who saved twenty-nine of my guards?"

"Thirty-three, Thal," Ken corrected.

"You're counting the four pleasure guards." The Grandfather's scowl deepened. "But once in the trade, they're expendable."

"It's war," Ken said. "Everyone's expendable." He broke attention to make eye contact, but kept his head still. "Depending on the objective."

"Some people are more expendable than others," the Grandfather huffed. "You wouldn't expect a general to die for a commoner, and engineers and healers fetch higher blood prices than your average soldier. Some people are force multipliers, and must be protected. Others are the protectors." He waved towards Sibila. "Our pleasure guard is the shield that defends us all."

Ken said nothing. He was trying to figure out what he needed to do. He'd thought this part would come naturally, but with the flesh and blood *person* before him suddenly the feelings that drove him seemed a lot less simple. Sibila's fear had him on edge. *Is there something going on that I'm missing?*

The Grandfather took a seat by Ken's assault pack. "Well. Go ahead."

Ken blinked, confused for a second before remembering that this was supposed to be a medical visit. He'd been thrown off by the surprise entrance.

The medic knelt by the Edenian leader and drew his blood pressure cuff out of his pack. "Do you have any particular medical complaints, Grandfather?" he asked, eyeing the compartment that hid his scalpel. His fingers sized up the warrior's bicep while he pretended to adjust the cuff. The Grandfather was twice Ken's girth.

"No complaints. Truth be told I'm only here because Sereno insisted that if you are to be serving me long-term you will need a baseline of my health," the Grandfather said. He never seemed to stop scowling. "Although I'm not sure you will be serving me long-term."

"Why is that, Grandfather?" Ken asked, pumping up the blood pressure cuff. Patients weren't supposed to talk while you took their blood pressure, but he really didn't care what the actual number was right now. He didn't want this to be a normal medical visit. Why was it turning into one? Was he about to lose his chance to—

"Because I'm not sure I like you," the Grandfather said. "I think you question our ways without understanding them, and seeing our sigils painted on your face seems as sick a mockery as if a death rat wore them."

"The paint wasn't his idea, Grandfather," Sibila piped up, voice muffled by floor. "That is my fault, I should have—"

The Grandfather's hand shot out, snatched the stethoscope from Ken's grasp, and hurled it bell-first at the girl. The heavy high-quality metal clapped her in the side of the head—Sibila twitched, but didn't move from her curled bow—

Ken dashed to Sibila's side, rage boiling in his belly.

"No one asked you, whore," the Grandfather snapped.

"The hell happened to the 'pleasure guard's our shield'?" Ken snapped back. "You don't believe in maintaining your equipment?" Blood began to trickle past Sibila's ear. "You almost hit her in the temple, you can kill someone that way!" He pulled a glove from his pocket and slipped it on, spreading his fingers around the wound with his other hand on her back—"Fuck, what am I saying, *equipment*?" he muttered to her. "Sit up. Are you okay?"

She shook her head and refused to move.

"What are you doing, plainskin?" the Grandfather growled. "You are here to attend to me. She had her time today already."

"Yeah, no, you hit her in the head," Ken growled back, pushing Sibila's hair aside and opening a gauze packet with his other hand—the cut was deep and head wounds liked to bleed. "She takes triage priority. I'll do your check-up once I know she's okay."

"No—you will attend to me first!" the Grandfather roared. "I will not be attended after a *tradesgirl*."

Sibila snatched the gauze from Ken and pressed it to her own head. "Go," she whispered, pupils dilated with the glitter of fear.

"No." Ken glared, reaching—

"Go or Grandfather will leave and you lose the chance to fix this," she begged.

Ken pulled back his hand. Dammit, she was right. He didn't want the Grandfather to leave. This may be his one chance to—

And even if it wasn't, he might get Sibila punished more if he didn't back off—to say nothing of the international incident or whatever was brewing right here between the Sevellan leader and the disobedient Terran-who-was-technically-a-hostage. If their most progressive leader was willing to kidnap innocent people to get his way, what was this old monster willing to do? Ken and Wimmer were alone now. He had to fix this.

Ken picked up his stethoscope and returned to the leader's side.

"Give that to me," the Grandfather said.

Ken hesitated. The Grandfather yanked the stethoscope from him—he tried to hold on but the older warrior shoved him backwards and before he could get up the beast stalked over to Sibila and hit her across the back with a sick *thwack*—

"I am still traded, Grandfather!" Sibila reminded him with a cry of pain. "You will anger the Bantai if I cannot perform!"

Ken's fist was already in his bag for his scalpel. *What am I planning to do? Am I really—what am I doing?* He couldn't flow. He kept finding himself thinking he was going to make it worse. He saw those Third topaz eyes losing their light—

"I don't think you need to perform," the Grandfather hissed, pulling Sibila up by the hair. "I think this one means to buy you. Do you like her? Do you like what you see, Terran?" Ken was almost on them, blade hidden in his sleeve; the Grandfather yanked Sibila backwards, throwing open the pleasure guard's robe. "That's how they get you, son. You're only captivated by her because your biology clouds your mind. You compliment this body? This?" The Grandfather laughed now. "The pleasure guard form is so *weak*. Always falling behind, always bleeding or cramping, it stinks like rotten meat if not constantly scrubbed or perfumed and something's always oozing or wet. Most of the time the brain doesn't even function with all those hysterical hormones running around! Oh, I remember every disgusting detail. No one can blame her for being born this way, but then she *chose* to keep it. Can you imagine *choosing* mediocrity?"

Ken's rage was burning so hot now his eyes were beginning to tunnel. He tried to tell himself to calm down, to *think*, but Sibila's exposed chest was heaving as she bit her lip and her eyes misted and Ken was already flicking the scalpel open now behind his back. "Grandfather, please—" Sibila panted.

"Please?" The leader threw the woman to the floor with disgust. "She's manipulating you, plainskin. See the tears now? They're for you. They're to violate your senses until you feel sorry for her. Everything that seeps out of her is poison only fit to feed the enemy."

"Let's return to our medical visit," Ken heard himself panting, but it sounded so far away. He found himself over Sibila, between her and the leader.

The Grandfather shoved him out of the way and kicked the girl in the ribs. "You could have been brave. You could have been like me."

"I don't want to be like you!" Sibila blurted. "I want to be like my brother! *He* would stand up to the Bantai where you're too afraid."

"What?" the Grandfather almost shrieked. "How dare you—"

"Stop it!" Ken snatched the edge of the stethoscope—and was suddenly thrown across the room as the Grandfather whipped him off the medical tool with one sharp motion. His back whacked against the edge of a desk—*ow*—

Ken was busy falling and throbbing and stumbling back to his feet but before he could rise a huge bulk was on top of him beating him over the head and shoulders and face and chest faster than he could register. Pain flashed through his forehead, face, brain—*Killed by stethoscope. Kind of funny, when you think about it.*

"Grandfather, stop! Please, I'm sorry—I didn't mean it, I'm sorry, please stop—" Sibila was pleading.

"Get your brother to make me stop," the Grandfather snarled. "Get him and watch him cower obediently at my feet!"

"Please stop!"

Each impact was blinding, disoriented—hard and fast and Ken had his forearms up over his face and felt each crack of the heavy makeshift whip against them—

"What's this in your hand, Terran?"

The scalpel.

Well, there's absolutely no turning back now.

Ken slashed his hand forward, taking the bell to the cheek as he did. The Grandfather fell back, cursing Ken and his whole lineage and whoever else was within a century of him. Blood sprayed across the carpet. Sibila stifled a scream.

"Now you've done it," the Grandfather hissed, clutching his bleeding eye. Ken dragged himself to his knees, panting, gripping the edge of the desk—his hand slipped on bloody wood. "Your brother's behind this, isn't he?"

"What? No, Grandfather, he would never, he would never." Sibila whispered, too terrified to speak aloud.

"I will have him dragged before the council of leaders and flayed alive," the Grandfather coughed, hoarse with rage. "His daughters will watch as I flay him myself, and with his last lidless view of life he will see his reflection in their eyes, the image of naked muscle and bared teeth of that shrieking nightmare replacing every kind memory they ever had of him—"

Ken lunged forward, swinging the scalpel—

Something was wrong. He stumbled—the world was slanting. *Oh God I don't have time for a concussion right now! Please stay conscious. Stay conscious!*

"As for you," Grandfather's fist found the side of Ken's head; the ground was coming up at him—meaty hands found his neck—

"Perfect," Ken smiled.

"What?"

Ken wrapped his legs around his enemy's neck and shoulder in a triangle hold and thrust his lower body upward, clutching the Grandfather's wrist for dear life. *Damn this elbow's strong*—pain pressed through Ken's body as he crushed the Grandfather's elbow against him—man, he missed his Mark X, tucked away still in that damn safe—surely the force of his entire torso was stronger than the force of this person's *arm*—

But his throat was closing and he felt the Grandfather's fingers shifting—

"Let me just rip out your trachea, eh?"

Panic surged through the Terran but it wasn't enough, the arm wasn't *breaking*—

And suddenly the damn safe dropped on the Grandfather's head.

Sibila couldn't lift it high enough to get good leverage but a safe to the head is a safe to the head, and the Grandfather collapsed sideways with a grunt. He wasn't dead. He didn't let go of Ken's throat. But Ken finally felt the elbow snap. One of the grips weakened. Sibila struggled to try to lift the safe again. Ken still had the scalpel—he stabbed over and over as his throat continued to scream for air—he was face to face with the glowing gemstone eyes as they burned with hatred, so much hatred that Ken knew there wasn't anything in the world this soul loved anymore, not the people it had sacrificed for, not the self it had sacrificed for them, and as the jaw twisted sideways under the impact of the safe's fall and those eyes disappeared in a squelch of crunching skull, relief and horror and sadness punched Ken as hard as the beating had, and he was so suddenly dizzy he almost passed out.

Alright. Now it was time to wake the doctor.

CHAPTER THIRTEEN

Jocelyn Wimmer

I WOKE up to the scent of blood and a hissing shush as Ken Kamakura shook my shoulder while Sibila panicked in silence behind him. In the dark tent corridor, I couldn't see for shit—just shadows and shapes—but I sure as hell recognized her hunching with her fists clenched by her mouth like a teenager in *all the trouble.*

"We've done something horrible," she whispered, almost weeping. "You must come quickly."

"We didn't do something horrible," he snapped. Snapped? *Hot damn he must be agitated.* "Doctor, I think we need to get out of here."

My brain throbbed as I crawled to my feet. *Shit-titty-hell, how the fuck much did I drink?* I tried to run my foggy brain through all the possible things Ken could have fucked up. In training I'd once inserted an IV without clamping my thumb down on the catheter fast enough, and it'd bled a lot. *Yeah, but his manual skills are good, and he wouldn't deny that.* Had he taken a tourniquet off someone too early? But I didn't think we'd even brought along any of the tourniquet people. Had he tried to do some procedure way about his pay grade and they were bleeding out? He'd be moving way faster if that were the case—he was even taking the time to roll up my bedroll and carry it with him. So it couldn't be that bad. *I mean, come on, here,* I smirked to myself, *it's not like he killed someone, right?*

Right?

Oh no. My stomach suddenly dropped and I was wide awake because before we even entered the room, I knew that was it. That was why he wasn't in that kind of hurry. There was no life to save.

And he wasn't apologizing because he'd done it on purpose.

"Oh, *fuck me,*" I groaned, gripping the curtain shut and pinching my eyebrows with my other hand. "Please don't tell me you did what I think you did."

"Look, if they didn't want me to assassinate their leader, they wouldn't have left him unguarded." Ken tried to give it the timbre of a joke, but I think both Sibila and I wanted to hang him for it.

"They left him unguarded because they *trust* you," I hissed. "Because you're the *medical professional who saves their lives!*"

"No, Sereno left him unguarded because—"

"Don't you dare implicate my brother in this," Sibila's hiss was almost as good as mine. "I only helped you to protect him."

"Good to know you're not worth fighting for but he is," Ken shot back.

She slapped him. *Whoa.* "Is that enough fighting for you?"

"Yeah, maybe I like that, who knows," Ken threw up his arms.

"Children, I am going to go back in time and abort the both of you if you don't shut up," I said. "And young lady, if you hit my medic again, I will deck you. It's not okay just because he's bigger than you. Okay, now—" I sighed, trying to psych myself up for whatever I was about to see when I opened the curtain. On the bright side, everyone was probably inebriated from the party. If I had to be awakened in the middle of the night with news that the kid had killed someone, this was probably the best night for it. Heck, it *was* kind of like it'd been orchestrated. And as long as it wasn't a huge mess, maybe there'd be some way to make it look like natural causes. After all, we'd been called in because the guy was sick, right?

There was no way to make it look like natural causes.

"The leader?" I squeaked as we stepped into the room. "The actual—Sylvie, no!"

My Scrit was walking through a thick wet squishy splotch of blood on the carpet, trailing little pawprints across all the pillows as she ran off with what was probably the guy's finger. A broken scalpel was embedded in the patient's breastbone. His head was under a safe that was open—the safe that'd held our weapons and only our weapons. The entire room looked like a hate crime against furniture, like it hadn't been enough to kill the guy—his upholstery had to pay, too—and curled around his wrist like a snake was a bloody stethoscope whose bell matched the indentations that'd been beaten into the desk.

"Did you forget to fucking *sign our names* when you were done?" I squealed.

"You told me to not let reality win, so I didn't."

"I didn't tell you to straight up *murder* the Sevellan regent!" My fists clutched my hair as I sputtered with hungover panic. "The hell you doing, taking advice from a drunk person?"

"I'm teasing you ma'am. It's not your fault. It's math. One death to stop a backdraft, just like on the ship when we crashed." Ken zipped up his assault pack and handed me mine. "With this Grandfather out of the picture Sereno's next in line."

"Yeah, so who's going to get suspicion for the murder, then?"

"Not him. I'm kidnapping his sister."

"Excuse me?" Sibila and I both wheezed.

"Look, Sibila, we can just leave without you, but I don't

think anyone's going to believe I took on that giant alone," Ken said. "Everyone saw you come in here with me. You're going to be the first person who's questioned. The only reason everyone isn't in here *now* is that the music's too loud and this tent material's magic-thick. Reasons, I mean. The two reasons." Ken took a deep breath and waved us to follow him towards the back entrance, away from the party outside. "I'm sure there's a way to make this look like the Bantai broke the trade, but I sure don't know what it is, and even if I knew how to get that blade out of the bone—trust me, doctor, I tried—" he turned to me "—I don't know how to make it look like I wasn't involved. And since everyone knows Sereno sent Wimmer and me to care for the Grandfather, that puts a target on him unless I do something he hates." He shook his injured hand, wincing a bit, and drew his Mark X, pointing it at her half-heartedly. My eyebrows tried to kiss my hairline. "You're welcome to hate me for this, but this doubles the motivation for him to hunt us down. Enraged brother betrayed by outsiders he trusted—it looks good. We'll leave you somewhere he can find you and then make our way to Sector Ben-haba on our own." His confident speech wavered as his voice softened: "Unless anyone else has a better plan?"

My better plan was to kill them both and go back to bed so my throbbing head could recuperate, so I said nothing. I had plenty of combat tours under my belt but almost no experience making anyone die on purpose before this year—the Terran military was too well-organized to have doctors out there shooting people when they could be saving lives—it wasn't like I knew any more about covering up murders than the kid did.

"Look who thinks he's thought of everything," I grumbled.

"Look who thinks we'd better hurry up before we're all caught standing over a dead body," he retorted weakly. "Sibila?"

Sibila tilted her head, studying Ken's face. Her eyes didn't flick once towards the gun—she knew he'd never shoot her. It was literally there for her plausible deniability—shit, from where

I was standing, I was pretty sure he'd flicked it to stun so he could knock her out if she didn't want to come along. *Decent back-up plan—make her a victim, too.* He wanted her to come so he could take her away from the Bantai for a while without drawing their wrath on the Sevellans.

"Okay," she said. "I'll drive."

Jocelyn Wimmer

We fled. The stolen buggy rattled in the wind like it might fall apart and my head was now blazing like *I'd* taken the safe to the skull. I was popping every pill I could find without overdosing and I didn't care at this point who saw—if Ken called me out for drugs, I was *going* to call him out for murder. Or just say it was for some imaginary condition and move on.

"Okay," I grunted, scooting to the back of the open trunk and positioning myself close enough to Ken to talk under my breath. I called Sibila's name a few times into the wind and then, satisfied that even her elf-ears couldn't pick me up, I leveled with the kid. "Okay, we need to be on the same page about what happened here. I mostly just need to know what you were thinking or I'm going to think you just saw a pretty pair of purple eyes and forgot to think at all."

"If it was like that, I could've just bought her," Ken muttered, looking away from me. "No, I didn't destabilize a government for a girl. If we could bring all of them I would."

I would've smiled if I wasn't busy grimacing. Sweet kid. "But I wasn't talking about those purple eyes," I said.

"His aren't purple. They're indigo."

"They're purple."

"They're more of a reddish blue."

"That's purple."

"Do you just want to be right, or do you want to ask me what you want to ask me about Sereno?" Ken smirked.

"I don't know, I'm not the one who cares so much about purple he's got four different words for it." I would've stuck out my tongue if I wasn't afraid of biting it in the jostling vehicle—that's how woozy and immature I felt. "You're the one who's stuck on being right."

"Why do people keep saying that?" Ken protested. "I am so chill. I am the most chill person on this planet."

"Somehow I don't think the most chill person on this planet just killed a guy," I said. "What happened in there?"

He looked away from me, hugging himself. He was shivering a little now; I unzipped my assault pack for a silver emergency blanket and wrapped it around him with a hard pat on the back. The post-adrenaline shakes were starting.

"I don't know." His teeth chattering seemed to surprise him—he made a face, and clenched his jaw for a bit, gazing out into the starlight.

"I'm pretty sure this isn't how he imagined it going," he said finally. "I think we were supposed to have the Grandfather accidentally die from a disease we *discovered.* Maybe slip something toxic into a medication—it was definitely supposed to be something medical and undetected, something only a doctor could do. Or maybe he had something in mind involving the jelly, so it looked like he was a target too. I don't know. I know I fucked up."

"Watch your language," I punched him in the shoulder. He laughed, but his eyes were glistening and his voice sounded like he might cry. "And you didn't fuck up," I said. "You're not a psychic. If the guy wants his bosses killed a specific way he can do it himself next time." I leaned back and closed my eyes. "It all literally sounds insane. I wouldn't believe you at all if I didn't *know* Sereno. But there's literally no other explanation for the total lack of guards. You were set up."

"If it helps you trust me more," Ken offered, shaking in earnest now. "I didn't make the first move. The Grandfather started—" He clenched his jaw, and suddenly his eyes were wet. "Fuck. What's wrong with me?" He wiped his face on his sleeve and didn't wait for me to answer. "The Grandfather started beating Sibila because she mouthed off."

"And you couldn't take it."

"I did take it. I think." He shook his head. "I don't know. I'm actually having some trouble remembering details for some reason."

Ooh, that was familiar. I sighed. *Yeah*... he was in for a ride.

I guess Kamakura didn't like the tone of my sigh, because he snapped at me: "Hey, quit judging me. It wouldn't have happened this way if you were on board instead of piss-drunk."

"Excuse me?" I could tell kid was having a post-adrenaline rage moment he couldn't quite control, but he sure as hell wasn't about to take it out on me. "You wanna explain why you're yelling at the only living creature in this vehicle who *doesn't* have blood on their hands? Yes, literally including you, little bitch," I prodded Sylvie gently with my boot. She purred at me and licked her teeth. I smiled and turned back to the kid. "If the region ends up being destabilized because a worse guy takes this guy's place, my drunk ass is innocent. I have no doubt this guy deserved to die, but you better be real careful about getting high and mighty with me before we've had a chance to see the full consequences of what you did here."

"Destabilized?" he was almost shouting now. "Look, I'm not going to let an evil dictator off the hook because some theoretical worse dictator's out there. I'm not responsible for some other chain event I didn't directly have a hand in, and I'm not in the business of propping up regimes!"

"Propping up regimes? My guy, you're talking like you're a neutral arbiter, but you're not. You're a vigilante," I said. I was trying to be gentle with the kid, but I was definitely erring on the side of *yo, I have a hangover, yell at me at your peril, killer*. "You have zero lawful authority on your side."

"It's not like I could take him before some lawful authority! He is the lawful authority!" He wasn't crying. But there were tears in the wind, and his voice was shrill. "And it wasn't like the people were holding their leaders to the *social contract* or whatever a nation's supposed to do to keep its government accountable. You can call me imperialist for coming in as an outsider to fix something without their consent, but the suffering is *wrong*. What they're going through is *wrong!* So when the system's that corrupt, and no one's policing the authorities, who's got the authority to act then? God?"

I lowered my voice to a hum. I needed to calm him down. "I guess so, yeah. But I've never been one for waiting around for God to act. Always figured if he wanted that he wouldn't've made me with arms and legs and a brain myself."

"Okay, so what would *you* have done?" Ken cried out.

"The same as you. I would have used the Grandfather's own weapon and not a scalpel to prevent forensics from connecting me to it so obviously. But otherwise, I would have done pretty much the same thing." I tugged at my laces, looking at the floor, and the furry masked face nuzzling at my boots. "That doesn't make it right. Or wrong. That's the shitty thing about having to make choices in a fallen universe. Sometimes it ends badly no matter what you do." I looked up at the shadowy hills and rock structures on the horizon, and back towards the dim flicker of light that marked the camp where we'd left. Still no obvious pursuers. "My Rabbi once said outcomes aren't guaranteed, just obedience. I kinda figured that's what algorithms are for. Like eating kosher, or the needle decompression steps—shit like that tells you what to do in specific scenarios. But then you've got scenarios that don't fall into the algorithms, and then you're stuck with just the general principles, like *love your neighbor*, or *kidney physiology*, and you've got to come up with the specifics on your own. And that's where you realize that we're all fucked on our own—that we need God to walk with us, in us, guiding, moving, like breath. Emmanuel, that's called. But that takes—" I stopped talking. Who was I to be talking about God? I scoffed at myself and scooted further down onto the floor of the buggy so I could lean my head back on my assault pack. "Your whole body hurts now, doesn't it."

"Yeah," he shivered. "But I was only hit in the head. Well, and the back, I guess, but I don't have any signs of vertebral fracture that I can tell. I guess the chest, too? I don't know. But definitely not all over—and the fight can't have been more than ten minutes long—"

"If that. That'd be long for a fight," I said.

"Right. So it shouldn't feel like my every muscle's full of acid? It's like I've had a six-hour ruck march and then did a day of push-ups." He ran his eyes across his sleeve again. "I'm so *weak* suddenly. Emotional. It's so stupid. I should be good. We won."

"Well, I'm pretty sure *should* is a thought distortion in this case," I said. He was into that cognitive behavioral resilience training shit. "But you *are* having an adrenaline crash. It's normal. Here." I shifted towards him. "Turn around so I can check your spine. You can't really rule out a vertebral fracture yourself, you contortionist wannabe."

He shifted his back towards me, and I laid my hands on his paraspinals. The muscles were tight under my palms—tensed, and screaming.

"Take a deep breath," I said. "Into your diaphragm—expand your belly, not your chest."

"Why?"

"Triggering the parasympathetic system instead of the sympathetic one. Just do it."

His back expanded under my palms as he breathed—he was doing it wrong. I'd correct him in a moment. I moved my hands midline and pressed my fingertips along the bony ridges of his vertebrae, watching him for any wincing or flinching as I moved from his neck all the way down to the top of his pants. "Any impact south of here?" I asked.

"No."

"Aight."

I lifted my palms and laid them behind his shoulders. Gah, his back was utterly *shrieking* with tension, like he might need to jump up and fight *right now this minute*. "Unhunch," I said. "Try to lean back and relax."

"Why?"

"Because you're still spilling neurotransmitters like crazy, and with all the cortisol and epinephrine and everything else running around your blood stream it's burning your muscles and nerve endings and hippocampus," I said. "Try to breathe again. This time put a hand on your belly and try to make it expand, and another hand on your chest and try to keep it still. Deep breaths."

He obeyed with a quizzical look backwards. I could see he'd cleaned up a few cuts on his head, and even in the moonlight I could see bruises forming and puffing— "Can you try again to tell me what happened?" I asked. "Having these chemicals run amok can do all kinds of stuff to your brain and body long-term. If you can kind of talk through it now and make it normal it shouldn't stick with you so bad."

"That sounds the opposite of what makes sense," he said.

"I know. But, I mean, you were taught the big study where soldiers who were taken out of combat after a traumatic experience suffered more PTSD than the ones who stayed in—we all learned that, right?" I said. "Exposure therapy is a thing. Early exposure normalization is a thing."

"So is retraumatization," he smirked. "But I'm fine. And I didn't lose consciousness, by the way. And I can count backwards by sevens, and recall sets of three things, and I'm oriented times four, and my neurological exam seems normalish except when I was having trouble walking at first—"

"Young man, I'm going to feel your skull now for signs of fracture," I interrupted. "And while I didn't get beat about the brain by a stethoscope, I have a headache myself, so unless you're going to help yourself by helping me with your story, I'd rather you just shut up."

"How'd you know that?" he asked. "That I got hit with a stethoscope, I mean."

"Right size and shape," I said. "Now shut up."

He did. He leaned back, and I gloved up and palpated his scalp. I wasn't just checking for fractures, though. I was looking for tension, and then gently moving the fascia under his scalp where I found it to lessen the headache a little, and reaching under the base of his skull to soften the trigger point near where his sympathetic nervous system activated for fight and flight and freeze responses. It was something I'd learned from an old civilian who was basically like a shaman, and I didn't feel like explaining it to the kid right now. I couldn't reach in and massage his brain, but I could kind of press the right buttons to reduce the pain around it and make him relax. I was a little worried about epidural hemorrhage, though. Our portable imaging wasn't always reliable—while modern technology had produced both CT and MRI scanners that could fit in a large briefcase, they definitely wouldn't work while bouncing around in the back of a fleeing vehicle. I'd have to check him once we stopped to rest.

"Is that why you use?" Ken asked presently. "Post-traumatic—tissue breakdown—from chronic—cortisol—spillage? Are you in constant pain?"

I stiffened, but kept my fingers working and didn't otherwise show my surprise. *No point in lying now.* "No. This would be the worst shit for that. You'd want to give your patient an SNRI—a gaba precursor, maybe, for pain, maybe THC… anyway that wouldn't be using, that'd be treatment." I set my jaw. "I pop because I'm weak."

"What do you take?" he asked.

"Mostly amphetamines. To keep my senses sharp. I'm afraid of fatigue." I took my hands off his head and gave him a pat on the back to tell him he could turn around now, and shifted away from him. "Sometimes I take benzos to calm myself back down again. It's all shitty and you shouldn't do like me. Keep your weapon clean."

"Speaking of," he handed me the service rifle he'd stolen from the Sevellan camp, and a cleaning kit, as he opened up his Mark X.

"We probably shouldn't break them all the way down, not with pursuit on the menu," I warned him. "Just some basic maintenance in case we don't get a chance later."

"Roger," he said.

A moving vehicle is a crappy place to clean anything, but the way across the desert had smoothed out some. There was something therapeutic about weapon maintenance, if you didn't have somewhere else to be, like bed. I'd always hated getting back late from the range and having to clean *anything*.

"Is that why you're afraid of fatigue?" he asked. "You think your medic could've saved the other guy when his gun jammed if he was sharper?"

I laughed. "Oh man, if only. No." I looked at the work in my hand, and then at him—he wasn't looking at me. He was working. There was no pressure. No eyes. I'd just told this kid some shit about exposure and talking—so was I about to talk, or was I a whole-ass hypocrite? Right now probably wasn't the time, though—you weren't supposed to do that shit suicidal.

But I wasn't suicidal anymore, I realized suddenly. I wanted to live and see what happened to this kid. I wanted to see him turn out better than me.

I sighed, and looked up at the sky. "It was my last assignment. Just before the end of the war," I said. My chest began to burn, right in the center under my sternum. I breathed into my belly. "My commander at the time had a bunch of mental health stuff he hid. I did my best to patch him up in every way I could, but I could only do so much as a generalist. He started to really go downhill that last month. He just refused to sleep. Too busy, too much work to do, he said. I'm pretty sure he was having nightmares he didn't want to deal with, but I can't prove that. Anyway."

I looked back down at the gun barrel and began to scrub. "You get to know everyone's dirty secrets as the unit physician. Who's assaulted who. Who's faking, who's not. Who's tough as nails walking off violent rape, and who looks tough but is actually hyperventilating in the middle of the night because they're just a tad too fat and sleep apnea scares the shit out of them." I smirked. "I took care of all of them. All the officers and NCOs who later fucked over my lower enlisted and me. I was there for them in all their stupidest moments. When they popped positive on their STD tests or started growing breasts because they were taking steroids. And I was there for them when they were exhausted or crying or when the administrative corps needed someone like me to yell and scream at the right people to get my patients the medical supplies they needed. I was the bitch you could weaponize when you needed help."

There was a warmth in my belly—something like love—at the memory. I loved all of them. I hadn't always been the bitch. It twisted and tore my gut more *because* I loved my unit. *Because* I loved my unit, I had complained.

"The Charee were on the back foot," I went on. "And there was a pretty heavily-defended outpost that was basically the gateway to a huge swatch of territory that would've expanded the Union by—oh, I don't even know. Some people were saying two or three planets, others were saying just one mining belt. But some of the logistics officers got it in their heads that if we could take this outpost, we could really crush those bastards." I sighed, and repositioned the rifle to get a different angle. "Someone came up with this big assault plan—it was so risky it was like something from fiction. They had so many smart reasons for it to work. And maybe it could have," I admitted. "But most of my soldiers were still recovering from our last offensive. We'd taken a lot of casualties already."

Now the chest pain spread from my sternum across my ribs, my breasts, into my stomach and back. I saw the sick bay of the ship, the rows of soldiers chatting or sucking through their MRE tubes or leaning on the edge of the bed panting, and my medics walking up and down the rows. My amazing medics. I saw sweet Terran Millie with her bright, innocent smile slipping my stethoscope over her head as I explained the difference between rhonchi and rhales; I saw good old Silvanus with his grim Grausian nictating membrane blinking at a shuddering male soldier who'd just reported a sexual assault, and his gray fist clenching as he told the soldier the *other* guy was the coward, the *other* guy wasn't a real man; I saw Chlai, my favorite Charee defector, arms full of checklists and clipboards as he rattled off patient report after patient report like words were bullets and I was the enemy; I saw all of them, and the others, and I saw Skinner—the one who reminded me of Ken, the one who was with me until the end.

And I saw all of them ripped away from me. "After it happened, my medics who didn't die avoided me," I said aloud.

"After what happened?" Ken asked, still not looking at me. I realized now that was on purpose.

"Um." I felt myself choking, and swallowed it. Shit, I felt so weak. "If I do this, you've gotta do it, too."

"I don't have PTSD."

"I know," I said. "That's not what 'this' means. I mean you've gotta—just—be—good with yourself. If I'm fixing my past you gotta fix your future."

"Okay. I can do that." It was his patient care voice—the soft but firm promise-tone he used when explaining what he was about to do, or answering a request. He always fulfilled those requests.

"Okay." I took a deep breath. "It's not that big of a deal, really. Other people have seen much worse. Shit, I'd seen worse, before that, and never had any problems. I don't know why the pictures that stick with me tend to be pictures of the officers arguing."

"Maybe because they didn't listen to you, and then someone died," Ken said.

"Whoa," I raised my eyebrows. "How did you know that?"

"Right size and shape," he said.

"Hm," I grunted. "Well, yeah. The commander basically didn't sleep for a month and went insane. This guy was laughing with wide maniac eyes when he dismissed all my medical council. But I was the only one of the officers actually working on the ground with the soldiers day in and day out. You didn't see them pulling mud out of tank treads. I did. But he didn't listen to me. Instead, he listened to logistics officers who said things like 'a leader is a leader because they know when to send someone in to make a sacrifice for their people.'"

Ken stiffened. "Yeah—that's true, I guess, but—weird."

"No, it's not true. A leader isn't a leader because of the power they hold over someone else to make decisions, but because of the utility they are to the whole," I glowered. "Because more people will suffer if the leader dies, you keep the leader alive. Not because they know better than everyone else but because they know the information that everyone else needs to know. The leader doesn't have a right over anyone else's life. When they give an order to charge a hill, it's not supposed to be like throwing sand in the wind." I threw my hand in an angry gesture. "Your soldiers trust you to give that order because they trust that their risk of dying in your attack is less than the risk of something worse happening if you *don't* attack."

"You don't send people to their deaths, you send people to make the other side die," Ken summarized, scrubbing harder for some reason, jaw tightening. This was resonating with him, hard.

"Yeah," I said. "Those were the officers who let my soldiers get screwed over in pay and admin while *they* got deployment awards left and right. And this attack, if it worked, was going to look really good on someone's OER." I clenched and twisted the cleaning rag in my fist; Ken took it from me and handed me the ultrasonic grime gun. I took it and began blasting its cleaning rays down the barrel of my weapon. In the dark it didn't have the satisfying visual effect you got in the light, but it was nice to pull the little cleaning device's trigger. Comforting, somehow. "You have to understand, my guys weren't sick call rangers, they legitimately weren't fit for duty yet. We didn't have enough people. They kept pushing me to fake the readiness numbers, kept telling me to stop letting my soldiers *fool* me, to toughen up on them—and then whenever I *was* tough on somebody they'd catch me for not being *tactful* enough."

"You don't do people who aren't patients," Ken said softly.

"I don't do people who aren't patients," I said. "And that's why my guys died, in the end."

He stiffened. "Whoa, I'm sure—"

"No." I put the gun down. Now I was finding my eyes with my sleeve. My voice wavered. "No, if I could just have been better—more convincing, less worn out, more persistent, a more respected combatant—maybe those jackasses would've listened to me. That's why I need chemical aids. Because I wasn't good enough without them."

Ken shook his head. The slightest rumble of anger vibrated under his voice. "That's not fair. You can't blame yourself, ma'am."

"Oh, I don't." I slammed the magazine clip back into the

weapon. I was done cleaning it. "The lucky bastard I blame died just like everyone else. At least he had the honor to do that. The offensive was a massacre. Oh, and entirely unnecessary. The Treaty of Kepler Sigconis was signed hours later worlds away. If we'd just waited a few days like I said the war would've been over without us. Two logistics officers were awarded Silver Novas for a pointless fight they started. They were the last men standing," I laughed. My laugh sounded crazy. But if I didn't laugh, I was going to scream. "All the better men were dead."

"What about you?" Ken's voice was small. Sweet of him to care, but I didn't deserve it.

"Discharged for erratic and unprofessional behavior." I hated saying that. I hated admitting that I was shit at the one thing I'd dedicated my whole life to being: a soldier. "Union bigwig was offended that I refused my deployment award, and that, wouldn't you know, for some unfathomable reason, some doctor broke ranks to scream at two higher ranking officers during their awards ceremony." Before he could ask why I'd done that, I added: "I had a medic named Skinner. He was shot in the head when we were boarded during the battle. I guess he was my favorite medic, I don't know. I don't know why that last death did to me what all the others couldn't. It wasn't more violent. Maybe because when they mentioned him during the ceremony like it was some great sacrifice, instead of a meaningless killing *they* caused… I don't know. They made reality wrong with their righteous bullshit. I guess it broke my view of myself and my place in the universe. Suddenly I wasn't the iconoclast advocating fiercely for my patients: I was the crazy woman who couldn't take an order. Don Quixote from the ancient tales, swinging at wind turbines. And that was why I decided to let myself be crazy."

The last sentence came out like a squeak. My stomachache was releasing, and I realized I had tears flowing pretty freely now, because the story actually didn't end there anymore. It used to, but now: "And then about a year later in a bar while I was kicking some bitch's ass, I met Skinner again in a peppy young Uri Naran from Alpha Prime who was looking for some wind turbines to swing at himself."

"They're not wind turbines. They're real," Ken grumbled. "We're neither of us crazy. We're just paladins. What they did to you was wrong."

I wiped my eyes and smiled. "I don't know what a paladin is," I said. "But Don Quixote is really, really glad to swing with you, Ken Kamakura, right up to the end. Just see if you can maybe avoid getting knocked around by the blades the way she did."

"I'll try," he said, looking out into the night with a sigh now himself. "I guess if we're going to defeat those damn turbines, we should be on the same page strategically, too. Let me tell you what happened tonight, Captain Quixote."

CHAPTER FOURTEEN

Ken Kamakura

KEN WOKE up untouched by headaches—an easy, slow waking, none of that startling jolting that felt like his heart planned to punch through his sternum—for the first time in days. A soft breeze caressed his forehead and rustled the wide leaves that fanned above him in broad, tattered horseshoe shapes, tickling his nostrils with a scent he could only describe as green: fresh and herbaceous like legumes and lawns without the aggressiveness of spices and flowers. Water tinkled and trickled in the distance, and near him, lapped against the soft lapis lazuli sand.

"Is all of Sector Ben Haba like this?" Wimmer was asking Sibila. "Because if so—yeah, I could get used to this. The last few days here…" she sighed with the little groan and squeak of a stretch. "It's almost been like a vacation, circumstances not withstanding."

"It is some of the most beautiful land on the continent," she said. "It changes hands often. This spot is a special one for me. We used to come here as children, before the Yada claimed the oasis."

"So if we leave you here, Sereno will probably find you," Wimmer said.

"Yes. This is where he will come."

Oh, man. Something sank in Ken's chest, and the beautiful world seemed suddenly painted in sadness as he sat up. Heaviness came flooding back, and with it the soft ache in his forehead.

The two women sat cross-legged on the other side of the small pond near the little outcropping of red rock from which the water trickled. Sibila had borrowed some of Wimmer's overclothes—they were a little small for her, but the way the fatigues hugged her rear definitely wasn't *un*flattering—and was now cooking something in the *breakfast pit*, as Wimmer had taken to calling the natural concavity in the rock where Sibila built fires. Tall bipedal bird-like lizards with brilliant scales and sharp feathers pranced around them, rushing in every now and then to steal scraps from Wimmer's Scrit. Here at the border between what Sibila called the water-lands and the mine-lands, hardy ironwood trees scattered among the twisting rock columns and the aggressive alien beauty seemed like something from a dream.

And it was a dream, because it was going to be over soon. The Terrans had managed to use the radio in the dune-buggy to contact Sergeant Howard, and they'd soon all rendezvous with Galaxy Aid not more than three hours from here. All that was left was to say goodbye to Sibila.

Ken hated this plan, suddenly, and didn't know why. He lay back down and stared at the thick, tall root structures winding around his bedroll. Maybe he should go back to sleep.

But then he wouldn't be able to see Sibila.

The medic dragged himself to his feet and shuffled over to breakfast pit.

"What is wrong with you?" Sibila greeted him with her eyebrows knit. "Does your back hurt?"

Ken hadn't even thought about his back. He reached behind

him, fingers digging into the spaces between ribs and the ridges of his spine—it was kind of sore? Maybe? But not really. The huge abrasion back there was gone, as was the cut on Sibila's forehead, after several days of judicious application of closing serum, and the headaches had fled before Wimmer's combination of hard pharmacology with soothing mind-body techniques and frequent blasting from the advanced handheld alpha-gamma-stim machine she carried with her. He really couldn't justify complaining.

"I'm fine," he managed a smile. Man, this day sucked.

"You do not look fine. Maybe the doctor should look at you again. Put your head back in that CT machine," Sibila said. She tapped Wimmer's elbow. "Should I go, and you—"

"Nope." Wimmer stood up. A wry grin tugged at her lips. "In fact, I'm going to go. I'm on my last day of vacation, you deal with him, lady."

"Me? I—should I use your—"

"Nope. Don't touch my shit." Wimmer clicked her fingers to get her Scrit's attention, and then smacked her lips. It lay down beside Sibila obediently, its triangular ears perked. "Stay there. Okay, bye!"

"Bye?"

With that, the doctor pranced off towards the cluster of rocks and spiny brush they'd designated as the bathroom area, humming.

"Well, she's in a good mood," Ken grumbled. He slouched to a seat beside Sibila and grabbed one of the roasting sticks that lay crossed over the fire-pit. The waterfowl here tasted a little frog-like, but it was in a really rich, *dark meat* way that he liked a lot, and it bummed him out that he wouldn't have it again after today. Sure, it might look like there wasn't a lot to shishkabobing spiny ducks, but Sibila had a particular way she managed the heat and he couldn't replicate it. This was all going away.

"I am surprised you aren't," Sibila said.

"Huh?" He stared at the stringy leg on his stick.

"I'm surprised you aren't in a good mood, like Captain Wimmer," Sibila repeated. "You reach your destination today."

"Eh, she's laughing at someone about something," he said. "You or me. Or both of us. She's not actually happy about the job." He looked at Sibila's face—her big purple eyes squinted in concern, but it was just concern for him, and for some reason that bothered him. "Why are you—" It wasn't really nice to ask why someone wasn't upset, but he didn't know how else to word it. "Why are you okay with everything?"

Sibila smirked. "Is your mission in life to make me *not* okay with mine?"

"No, I—" He paused. He'd uprooted everything around her, hadn't he? But her life was already chaos. He'd literally met her with bullets flying around them. She'd been just another one of the mass casualties he needed to sort then—almost unrecognizable in his memory. "I haven't changed that much in your life, I don't think," he said. "That's what sucks. You're still—you're still going back to the same thing."

"What? Not changed that much?" He couldn't understand her tone—it was something between a scoff and a confused question. "The one constant in my entire life is dead. You know I have memories of Grandfather from before either of my parents? And both of my parents are long gone. Everything in our lives always changes—location, enemy, food—everything. Tradition and Grandfather were the only constants. And you've twisted the one around on top of itself and killed the other."

"What do you want me to say to that?" Ken asked. It sounded more argumentative than he meant it to—he stopped himself before continuing. "I mean—what—" He pressed his palms against his eyes. "I'm not sure I know what I want to say."

"I feel the same way," she threw her hands up in the air. "I don't know what you want from me. I won't be returning to the trades—or if I am, they'll be different—is that what you want?

Sereno will have found a way now to make Grandfather's death the Bantai's fault. He may even be able to make an alliance with the Third over it, if temporarily—they despise breaches of contract. Whether that means full rebellion against the Bantai I don't know. I know he wanted more outside aid first."

"So there's no real guarantee you're going back to freedom and not just more—intrigue." Ken's chest heaved. He'd just woken up, and he'd slept well. Why was he tired already? "I hate this."

"What *this*?" For some reason she seemed offended. She planted one fist on her curvy hip, the other on the stone beside her. "What do you hate about us?"

"Are you happy?" Ken asked. "And stop it with the *oh it doesn't matter if I'm happy, lives depend on my misery, blablabla*."

Sibila ground her jaw and lifted her chin. "Do not mock me, Kenta Kamakura." She nodded towards the stick in Ken's hand. "Why don't you eat? You seem completely wrong this morning, and I don't know why the doctor left me to fix it. Are you in pain?"

"In pain?" Ken almost threw the meat morsel—almost. Instead, he took an angry bite. "Look, I'm eating. Stop worrying about me and worry about yourself."

"I don't need to worry about myself. I am fine!" she shouted.

"You don't sound fine!" Captain Wimmer called from beyond the rocks.

"Ooh—sorry," Sibila blushed. "I am fine," she whisper-yelled now. "I am strong. I can take anything for those I love. You seem to want to force selfishness on me, but selfishness isn't what I want. *Oh, think of yourself Sibila, you're so beautiful, you're so smart, do what makes you happy,*" now she mocked *him*, with a deep, round, idiot voice. "What if helping others *makes me happy*? Have you thought about that, hm, you hypocrite?"

Her outburst was so—cute—Ken found himself laughing. Oh, it hurt. It hurt to laugh when he wasn't going to see her anymore. "How am I a hypocrite?" he asked.

"What do you mean, how are you a hypocrite? What are you doing here to *be happy*? No one is paying you, not yet, and definitely no one is paying you to do my brother's bidding—you are supposed to be a *medic* for a foreign corporation," Sibila couldn't seem to decide whether to laugh or—cry? "Are *you* happy?"

He sat back. His mouth opened, but—huh. "I—was."

"What do you mean, you *was*? I mean *were*." Sibila stuttered in frustration. "I—what do you mean by that?"

"The first day I met you, when everything was going to hell, and it was so—exhausting," he said. "It was awful. But I was happy."

"Because you were helping others," she said, stabbing a finger into his chest. "See? You and I are the same. You would be pleasure guard, if you were me."

"No I definitely would not," he blurted—and then, more carefully, to not hurt her: "I—you're right. You're right that if it were me vs my people, I would choose my people. So in that way, yeah. And you're right, I—I guess it's kind of condescending of me to try to push your own value in your face when maybe it's because you know you're valuable that you'd give yourself for those you love. After all, you wouldn't give a trash gift."

"Exactly," she gave a firm nod.

"But—I would have to find another way. I couldn't—not because of the pain or health stuff to myself. You're right, I could probably handle that. But even if it was just to ruin my enemies, I couldn't use intimacy as a—weapon, or a—or a trade. Not knowing what I know about the long-term health effects." He forced himself to tear his eyes away from the stick twirling between his fingers to meet her eyes—even though the whole conversation had him suddenly feeling naked. "And even if I'm just a tool myself—or a shield—I'd be damaging that tool and maybe even dying young when I could still give so much more."

She looked away from him. "You could say the same about battle guard."

"I know. But at least there the whole point's *not* to get hurt, and the hurting of the other person is pretty straight forward. I don't have to shoot myself to shoot the other guy—you do." Ken put the now-cold meat back over the fire. "To me the pleasure trade's a temporary fix that, in the end, isn't healthy for anyone involved. Not for you, or the Bantai—or those who love you."

"Who loves me?" Sibila crossed her arms now, still looking away.

"Are you serious?" Ken narrowed his eyes. "Lots of people."

"Like who?" Sibila glared into the distance. "I care for people. They don't care for me."

"How can you say that? Of course people—" Ken paused. "You don't think your brother cares about you?"

"I don't know. He hasn't come looking for me yet."

"Because he knows you're safe! And maybe it's not safe for you back there yet." Something caught in Ken's chest. She really couldn't tell?

"Kenta Kamakura, if someone loved me, people would have found a way for me to be bought back and married so I could be out of the trades," Sibila said. Her glare found him now. "They wouldn't have left it up to some foreigner upending our whole world to get me out. It's not even that expensive. Sereno already has six or seven possible marriages lined up for each of his daughters. He's constantly panicking about them falling through and they're not even trading age yet." Her hard face cracked—her little mouth did half a smile, but her eyes stayed cold. "I don't need to be loved. *I* love. Everyone else only talks."

The way she said it—like a queen commanding the earth itself to move, like a celestial juggling planets while mortals whined and tugged at her coat—*everyone else only talks* was simultaneously such a badass challenge and so sad Ken found himself laughing gently.

"Hot damn," he whispered. "That goes so hard." He reached for her hand; she gave it to him with a quizzical look. "Well, if you could choose, what would you—"

He stopped himself. What was he about to ask her? What she wanted in a buyer? *Why* would he ask that? That wasn't how things were supposed to go. She should choose someone because they loved each other, not because she needed an out. Ken didn't want to *be* just an out.

Ken's thought startled him, and he let her hand go. *He* didn't want to be an out? Where did that thought even come from? It was both crazy irrelevant and—he suddenly realized—crazy untrue. He would be just fine being her out.

Have some self-respect. This wasn't how things should go.

Sibila's hand hung in the air, as if when Ken let her go it'd forgotten gravity. "What were you going to ask?"

"I—"

The buggy they'd escaped in suddenly zipped around the pond, throwing up azure sand and rattling like it planned to fall apart right there. "Sereno's coming," Wimmer called. "We're off. Bye Sibila!"

"I'm sure he won't—" Ken wanted to find an excuse to stop the rush, but he could see the dust on the horizon. It wasn't *just* Sereno coming. *Dammit.*

And with that the medical team drove off, leaving unasked the one question that Ken knew could change Sibila's life.

CHAPTER FIFTEEN

Jocelyn Wimmer

Poor kid was actually pretty distraught when we tore off for his final destination, and not because we were being hunted by what looked like a decent-sized army.

"I'm sure you'll see her again," I said.

"Not if she doesn't come find me," he said, cheek pressed up against his fist. *My gosh he has it bad,* I grinned. "She knows where I'll be, but she's nomadic." He straightened and replaced his pout with a hard, set jaw. "Besides, it doesn't matter as long as she's happy."

"She'll be happier with you," I said. "Bet you two bottles of makka she shows up at the Ben Haba outpost looking for you in two weeks."

He gave me side-eye and didn't answer.

Which was fine, because I was having trouble shifting gears across the sand and rocks and random spots of fertile earth as we wove through the half-stone forest. I was rated for a vehicle that I *thought* was this same land-rover, but apparently, they'd hodgepodged enough different parts into this buggy that it wasn't really the same car anymore. It screamed like a Scrit giving birth and coughed like a smoker every time I accelerated, and I really did need to accelerate. I'd made sure to keep it fueled, and I didn't see dripping, so I didn't know what was—

"It's a little strange that they're not giving up," Ken said, looking back behind us. "And they're kind of gaining on us. I kind of figured Sereno would take Sibila and go home."

"Maybe it's an honor thing. Those are definitely Sevellan sigils on the lead truck."

After about an hour the buggy started smoking out the front. Whatever I was doing, it didn't like me.

"Are we about to be caught?" Ken asked, raising an eyebrow at me.

"Thank you for not panicking," I said. *Because I'm starting to panic.*

"You're welcome." His pretty little Mark X hummed as he locked and loaded. *Oh, and there goes the GPS screen flickering now...*

"I'm going to be pretty annoyed if we end up shooting a bunch of people we saved just last week," I said, steering towards a tighter copse of stone 'trees' that kind of formed a V—it'd be easier to defend a narrow entrance like that. "I mean, do they believe in trials? Do we just surrender ourselves?"

"I didn't read a lot about Edenian justice systems before coming here," Ken admitted. "I wasn't really expecting to—need to?"

"'And thus, they learned why the military always gave long briefings before deploying.'" I smirked over a pompous voice. "So Specialist Kamakura knows the legal consequences of assassinating a world leader."

"I feel like you joking about that has to stop at some point," he grumbled.

"My guy, it's been a week—you think you're just going to live down murder?" I laughed. "I will be busting your chops until you *die.*"

"Or until you die."

"Nope. If I die, I'll come back from the dead and tease you some more." The car sputtered and vomited some reddish fluid—I didn't even know they could do that. "Which might be soon, actually."

"We can't make it just a few kilometers further?" Ken begged the buggy.

And the front burst into flames.

"Simon says *nope*!" I said, jumping out my side and running around to the back to drag out my duffel and assault pack. Sylvie jumped on my shoulders with a heavy thump—I tossed Ken my bag so I didn't fall over, and pointed him towards the defensible V of stone columns I'd been aiming for. "We hide there. Maybe if we're lucky, they'll think we died in the car," I said.

"In all your very long, very old wrinkly life, have you ever had that kind of luck?" he joked.

"Until I met a certain murder-hobo medic, yes, yes I have," I teased back. "Occasionally."

The gap between the two front columns in the V-formation was smaller than it looked from a distance—I had to suck in my stomach to squeeze through and my bag almost didn't fit at all. *Maybe I should drop it*—but I really didn't want to ditch my medical imaging equipment—

Ken pulled me through. It wasn't just a V—we were surrounded by an almost perfect ring of stone columns that twisted together above us like multicolored pastry—*crap, I'm hungry now?*—casting cool shadows across the green shrubbery at our feet. Huge black tree trunks surrounded us inside and outside of the columns—it wasn't a bad hiding spot.

Or so I thought. A thinner buggy pulled up and Sereno got

out. Engines still roared in the distance over the sounds of doors slamming and boots hitting dirt—Sereno's was the only vehicle small enough to maneuver through woods this thick. Everyone else was showing up on foot, but they weren't far behind—

"Why's he alone?" I whispered.

Sereno whirled, rifle raised. It was an old hunting gun, like the kinds Grausian aristocrats used for sport. "I'm alone so I can apologize before we kill you," he called.

Curse those fantastic ears. Well, at least that settles the question of a trial. I raised the fully automatic we'd borrowed from the Grandfather. I thought I might have a clear shot—

"Can I ask why?" Ken called back.

"Dsh—pf—sh!" I sputtered. "Shush!"

"Because it was too messy, Kenta, and you involved my sister," Sereno's voice was quieter—and closer. I could see him through the trees, looking back over his shoulder. I still didn't see anyone else.

"She wasn't involved," Ken said, pushing my elbow to keep me from aiming. "Please let's try talking first," he whispered to me. To Sereno: "She was kidnapped."

"That, people won't believe unless you're dead," Sereno said, turning, turning, turning— "The way she *looks* at you, the way she says your *name*—she's a terrible liar, Kenta Kamakura. As long as you're alive, she'll either find you or pine for you, and the moment anyone sees her set eyes on you they'll know."

"No they won't—let me leave the planet and she'll never see me again," Ken said. *Fat chance you don't come back,* I thought, my signature eyebrow raised.

Sereno wasn't having it either. "Now that *I* don't believe," Sereno sighed. His ears twitched in our direction; he raised his rifle and peered towards our hiding place, hunching. He still didn't see us yet— "It's too messy, Kamakura. And I'm so close now." His voice lowered further as he turned again, almost whispering, his voice genuinely sad but steady. His back was now less than half a meter from us, so close I could see the uneven stitching on the triangles on his collar. Even I couldn't miss. "If I let you live, there will be doubt about my involvement, Kamakura. I could lose everything we've worked for—and I *must* rule the Sevella, you know I must. You've seen how horrible our lives are. I can make the world better, Ken, for the pleasure guard, for my sister—and not *only* for them! For everyone. You wanted to help us, yes? You have. You *are*. You are our hero, Kenta Kamakura. This sacrifice of yours will be so noble. Please don't make it difficult."

Ken opened his mouth to answer—I gave him a death stare. We were standing way too close, and did he not *hear* this guy? He was literally saying he'd kill us so he could tie off any loose ends that *might* hurt his bid for power. *Come on, Kamakura, what's this guy got over you?*

Ken closed his mouth, but Sereno's ears were twitching in time with our breathing. Shit. He started to creep towards the gap, the entrance to the ring of stones—

I raised the semi-automatic and switched off the safety.

"No," Ken muttered, and dove for the entrance.

"What the—"

He grabbed Sereno by the collar, yanked him against his chest, and held that little Mark X to his temple—blocking the entrance to the stone grove with Sereno's body, and my shot of Sereno with his.

"Clever," Sereno said, looking backwards now. "Captain Wimmer was going to shoot me, wasn't she?"

"Yes, she was," I answered. "I warned you not to play games with my medic. I could've helped you, man, if you'd just been brave enough to *talk*. I'd still be down to help you now if you'd bothered to show up here with a solution other than *die so I'm safer*."

"Help me what?" Sereno asked, his face the perfect mask of confusion.

We had an audience suddenly. There were Sevellans pouring through the woods, their skin shifting lime, emerald, black and tan with the shadows. I recognized so many of them —shit, we really had betrayed them, in their eyes. I was suddenly really glad they couldn't see me. I'd already lived through one military experience where the crowd of familiar faces contorted through the whole spectrum of cold disbelief to bitter judgment to despising me. I'd let Kamakura take this one.

Ken kept his head tucked behind Sereno. "Back away, please!" He shouted. "Let us just get to the Galaxy Aid outpost and you can have your leader back."

"Agh, you're yelling right by my ear," Sereno complained under his breath. "Let me go, Kamakura. This doesn't end well for anyone."

"Well, see, I don't really want to die," Ken said. "Because then *I* can't make the world better. Do you see how that sounds, friend?"

"You're—ugh." Sereno didn't look angry so much as disappointed. "I cannot believe you're actually a coward. You, really? It was going to be so quick. Much quicker than how you brutalized our Grandfather."

"He doesn't deserve *quick*, if the story the room told holds weight," growled Lachish's deep timbre from behind cover just a few meters in front of us. I had a good angle on him, if I needed it—the tiny gaps between the columns here were perfect for me to shoot out without anyone else shooting in. "We trusted you, plainskin. What happened in there?"

Man, I'd liked Lachish: even pissed he was trying to get an explanation. Shit, I'd liked a lot of them, I realized. There was the husband of the girl whose baby we delivered the first day. There was the abdominal wound guy, whose IV I took over when Ken almost fell asleep on him. There was the panicky chest wound guy who almost trampled me—

Wait, what was he doing with his face? His whole deal was scrunching as he stared back at the vehicle fire back behind him.

"Thal," he said to Sereno. "I have some bad news."

Sereno glared at him with bored, half-lidded eyes. "I can't imagine it's worse than the news that I have a gun to my head, soldier."

But Ken's eyebrows shot up—he was a bit more concerned about chest wound guy, and suddenly roared: "Everyone shut up! Back away or I'll make it two regents dead in a week."

Screams and curses broke out from the battle guard: "He admits it! He admits it!"

"I didn't admit anything!" Ken yelled. "But I will kill the puppetmaster here if you don't clear the way, now, for me and my companion to Sereno's maneuver-buggy there."

"But who's going to drive?" smiled the chest-wound guy. "Neither you nor your companion know how."

Oh… shit. I knew why Ken was freaking out.

———

Ken Kamakura

It took Sereno a second to put two and two together, Ken could tell, but he didn't have time to wait for the new Grandfather to get on board.

"Sereno will drive, obviously," Ken growled. "Now move!"

"You wouldn't prefer to bring along your normal getaway driver?" sneered chest-wound guy.

"You think you know things, but you don't," Ken snapped.

"Your face says otherwise," chest-wound guy laughed.

"Would you mind enlightening the rest of us, idiot?" Lachish rumbled.

"If our new Grandfather would consent to bringing Guard Sibila here…" chest-wound guy bowed.

A shot rang out that almost made Ken jump. Chest-wound guy shrieked as Wimmer's round impacted his leg. "Stop it!" Ken snarled to her. But over his shoulder he could see the concern deepening the wrinkles around the Captain's mouth and eyes, and he realized he didn't know a better way out of this anymore. Killing chest-wound guy could make Sibila look guilty; Sibila showing up and making a face could make Sibila look guilty; letting chest-wound guy explain why he knew Sibila had to have driven them could make her look guilty—and did he even deserve to die, when he was simply helping his people's process of justice? Was that even right?

"The Terrans don't know how to downshift!" chest-wound guy groaned, gripping his leg. "The younger one isn't even rated for their *own* vehicles—he told me at the hospital." He interrupted himself with a dramatic moan. "That's why they destroyed the buggy once they left Sibila at the oasis. They treated it like a Terran vehicle and broke the fuel line. Guard Sibila wasn't kidnapped."

Jocelyn Wimmer

Sereno's face froze on an expressionless mask. No more cool smiles of shimmering black teeth; no more calculating eyebrow raises. He had to be struggling just to not show emotion at all.

"I held a gun to her head, tell them I held a gun to her head," Ken hissed in Sereno's ear, but even I heard it.

"Where is my sister?" Sereno asked, voice quiet.

"I'm here!" she cried out.

And she was, running barefoot towards us through the rocks and shrubs. She had the stupid naked-dress on, again—she'd probably had to change out of my fatigues the moment we left her so she didn't look too much like us. "I drove, it's true, but he threatened me with a gun to my back the whole time! I had no choice. He said he would—" She started to tear up—with real tears. Either Sereno was wrong about her being a bad liar, or she was just really scared enough to cry. "He said—"

"She's lying." And suddenly the chest-wound guy lunged at her and put his dirk to her neck. Ken gasped— "See? Did you see that?"

"What I see is you attacking a pleasure guard who's in an active trade." Sereno's smile was back—and as icy as a tomb in deep space. "You had better release her before we make *you* explain to the Bantai why you've damaged their property."

"But how did they drive out here?" chest-wound guy cried.

"The same way we're going to drive away," Ken spat. "Do you not see the pistol in my hand? Are you really so stupid? Gah, I can't believe we wasted the time saving your life. Have you done anything useful with it since?"

It was so uncharacteristically nasty I found myself almost laughing; the Sevellans seemed less amused.

"I said release her." Sereno's eyes blazed, and I saw the little red lines pulse when he turned to look back at me over Ken's shoulder. "Captain Wimmer," he said. "I'd be willing to spare your life—I cannot spare Kamakura's, I'm afraid—if you would either shoot the imbecile who has my sister or the traitor who has me."

"Uh—I'm not the person you want shooting someone who's got a hostage," I shook my head. "I'm not responsible for Ken's crack shot. I didn't teach him that."

"May the fires take me, this is so messy," Sereno breathed a moan.

"I'm walking now!" Ken announced, pressing his back against the rock beside him and beginning to scoot. "Come along, Thal—"

"If you take another step, I'll kill her," the chest-wound guy hissed—and Ken froze.

"Why would I care about that?" he asked. But he wasn't moving.

"Right, why would you?" the captor mocked.

"Because he's got a respect for all life," I butted in finally. "Just not Sevellan leaders. Okay? Can we go now?"

"I already ordered you to unhand her," Sereno growled.

"But Thal, it's *working*." Lachish held out his hand as if holding chest-wound guy in place with telekinesis. "You cannot see the medic's face. But I do not believe he will take you as long as Sibila is threatened."

"I will," Ken said.

"She is in the trades," Sereno insisted.

"But we see you, we see you both," Lachish said, rising now. "When have you cared for the sanctity of the trades, and when has this Terran ever proved cruel? I guarantee you he killed Grandfather *for* Guard Sibila. Our brother is right, I think. See the mark there, on her head? It matches his, even. They were hit with the same weapon. Sibila fought Grandfather."

The gig was up. Their chests heaved almost in waves, one after the other, Ken's against Sereno's back—they were caught. I was feeling strangely far away. How did I even get in this mess? Was I really going to die surrounded by painted elves in a stone forest for a crime I actually had no part in? The hell was I thinking?

"I must be high. I must just be so high," I muttered.

And then she woke up and it was all a dream.

But it wasn't, of course.

"What do you say, Thal? What shall be done with her?"

Sereno would need to condemn Sibila to keep his position secure. It was clear he didn't have the authority I'd thought he had, if his soldier didn't obey a direct order—no wonder he was paranoid about killing Ken to prove himself.

But he'd secured this position *for Sibila*, so that he could finally keep her safe. I saw his jaw move; I couldn't see his face anymore, not with him staring forward at her, but I saw her. She watched him with clear, cool eyes—totally analytical eyes, totally unafraid. She was curious.

And he was undone. He was scrambling for words, gasping, almost, for air. He couldn't choose.

"I'm the one who loves; no one loves me," she'd said to me that morning before Ken got up.

So she chose for him. "I did it, Sereno," she declared. "I did it to punish you all in the name of our Bantai masters. None of you would ever buy me, but the Bantai value me. They treated me far better than you and Grandfather ever did, and when they told me you'd accepted *their* Galaxy Aid medic into your fold, I laughed at your kindness, your *weakness*. My heart is Bantai now. So for them, I and my consort have slain your predecessor, and if I am not unhanded, we will slay you, too."

Lachish almost looked like he'd fall over from the double-take. "For the *Bantai*?"

"She has spoken, yes?" the chest-wound guy was salivating now. "I should slit her throat, yes?"

"You fool, then the Terran will kill Sereno," Lachish growled. "Look at his face!"

I couldn't see either young man's face now, but I heard Sereno's hoarse warning: "If you leave alive, sister, saying this," he croaked. "You will never be able to return. You know this. Are you certain that's what happened? Are you certain you weren't coerced?"

"Coerced? How could she be?" protested the chest-wound guy. "She clearly fought, the whore loves—"

"Silence," Lachish said. "This is what we will do. We will return, conduct a thorough investigation, and hold a committee of evidence. Perhaps there was more than murderous intent at play. Terran, if you unhand our leader, we will treat you fairly. You cannot keep this up forever. Our guards are circling your defenses now and will find a gap—we will kill you where you stand, and your teacher with you. If you surrender, perhaps your teacher will live. We will also investigate this supposed Bantai connection."

The guy was being pretty reasonable, all things considered, so it was a real pity he suddenly took a high-power plasma round to the skull.

CHAPTER SIXTEEN

Ken Kamakura

THE GUNSHOTS suddenly blaring from all directions weren't the old pop and crack of the used, scavenged rifles Ken had gotten used to on Eden Crescent. These fired blinding blasts and whizzing flechettes that sung and screamed through the air, shrieking their technological supremacy with every target hit. There were no Third robes or Bantai jewels. The uniforms the shadows hinted at between the trees were fatigues, and this scene Ken had seen before on Interthought Media broadcasts.

They were under attack by the Yada.

Ken hurled himself forward on top of Sereno and—as they hit the ground—aimed the Mark X in his hand at the underarm of the Sevellan holding Sibila. One quick trigger pull and the chest-wound guy crumbled just as he had the last time Ken shot him. Of *course,* Ken had had the weapon on stun the whole time he held Sereno—he'd never flag someone he didn't hate with a loaded gun.

"Stay on the ground, on the ground now and surrender!"

screamed a familiar high-pitched order. *Howard?! What's she doing with the Yada?* "Wimmer, Ken, hold tight!"

"The fuck is going on," Ken heard Wimmer mutter behind him.

"Get off me!" Uniforms rustled as Sereno fought to get out from under Ken, pummeling the young Terran's gut; some other Sevellan tried to help his leader but the forest was now a leveling field—if you stood up, you got cut down. The air was hot with plasma rounds and it was almost impossible to see anything.

"I'm trying to save your life," Ken hissed, wrapping his arm around Sereno's neck and pinning down Sereno's hand with his knee as the Sevellan tried to go for his dirk. "Will you just let me?"

"I have to kill you, you fool, or my life won't be worth saving!"

"Please stay down, please stay down, both of you!" Ken pleaded, trying to look across the rocks and dirt by his face to find Sibila's eyes. She was on the ground prying the knife from the chest-wound guy's stiff hand—*I have got to ask that guy his name,* Ken thought—

The blazing barrage ended almost as quickly as it had begun, and in its place for a moment the forest was silent.

Then began the moans of the wounded. Uniformed Edenians with black masks emerged from behind the trees and began shooting anyone on the ground who tried to stand. Sereno twitched under Ken with each shot fired as if shot himself, and finally began to curse and scream:

"Cowards. Thieves! Afraid to face the wounded now? Hide behind your Grausian gifts, you will never regain your souls!"

"Oh, that sounds like Sereno." Howard's voice, again—Ken could see her now, with Tack and Bones, stalking behind a particularly tall Edenian with violent red hair protruding from the top of his mask. "He probably has the authority to surrender."

"Stop shooting the injured!" Ken shouted, still pressing as much of his weight down on Sereno as he could. Howard was above him now; still he didn't move, keeping his body over the Edenian he was afraid he couldn't protect if he so much as breathed too hard. "You killed Lachish," he panted. "You didn't even give him a chance."

"We gave them the same *chance* they gave your Galaxy Aid outpost," boomed the red-haired Edenian. "You don't seem very glad for rescue."

"Sevellans massacred every last Galaxy Aid volunteer yesterday," Howard explained, crouching. Her dull blue eyes regarded Sereno's enraged indigos with something between boredom and disgust. "Something about revenge for a medic killing their leader."

"Well, fuck." Ken heard Wimmer mutter behind him. He'd thought he felt sick when finding out about Sibila's slavery—that was nothing compared to this feeling now, where the nausea consumed everything from his gut to his eyes and the world spun around him so fast, he wanted to pass out, no, he almost *begged* his blurring vision to let him pass out. He'd gotten an entire hospital *massacred*? He couldn't breathe. He tried to breathe, he couldn't breathe—

"That was not us," Sereno spat. "We did not have *time* to reach Ben Haba—we have a custom of rites, and I needed to find my sister. We barely reached the oasis today!" For some reason he looked now not at his enemies, but to Ken. "I swear on my life, you were the only medic I planned to kill today."

Ken couldn't answer. He shook his head, pressing his forehead now into the dirt, still wrapping himself around the young Edenian. He didn't know what to do except keep the person underneath him alive. Sereno, Sibila, Wimmer. That was it right now. He couldn't help everyone—he couldn't help anyone. Someone was crying. There were still gunshots going off here and there. "Please make them stop shooting, Stacey," he croaked.

"Thank you for the rescue but please. It's all a misunderstanding. I believe him. It must have been someone else."

"The Sevellan robes were clear," said the giant Yada.

Sibila screamed; Ken's heart clawed at his throat. "This one's a Bantai trade!" someone called. Ken looked up to see two Yada soldiers yanking her to her feet, huge gloves wrapping around her arms and pinning her wrists like she was a child.

"Better return her," said the red-haired giant. "We don't want to jeopardize the peace talks." He cursed, and shook his head. "Barbarians."

Back to the Bantai? After all this? "No, wait!" Ken cried. "She's not a trade."

"What are you doing?" Sereno whispered.

Ken began to rise off Sereno—slowly, his body still generally shielding the Sevellan leader as he reached out towards the pleasure guard with one hand like he could summon her to him through the air. His knee still kept Sereno's knife-hand pinned. "She's been bought. Or she's being bought, if she wants to be." He met her soft violet eyes, his chest pumping like a bellows. He was so afraid. Had he ever been this afraid? His panicked mouth rattled words *so* much faster than his brain could think: "What do you want in a buyer, Sibila?"

"You," she blurted immediately. "I want you."

"There, it's happening, right?" Ken asked Sereno. "I pay you and I send a payment to the Bantai, right? So the cost of the loss is covered, and you can't get in trouble—no one gets in trouble, none of you." He looked up at the Yada. "I'm paying. Please."

"Fine with me," the red-haired giant shrugged. "We'll deliver your payment at our summit tomorrow. Sereno, do you surrender?"

"No," Sereno spat.

"Yes, he does!" Ken cried, lowering himself again. "He does! See?" With a quick trigger-pull and a stun-shot he put Sereno to sleep; Sibila squeaked with shock. "You can't kill an unconscious guy, right?" Ken begged. "There's got to be some Edenian honor rule against that?"

"Give the kid a break, Howard," Wimmer growled. "Like he said, it might not have even been Sevellans who killed off Galaxy Aid. We were at their camp just a few nights ago and Sereno's right, it would've been kind of hard for them to reach Ben Haba ahead of us."

"I don't know what to recommend, sir," Howard said, looking to the giant. "I mean, I saw the Sevellan robes at Galaxy Aid, too… but I kind of have to admit I don't think I saw any of these particular people. I don't know if you did?"

"I'm comfortable limiting bloodshed if we're not sure," the giant shrugged. "Take 'em all in, boys. We have a peace summit to prepare for."

Jocelyn Wimmer

The red-haired giant was named Yako Bisraya, and he immediately had someone bring us blankets and hot tea—and when we returned to his base, more hot tea. The guy was obsessed with hot tea and blankets. Even Sereno and the other Sevellan captives—in chains—got tea and blankets. None of the Yada seemed to *like* the Sevellans, but it almost seemed like they'd only shot the wounded because they feared them—because they knew they *wouldn't* surrender. An injured beast's deadly.

Now the Yada were following all the standard prisoner-of-war practices we Terrans kept, and when Ken offered to start tending to the injured prisoners, Yako let him. That was how we ended up in a dark green canvas hospital tent that was literally just a repurposed Terran Role II in the middle of a mystical-looking forest village. The Yada homes we passed on the way there seemed to blend into the tree trunks themselves: instead of leveling the forest, the Yada had bent it around them, weaving their thatch roofs and thick fibrous walls around the columns of ironwood and stone. Where they absolutely had to take down a tree, they'd left its stump for furniture, so the community forum we passed almost looked to me like what you'd think a child would come up with if you asked them to build an amphitheater for their secret club—not because kids are stupid or the town center looked backwards, but because I was used to places of government replacing nature completely with cold, sterile forms, not just hacking into living wood and saying *good enough for a chair for me*.

I recognized the tell-tale blue glow of localized clean nuclear power stations here and there, and transmission cables for advanced communication wove through the trees. The city in the woods seemed set up for families, but I didn't see any—at least, no one who *looked* like a civilian, and no kids.

The soldiers who escorted us were both male and female, all unmodified, and there wasn't any obvious hierarchy between the genders—it would've been exactly like being back on a Terran military base, actually, if not for the camo-green-and-black skin and long, pointed ears of the Yada soldiers in uniform. Like other Edenians, they all had huge, vibrant eyes. They seemed a bit more dark-colored and sharp-nosed than the Bantai and taller than the Sevellans, with more mossy, kinky hair, but it was still kind of hard for me to tell Edenian races apart. I could tell, though, that they had no *pleasure guard*. Sibila was offered plain, unembroidered robes, if she wanted them, and kept unchained.

She opted to put my clothes back on instead.

Sereno was rabid when he woke up. It was almost like he was a different person. Gone was the master of intrigue and cool expression: in his place was a swearing, thrashing, teeth-gnashing neodog spitting more racial slurs than a Sons of Terra pride rally. And words weren't all he was spitting—he was more than willing to spray any Yadan who came near with whatever he could hock up from the depths of his throat. He was incredibly lucky not to get his face bashed in with a rifle butt—not that I considered that an okay response to insults and mouth-juice. Still. While Yako seemed pretty serious about rules of engagement I knew from experience every army's got its soldiers with deadly short fuses who can only take so much abuse. And getting told over and over that your whole people group should be eliminated tends to get people riled up.

Ken was dumbstruck. Sereno wasn't nearly as angry at him as he was at the Yada, but even chained to the stretcher there was no examining the flailing leader for injuries. He was left to rail in a room of minimals under guard while Ken and I dealt with the more immediate casualties. There weren't many, unfortunately: there's not a lot you can do about a plasma round through the chest, and the sudden, precise Yada ambush left the Sevellans no chance. These guys knew how to aim for center mass.

"You all crack shots, or you got some homing tech?" I asked Yako, peeling off bloody gloves and dumping them into the sanitizer bin as I let the flap to the trauma room close behind me. He was sitting with Howard and her mercs at a small table in the middle of the patient sleeping area.

"We're simply fast and aggressive. We did loot some excellent hardware from the Galaxy Aid skirmish, though—half the plasma rifles used today came from there," Yako nodded. "It is a great pity we arrived only at the end of the conflict. We pursued a company from the fight and almost lost them, too. Fortunately, we were able to catch up again, and found you."

"That's why the location you say Sereno came from doesn't really make sense," Howard said. "We literally followed the killers to the grove where he was."

"Well, unless bro can teleport, he'd have to have passed us to get to the hospital, and then turned back around to get us," I said. "There's like ravines that drop off on either side of the oasis for miles. And *why?* No point in throwing a whole army of vehicles off cliffs to fool two Terrans he was planning on killing anyway."

"Okay, but then who were we following?" Howard asked. "We were only a kilometer or so behind. We lost them for a bit when the trees got thicker and we had to dismount, but…" She trailed off with a wave of her hand as if the conclusion should be obvious.

"It's not weird to you that people *fleeing* from you would suddenly all stop to have a conversation with Ken?" I smirked.

She shrugged. "Sure. I don't know. I don't care anymore, now that I found you two. I was beginning to worry I'd gotten you killed." She sighed. "I'm just ready to get off this damn ball of sand. It's not all a loss—GPSS still gets paid for orchestrating the rescue for the Interthought Media reporters. With Yako's help, here." Howard nodded. "The landing zone's now under Yada control so it won't be that hard to fly out."

Ken and I looked at each other. I drew my lips in a grim line; his eyes glistened with discouragement, but he said nothing. *Yeah, I know, kid.* There was no way the Sevellans left behind had given up control of the air strip to the hated Yada without a fight. We'd worked so hard to save some of those people back at "Welcome Village" only to have them lose their homes or… well. Die.

Yako misread Ken's face and tried to comfort him about the Galaxy Aid massacre: "If you had arrived to Ben Haba on time, young Terran, you would probably be dead, too," he said. "Survivors' guilt hurts, but there is nothing you could have done."

Ken shook his head and sniffed. He looked at the floor, and then at the wall, and basically anywhere but the Yada commander's face. His eyes finally found Sibila, sitting in the corner on one of the patient cots, hugging her knees and watching us, and his gaze steadied. He cleared his throat. "Sereno isn't like this, you know," he said. "He didn't have a reason to kill the Galaxy Aid folks. He was hoping to get supplies from them."

"Isn't like what?" Howard laughed. "That crazy monster in there would kill his mother for soup. Face it, Kamakura, the guy you think you know? He's all an act."

Ken clenched his jaw. Yeah, I knew that feeling, too—when you know you know someone and no one believes you because the person you'd like to help is doing themselves *zero* favors. "Well, I guess he can just teleport magically, then," Ken said. "I don't know why he's acting like this now, but maybe I'd throw a fit, too, if all my plans failed spectacularly in the span of forty-eight hours."

"It's simpler than that," interjected the Yada leader's slow rumble. We all looked at him. His voice flowed like honey over gravel—it was smooth and thick, but commanding, with texture to it. You couldn't help but listen. "The behavior you're seeing right now is hatred. That's all. We see this all the time from everyone. The most reasonable, rational person will become a demon when they find out you're Yada."

I grunted. That was the kind of story I was familiar with from family history.

"Is that—your—personal experience?" Ken asked Yako.

"It's the experience of every Yada child who ever grew up outside of a Yada enclave," Yako said. "Before the New Empire pulled out, they used to sometimes run integrated schools and cities. I mostly learned everyone who isn't Yada wants us wiped out."

"Why?"

"Because we don't belong here." Yako's tone was matter of fact. "Although if you want to be historically correct, then neither do they. They were moved here after our ancestors were almost wiped out a few hundred years ago. Our ancestors migrated here several hundred years before that and eliminated the people who were there before. That's the story of this region.

To people here, there's no such thing as an immigrant, only an invader." Yako turned a cobalt-blue glass over in his hands, eyeing the liquid within as if staring through it into the past. "My grandparents fled here when they had nowhere else to go. They were immigrants until they weren't."

Ken fidgeted. I knew why: he'd told me during some of our down time in the past few weeks that a reputable Grausian news source had reprinted documentation extracted from the former satrap's files that made it pretty clear she'd intended to displace local people groups by moving the Yada here in the last fifty years. The document claimed that was in the interest of promoting agriculture and stability in the region; Ken had speculated the satrap possibly felt sympathy for the Yadans because of their mistreatment on other parts of the planet, or perhaps she simply identified with them because they had a culture that was more similar to hers. Or maybe she really did think they'd make her more money—better serfs, better agriculture, better mining, better profits. Either way, the Grausians definitely intended to screw everyone else but the Yadans.

Yako watched Ken with pursed lips, and then gave a small exhale too somber to be a laugh but too short to be a sigh: it was almost like he put *yup, mm, this again,* into a breath. "I see you've read the relocation manifesto," he said.

"I have," Ken said.

"Well, know this: whatever the Grausian's intentions, they were not ours. There was no violence, and we took no one's land, until the Sevellans attacked us. It was they who turned us from immigrants into invaders by attempting to forcibly deport us when we had nowhere else to go." He turned towards Sibila in the corner. "Although I'm sure you have a different story."

"No," she said. "We did attack first. But that isn't the full story. Some impatient Sevellan youths robbed some rich Yadan in the street and the whole countryside exploded into violence like a fuel tank just waiting for a fire. Because you were waiting.

That foolish little street gang gave you everything you needed, and at the first excuse to take our homes, you pounced."

"Your leadership didn't exactly condemn the unprovoked violence," Yako smiled.

"No, they didn't." She wore the same blank mask she'd worn when talking down the Bantai in the hospital now. "Your response was too fast for that. Street by street. Then field by field. Countryside by countryside. Two days. You were running the territory almost before our councils could form a diplomatic strategy. You never gave us a chance."

Yako's hard, square face reflected hers. "We learned from a young age that if we don't strike hard, fast, and first, we will be destroyed," he said to her. "I grew up hearing every day how I should die. From my Bantai classmates. My Third classmates. My Sevellan classmates. Every day. *If it weren't for the Grausians, we would kill all of you now, foreigner.* Never mind that I had ties to the land, too. Do you really think any of our generals were going to sit and wait around to see what happened next?" He chuckled—it wasn't a cruel chuckle, or mocking, but it almost sounded like her naivete saddened him. "When the war started, I was still young. A combat medic, actually, about your consort's age. I remember tending to a young Yada soldier who had been playing with some Sevellan children in an area we'd conquered. He trusted them—they were only children, right? And then without warning during the game suddenly the soldier went down clutching his side because one of them had stabbed him with her father's vibroblade." He swirled his glass, gazing into the blue pit of the past. "Meanwhile I know another young Yadan soldier—same age—who saw a Bantai teenager walking towards him with his hand in his pocket, and because the Yadan simply had a bad feeling he fired. When he rolled the teenager over, he'd been in the act of pulling a needle-gun."

"You're that second guy," I said.

"Yes," he said. "I am. And I am alive because I struck hard, fast, and first." He looked back at Sibila. "And so it was with our people. We struck hard, and fast, to make it very clear we were not going to allow anyone to repeat our history. We will not be eliminated. But instead of listening, you recruited the Bantai and the Third against us. And even with all the abuses so many of you suffer at the hands of your own leadership, and each other, you all continue to refuse to learn." He turned to Ken. "You know we tried to allow some of them to resettle? Half of those we allowed through our borders tried to bomb us. We don't have the funds for the kinds of intensive background checks that can rule out who will and will not murder us for our kindness."

"The entire concept of your background checks is insulting. Many of us were *not* involved in attacking the Yada," Sibila said, her chin raised. "Why should we be investigated like criminals merely in order to have our own family lands back?" She pointed towards the tent wall. "My father used to own the square where they now have their meetings. The Yada stole the land, the Yada should return it and *we* should sort out who lives where."

"*My* family didn't steal anything. My grandfather bought the house in front of the square long in advance of the conflict," Yako smiled. "So then who decides what happens to his house—and the other houses around the square? Is his family evicted, simply for having been immigrants of the wrong race? There is no clean place to simply split the land. One of our governments must rule, and the other people must become—as we were—immigrants. And I choose to give that responsibility to a government that does not use its vulnerable as human shields or take food from children to feed warriors."

"'Maybe if the right people were signing the paperwork more of my guys would come home,'" Ken quoted me, wrist draped over his knee and head bowed. Most everyone ignored him—it seemed almost poetically nonsensical, and the mercenaries weren't exactly fans of his right now. I was standing within reach of him, and gave a soft prod of my boot against his to let him know I heard him.

"I can't imagine a world where either of our peoples actually sit down and allow the other to have authority over those choices," Sibila said.

"Me neither," Yako said.

"And because we cannot imagine, here we are today."

"Here we are today." It was sad how resigned and calm they both sounded—more dead than calm. After a long silence, Yako turned to me: "What's your next step, Captain?"

"Eh I'm basically Sergeant Howard's property," I grinned. "She's in charge of the job."

"About that." Howard blew out her breath hard and folded her hands on the table. She had the severe face of someone who's disappointed in you but too tired of your shit to argue with you about it—like law enforcement just telling you the consequences straight-faced because you're too much of a lost cause to even get mad about. "Galaxy Aid is over. They've pulled out —and I mean pulled out. All hospitals run by them on this planet, shut down. There is no job. The contract's canceled."

"They don't have positions on another planet?" I asked.

"Not that they need filled at this time," Howard said. She straightened her shoulders and blew hair out of her eyes, closing them for a moment as if trying to shake off a weight that just wouldn't fall. "I feel bad stranding you here, but Gamma Pavonis didn't agree to transport you off-world. Life support's expensive. I can probably convince my pilot, when he gets here, to at least bring you to the jump point so you can try to get a working pass on another ship. Medical folks are always in demand, so that shouldn't be too hard. But I've got no guarantees for you." She ducked her head down and gave the briefest glance over at Ken, then back at me. "Did he really kill the Sevellan leader?"

"Yeah."

She blew out her breath through tight lips again. "If that gets around it's going to be hard for him to find a job in the mercenary corps. I mean, he couldn't have screwed over the client more if he'd run in and shot up the hospital himself."

"If I may, I think, again, you're overcomplicating the story," Yako interjected, leaning back and folding his arms over each other. "Or perhaps oversimplifying it, depending on how you look at it. Whether Bantai or Sevella, your friends were slaughtered by the people they were trying to help. Galaxy Aid has long been supplying the Bantai with food and medical equipment. That food and medical equipment almost never reaches the people—it's always sold for arms or used for soldiers. The Third and the Sevella—and, if I'm honest, we Yada, as well—were always destined to see GA in some ways as arms traders, and at some point, someone was always going to remove them from our region."

"Wait, what?" Howard asked. "The actual people don't get the supplies? How do they put up with that?"

Sibila laughed.

"What?" Howard asked.

"Of course the people would leave the supplies to the soldiers," Sibila said. "It would be the best they can do for the war effort. Many of us would gladly starve if it meant reclaiming our land. Wouldn't you?"

Howard hunched her shoulders. "I need to get off this planet," she muttered.

"Well, there should be transport available back to Welcome Village tomorrow," said the giant.

And with that, Yako rose. He had preparations to attend to for tomorrow, he told us: the Bantai had agreed to peace talks finally, and skeptical or not—heavily armed or not—he had to try them. On his way out the door, he looked back at me. "Captain?"

I looked around—yeah, he was talking to me—and followed;

Howard trailed behind me like a bodyguard, nodding for her two mercs to keep an eye on Ken. As soon as we stepped into the cool primrose evening light Yako was immediately surrounded by various aides and lieutenants who needed this or that documentation signed or order confirmed. He waved for me to continue after him as they talked, and we quick-walked through the narrow street lined with obelisks to until we reached a machine shop, where he sat beside several other soldiers turning lathes and polishing metal.

"Gunsmithy?" I asked.

"Among other tools," he said. He had someone bring me more tea, and sat to work with his soldiers creating something I didn't quite recognize—I was never a gun porn gal. The documents he signed all carried the smear of machining grease. Howard began to occupy herself coordinating our transport logistics with some of the lower-ranking officers. I'd learned to hurry up and wait during my time in the military, and it wasn't like I'd rather be dealing with the tedious minimal injuries back at the tent, so I hurried up, and waited.

"If you're able to stay here for a few months," he said presently. "We could always use two more pairs of hands. I'm hoping Interthought Media changes their tune about us now that we've rescued their reporters, which means I'll be able to negotiate with them to bring you home on their next visit—I will admit I'm not confident. It wouldn't be an *easy* position. We'd keep you here, though, away from the bulk of combat, and provide whatever benefits you request."

"That's pretty generous," I said, straddling the workbench beside him. "You've known me for less than what, six hours?"

"Howard spoke well of you—of both of you—and we need medical support desperately," he said. "If you're able to keep your medic under control, and he's not in the habit of killing every boss he doesn't approve of," Yako's eyes twinkled, "I believe we could work something out. Then he could stay longer with his Sevellan lady-friend."

"It looks to me like that whole thing was some version of self-defense," I said. "As long as you don't try to beat his girlfriend with a stethoscope you should be good. But you'd let Sibila just stay here?"

"We have several Sevellans and Bantai—even a few Third. Mostly former pleasure guards and other down-and-out survivors. Quite a few detransitioned modified males," Yako said. "I know life isn't easy for them among us. There are plenty of Yada who despise any *Sub-Edenians*, as the slur goes. But we can provide them more rights than their own people can."

I stared at the dusty green of the tea in my cup and pursed my lips. Shit, I'd really gotten attached to Sereno's people. I kept thinking about the baby we delivered back at Welcome Village, and the Sevellan kid who lost their arm there. They were probably okay. But their parents? We'd patched up so many warriors, and while I understood it'd technically been a hostage situation with the reporters, and it was *cheaper* to bring the Yada in to break it up with violence, I couldn't help wanting there to have been a different way. What way that was, I didn't know.

"You know, *shoot first, ask questions later* does work to keep yourself alive," I said. "But it's not really going to bring you peace unless you're willing to straight up genocide the other side."

"I hope that's not what you're suggesting," Yako laughed. "I may dislike the Sevellans, but I value my soul."

"No, I'm saying you're stuck. Yeah, you can strike hard, fast, and first, and never take the risk of anything bad happening to you. But then, at the same time, you've actually got all these moral qualms about treatment of prisoners, minimization of casualties, bla-bla-bla—all that shit you're afraid to lean into because you've got to *hit hard and fast*. The two things are working against each other."

Yako nodded, hands busy sanding something now. "What do you suggest?"

"I don't know," I said. "I'm just a doctor. If you could show them, somehow, that you're serious about bringing them home —" I took a sip of the tea. It was bitter, but soothing in the throat, and I could feel a relaxing tingle in the back of my scalp. "I don't know shit, sir. I just know the Sevellans are screwed because of their leadership, not because of something inherent to them. And maybe now's the right moment for change." I nodded back towards the tent. "That very angry young man in there is dangerous. Definitely not a good person. I doubt you could share territory without always watching your back. But there is good in him. If you can lean into the idea that the Bantai set him up…" I trailed off. "You're trying to make peace with the Bantai tomorrow, though."

"Oh, I have terms to offer the new Sevellan Grandfather, too," Yako said. "Quite frankly, however, even if I were to save his life in battle, I would fully expect him to embrace me over his blade. Kindness is weakness to them."

"Is there a *them*? Kid can't be an individual?"

"That depends on him."

"Guess so," I muttered.

I leaned back against the hot, thick-walled mud furnace behind me—its intense warmth just bordered on unpleasant, like a sauna, and on my sore back muscles that felt like therapy. I was actually really fucking tired.

"I don't know, commander." I sighed. "There's an old saying my Rabbi told me, to try to get me to calm down, back when I was in the service: *The king's will is in the hand of God, and he directs it like a waterway wherever he pleases*. It always seemed to me like either it wasn't true, or God's more interested in drama than peace, because—well, that's where leaders' wills tend to turn." I took another sip. "Of course, I know there are two ways to read that—one is that if the king *pleases* chaos, God will help direct him that way. We become what we want to become, in the end, bla-bla-bla; God might direct, but the king flows. The other reading played on quantum choice, and God outside of time, and free will and predestination—God directs kings towards shit decisions, sometimes, because he's seeing multiple timelines to choose from, and choosing the overall best might mean things suck for a few people for a while. I dunno which I hate more." I closed my eyes for a second, feeling the blazing heat at my back contrast with the prickling on my skin from the cold flowing through the open door. When I opened them again, I saw the leader had lain down his tools for a moment to listen to me. "You know I've noticed something about waterways, though?"

"Mm?"

"You don't direct their course from the outside. Usually, you toss a dam or a boulder or something inside the stream."

Yako smiled, and turned back to his work, picking up a large, hard-bristled brush to dip it in black goo. "I suppose in the young Sevellan's case I would be a dam, then."

"Yeah. You can't do shit about God but you literally have Sereno right here. If he can just stop screaming and spitting for a second maybe some time in your company could—I dunno. Divert the stream. He's had shit mentors up 'til now."

Yako scrubbed the metal bar with the goo—I had no idea what he was doing but he did it with max effort, biceps pumping fast as he brush hissed. He was about my age, or maybe a little older, but dude was fit. Here in the workshop his skin took on a deep iron color—or maybe durasteel—that made his bright red beard stand out like blood on fire. With the stern face, and the vivid, high-contrast dark gray eyes that made mine seem washed out and sleepy, I could imagine this guy could give kids nightmares. Everything about him *looked* legendary.

"You know, doctor, I would argue that perhaps I can, as you say, *do shit* about God," he said presently. "You make it sound as if I'd be acting apart from the divine, but can't the boulder or the dam be part of his plan?"

"Sure. I think that's implied in the metaphor, God working through people. I only sound contrarian because I'm salty," I shrugged. "I used to know a lot of theological stuff, back when I was a good person."

"Are you not still a good person?" Yako asked, smiling.

"Oh no, I'm the worst," I said. "Ask anyone."

"I suspect if I asked your medic, or your patients, they might speak positively of you," he said.

"Eh." I smirked. "If I'm a good person, no one's a good person."

"*All fail and fall short of the brilliance*," Yako quoted. "Do you have that saying, too?"

I narrowed my eyes. "Yeah, we do. That's odd."

"Not so very odd. We have the same kings and waterways saying, too," Yako said. "I always find it fascinating when travelers come through here, with all their polytheisms and theisms—because every now and then I'll get a traveler who knows my true God. You know there's a belief among us that all sentient bipeds are descended from one ancient ancestor people? We have a legend that the first people were constructing a space elevator to an interdimensional portal, and God saw this tower and scattered the people to all different worlds as we are today."

"Didn't want them united," I grunted. "Yeah, we have that story, too. I always thought that was kind of a dick move. They just wanted to get to heaven or some shit, right?"

Yako smiled. "They were too powerful united, Captain," he said. "They would have made it to his realm, and they would have instantly perished from the radiation. We cannot hope to meet God while we are demons." He grabbed a rag now, and wiped the grease off the rod he'd been fashioning, and jammed it into a gear'd contraption with a grunt. "That is why we need an

Anointed One, a bridge soul, to transmute our nature through his and allow God to turn to us. Then we can traverse his realms."

"Hm. We have that story, too." I swirled the dregs of my tea to get all the green powder into one last gulp, sucked it down, and stood. This conversation was making my chest itch for some reason, and I was remembering Skinner suddenly. "Well, I'll give your proposal some thought, commander. I'd better hit the sack."

He waved me off. "Consider joining me tomorrow for the peace conference. If we do end up working together, I'd like you to have an in-depth understanding of how we operate."

"Fair enough."

Silvie bumped her head against my shin as we walked out of the workshop into the cool night air and let out a little complaining mrowl. "I know," I said. "I want to go home, too. I just don't know where that is."

My chest was so tight, and there was a tremor to my hands that I didn't want to deal with. I glanced over towards the medical tent—it was about a street down, to my left, shining light from its open front flap out onto the vehicles parked out front. Thinking about Ken dealing with whatever he had to be feeling about Galaxy Aid and the Sevellans had my hand hesitating before it went for the benzos in my pocket. I knew what I'd tell him if he were me. *You gotta stop. You gotta get a real medical eval, get on an SNRI and a psych antihistamine or some shit. Prazosin for the nightmares. Benzos and amphetamines, kid? You don't have seizures, or ADHD. You know that's not indicated for you.*

But the difference between medications, and drugs, is that medications don't give you that little benefit of knowing you're kind of killing yourself slowly—punishing yourself for how hard you fail. Ken shouldn't do drugs because he was still worth something. Me? The health risk was literally part of the draw here. Sometimes it feels good getting stepped on when you're in control.

And maybe that was why these people couldn't quit their leaders and their wars, either. Maybe self-destruction was part of the draw.

"Nah. Being too philosophical and making things too complicated," I said to my Scrit. She mrowled in what I could only assume was agreement.

My hand hovered by my pocket. I was right about not being good enough. People could pump me up with false compliments if they wanted—not that I got a lot of those, with how antisocial I was—but I knew who and what I was.

That is why we need an Anointed One to transmute our nature.

Emmanuel to walk with us.

It's a lot harder to rely on slow, invisible people than a little pill I can hold in my hand.

CHAPTER SEVENTEEN

Ken Kamakura

KEN SOUGHT out Sibila as soon as he could and as often as he could in between running errands for the minimals. That was what they really were—all the serious injuries had been stabilized, and what was left to do was essentially the errand-work of finding various medications every few hours, or checking vitals and measurements now and then, or comfort-care-type activities like bringing water to the Sevellans chained to stretchers as the hospital Scrit bounded behind his ankles. In medicine, the work was never actually done, which made it a huge dopamine drain for the people who got their hits by *finishing* things—people like Ken who didn't like to take breaks.

But medicine was also a great place to hide from the quiet of thinking, and guilt. When you literally didn't have time to pee, you didn't have time to bleed inside. Sibila kind of counted as a patient, so Ken could stop every now and then and offer her a drink, or ask her if she needed anything. Most of the time she told him no, which was kind of annoying, if he was honest—*let me do something for you, dammit—*

"What if you let me help you?" she asked finally, the tenth time he passed her cot. "Then we can be together while you work."

"That's not why—" Ken cut himself off. No, it would absolutely be a lie to say that wasn't why he kept stopping by her, he realized. "Wow. Am I that transparent?"

She laughed. "It's rather charming."

He shook his head. He was annoyed with himself for not noticing his own behavior. "It's dangerous, is what it is," he said. "Everything I do should be by triage, order of need. I shouldn't be prioritizing patients I like better."

"But I'm not a patient. There's nothing wrong with me," Sibila said.

"Sure you are, the cut on your head still isn't completely gone," he answered. "That's why I was asking you about headaches earlier."

She pouted out her lower lip and placed her fists on her hips. "And if my cut were healed, Kenta Kamakura, then you couldn't talk to me?" she asked.

He pursed his lips. "You know what, it's a good idea for you to help me."

"Mmhmm. I thought so."

So Ken started to give Sibila the little easy tasks that didn't require any training, and that way they passed the rest of the evening *together*. The Yadan guards posted here and there through the hospital tent were actually quite helpful, and Ken didn't particularly *need* an assistant, but there was always some kind of work to do, and Sibila could talk to the patients who, at this moment, wanted nothing more than to stab Ken in the eye. He didn't exactly want to expose her to their wrath, either, but at least she spoke their language—every now and then the hospital's Scrit kept wandering off and making it hard for him to communicate.

And he trusted Sibila with the prisoners more than he trusted the Yada, even though really none of the guards had done anything to give him pause. It was just that, after the hundredth time of being called a ‘bitch’ and a ‘whore’ and hearing the next creative insult about how so and so might punish her sexually, Rachaba the tent director—a tall, broad-shouldered woman with bright orange eyes—seemed like she might snap. And after seeing her break a metal bar with her bare hands when some of the medical equipment needed unpacking, Ken didn’t need to imagine what would happen to whatever Sevellan finally wore out her patience. They’d totally deserve it, too, but best to keep everyone’s faces and knuckles separate if he could.

There were some people Ken didn’t want Sibila around. He almost didn’t want to check on the Sevellan his mind still called “chest-wound guy” at all—part of him regretted shooting the man on stun instead of kill. It was kind of a gray area. Ken’s personal code firmly held no one deserved to die who hadn’t killed or raped someone else—you couldn’t be killing people for thoughts or things they said—and you couldn’t even kill murderers unless law and proof gave you the authority, because there was always the off-chance you were wrong, or acting on emotion, or missing something important like self-defense or coercion. The guy had intended to kill Sibila, but if you flipped that code from chest-wound guy’s point of view, Sibila had killed someone, so she deserved to die. He’d even waited for orders, sticking within the authority of law. So—just because he was a dick didn’t really make Ken feel comfortable wiping him off the face of Eden Crescent.

Still, Ken had really only fired on stun to protect Sibila in case he missed—and because it was faster than switching over to kill when he’d already had the gun set for Sereno.

And if he was going to give Sereno a pass—Sereno who had actively been trying to murder him for literally acting on his authority—he couldn’t justify killing chest-wound guy.

Also, it’d been so much work saving the guy’s life in the first place from that first injury back at the landing zone! If he died—oh man.

These were the thoughts wrestling back and forth in Ken's mind as he checked chest-wound guy's pulse, oxygen saturation, and blood pressure, and peeled back the gauze to look at the original wound. A Yadan guard held the patient's head still for Ken so chest-wound guy couldn't bite him, and it didn't take Ken long to see the wound hadn't dehisced. They'd done good work.

"Why don't you answer me? Are you afraid of me?" the chest-wound guy sneered. "I see you. I know there can only be two reasons you kept me alive twice. Either you're too weak to do what needs doing, or you have some twisted plan for me as your greatest rival. Your little whore pretends she doesn't, but I know she likes me."

Ken had to think lightning-fast to keep his pulse-checking fingers from clenching down painfully on the blood vessels in the patient's wrist. *No. I'm better than that.* "Rival?" he laughed. "Guy, I don't even know your name. I kept you alive because I didn't want to waste all the hard work Captain Wimmer did patching you up. I'm trapped in the Sunk Cost Fallacy." Ken closed the bandage and tapped it. "These cost money. You owe the world now. Like I said out in the field today, you better come up with something useful to do with your life."

"I do plenty of useful things," the patient snapped.

"Do you? I've watched you for two weeks, and so far, I've only seen you throw insults at people braver than you, panic and run in combat, and almost kill someone over a situation you actually don't know anything about." He wanted to convert this idiot, to show him how *wrong* he was—about the Grandfather's crimes, about the opportunity now for freedom, about how Sibila had really liberated their people—but that would only conflict with her story about Bantai manipulation and make it easier to implicate Sereno. And she hadn't planned to liberate anyone.

She'd just wanted to protect her brother. So he confined himself to a parting shot, and walked off: "The way I see it, if you want to be worth the materials it took to keep you alive you've got some work to do."

The Yada guard grinned as he and Ken left. "What's your name, medic?" he asked.

"Kamakura," Ken said.

"I'm Benjamno," said the Yadan. He had rather striking blue and black marks across his skin—*weird that he's not gray-green like everyone else right now. Is it a skin condition? Or is he like wearing something his skin is somehow syncing with?* Ken felt it'd be rude to ask, and when the medic laid his hand on his shoulder, he thought the guy was going to tell him something about himself anyway. But: "The Sevella leader's rubbed his wrists raw against the restraints. I was thinking you probably wanted some antibiotic ointment or something to prevent an infection—it's awful moist and gross under those shackles. We can probably get something soft under the restraints, too, so he doesn't deglove himself in his effort to slip out."

Ken lit up; Benjamno's attitude gave him hope. Some people really did care. He accepted the thin, hard tube of ultramycin ointment from Benjamno and took a bouncy step towards the cot at the far end of the minimals tent, where Sereno lay fists clenched, staring up at the ceiling.

Sibila intercepted him and slipped her warm hand into his, wrapping her fingers around the ointment. "Let me do it," she said.

Ken looked down at the tube. "You think they're poisoning him or something?" He went to open the tube—

She took it from him. "No. It's sealed, see? And I know this bottle. Anyway, when they want to kill us, they have no reason not to do it openly. You are a limited audience. No." She stepped back from him. "He does not want to talk to you."

Anger heated Ken's chest—*why do I care what he thinks?*

Stop it. "That's fine," he said. He sounded colder than he intended.

"Is it fine? I think it sad," she said. "He does not want to talk to me, either, but people will understand if I attend him anyway, even as a traitor. You, on the other hand, would be expected to be hostile. You cannot be friends."

"I'm so tired of this social game. He should just admit, at this point, that the Grandfather was—" Ken interrupted himself with a sigh. "I'll keep playing along as long as you tell me to, but I'm tired of it, Sibila."

"Well, you have only just started," she raised an eyebrow much like her brother's. "Even if you leave this planet, we are family now—after all, only a father, or a trade herself, has the authority to reject a buy-out. And I saw you empty your pockets with the Yada when you arrived—" She lowered her voice; her eyes flickered to the floor for a moment. "So you need only pay Sereno now to claim your prize."

Ken scowled. He hated that phrase; the idea of her as anyone's property disgusted him. "What does he want me to pay?" he snapped. "How about saving his life today from the Yada—that not good enough for him? How about three weeks of free medical care, did that not count for anything? What does it take for them to let you go?"

She stepped back from him, blinking. "I—I suppose I can ask him."

"Great. Thank you." Ken whirled and stalked off. He still had patients whose q4 "every four hours" vitals he wanted to note down, and he was done with non-patient interactions right now.

BY THE TIME Ken slowed down enough to find Sibila at her cot, she was already asleep. His shoulders dropped—he was disappointed—but he knew he should have expected this. After all, while he might feel responsible for people's well-being, helping bury bodies and load crates definitely had nothing to do with him, and at some point, all his helpfulness was stalling. He literally stopped working because it was starting to look obvious.

"Didn't you get, like, married today or something?" Howard had asked the fourth time he passed her table.

"I have no idea," Ken lied, focusing his attention on balancing the crates in his hands with the bags dangling off his arms. Rachaba had wanted someone to restock the Sevellan medical truck they'd captured.

Howard followed him outside this time. "You don't *know* if you're married? Shouldn't you check?"

"Look, I don't know what everyone wants from me," he said. "She can do what she wants. I just want her to be okay."

"So this was purely altruistic," Howard narrowed her eyes. "You have no feelings for her."

"Of course I have feelings for her, who doesn't? Are you stupid?" Ken kicked the closed truck door as if he could knock it open with his toes—it definitely didn't work that way, and Howard opened it for him with a smirk.

"Sergeant. 'Are you stupid, *sergeant*,'" she corrected him.

"I'm fired remember?" He shoved the boxes inside so hard they slammed against the far wall. "I don't report to you."

Howard crossed her arms. "I wonder if these little fits you throw are cute to her," she mused. "I'd think they were hot if they weren't so dumb. What do you mean, *who doesn't* have feelings for her? Most people. Most people don't, you goof. What, you think just because she's a prostitute, she's in high demand or something?"

"She's not a—fine. She is that," Ken said. "And maybe that's why I don't know if I'm 'married.' Because I'm pretty sure all she knows is transaction. And that's not what I want." He slammed the door shut. "Like I said, I just want her to be okay."

"So you're still on the market, then." Howard said it like a challenge—not a statement or a question. It didn't sound like an invitation, either. "You're going to fly right away from here and find someone else."

"No." Ken started to step around her to get back inside—she stepped in his way, backing up with her palms towards him in the 'stop' motion so as not to bump into him.

"Okay, then, word of advice?" Howard asked, and then answered herself before he could assent or protest. "From a single mom with a lot of experience needing help and not getting it. Sure, I can take care of myself. I don't need to be loved, to be rescued. But that doesn't mean I don't want to be. It's easier sometimes to make things feel like a transaction up top because then I'm not surprised or disappointed when it turns out I'm not worth the trouble." She dropped her hands. "I kind of couldn't help overhearing your uh—outburst—about Sereno owing you. Just telling you right now, it probably sounded to her like you were saying she's not worth that much."

"That's ridiculous," Ken started to say.

"You're the guy who's all culturally-attuned or whatever," Howard shrugged. "And I don't really care either way. But seems to me her 'price' is literally a measure of her worth, to the point that in normal circumstances she'd be well within her rights to turn down a buyer who rates her too low. Love's a language that's sometimes communicated in cost instead of words."

"I hate that."

"Okay. And?" Howard laughed. "If that's how she communicates? She's got to just change her savage ways and be like you?"

"I don't think I'm better than her," he grumbled. "I'm right though. She shouldn't have to think that way."

"Good job being right," Howard whacked him on the arm. "I'm right, too, which is why I'm not out here marrying random Sevellan chicks. But you'd better let her know pretty quick if she's wrong and it's not real. Don't be a dick and screw around, Mr. Right."

Ken started to argue further, but Howard laughed, and walked off, waving Tack and Bones after her.

And so Ken now stood above Sibila in the corner of the triage tent, his assault pack dangling from his hand, disappointed because he didn't get to see her violet eyes, and concerned because he really did need to talk to her. What she said would one hundred percent determine who left with Howard in the morning or not, and that was kind of a huge decision.

Should he wake her up?

It would be so sad to wake her, though. The way Wimmer's shirt fell off Sibila's shoulder framed a proud, elegant collarbone that pointed down towards the space just above her chest, suggesting a perfect hiking path for fingers to trace above the hills of her breasts that rolled almost imperceptibly up and down with the soft breath that parted and fluttered her full lips ever so slightly—

Ken found his own breath held, and it seemed like he'd never get it back if he didn't breathe hers.

Easy, there, man. Take a seat.

But he couldn't get his breath back. As he shifted to sit on the cot that lay across from hers, his shadow fell over Sibila and she woke up.

"Come to claim your prize now?" she asked.

Ken's lower core died. All the soft glow of the moment withered and shriveled and shrunk and died, as if the room had been lit in candlelight when a cold wind blew out the flames and harsh, ugly fluorescent lights now radiated everything in stark sterility.

"Ugh—you have no idea what a turn off that is for me," Ken said. He unzipped his assault pack and pulled out the last of the MREs he'd taken with him at the end of his time in service. "I didn't see you eat dinner. I've been saving this to share."

"Oh…" Sibila sat up and—*oh no*—adjusted her shirt, hiding that perfect shoulder. Ken tore his eyes away from her and towards the MRE bag as he opened it. Space-capable MREs came in tubes and gels to account for low-grav environments: this was a surface MRE, with actual pouches of textured food, and a little chemical heater, and it was salty, umami ground Bovie with small pasta shapes, a favorite recipe designed kind of in homage to some of the earliest and best soldier foods of ancient Old Terra. Good stuff.

But Sibila was watching Ken, not the bag; her eyes flitted from Ken's hands to his face. "Why are you angry with me?"

The way she said it seemed so matter-of-fact, so pure, Ken felt like he was melting inside. "You? Why would I be mad at you?" he laughed softly. "No—it—how do I say this." He turned his eyes up to the ceiling for a second as if he could read the words up there. "I just hate the implication that I owe Sereno something," he said, finding her gaze again.

"Am I too expensive?"

"No! You're not property, you shouldn't have to—" But he realized in her downcast eyes that Howard was right: he was misunderstanding what this meant for her. "I would pay much more for you. But that's for you, not for him." He suddenly wanted so badly to grab her hands and press her palms to his chest, to beat his heart against her touch, to cradle some small part of her, because he honestly couldn't even afford a finger of what she was really worth. He kept the thought and his hands to himself. He *couldn't* touch her, not if she didn't know there was no duress, no financial requirement, no owing, no pressure—he *needed* her full desire and consent. He needed her to want him, to crave him, for himself. *I'm not just your out.* "You don't owe me anything."

"What if—what if I want to owe you something?" Sibila asked. "When you asked me what I wanted in a buyer, I thought you understood that I want… you."

"But that's hard to be sure about," he said, fingers rustling and creaking through the biodegradable plastic of the MRE bag to find the pouch for the main course. His mother definitely wouldn't approve of him running off and falling for some alien. But that didn't make him want it less. He *shouldn't* do it, maybe, but wasn't "should" a thought distortion? The GI who runs off to war and falls in love with a foreigner was a tale as old as time, as storied a classic as the legend of the faithful lover waiting at home. "You've only known me for three weeks," he made himself say.

"Is—that important to you?" Sibila tilted her head. "Is there some kind of required courtship period in your culture?"

"Man, fuck my culture," Ken heard himself say. It was such an uncharacteristic spurt of aggression he startled, and looked up —Sibila laughed at his surprised face, and he found himself chuckling, too. "Wow, uh. What I mean to say is, we're on Eden Crescent now. We're on Sevellan land now, or at least—at least Edenian land." Something inside him winced—he knew that was the wrong thing to say, but he could see so clearly now how all peoples here really did have claims to their homes, and really did *need*—ugh. There were no right answers.

But to his surprise, Sibila's face didn't harden. "You would have fallen in love with the Yadans, if you had met them first," she said. "I am lucky we stole you." Her hands pressed against the wrinkles in Wimmer's shirt and pants—wrinkles that hadn't been there before she fell asleep in the uniform—as she looked down at herself. "I know I cannot go home. I will not become Yadan, nor do I accept their occupation of our homes, but I know I would need to at least accept the people themselves if we stayed here, and, in any case, I begin to see living out my days with my hated enemy would at least bring me less physical pain than living with the Bantai. Spiritual pain, I cannot say."

"We don't have to stay here," Ken said. He hesitated—he actually found himself dreading the idea of leaving the planet:

"We can—go with Howard, I guess. Try to find a freighter to work on or something. I think that's what I'm expected to do."

"I think I expect you to stay with the doctor," Sibila said. "She needs your help."

"Well, but I mean, this was my job first, not hers." Ken tilted his head. "Yeah, we work well together, and I guess she can't get even half as much done without me—technically I'm her assistant—but she kind of came along to help me, not the other way around."

"But you would be fine without her," Sibila said. "She would not be fine without you."

"That's not true at all," Ken laughed. "We would've been screwed on our own at the oasis, you and I, without her taking care of us. TBIs are serious, I wouldn't have been able to fix myself."

"That is not what I mean." Sibila laid her hands firmly on her knees with a little pat and literally put her foot down, as if decided. "We should stay with Captain Wimmer. She will know who to work for, and she knows more of the healing arts than you do, so you can become more effective and earn more. And I will need to be useful, and you and I have no camp to tend, or children—I don't think we even *can* have them, a Terran and an Edenian—so I could learn from her, too, and perhaps I could even work with you both."

"Most commercial flights will probably want evidence of formal education before they hire you, though," Ken winced. "It's not so—it's not just about skill. Unless we worked for pirates or something."

"Captain Wimmer is not going on a commercial flight," Sibila said. "The Yadan guards made it sound like she will be staying here. There are legal questions about whether or not I can even leave this planet anyway—you know, with all the paper-work of the Terran Union and other giant nations out there in space."

"I think you'd be fine, but we'd get around the paperwork if we needed to," Ken said. He was more interested in knowing: "Did Wimmer actually say anything to you about her staying here?"

"No. I think she is trying to give us time alone—we can talk with her about it in the morning. They won't leave without you. I think secretly they're all jealous of you."

"Why, because I'm the only one who comes out of this mess with a hot wife?" he quipped. It was a joke, and one he instantly regretted. He sighed and ran his hand over his face. "Listen to me, making all these plans with you—I'm such an idiot. I don't even know if we're really—"

"Sereno accepted your terms," Sibila cut him off. "I have the bill of sale here."

She dug under the pillow for a sheet of that plastic-like, tough paper, inked in red. Ken realized suddenly he was at a pretty big legal disadvantage. "I can't read it."

"It has the signature of the Yadan leader, who took your payment for the Bantai, as a responsible party, and my brother's signature—here it says 'a life for a life.'" She pointed. "Normally for a sister you love you're supposed to ask for a price increase after the first offer, but of course he did not."

"But he couldn't, not in front of everyone else in the minimals tent," Ken protested. "He can't look too attached after you outed yourself."

"I know this." Sibila's face scrunched. It wasn't quite a scowl, but it was close. "I am not pretending to be worth the risk."

"I'll pay more," Ken jumped in. "You're worth whatever risk—whatever you say, I'll pay."

She narrowed her eyes. "For—what, exactly? You'd pay whatever I say for what?"

"For your freedom."

"Oh." She grumbled to the floor. "Is that all."

Ken wasn't an idiot. He could almost hear Wimmer or Howard yelling in his ear: *"She wants you, you numbskill! Grab her and kiss her already!"* And he wasn't insecure enough to think he wasn't good enough for her, or that an alien princess couldn't fall for him.

He just really wanted to be sure. It was almost a power move as much as it was fact-checking—he craved her craving and wanted to hear her say it first.

But she needed help. He took her hand, rubbing her small rough fingers between his thumb and forefinger. "You know, freedom includes choosing who you give your freedom to," he said. "I notice no one asked me to sign this paper—I'm assuming my payment is my signature. Where's yours?"

"My—signature—is an action," she said. "But I don't know if you want that action… I mean, I know you find me attractive, so I think maybe you don't want it because you know for us that action would mean I'm yours forever. We don't have hundreds of life partners like Terrans do. We have one. Outside the trades there is no pairing and divorcing and pairing and divorcing. Even battle guards must stop, once they buy. And maybe you know that, and don't want… maybe you don't want me forever."

Her voice as she said forever was tiny.

Ken stood, still holding her hand. He was suddenly quite sure what he wanted, and privacy was urgent. He wanted to wrap his arms around her tiny "forever" and breathe into her breath, her life in his, so his wouldn't stay trapped in his throat without purpose. There was a physical ache building within him to *prove* to her what she was worth to him, to speak whatever language she needed, whether that was pay or touch, and if it was touch, he wanted to find ways to touch her that none of the worthless people she'd been with so far had ever dared—to draw gasps and cries from her lips that for the first time were fully *hers.* And that would take time. It might take forever, in fact. He needed to start immediately, and the satisfaction that he wanted—the words he needed her to say—he wouldn't make her say in the corner of a crowded medical tent.

"Come," he said. Something about his own command tone sounded almost Sevellan to him suddenly. "I'll show you what I want."

She followed him outside mutely, carrying the half-open MRE bag in her other hand. His assault-pack dangled from one shoulder as he looked around the outside street, ducking through the medical tent entrance with the furtive eyes of someone hunting cover from a sniper. The painted medical truck where he'd tended to her before sat parked outside—it wasn't the classiest rendezvous point, but forever was a long time: there would be other places to speak with her, and right now if he didn't taste her breath soon, he might suffocate. He kept a firm grip on her hand as he opened the back door, swung his pack and her MRE inside, and then hoisted her by the hips up to sit in front of him on the loading platform.

She was panting. Even in the moonlight he could see that translucent pulse thrashing by her throat. He held her there, hands on her hips, as she clutched his forearms, her fingers almost clawing at his skin to pull him close to her. Their bodies were only an arm's length apart but it felt like kilometers.

"Say what would make you happy, Sibila," he ordered, maintaining that painful distance between them. "Say what would make you happy and I'll give it to you forever."

"It would make me happy to—" She choked on her words. Her purple eyes were glowing, actually glowing in the dark, and her chest was heaving so hard tears began to spring to her cheeks. "I'm sorry," she said suddenly. "You're the only one who asks me this."

He waited. The ache burned, but he waited. The slow, intense pounding in his chest echoed into his head and lower core like his whole body had become one dizzy pulse, screaming that if he didn't get his skin against hers soon the world would end—but he waited.

"Please hold me," she begged.

"Answer my question first," he whispered, bringing his mouth forward to tease his lips against her forehead. He was right between her legs but *so far away*…

"It would make me happy to stay with someone like you forever," she squeaked.

He stepped back. "Someone *like* me?" he interrogated.

"No," she said. "Just you."

Still he held the distance. "And who am I?"

"I know you said I've only known you for three weeks, but I see you, Kenta Kamakura," she trembled. Her left hand reached for his face, gracing his jaw with the lightest touch as her glowing eyes pulsed and her right hand gripped his forearm tighter. "I saw you from the first when you were tightening that horrid thing around my leg to stop the bleeding, and it was the most terrible pain I've ever felt, before or since, but I saw your jaw and your eyes and even when the silly Scrit ran off and I couldn't understand what you were saying I knew you would save me, and not just me, but us, because I saw that inflicting pain hurt you and you did it anyway, no hesitation, because you *knew* you were right to do it." Ken's face pressed down against his shoulder to trap her hand against his cheek; he was falling into her caress, and his feet drew him closer to her just a step. Her thighs squeezed against his hips— "You were like that with Grandfather, too," Sibila added.

His arms held him steady. "That's what I did, not who I am," he said.

"We know trees by their fruit, Kamakura," Sibila begged. "Of course I would love you for what you do!"

"Love?" he smiled.

"Yes, I love you!" she cried. "And I know who you are, I know where you come from, and what you like, and what you don't like, and how you grew up, but all of that is just talk anyone can lie about! I've seen who you really are. Love is action, and you are more to me than the alien from Alpha Prime who's never had a birthday, you're *my* alien, *my* tree, and I want to taste your damn fruit so come here and—"

"You want to taste my *what*?" Ken chuckled through what almost became a moan as Sibila pulled his chest against hers and electric tingles shot through every particle of his being that had contact with her, and every bit of him that didn't ached with painful jealousy.

But the hospital Scrit had wandered out of range, and suddenly Ken heard Sibila's voice in a language he didn't know, cooing purrs and desperate consonants thick with hunger, and she was right, and he was convinced. They would both die one day. It could be years from now, it could be tomorrow, but they would both die, and there was so little time in which to love, and just the *spending* that lifetime—just the learning about each other and *staying* as time marched on—that was a kind of love, too, a defining, proving action that wrapped up all the gifting and smiling and healing and helping each other around the house and whatever other actions would come with them, and every Scrit in the Universe could die and they would still understand each other as long as they spoke that language. And the sooner they began speaking, the better.

"I love you, too," he whispered, burying his face into her neck as he let her wrap herself around him and begin to soothe the ache. "But we'll need to be careful of your leg, okay?" He climbed up into the truck with her clinging to him like she might fall into the deepest abyss of damnation if she let him go, and finally, *finally* as he crushed her against him, one hand gripping her bare back and the other tangled in the hair at the nape of her neck, his mouth found hers, and he could breathe.

CHAPTER EIGHTEEN

Jocelyn Wimmer

It was just as well, I thought, when the first explosion went off. This story would be boring if it was just Ken's cute little alien romance instead of my drugged-out adventure of death and destruction.

I woke up sore and shaky, groggy like I had a hangover and disappointed in myself as always—but clean. It was the first night since my discharge that I hadn't taken benzos to go to sleep, and it'd been a rough night. Lots of nightmares and rolling around waiting for the nightmares, and, also for the first time in ages, lots of praying. And crying. *Lots* of crying and other fucking embarrassing shit like that. I didn't wake up to the explosion, either. I was already up as the sunrise peered through the slats in the hut where I was staying, wrestling through my weary head with memories of liturgy and questions about the divine—and then it was time for some poor souls to meet him.

When the explosion kicked off, I was out of my bedroll and loading the rifle I'd gotten from the Grandfather before Howard could call me. I heard her voice over the radio—and Yako's too

—in between jamming my feet into my boots and tightening my belt buckle like it was strangling someone, fast, shortsword slapping my thigh.

Of course, the Bantai had bombed the meeting site for the peace summit.

And of course, Yako had expected that, and sent holograms instead.

Of course, the Yada had already evacuated their kids the day before.

And of course, the only people who'd died in the first blast were the Bantai delegates and leader, who lo and behold, had actually wanted peace, and got taken out by their underlings.

"All this double-crossing's starting to give me a headache," I muttered.

"You sure that's not alcohol giving you that headache?" Howard quipped back over my comms. "I just realized yesterday the first time I saw you wasn't at the launch pad. You looked so different I didn't recognize you from Kamakura's interview."

"Yeah yeah, laugh it up. What's going on?"

"It's crazy," Howard said. She'd gotten up bright and early for the peace summit with Yako and now spoke to me from an underground observation room watching the city on cameras. "We can literally see them mocking their dead leader with the radio off, and then when the radio's on it's all *oh, curse the Yada who double-crossed our brave leader when he desired peace.*"

"Sounds about right," I grunted. "There are whole sagas here that we're not even players in."

I had a habit of sleeping in my personal slipsuit—the custom military-grade uniform we wore under armor in space—so I was already pretty much out the door within seconds of the blast. It wasn't great camouflage, but I'd lent Sibila my fatigues before we reached the oasis figuring it wasn't like they'd help me much here, anyway, where I'd almost be better off colored purple or sandy-pink or blue-gray than mottled green. I hadn't counted on a city in the woods.

Shit. The smoking amphitheater lay between me and my destination. I could see Bantai warriors milling about and starting to spread through the streets. Anxiety stirred in my stomach. I wasn't much of a shot and I was by myself. There was a *lot* of cover, though, and they were going to find me pretty quick anyway if I stayed here in this hut wrapped around the trees. I left the door open behind me—no point in making noise shutting it—and crept forward to crouch behind the first twisted rocky column, wedging myself between it and the nearest house.

"Wimmer," Howard asked in my earpiece. "Where are you going?"

"Hospital tent," I murmured.

"Why?"

"There a reason I shouldn't? How are you seeing me, anyway?"

"You're on a street with a camera," Howard said.

I twisted my head over my shoulder—I couldn't see the camera, but I guessed they'd installed it on the corner of the house where I'd slept. Didn't matter anyway. I kept my head low and looked for my next hiding spot: the big tree right next to me. I could probably follow this line of ironwood trees and stone around the clearing, right down the street to the medical center. *Crossing* the bare street to get to the hospital tent would be a problem, but—I'd cross that bridge when I got there. Literally.

"You should know there's a Yada ambush waiting around the amphitheater," Howard said. "Yako wants you to stay put until it takes off so you're not in the way."

"I can probably do that," I said, still creeping through the narrow space between the trees and this house.

"I can see you *not* doing that," Howard said.

"They can't friendly-fire me from this spot," I said. "I need to get to the hospital tent."

"They're evacuating the hospital tent as we speak. There's a basement under there. It'll be fine."

It'll be fine. They'd said that the morning Skinner died, too. I'd obeyed orders then, and people had died. I'd argued a lot, but I'd obeyed.

Now my policy was not to argue, and not to obey. "I'll stay put," I said. "If I get killed being stupid it's my fault. Tell Yako to do what he needs to do."

"He says to ask if you've got a saying about multitudes of counselors… whatever that means."

In a multitude of counselors, there is wisdom. "Yeah. I've got a few sayings like that. Tell him in my experience it depends on the counselors."

"He says don't listen to just one." Howard sounded annoyed. I could hear her turning away from the comm desk to talk to someone behind her. "Is this what passes for flirting for old people? What's going on?"

He's probably waiting until enough Bantai gather in the field of ambush—probably the amphitheater's the center. The Yada must be all around me.

I knew what he was saying. My own council wasn't enough. My own experience wasn't enough. I couldn't flip to an extreme just because the other extreme screwed me over—just because it all went to shit listening to someone else before didn't mean it was going to do that now. A multitude of counselors, not just one or two past events.

But everything *was* all going to go to shit. I could feel it was. *I lost all of them.* The ones who didn't die never spoke to me again. I could smell blood, and engine fuel, and melting medical kits, and feel sweat trailing down my spine, and Skinner's wrist spasm around mine. Everyone was going to die. I knew the past, so of course I knew the future, too.

Stop it. I knew I was being crazy but couldn't prove myself wrong. My knees started to shake—they shouldn't. I was used to crouching this long. The smoke wafting to me in the air carried the scent of roasting wood and smelled disturbingly like a barbecue. I could see through the gap between this stone obelisk, and this tree, over to the amphitheater now—

"Howard, some of these Bantai look familiar," I said. "Do you recognize the modified female, with the breastplate—the short, wide one? The three pleasure guards with that group are the Sevellans they took with Sibila."

"Yeah, Yako says they were at the Galaxy Aid massacre, too. I didn't recognize them then, but he says they were there. We can hear them on the cameras closer to the square—they're looking for Sereno." Howard started to *"told you so"*—I could tell, to her, this scene had the makings of a rescue attempt to free Sereno, and *that* definitely made it look like the Sevellans and the Bantai had worked together to slaughter Galaxy Aid. But I waited. I knew what I'd overheard: Sereno hadn't wanted those pleasure guards to leave for the Bantai that day. Maybe he'd had more reasons than just Sibila's safety. I heard some rustling, and some static— "Holy shit," Howard realized. "They're here to assassinate him. The Bantai don't want him in charge and apparently a bunch of Sevellans agree. Hold on, Yako's sending a contingent to the hospital now. Just let the ambush pass first."

Let the ambush pass first? Ken would die before he let someone kill his stupid dictator friend—and my path was plenty hidden between the treeline and the houses. I didn't stop advancing. Next column. There, a fence… I could make it to the hospital first. Why should I let the ambush pass first? I wasn't even heading towards the line of fire. If the Bantai got there before I did, they'd kill Ken. They'd torch the flimsy Role II and kill everyone in it while he tried to save patients who hated him. He would die, Sibila would die—I saw jam on his forehead and no way was I going to wait and let the ambush pass first.

"Jocelyn," Howard whispered, trying not to alert Yako to

what she saw me still doing. "What would you tell Ken right now?"

"Fucking dammit," I spat. I couldn't fight with that.

"I know." It was the sweetest tone I'd ever heard from her. "I know, Jocelyn. I'm sorry."

Fucking—*damn her.* I'd made Ken obey orders so saving one guy didn't endanger a bunch of other people. But I could trust the science, then—trust my training, trust what I knew about backdrafts, and see that the orders made sense. I couldn't trust right now. I didn't know these people. I knew Yako mystically and authentically believed in my Rabbi's God, I knew Howard would go to great lengths to keep her people alive, and I also knew Yako killed the wounded and Howard looked down on poor people. I knew my commander had once seen a soldier kill himself in front of him—blaming him for it as he pulled the trigger—and my commander didn't want to feel that weakness he'd felt then ever again, and I knew my commander *was* weak, and listened to all the wrong people because he wanted to be strong. Trusting any sentient being other than yourself was actually insane. Charismatic schemers could turn out to be raving lunatic racists; drunk kids could start wars.

I couldn't even trust myself. I'd been wrong, too. I'd obeyed, and people died. And unlike what I made Ken do, when I'd obeyed people died for no reason. That pilot's death meant a dozen other people lived. My medic's death meant more people died, because then I was alone, and alone, I was not enough.

And I was alone now, and not enough now.

I had them in my sleeve. The slipsuit's supposed to be too tight for that, but I had a little pouch under the sleeve where I kept the envelope. They might make my brain work. They might make the world make sense.

I stopped moving.

"Get lower," Howard whispered.

I got lower. I sat my ass on the ground. I wasn't really stopping, I told myself—not really obeying. I was going to get my fucking amphetamines loaded in and then I'd keep going.

As soon as I sat down blinding plasma shots blasted *from the building beside me* across the square. "Holy shit you could've said they were in there!" I yelled into my comms as the air zinged with blue heat just like it had yesterday in the grove.

"I didn't know!" she shouted back. Firepower from every direction bathed the amphitheater and surrounding streets in light; I almost couldn't hear her over the shrieks of the guns. "Yako was busy telling other people things, he just said for you to wait and get low! There's apparently a whole unit of Third approaching from the Northwest, and what looks like Sevellans from the Southwest—he's getting on a general frequency now to talk to them and *also* coordinating an ambush *and* the soldiers rushing the hospital so forgive me for not just putting him on the line to explain his every move to you!"

"I know! You're fine. Thank you. You're the best!" I couldn't find enough grateful words for her. Shit, I was such an idiot. I couldn't be trusted to make decisions anymore. I was so stuck rebelling against the past I couldn't *think*. And I'd stopped out of addiction, not wisdom? Man, fuck me.

The journey to recovery starts with just one step, and a lot of stumbling, I would've told Ken, had he been me.

I steeled my jaw, shifted my shortsword to my backside, and began to crawl. My goal with my remaining life was to make sure he'd never *be* me. And to start with that, he had to stay alive.

Ken Kamakura

Back in the hospital tent orange-eyed, broad-shouldered Rachaba shouted orders in a command voice as solid as an ironwood tree itself the moment the first explosion went off.

"Ambulatory patients will assist soldiers in carrying stretchers to the basement!" she thundered. "Prisoners be advised that walking beside each of your cots will be a soldier aiming my favorite PW93C center mass! Do not try anything if you plan to see tomorrow, understood?"

Ken had already been up taking vitals and coordinating diets for various patients, his every step jaunty, as if the touch of the morning sun itself energized him every time its rays caught him through the tent windows. He was focused on his chosen tasks, but his chosen tasks always involved passing Sibila on the way, brushing the edge of her hand with his, and feeling that little zing of delight from his skin to his chest. He'd never seen her so happy—almost wickedly happy, with a rebellious little gleam in her eye every time one of her stolen lilac glances met his. There was a confidence, a peace, in the sure movements of her hands and steps as she brought water to her countrymen, and this morning he saw her chuckle, or even quip back, if anyone said anything untoward. Her delightful little sighs made him feel like a magician. *I did that,* wriggled up through his spine like a neodog puppy.

So he was beyond alarm bells—all the way into sirens—when Rachaba nodded two of her soldiers towards Sibila: "Get restraints on that one, too."

"She's with me," Ken stepped in front of her.

"Oh, we all know she's with you, Terran," Rachaba smirked. "I've half a mind to slap cuffs on you, too—I don't know what kind of prison breaks you all cook up when she's playing advanced alien zoology on you. I know she's the leader's sister. Get out of the way."

"What the hell has she done?" Ken protested. "She's a noncombatant—you can search her, she's unarmed!"

"I hear you were unarmed when you took out her brother's

rival," Rachaba retorted. "They're all combatants. I lost my whole crew when a *noncombatant* pleasure guard strapped with bombs set herself off in my camp. We see these people. We've all been listening to their sick threats for a day and a half." She raised her rifle straight towards Ken's chest—shooting panic into his sternum as her stare blazed with spite like Sereno's. "Move."

Ken's eyes darted to Sibila, stomach tightened into a roiling black fist—her pride would never let them take her without a fight, she hated them! Sereno certainly would've rather had death than chains, and if Sibila fought like him, they'd—

To his surprise, she did not.

"You may move—it is fine," Sibila said, stepping out from behind him and extending her wrists. "Let the cowards have their comfort." She flicked her lilac gaze towards her brother's cot. "Go."

Ken gave her a quick nod in return and trotted past the other evacuees towards the chained leader in the far corner of the minimals' tent. He wanted to reassure Sereno, to tell him he'd stay by his side, he wouldn't let anything *accidentally* happen to him during the attack—*he'd* be the one carrying his cot. But he could say nothing—how many Sevellans and Yadans already saw them as closer than they should be?

"Right behind you," a comforting hand found Ken's shoulder. He recognized Benjamno, the blue-streaked Yadan, with a grateful nod. Good to have a friendly helping him carry.

Sereno turned away from Ken with practiced look of disgust as the Terran medic crouched at the foot of his cot. Ken almost smiled. It was weak. Benjamno crouched at the head— "Juda, over here," he called before Ken could count off lifting.

A tiny Yadan female no taller than Ken's chest-height stepped up, rifle raised at Sereno—Ken's gut clenched, but instead of spitting or cursing, Sereno raised a quiet eyebrow with an almost approving twist of his lips. Juda stared straight ahead at her target, not apologetic, not vicious, and somehow not cold either—just focused. Just doing what she had to do. No hard feelings.

"Trust me, Juda's who you want watching your back," Benjamno said. It was hard to tell if he was talking to Ken or Sereno. "One, two, three—lift."

Oh, that's right—the head counts off. Ken had gotten so used to just always being the guy who knew what to do he'd lost the habit of letting anyone else count. But Benjamno was on his game, too.

The other Yadans were also on their game, but the game they were playing, Ken realized, was everybody gets down into evacuation before the Sevellan leader. That was probably why they'd placed him so far away from the trapdoor. Even minimally-injured Yadans were going ahead of totally stretcher-bound Sevellans.

"Hey, Rachaba, didn't you order us to go by regs?" Benjamno called innocently. "Stretchers first, right?"

Rachaba shot him a dirty look; Ken smiled as Benjamno shouldered his way through the group with Sereno in tow. The Sevellan wasn't light, either—Ken was huffing already as they approached the trapdoor—

Rachaba stuck her arm out in front of Benjamno's chest. "He's not injured, just confined. Wounded first." She flashed a black-toothed smile. "Regs."

"Fair enough. Lower on four—one, two, three, lower," Benjamno said, easing to a crouch with Ken.

Ken seethed. He could hear gunfire outside now. Tension rippled through the air. The gunfire was getting closer. Yadans outside opened fire.

"Hurry up!" someone begged.

"Safety first!" shouted Rachaba.

"Shit, she's trying to get them killed," Ken muttered.

"No, she's not," Benjamno soothed. "She's just salty and juggling a lot of people. I've got you both."

The line into the basement was bottle-necking as medics struggled to get stretchers down into the hole — "This is stupid design," Rachaba announced. "Alright, if you're not carrying a stretcher and you're injured, get your ass down into the hole, go go go!"

"She's just trying to get as many people down as possible," Benjamno murmured. "We'll get there."

Ken fidgeted, looking Sereno over. He was definitely going to be last, stretcher-bound *and* uninjured. Ken's fingers tapped around his holster as he crouched, waiting. Should he—

"Don't you dare shoot me to push me up the line, Kenta Kamakura," Sereno snapped.

Ken's guilty hand shot back to the corner of the stretcher. "I'd never dream of it, Grandfather," he said.

"Yes, you would dream of it," Sereno grumbled.

Benjamno chuckled. But as easy as his mood was, his eyes were sharp and his position poised, ready to explode into action, and the moment they could— "One, two, three, lift! Double-time!"—he charged forward with Sereno towards the trapdoor. "You're down first, Kamakura!" He shifted backwards so Ken could angle himself towards the ladder and get Sereno feet-first —they'd prevent bad head injuries from drops this way—

There was screaming. There was screaming outside, really close. Ken's pulse quickened—Benjamno was still crouching up outside the door. He could see the Yadan's silhouette against the square of light turn and look over his shoulder as blue energy blasted towards him—Ken tried to jump the last few rungs—pain shot through his knees—Sereno slipped and yelped, sliding down the ladder as Benjamno dove into the hole to cling upside-down to the ladder and Ken found himself stopping the Sevellan's slide with his body and it was *heavy*—

The second explosion hurled heat down into the basement after the three men. The earth shook, and dust showered the injured down below. Flames whooshed through the tent above—

"Is he alright?" Benjamno shouted, righting himself on the ladder now.

Sereno had slid down the ladder and come to a rest on his back— "I am fine!" he roared, wincing—he'd probably strained something or bruised his spine, Ken thought. "Leave me—there are more of my people in chains up there!"

"I thought we got everybody?" Ken gasped.

Benjamno shook his head and nodded toward Juda. "Cover us?"

"Where's Sibila?" Ken asked, whacking Sereno on the shoulder.

Sereno nodded to the far end of the room where evacuees were being herded into a narrow hallway. Sibila gave Ken a worried look over her shoulder before disappearing after the others. "Get upstairs!" Sereno snapped.

Ken prepped his Mark X and followed Benjamno, scolding himself inwardly. With all his attention on Sereno and the tension around Rachaba, Ken hadn't even noticed anyone behind them. Benjamno and Juda both slipped-on gas-masks—Ken pulled the folded-down "balaclava"-top of his slipsuit up over his nose and mouth.

He'd never been in a fire before—he hadn't been *inside* the flaming area of the ship when they crashed—and Ken was suddenly overwhelmed by the intensity of the heat, blinking against the blinding smoke. He couldn't see—he really couldn't see! It was all he could do to follow Benjamno's hunched form with his eyes squinted as Juda parked below them on the ladder to fire at something else Ken couldn't see in the distance. Screams and grunts—she was doing a good job covering them—

Ken and Benjamno passed three pleasure guards, their Sevellan cloaks pulled up around their faces— "That way!" Ken pointed at the trap door. *Weird that Rachaba didn't force them in chains like she did Sibila—*

It was hard to pay attention to anything but taking one step after another, one detail and the next. Burns, all over this chained Sevellan on the ground—black soot all around his mouth—no pulse. This one, coughing, legs blown off. Two tourniquets high and tight, hoist him with Benjamno, quick-step back to the trapdoor. Maneuvering around Juda—handing him off to the medics still down in the basement—it was mostly all Yadan soldiers in there now, waiting to attack any Bantai forces that followed, with only a few scattered Sevellans like Sereno, and the three pleasure guards—the cool was so refreshing. Ken lowered his balaclava to gulp air—

"You good?" Benjamno asked.

"I'm good." Ken pulled his slipsuit over his face again. Back up the ladder.

Jocelyn Wimmer

I reached the hospital tent before Yako's soldiers did.

The chatter on the radio told me why: every force on the horizon was hostile and Yako had his hands piled full with steaming *shit*. The incoming Third had agreed to support the hated Bantai in this particular campaign as long as the Bantai leader died. That'd happened, and they were now all-too-happy to call a truce and focus for a day or two on the other evil alien-corrupted techno-force they saw ravaging their sacred lands: the Yada. The Sevellan contingent, terrified at the prospect of renewed Bantai focus on them and worried about Sereno's possible reforms, had agreed to take out Sereno to ensure Sevellan obedience to their Bantai lords.

And even if I didn't care much for Sereno right now—I don't take kindly to people trying to kill me for things I didn't do—my top priority was making sure the people who wanted to kill him didn't get to him. Because where Sereno was, that was where Skinner—

That was where my medic was.

I was still behind the tree line, crouching behind a short column, my back to another building. *If the Yada show up, they'll show up behind me, from cover.* In front of me, in the clearing, a company of Bantai soldiers had gathered—some of them came from the direction of the amphitheater, like I did, and others from further out, but they took cover now behind the vehicles parked outside and fired on the hospital. Someone inside was returning fire.

"What are you doing? You're a doctor, not an infantryman."

"I know, Captain, but—"

The scent of melting wire. Blood—the taste of iron splattering in my agape mouth. The deep, dark crimson, the chunky texture of the brain leaking through the open hole.

I blinked, squinting to focus on getting my medic out. I could see the Bantai firing and taking fire, sunlight glinting off the muzzles of their weapons, skin mottling in the shadows of the trucks. I lifted my rifle and seated it against my shoulder, kneeling against the rock in front of me. My sight kept shaking. I was shaking. I was shaking and I was a shitty aim even without shaking.

I was so powerless. I was so pointless. I knew I was going to try anyway, and I hated that. That's what I did, how I lived, gritting my teeth as my useless body and broken mind rebelled against me, and I began to fire on the Bantai from behind.

To my surprise I actually hit a guy. "Wow, okay," I muttered. Then another. My next round ricocheted off the truck in front of someone and made them freak out a little bit—hey, even suppressive fire could mess up people's aim. I couldn't break through this line alone right now, but I could at least make it hell for the Bantai to win. Spread the misery. I fired again, breathing so fast I started to give myself hiccups. No one tells you that every single soldier shits themselves the first time they go into battle, and I was suddenly like a first-timer again, clenching against the jitters and forcing my fingers to hold steady on the trigger—*don't just hold it down!*—again and again. It was so familiar. The catecholamines surging through my body burned, giving me a high and a sense of terror all at the same time, blending invincibility with the choking certainty that everything was going to go wrong. My vision tunneled. I steadied my forearms—

What would you tell the kid right now?

It sucked that the Yadans hadn't arrived yet. I was the shittiest option for rescue right now. But I was the option that was here. *Just keep going.*

"God, please just—"

Civilians assume that battle changes you, but in real life, some people come back from war and it's no big deal. Some people just become a little more alert, watch their back at the grocery store when it's crowded, get a twitch in their eye when they see a shadowed treeline. Some people kill and don't care because they're diseased and it's just a game, and other people kill and move past it because they know they did what they had to do. It's not really battle that changes you. Sometimes it's not even death itself.

Whether you're fucked up because of dead babies or rape or living with an awful spouse, it's knowing there's no one at your back and you're not enough—and your body struggles against that, tries to throw out every chemical it can to make you enough, and it can't, because burning out your hippocampus with adrenaline can make you jumpy and alert and give you momentary super-strength and aggression, but it can't undo your friend's suicide or convince your command team they were screwing your soldiers for no reason. That changes you, that creates the time lapse where you live over and over in the moment you can't fix.

The shooting, the killing, the loud sounds, the battle itself wasn't the problem. The problem was that I knew Skinner was in the med bay and it was overrun by the Charee that boarded our ship, and I couldn't get back in. I knew no one had my back and my command team wouldn't help because they'd gotten themselves killed, because they wouldn't listen to me. I knew unless someone swooped in and saved us all—

And no one would. They'd arrive, but they'd arrive too late. The Charee would lose, but so would we.

Nothing existed in the real world but my rifle and the targets. Everything else was trapped in the time lapse. The second explosion rocked the ship. The medical tent went up in flames. A toxic smell of burnt medications and melting plastic blasted out to me under the thick, sweet odor of fuel.

I saw the three familiar Sevellan pleasure guards poised near the entrance of the tent, waiting for a chance to burst through the smoke—

"Shit, they're going to infiltrate the group evacuating in the confusion," I muttered. I tried to fire on them—I missed, and they disappeared into the collapsing structure—

The explosion was my chance to charge, too. The Bantai near the front of that painted Sevellan truck we'd traveled in had gone down—I could cross the street now while the others focused on the heat and shock, dash around the front of that truck, and the others might not see me. Oh, it was risky—my knees wriggled like they needed a restroom—should I? If I didn't go now, I'd lose my chance and have to wait for back-up—

I went, boots pounding the earth like the planet surface owed me money, head low, stomach and chest churning like a turbine, silent scream caught in my throat under a grimace like pain, like terror, but something else entirely—I skidded to a stop in front of the truck—no one had shot me yet but I needed to keep moving, they'd poke their heads around the front hear to see, to aim, in just a moment—I saw brush about to catch fire to the left of the medical tent, my left not patient left, and if I darted behind that, and then crossed behind the tent, I could go through the back entrance where the fire hadn't reached yet. I remembered where the trap door was.

My body was already carrying me there. It was trying, poor, stupid, weak thing, it was trying, every movement a prayer. Good people don't understand the desperation of real prayer, the need for the divine that's impossible to voice—columns of stone blocked me from the heat now but I could feel the raging inferno when I moved. The front of the hospital tent was impenetrable now, pure fire. Sparks flew into the trees, embers lapping at their feet like waves—

I was almost there, and still clean. It didn't feel like a victory. But I was just a few meters from the trap door—I could see it through the back entrance to the minimals tent, flapping in the wind, an open wooden hatch framed in my vision by smoking canvas.

Just a few more steps through hell.

Ken Kamakura

When Ken and his new Yadan friends made it back down into the basement for the last time—when they couldn't make it anymore into the front of the tent to find bodies in the flames—the cool relief of the covered room seemed like the sweetest draught of heaven distilled into breathable elixir. But heat seemed to hang around Ken anyway, his slipsuit crushing him with the scent of smoke, sticky with the grimy sweat that clung to every centimeter of his skin. He could almost feel his own pulse in his throat. The world tasted sour and he couldn't stop coughing. "Should've packed my mask," he grunted, trying to smile up at Benjamno as he doubled over.

"Get your charges down the tunnel!" snapped one of the Yadan soldiers watching the trapdoor. "We'll have Bantai on us in any second and the prisoners can't defend themselves. We just got word he's a target," someone nodded toward Sereno, still chained to the stretcher in the corner. "The medics already moved the other folks you brought. Take the hospital Scrit with you so the Terran knows what's going on!"

"Obeyed," said Benjamno. Ken felt a firm hand on his spine. The black and white Scrit looked up at him from between his boots. "You good?" Benjamno asked.

"Yeah, I'm good." Ken straightened and made for Sereno, swinging his legs with effort—his clothes felt heavy, but he had pep still. He actually felt pretty good. "Why are you still here, Grandfather?" he asked, crouching.

"He wanted us to move the wounded first," said the nearest soldier.

"I asked them to release the bonds so I could assist, but they refused," Sereno grumbled. "Hurry up and get me out of here now."

"Obeyed," Benjamno grinned, humoring—but not mocking—the pushy Sevellan. It was such a relief, that pleasant smile in this disaster. "Juda, you with me?" The woman nodded, weapon pointed at Sereno, but eyes flickering every other second to the trapdoor above for the actual enemy incoming— "Alright, one, two, three, lift!"

Ken grunted, lifted—something was up with his knees, he didn't have time to remember how or even when it started. Lifting Sereno—that was his only thought right now—he followed Benjamno to the tunnel. The three unchained pleasure guards met them there. "This way!" they whispered, pointing to a fork to the right. "Everyone went this way!"

Juda hesitated. "Wait, are you sure—"

Loud bangs and pops suddenly shot off behind them. Ken jumped—his fingers spasmed as he steadied himself—*whoa—*

"Hurry, we don't have time!" cried one of the pleasure guards. A stray round hit the wall beside Ken—

"Right, double-time," said Benjamno. They followed the pleasure guards down a winding passageway, deep bronze-green earthen walls almost pressing against their broad shoulders. "Watch your head." Ken ducked—the only light now was from periodic pin-holes up to the surface, and as those disappeared and they left the lit main tunnel further behind them the tiny hall grew darker and darker—

"Grenade!" someone screamed far behind them.

"Fall back!"

The blast puffed through the tunnel, muffled by the earth. Ken had a sudden instinct to run back to the main basement—the wounded!—but he heard shouts and footsteps as medics raced down the main tunnel. Strange that they'd come from *that* way, and not had to come past here, if everyone evacuated this way…

"We are going the wrong way," Sereno said, twisting his head to try to see who they were following.

"You know, I think you're right—" Benjamno began.

The women in front whispered something.

"Get down!" Juda roared.

Ken and Benjamno both dropped, heads bowed—*what a command voice on that tiny lady!*

Sereno yelped—and growled mid-yelp, ever conscious of himself—as his carriers' power-squat dropped him a centimeter from the ground, too—

And the first pleasure guard just in front of them dropped, holes through her chest smoking from Juda's shot.

Benjamno threw himself backwards over Sereno, letting go of the stretcher as *a pistol shot went off in the hands of the second pleasure guard*—it was so fast and frantic from the back in the dark Ken didn't understand the movement until too late. Juda's rifle thundered over Ken's head; the second pleasure guard hit the dirt, too.

Juda double-tapped both of her kills with another round each. "They pulled on you," Juda panted.

"I see that, thank you," Benjamno grunted, lifting himself off Sereno as the third guard threw herself on the floor for mercy. "But I wasn't the target."

Sereno grimaced, his nose bloodied by Benjamno's back falling over him—and his own back likely stinging from the sudden drop. "Who the hell," he wheezed.

"I'm sorry, please spare me, please!" begged the guard on the ground. "Please listen to me!"

"We're listening," Benjamno said, reaching forward to check pulses on the dead women. He glanced back at Ken with a shake of his head.

"You have to let me kill him," the third pleasure guard wept. "For both our peoples."

"We don't have the authority to make that call." Benjamno's voice was calm; Ken couldn't see what he was doing, but he'd taken something off his belt. Ken opened his own assault pack with an awful heaviness stirring in his gut.

"What authority do you need? The Bantai stand at your gates. If you deliver them Sereno's body you can make an argument for a truce, at least!"

Juda gave a quick Edenian headshake, weapon still trained on the woman on the floor. "We're Yada. They'll always want us wiped out."

"How do you know what anyone wants if you don't ask them?" the pleasure guard cried. She lifted her head to look at Ken now. "Please. I know you love our people. I was there at Welcome Village. Whatever happens to the Yada, you must understand that the Sevella will only survive as a people if we honor what the Bantai ask of us."

"How are you even an independent people, then?" Ken asked. "If they're choosing your political leaders for you, aren't you just vassals?"

"Please! Please—Sereno, you understand!" By the light of the flashlight Benjamno pulled to go through his pack Ken could see tears streaking through the dirt on the woman's face. "Please, Sereno, this is a sacrifice you must make for our people. You will be our hero, Sereno, and the pleasure guard will ever tell your story in our secret chambers. Please let us take you."

Ken made eye contact with the leader in chains now. He couldn't help a sour jab: "Huh, this sounds familiar."

Sereno said nothing. He clenched his jaw and stared at the ceiling. The sound of everyone's heavy breathing filled the tiny space; behind them, down the passageways, the sounds of the dying and killing seemed far away. "Is he alright?" Sereno asked finally.

"Is who—oh *no*," Juda gasped, lowering her weapon for just a second—

The pleasure guard's eyes lit up at the momentary lapse. She leapt to snatch a pistol from her fallen companion—

Ken was ready this time. The third pleasure guard died on top of the other woman, Mark X round in her skull. Ken climbed forward over Sereno to the dying Yadan in front of him, yanking his assault pack with him—because Benjamno had taken the kill-shot meant for the Sevellan leader, of course he had! "I'm so sorry, I didn't understand what'd happened—I thought she'd just missed, I'm so sorry—" Ken rattled, kneeling over the other medic's legs to rip open his uniform. After so much time treating Edenians and their color-changing wounds, the simple hole in Benjamno's chest seemed so—wrong. Just red over flesh. Was something—more wrong? Should he do something different? Panic pummeled Ken's lungs—

"You're fine—my skin's all burned, I can't change color, that's my normal," Benjamno soothed. He lifted a weak hand to point towards one of the unchanging blue streaks across his face. "I got these scars in a chemical attack. Sevellans."

"And yet you've treated them better than anyone else here."

Ken's chest caught; he closed his mouth, steeling himself, trying to focus on finding the exit wound—there was no exit wound, and there was a huge, *huge* purple bruise spreading across Benjamno's chest and abdomen. He was bleeding internally. And it was fast.

"'He who's been forgiven much, loves much,'" Benjamno shrugged. "I'm big on giving people a chance to do the right thing. I'll always defend my people if they're under attack, but my 'people' kind of include all Edenians as I see it."

"That's a hard stance to take," Ken breathed. Oh no, what was he going to do?

"Oh, it sucks," Benjamno laughed. "I get the teeth of my heart kicked in every day trying to protect everyone from each other, but what do you expect? I know people don't change without miracles. I had my miracle. Maybe this asshole will have his." He nodded down at Sereno with a wry little grin.

Sereno said nothing, and Ken hated him in that moment for it—actually despised him, with a pulsing hatred that jerked through his fingers and clenched them into fists that longed to *beat* the racist who couldn't say thank you to the people saving his life. He forced his hands to rip open the chest seal for Benjamno—but, he noticed, the chest wasn't rising and falling unevenly, so probably no pneumothorax right now. Oh, the *darkness* of that bruise—

"I think she nicked your aorta," Ken said, pronouncing the death sentence with utmost gentleness. "I'm—really sorry, man."

There was no answer. The blue Yadan was already dead.

Jocelyn Wimmer

I was seconds away from the trapdoor when the Bantai charged the tent. They sent a huge orb-shaped ordinance vehicle with a firehose first, spraying a central path through the flames as it rolled over the medical center, crushing cots, bodies, everything in its way. I ducked behind a huge black stone in a clump of not-yet-burning bushes and raised my rifle again—I could just make out the helmet of some Yadan soldier perched on a ladder down into the basement, their shoulders hugging a rifle that fired again—again—again—trying for the driver of that armored almost-*tank*—

It was just one guy or gal at the bottleneck, one guy or gal against the inevitable metal future. Of course it had to be—there wasn't room in that tiny doorway for more than one. But to *be* that one, whether you wanted to or not, and to be doing a damn good job at it—

My chest swelled with something like pride, but more like the honor that is love. I loved my soldiers, and I loved this soldier, their elbow planted on the ground, their grip steady, their cheek against the stock, their weapon marching through time with the weight of their breath. Watching that lonely soldier had my hands naturally moving to reload my rifle and keep pace. I angled myself to make sure my field of error didn't include them—you can't just fire over top of someone—and I too fired—again—and again—and again—

A hatch opened at the front of the vehicle. A grenade-launcher—

"Well, shit."

It looked like the soldier or me—probably the soldier—managed to get a round inside the hatch, because it didn't shut again. But the launcher still snapped down at forty-five degrees, right for the soldier's face, and fired.

I like to hope that face got one more defiant look in before taking a grenade to it.

Soldier and explosive pounded back into the hole, and I was suddenly pissed. Maybe it was the heat, maybe it was the hormones, maybe it was just that the soldier reminded me of a hundred other things or I hated for Goliath to defeat David or maybe this soldier's personal aura alone overwhelmed me—but I was too pissed to think about anyone dying, too pissed for the past to exist, too pissed for anything but the knowledge that *with the explosion splashing out of the trapdoor I had a good few seconds of obscured visual field to charge the tank solo.*

I dashed through flames—my slipsuit was retardant, if I was fast—and darted for the hatch with the grenade-launcher sticking out of it. I gripped the tiny door, jammed my rifle into the hole, and fired blindly, automatic rounds rattling and ricocheting through the whole vehicle inside. I heard cries of surprise, and grunts that sounded like death. Good. I yanked the grenade launcher out of its seat and rolled under the bottom of the vehicle, crawling between the tank treads, ash and dirt caking into my hair as I looked for the repair-man's hatch—I didn't know what it was actually called, but I knew there was a path to the engine here.

"Found you, fucker," I grinned. I yanked it open, my eyes scanning for a good little nook that looked close to fuel lines as I fiddled with the grenade launcher to get it to drop one of its gifts — "Be careful, fingers," I grunted. "Unclip—yeah."

I pulled the pin and jammed the grenade up into the bowels of the beast. Then I scrambled the fuck back out of there. Fire was catching up with me. I tore down a piece of flaming canvas and threw it under the tank.

And then I ran.

The tank exploded from the inside with more of a "crunch" than a "boom"— the armor absorbed most of the impact, and the Bantai running up from behind it seemed more confused than scared. That was fine. I had the grenade launcher.

And it was a good thing to have. I was a shit shot and grenade launchers have shit accuracy anyway, but I just needed to land my load in my target's general area to slow them down with shrapnel.

Parked behind my black rock as embers glowed at my feet, I sucked in the soul of that soldier and fired—again—again—again—each time waiting for a group to gather first. I'd read a study that said the number one predictor of winners in a firefight was use of cover, and cloaked in smoke behind a tank, a rock, and bushes I had the best hiding spot. I didn't revel in the poor bastards hurting. The medical part of me kept insisting I needed to fix the screams.

But it felt good to land my hits. It felt good to catch a win.

At some point there was a lull. I tried to wait—had they just fallen back for a bit? Were they circling around now? It was getting too quiet for too long, and I could hear groans down below.

I looked both ways like I was crossing the street back home on Zeta Leporis—I'd had to book it then, too, and for a moment my legs and arms were youthful and hungry and scared again, shoes wearing out on gray pavement under a grayer sky. I was so lucky, I realized, as I scrambled down the ladder, to have seen a world as beautiful as the one that now surrounded me. Death would have followed me anywhere. But at least here I forced it to see life.

The basement under the medical tent was a technicolor portrait from the mind of He Who Hates Us All, straight from the horror stories my dad used to read to us about existential madnesses steeped in blood. Pieces of people everywhere. Walls painted with Rorschach blotches in which every blot was a visual scream, a portal into a world we form entire religions to avoid spending our afterlives in. I couldn't remember if I'd announced myself or not—I should have, it would've been stupid not to—but even if I'd forgotten no one tried to shoot me because everyone was either dead or in the process of getting there. I could hear footsteps running away down the hall—heavy footsteps, like those of medics carrying bodies. I grabbed one of the medical bags I saw lying around and began to run after them.

Wherever they were headed was where Ken was. I didn't see him in here.

I didn't want to see him in here.

Ken Kamakura

Ken wanted to scream. He wanted to scream at Sereno and he wanted to scream at the dead pleasure guards and he couldn't help an insane inner laughter, either, because this was exactly what the dead Yadan medic had said—trying to save all these people from each other was a pain, and not in the idiomatic way, but with the literal tearing in his chest now as he choked up over the body of someone he didn't even really know. By now he'd seen plenty of people die. But this one seemed different.

He couldn't stop cursing under his breath.

Juda stared blankly at her companion for a few long moments. There was no sadness or anger in her eyes—literally nothing. No sound, no tears. It was like she wasn't even here. Presently she blinked. "We need to get back to the main hallway," she said, still staring at Benjamno. "That's the fastest path out of here to the evacuation zone. But what do we do with him?" she nodded towards Sereno.

"You let me walk," he said. His voice was very, very quiet. "Unless you believe you can carry me."

She gave him a once-over, clearly considering it.

"You're—not large, ma'am," Ken said. "You'll fuck up your back."

"And mine, when she drops me," Sereno smirked.

"Hm." Juda gave a sardonic half-chuckle—just a huff. "I'm more worried about having my hands full. I don't want to die without my palms on a gun. And even shackled I don't trust you without my rifle on you. Respectfully. Grandfather." She looked at Ken now. Her eyes were so empty. Not as in soulless—as in she'd buried her soul beneath the memories of a hundred dead companions, and it couldn't come to the window right now. "I don't even know what the protocol is for this."

"You're in charge," Ken said. He wasn't going to be responsible for whatever nonsense Sereno did next. "I can walk with him shackled to me, with your sights on him. Or I can drag the stretcher."

A soft buzz interrupted them—Juda scrambled for the comms unit on her chest. Her eyes widened like tree stumps: "It's—the Grandfather!" she whispered in awe. "Our—our Grandfather!" Apparently as humble as Yako had been with his Terran visitors, his lowly soldiers either didn't get much contact with him or had enough contact with his exploits to see him as a legend. Juda tapped the radio; her earpiece had fallen off somewhere along the way, or maybe she'd never had one—so Ken could hear the crackle as the channel opened. "Y—yes Grandfather, heard!"

Ken recognized the deep rumble of Yako's voice, but only the words "Juda" and "Sevellan Grandfather." The black and white hospital Scrit sat about a meter beyond him, licking its paw with wide eyes gleaming in the dim light, staring at him like a predator, but it didn't translate radio.

"Obeyed, Grandfather," Juda said, unclipping the comms unit from her vest. To Sereno: "He wants you to hear something."

As Juda held the radio near Sereno's ear it lit up with whoops and screams and curses from some recording Ken couldn't understand. Ken could hear laughter, and cries, and explosions.

Sereno understood, though. "What are your terms?"

Yako's firm voice gave a quick, one-sentence summary.

"I won't surrender our land to protect my name," Sereno said.

Yako spoke longer this time. Ken realized he actually understood the words "land" and "return," now, but he didn't know what to say when Sereno looked at him.

"He says my people have promised to purge everyone loyal to me for the Bantai—that I have no choice but to ally with the Yada if I want to remain in power," Sereno said. He shook his head and looked at the ceiling. "But even with the heavy losses we suffered this week, it is only one platoon of Sevellan rebels attacking his people now, and without a promise of our land returned to us—" Sereno tightened his jaw. "I must have a future for my daughters."

"He wants you to call and order your battle guard back at camp to come attack on your behalf," Ken guessed.

Sereno nodded.

"But it doesn't matter if it's just a platoon of your guys trying to kill you now. There's an entire Bantai army out there." Ken said. "What do your daughters want land for if you're dead?"

"The Third have come out in full force, too," Juda said.

Sereno stared at her. His gaze hardened; Ken's pulse quickened. "Tell me, Yadan, what is the worst your people have ever required of you?" Sereno asked.

"To protect the leader of my enemy," Juda said without hesitation.

He smiled—a cold, decided smile—and when he answered Yako, it was to Juda, not the radio. "Tell your Grandfather I will grant a six-hour truce, until I am released. I make no promises after that point."

Yako answered something, and then hung up. Sereno instructed Juda on opening a general frequency his people would be attuned to, and gave orders into it.

"It is done," he said.

Juda closed the comms channel. Her eyes narrowed. "Why did you ask me that, Grandfather?"

"Because I want my daughters to have what you are allowed to have," he grunted. "My sister deserved what you have."

"The land where I grew up, you mean."

"No. That is not what I mean. Now get these off me. We have

an enemy to kill before we kill each other." He shifted his head. "I thought I told you it was done. Why is your radio still on?"

"It's not," Juda tapped the dead unit on her chest. Ken tilted his head—he heard a crackle, too—

He put his head down to the ground, and turned his face to meet the dead eyes of the pleasure guard at Benjamno's feet. He rolled her over—

Oh no.

"She has a comms unit. And it's transmitting our location."

Jocelyn Wimmer

It took me a hot minute to figure out that Ken and Sereno had gone the wrong way. I caught up with the medics—it's not really easy or polite to ask someone where your friend is when theirs is dying in their arms, and the more pragmatic "where's the Sevellan leader" got me a lot of well-deserved "I don't know, plainskin, fuck off!" I *also* don't like people asking me stupid questions unrelated to my mission when I'm focused.

But my mission, right now, was to find my medic. That's why I'd arrived on this damn planet in the first place—because I knew it, I knew this kid would get himself into something well beyond his ability and I wanted him to *live.* That was it. It was maybe a shitty mission, maybe a selfish mission, but no one was paying me to do the right thing.

No one was paying me at all.

In the end, the Sevellans led me to Ken. Not the prisoners, though—those were sequestered somewhere way down the hall, and I was on my way to look for Sereno among them when I heard shooting back the way I'd come.

"I thought there wasn't anyone back there to bother shooting," I muttered to Sylvie. Faithful Sylvie had waited patiently by the black rock while I played under-tank commando and found her way to me the instant she saw she could; she trotted happily behind my heels now as I crept back down the hall. "Holy—!"

I ducked into a nook in the wall, trying to make myself as thin as possible. A huge swarm of Sevellans now occupied the basement. But they weren't coming this way. Their robes disappeared around the corner into a tiny, narrow hallway I hadn't even noticed in my hurry to follow the medics.

I signaled for Sylvie to stay back and scooted back towards the basement, back against the wall, grateful that I was tan enough to look somewhat like the color of the mud here. I held my mouth open to improve my hearing—

Oh man. My pulse became a drum for that speedcore hissing Lachan music I'd had to listen to nonstop during that diplomatic mission in my youth—fast, light, and terrifying. I heard them. Sereno, Ken—and lots of gunshots—! Someone shouting about not letting the traitor's lies get to them, someone else shouting about traitors violating the core law of descent—

"Lots of talk about traitors," I muttered.

Oops. Sevellan ears are amazing.

Someone whirled and fired on me. I clung to the wall and fired back. *Stay. Away. From. My. People.* It was easier for me to hit my targets—they were bunching together; I was leaving open space. But they were better marksmen. Rounds zipped against the wall, the floor, centimeters from me. They were going to hit me sooner or later. Was I only *buying time*? Was that literally all I could do?

Well. I still had one grenade, though.

———

Ken Kamakura

"Go, go, go!" Juda shouted, running backwards as the Sevellan force poured single-file into the narrow hallway. Ken wanted badly to help her fight, but there was almost no room to shoot around her, and he had a policy of not flagging people he liked with a loaded gun. Sereno and his detractors shouted heated words at each other over the two non-Sevellans even as he ran—and Sereno seemed to believe, for some reason, that whoever yelled loudest would win.

"I think there's another turn back towards the main hallway," Juda tried to say over her shoulder to Ken, as *under* her breath as she could while running and shooting. "If I remember right, it comes out at a really narrow bit that shouldn't be too hard to defend."

Ken painted a triangle in his mind, imagining the narrow hallway looping around— "What if we come out in front of the other evacuees?" he asked. "They'd be cut off then by enemy ahead and behind them."

"That's assuming these Sevellans are as fast as my squad-mates," Juda said.

"Carrying injured people?"

"Good point. You can scout ahead with the Grandfather. I'll slow them down."

Ken realized suddenly that Sereno's yelling had been entirely to give Ken and Juda some sonic cover, because as soon as they'd come up with a plan, he stopped talking and sprinted. Ken ran after him, knees complaining but quite grateful Juda had opted not to chain him to the Sevellan leader. Every now and then one of them stumbled on the uneven terrain, but otherwise, they ran in silence. For stretches it almost felt like a competition. Sereno would speed up along the straights; Ken would get right on his heels, almost running him over. Then around a turn, or in a darker area, he'd pull away from Ken, his eyes better in the dark, and so on. Neither looked at the other. But they both knew.

They both still had something to prove.

Jocelyn Wimmer

In the underground tunnel my explosion wrought havoc. I heard rumbling—maybe I'd caused a cave-in near them? I couldn't see through the bodies and the smoke and the dust—I was busy trying to rip a tourniquet out of the IFAK I'd taken from the dead medic.

My own explosion had disoriented me, and it took me a second to figure out what hurt most. Just as I'd lobbed my grenade, I caught two rounds—one to the upper thigh and the other to the left arm. *Thank God that's not my trigger side*—there was a lull in the action while the Sevella regrouped, but fallen on the ground here, I was a much, much bigger target than I had been standing against the wall. I needed to strap myself up, fast, and move. *Shit shit shit shit shit*—

"Give me one!" cried Sibila's voice.

Sibila?

"Where'd you come from?"

"From the evacuation point," she said, yanking one of the tourniquets out of my bag and wrapping it around my arm. "Kenta and Sereno have not made there yet." She looked up at the far hall with worried eyes. "They were tricked, I think. As soon as I got out of chains I returned."

"Wait, you were in chains?" I tightened my leg tourniquet, clenching my teeth. "And you got out? What?"

"One of the medics told Rachaba about the *other pleasure guards*," Sibila said, tightening the arm tourniquet now. "With the plot against my brother on the radio she was immediately suspicious and brought me forward to identify them. We almost reached the basement again when the third explosion happened. I took her keycard when she was shot." She glanced up at my face, eyebrow raised as she tightened—tightened—tightened—*fuck that sucks!* "Are you going to ask me if I killed her?"

"No," I groaned, coughing and growling to myself to try to keep from screaming. I pawed across the dead soldier's bag to find—oh, come on—okay, he had a fentanyl lollipop in the smaller front pouch. I jammed that in my mouth, my throat clenching. "No, I'm going to ask you to run."

"What? No! You're hurt, I'm not leaving you!"

"Woman, I need you to leave me. I can't think if you're here. I can't be worrying about keeping you alive."

"I can help!"

"Yes, you can. And you can also die. It's not that you're too weak to help. It's that I'm too weak to—" Tears sprang to my eyes. Fuck. I ordered them to leave. "I won't be able to do what I need to do if I see you. I'm going through hell in my head right now. I'm going to see you and a million other people in you, and I'm—I can't do it, Sibila, I can't."

She stared into my eyes for a moment, and then nodded. "Okay. You aren't afraid if I leave you I'm going to release my brother?" she asked.

"I think you'll know the right thing to do in the moment," I said. I gripped her wrist now and squeezed like I could squeeze the pain out of me into her. "But if you let him kill Ken, I will haunt your ass so bad your grandchildren will come out the womb screaming, girl."

"Don't—all children scream when they're born—?"

"Not like this," I chuckled. I put a palm on her face. Her lilac eyes shone back at me wet. "Hey," I said. "You're an amazing woman, and you can be anything you want to be. I know that's cliché, but—I actually think you've never heard it."

"Not in those words, no," she said, looking down. She

clenched her jaw. "Stand with me. I will give you a better hiding position."

"There's a hiding—ooh!" I groaned as she pulled me to my feet. She was stronger than she looked. I hobbled against her shoulder and she brought me to a second little tunnel point. "You can shoot better from here."

"Right you are. Now go. They're coming back."

She gave my hand a squeeze, and vanished.

New Sevellans were pouring into the basement like a Grausian decicrus swarm—I'd seen that ugly sight once, too, and killed a fair few of the spider-like flesh-eaters defending my patients myself. That'd been a really successful mission—I'd be glad to repeat it. I didn't mind monsters.

I reloaded my rifle for the last time. I never saw Sibila again.

Kenta Kamakura

Juda was right. The narrow passage did come out into the main hall.

"What was the point of this curve?" Ken whispered.

"To give evacuees a place to set up ambush," Sereno answered. "It was a common Sevellan construction once. I'm surprised the Yadans don't know how to use it."

"They're not Sevellan," Ken said. "But we are. We can come back around on them from this way—"

"We?" Sereno narrowed his eyes. "You're much more similar culturally to the Ya—what the hell is she doing?"

They both interrupted themselves—Ken hadn't even noticed his own error—because to their mutual surprise, down the hall was Captain Wimmer firing into the Sevellan army.

Jocelyn Wimmer

The new Sevellans were less focused on the small side tunnel and more interested in charging in my direction. "It is a trap-circle," someone was yelling. "The side-tunnel must come out further down the hall. We can cut them off!"

"See, what did I tell you?" Sereno's voice—right behind me?

"Wimmer!" Oh, Ken. My chest relaxed, and even with my screaming leg I felt immediately better.

The young men came up behind where I knelt to fire on our approaching horde; Ken immediately posted against the wall above me, shooting over my head from a standing position.

"I didn't know officers could teleport," he laughed. Man, he sounded really glad to see me.

"There's a lot of that going around," I said. "Why's this jerk unrestrained?"

"You have six hours of non-jerk Sereno before he resumes his jerk status," Sereno answered. "Killing you no longer serves my purposes."

"So nice to hear that," I smirked. Sylvie hissed at him.

As Ken was asking me questions about my tourniquet—and I answered something vague I don't remember now—I realized suddenly this was like nothing I'd ever done before. The smells of the metal-rich earth seemed almost fungal; the accents around me not Grausian or Charee or Lachan; the enemy with me so much less self-righteous than the enemies hidden among my companions before. I much preferred this outright literal back-stabbing to the political papercut murders I'd seen—you could do something about this backstabbing. And most of all—

Kamakura wasn't Skinner. Kamakura was alive.

But we couldn't keep up with the Sevellans in terms of sheer bulletstorm. They were advancing down the tunnel and we'd run out of rounds before they did.

"We cannot let them cut us off," Sereno said.

"It's narrower here, though," I said, dropping another charger. "One person can kind of defend this gap if you all are fast."

"Alright," Ken said, dropping two. "I can do that."

"No—you're leaving," I said.

"What? This is absolutely not the doctor's job," Ken protested.

"You're leaving because I can't carry her." I nodded as a Yadan warrior stumbled around the corner, gripping her side. She'd already applied a tourniquet around her own arm.

"I don't know if they're behind me," she groaned. "There was a cave-in."

Sweet, it kind of worked, then.

"Juda!" Ken shouted; Sereno darted to the soldier's side before the Terran could and caught her as she fell.

"Keep shooting!" Sereno ordered. "Unless you want to give me your weapon."

"*I* don't want you to give him your weapon," I snapped. "The whole region gets ten times worse if the Bantai do whatever-the-fuck they want—Ken, you need to get him out of here, and she needs medical attention. And I can't both carry her and protect him. You can. Get the fuck out of here. I'll be fine."

"You can do better than me for her, though—"

"So you're choosing her over all Sevellans, then?" I asked, getting thoroughly annoyed and dizzy now. "Because yes, I can save her life. Maybe—it's easier to think about shooting people than medical treatment *with a fucking tourniquet on me*, believe it or not, kid! So then while I'm struggling slo-mo through casualty care these renegades end up right up our no-fly zones, and world's youngest Grandpa here dies. Is that your plan? Go make sure the evacuees and wounded get where they need to go and then come back."

"But it's return fire *first*—"

"I'm out of ammo," Juda muttered.

"Ken, this is an *order!*" I roared.

I grimaced as Ken left. I felt like an asshole—it would've been nice to have time to explain to him that I could see she'd need surgical intervention fast, and a couple tourniquets wasn't going to cut it so he *had* to get her to their evac platform, but we didn't *have* time for classroom learning in the middle of an active firefight. I hated yelling at anyone under my control. I could still hear my voice echoing through the metal ship medbay… I wasn't known for being easy to work with—my commanders had somehow simultaneously said I was too easy on the medics and too hard on them, because since the "paperwork officers" never showed up around the medbay they actually had no idea what hands-on officer work was like, and the other doctors believed whatever the paperwork guys told them because since the dawn of time a shiny star has never failed to impress Grade A performers—

"You know what, maybe it's time to let that go," I interrupted myself. Click-click—

Ooh, out of ammo.

I waited in the small side-hallway, my back against the wall. Once the Sevellans got close enough from either side I'd get to work with close-quarters goodness. I closed my eyes, counting their steps.

It was time to use my shortsword.

Ken Kamakura

It wasn't just Juda who needed saving.

Ken and Sereno caught up with the other medics just around the turn, almost stumbling onto the first bodies on the floor. The entire stretch of hallway was littered with wounded Edenians—and far in the distance Ken could see the literal light at the end of the tunnel, and hear heloblades whirring. Everything from chest wounds to limb loss to horrific burns—

"I need to get the doctor," Ken breathed.

"The doctors are all on the med-helo with all the robotics equipment," snapped the nearest medic crouched with his back to them. "What you need to do is help me get these people on it before it takes too much fire and has to leave!"

"Obeyed," Sereno said.

At the Sevellan accent the Yadans all looked up in surprise—but Sereno was already trotting down the way, Juda on his back. Ken crouched by the medic next to him.

"Oh, your doctor was looking for you," the medic murmured. He was so clearly exhausted. Ken clicked open the tube of his camel-back and gave the guy a sip— "Quick caffeine," he said. "You good?"

"Yeah."

"Chair-carry this guy between us?"

"Yeah."

"One, two, three, lift."

The load was huge. He was larger than either of the two medics, and stepping over other bodies didn't make that easier.

"Why are we starting down at this end?" Ken groaned.

"Triage by ability to return fire," the other medic panted back. "You don't hear the enemy coming down the hall? Whoever's out there can only hold them back for so long."

Ken tried to come up with a faster way to do this as they limped down the passageway, but it was all he could do just to focus on not dropping the soldier drooping against his shoulder. They tried to balance the weight between them but Ken was stronger, and the patient kept leaning on him—

There was so much screaming and swearing in the distance. A lot less gunshots now. Maybe that was good? He wanted to run back and help his friend. But all these people, they all had friends, too—each of them somebody's whole world. *Shit*, he breathed, after everything that'd happened in the past week, he was actually done with this. His throat was tightening. All these people, something within him wept, all suffering for what? Because they couldn't come up with a way to share the entire damn planet? He knew it was more than that, he knew that each person had some beloved dream they fought for, but the gauntlet of pain didn't seem to end. Here, she was missing half her face and still conscious as a medic shoved a tube down her throat to keep her airway from closing. There, he would never have children if he even lived to meet someone. And a person could only help one at a time. One at a time.

The first day it'd been exhilarating. Today, it was heartbreaking.

What could one person even really do?

And then, he saw Sibila.

She was helping a few of the more ambulatory patients position themselves along the wall— "You will be able to shoot from here," she was saying—and handing out fentanyl lollipops like, well, candy. And then somehow Ken's question to himself seemed stupid—all negative questions seemed stupid. He'd asked why people created their own suffering by destroying each other—well, obviously, because they couldn't see what each other were worth, like how every idiot in this woman's life couldn't see what he saw. He'd asked before if the little moments were worth fighting for—of course they were worth fighting for. That was where God lived. He'd asked what one person could do—well of course, one person could save Sibila, and Sibila could save the world.

Jocelyn Wimmer

I knew exactly what one person could do.

One person could make the call that got a whole starfleet killed.

One person could start the rumor that altered the course of a nation.

One person could stop the bleeding that changed a king's mind.

And one person could kill a lot of guys with a vibroblade in close quarters in a tiny narrow hallway.

Because the Sevellan platoon still didn't know where the tunnel let out. So they could either stay back, away from me and my little hiding place, while their prey escaped, or they could rush past my hiding place and get chopped down. They tried clearing me out a few times with explosives, but they had to run so far back each time they tried to do that that I had time to run back up my dark little tunnel, too, and they just ended up wasting some good grenades. Someone in charge started to yell at them that they might cause a cave-in that blocked them off from Sereno for good, and I heard someone suggest trying to clear out the dark little back tunnel now and get to me that way. Which would take hours.

So by and large it was starting to look like the only actually effective strategy was for them to rush me melee-style, and unfortunately for the guys at the head of the line there was really only room in this narrow part of the hallway for one person at a time. And every guy who collapsed in front of my little tunnel of death blocked it more. Here came two skinny guys trying to run past, one trying to tank the blow for the other—I aimed for the gut instead of the chest to avoid getting caught on ribs, and skewered them both, pulling out fast to swing around to the first guy's neck. The second guy stumbled forward a few more steps, but I'd bisected his aorta. His marathon ended while I was dealing with a particularly bold strategist who pierced himself with my blade to grab my hilt, trying to yank me out of my hiding place to get shot. I twisted the blade and dropped to the ground, planting a foot in his stomach and throwing him back over my head behind me. Risky—but because he wouldn't let go, he hit his head hard on the ground, dazing himself. Then he let go, and it took me a millisecond to stab him in the throat on the downswing and still have upswing left to slash the next passerby. They were fast. At some point, one of them would be faster than me.

But that point wasn't now.

"Alright, who's next?" I called, yanking my sword out of the newest guy now collapsing to a kneel in front of me.

"I am."

It was a voice deeper than a mass grave. The body that stepped up into my space took up the whole hallway, blocking out the light. His body was rounded with the tell-tale bulges of pretty decent armor. He was so big he couldn't even step all the way into my tiny tunnel.

Pros, no one could run behind him to chase down my people. Cons, once I hit him, I had *that move* to end the fight, because if my blade got stuck in this guy, I was dead.

He raised a pistol. I knocked it out of his hand. He swung a dirk. I backed up, and he couldn't reach me.

"I'm so sorry," I panted as I realized what my one attack was going to be. I'd spent enough time healing horrific injuries at the seams in armor to know this wasn't a nice way to go. "There's still time for you to surrender."

"Funny bitch," he said. "I was just about to tell you the same—"

He was tall. I slid, and went for the worst seam from underneath, showering myself in blood.

I blocked out the details. *Just trying to reach the abdominal aorta through nontraditional means,* I told myself; I fully expected to have nightmares about that one if I survived.

That was the worst one of the bunch. But I'd warned him.

No one was going to touch my medic.

"Is anyone interested in surrendering now?" I shouted, wishing with all my heart they would say yes and knowing full-well they couldn't. It was starting to look like they couldn't beat me on skill, and there wasn't room to beat me with strength.

So my time would run out when I got tired.

And I was starting to get tired.

Ken Kamakura

Sereno didn't leave the evacuation zone right away.

The Sevellan leader returned twice to carry people with Ken, sweating and stinking and groaning—both times for severe cases where a minute would make a difference of life or death. They weren't large people, and he wasn't winded at all.

But as they lifted the second one, Sereno began to talk. "I will send out a general communication when I am gone from here," he panted. "So that my people know I am not here."

"You can't do that," Ken grunted.

"If I do not, they will continue fighting through these halls, and you will all die. Wimmer will die first."

Ken gritted his teeth. He wouldn't think about that. He was obeying her orders. He was trusting her. He was going to save as many people as he could and find a way to get her, too.

"When you're home safe," Ken panted, shaking his head. "Please consider trading the jelly, or the sound-blocking microfiber, or the other technologies you have. With what you already know your biomedical can be way ahead of the Bantai if you just nab a few laboratories. You don't have to take people hostage to feed your people and you don't need the mines. You are brave, you are creative, and all of you would do almost anything for the rest of you—the galaxy needs that. The galaxy needs the story of free Sevellans—all of them, both guards." He wheezed. Too many words. They were almost there. Almost halfway.

"Our people have truly painted you," Sereno smiled.

"Yeah, yeah you have," Ken admitted. "And that's why it sucks so much to be enemy number one now."

"I cannot help you with that."

"I know. I wish I'd known that going into this."

Sereno huffed harder as he stepped over someone's leg. "Would it have changed what you did?"

"No. But I would've felt a lot better if I could've expected the surprise."

Sereno said nothing for a few paces. His brow furrowed. "If I had known my people would turn on me anyway, I would perhaps have acted differently. Perhaps trusted you with direct orders. Defended you." He set his jaw, chest stiff. "At the very least, like I said, killing you no longer suits my purposes," he said. "And even if it did… I don't know if I could."

"I don't believe that for a second," Ken shook his head; Sereno laughed.

"When you arrived, you moved your head like an alien," he breathed. "Now you move like a brother. We are brothers, now, you know." Ken was focused on not tripping and couldn't see the Sevellan's face, but his voice was somber. Real. "Please do not hate me, Kenta Kamakura. I have done what I believed I must do."

"I only hate you for not thanking that Yadan medic," Ken grunted. "Everything else I forgive."

"I could not," Sereno said. "I still don't understand why he would—" Sereno interrupted himself with a wheeze. "I would not have."

"No, you wouldn't," Ken heaved. They'd reached the light at the end of the tunnel; he blinked as they stepped through it, and out into the smoke-swept wind. "One, two, three, lower." They laid the patient onto the mechanical stretcher and strapped her in; the huge, almost building-size medical helo far in the sky began to suck her up towards it. Sereno hopped up onto another stretcher, standing astride it like a pirate on the rigging of an old sea-ship, gripping the rope with one hand and waving Juda's radio with the other.

With Ken's last look back, he saw the Sevellan leader flash him a black-toothed grin.

Jocelyn Wimmer

I was getting tired. And Yako hadn't shown up yet. I thought about opening a channel to Howard to ask if he'd abandoned the young leader on purpose, selling out his own people for the "greater good" of eliminating Sereno—I thought about it like a distant dream in the back of my head, like a flashback to an alternate universe, because in the real world, right now, I was thinking about killing the guy in front of me, and the guy in front of him. He was a windmill, and I was swinging at him. For what, I almost didn't know anymore. For Skinner. For Kamakura. For the giant lilac eyes and the planet of pink sand.

I needed medical care. I was bleeding from cuts all across my arms and legs. The guys who'd made them didn't need medical care—dead men don't use bandages. They'd formed another pile in front of my tunnel, and now I heard their comrades backing up to try to blast through the bodies again. I knew they kept hoping they'd cause a cave in where I was, but it hadn't happened the last two times, so. Either insanity was doing the same thing over and over again and expecting different results, or if at first you didn't succeed, you should try try again. *We'll find out now, I guess.*

And unfortunately, my first day clean had to come to an end. I was getting too dizzy to focus and I needed any advantage I could get. Because it was the end.

I pulled the envelope out of my sleeve and emptied the last pills into my throat. "Kinda hoped I'd die without that shit in my system," I remarked. "Oh well."

The explosion went off. This time, there was a cave-in.

And this time, it got me.

I dove forward out of my tiny side-tunnel, back towards where the medics had gone. Rubble showered around me. A violent pain smashed between my shoulders, and suddenly my leg didn't hurt anymore.

"Ooh, you guys fucked up," I grinned.

They'd made the main tunnel narrower. And now the only way through was *literally* through me. Where before they could line up one after the other after the other, wearing me down with sheer numbers, now they had to crawl and squeeze far apart from each other, one—by one—and then after a while the other one—only to eventually reach my blade. I was still utterly necessary. Without me there, twenty soldiers would have passed after the explosion.

But now I literally didn't have a choice *but* to be there, because I couldn't move my lower body, and that was actually kind of nice. It was very simple, suddenly: keep my head below the big pile of dirt in front of me, and then swing faster than the other guy could when he arrived.

I'd always liked fighting. It was one of the only places I was actually allowed to be angry.

But as the last enemy hit the dirt, and the hallway grew quiet, I wished I could have had a chance to actually overcome the demons that I was dying with.

Ken Kamakura

The Sevellans didn't find the evacuation zone. The Bantai did.

When the Bantai arrived, they arrived with Yako's forces hot on their heels and the area under the evac zone became a full-on traditional battlefield. There were no more fancy plasma rounds —it was all standard needles and slugs, zipping through the air as Eden Crescent struggled with her own soul. Explosions threw colorful earth shooting into the trees, showering rainbows laced with blood across the obelisks.

And even as Yadan soldiers from the battlefield *finally* rushed down into the tunnel to help Wimmer defend the wounded, Ken was still trying to get dying people into the helo.

The helo itself was too high for anyone to reach with the standard armaments they had, but everyone trying to reach its dangling threads was fair game. Ken now found himself dragging people alone, dropping them to return fire, dragging them further—trying to remember things like maintaining c-spine became almost impossible next to the need to remember how to stop the next person from shooting at him. *Get this person to the threads. Get back into the tunnel. Get this person down the tunnel. Get them to the threads.*

He was wheezing. It was too long. It was too many. He couldn't do it. He couldn't do it, and his friend was going to die for nothing. He wasn't good enough. He was the star medic, and he wasn't good enough. No one was.

He collapsed to his knees at the entrance to the tunnel.

"I'm so tired. I didn't know I was so tired," he wheezed. His knees were burning. His throat was burning. Why? When had that happened?

"There is grace sufficient for you," Sibila whispered in his ear, wiping sweat from his brow as soldiers dashed past them.

"What does that mean?" he croaked.

"I don't know. It is just in my spirit right now." She gripped his face. Tears were running down hers. "We will find out together. Do not lose heart."

And so he got up. Again.

And again.

And again.

Through the smoke. And the screams. And the waning sunset.

And eventually, it was over.

There were still cries and shouts. Scattered shots here and there. People on the battlefield still needed medical transport. But Ken couldn't be expected to clean up the entire world for these people before returning to his friend. That hadn't been the order. It'd been "go make sure the evacuees get where they need to go," and he'd done that.

Ken saw Yako approaching from outside the tunnel, but he didn't have time for world leaders right now. He had one more patient to get. He stumbled around the corner, weapon ready. Where had all the soldiers gone?

"Oh no," Ken breathed.

The doctor looked so old and thin when he found her bleeding in the dirt. She lay on her side, eyes closed and bloody scratches criss-crossing every extremity. Her leg twisted underneath her backwards, and her spine was split open like an overripe gnu-mato, oozing clear fluid down her back.

"Where are the Yadans?" Ken cried out, rushing forward. Her Scrit raised its back and yowled as he approached—it'd never done that before. "Why didn't they move you?"

"I told them not to," she grunted. "I'm good."

He stepped over her to loop an arm through hers and another through her leg for the fireman carry—keep that exposed spinal cord out of the dirt—

"Will you fucking let me not spend my last minutes getting

dragged like luggage, please?" she snapped. "I'm good. I said I'm good! Do you not see this cerebrospinal fluid leaking all over here? What, you gonna become a neurosurgeon all of a sudden? Sit the fuck down." She heaved—her tirade drained the color out of her exhausted face like someone turned off the power. "Hot damn, you have the obsessive compulsivity of an autistic hedgehog," she breathed, a gentle, weathered hand on the side of Ken's face.

He clenched his teeth. It wasn't post-adrenaline shakes he was fighting back this time. "Why the hell did you come with me?" he asked.

"Because I know you," she smiled. "You were going to come here all starry-eyed and get yourself killed. No point in arguing with you. Better to protect you."

"We worked together for less than three months before this!" Ken cried. "What do you mean you know me?"

She snorted. "Kid. 'Course I know you. You're me. You think an old gal can't recognize a mirror when she sees one?" She gazed off into the distance. "There wasn't a lot of electricity in my neighborhood growing up—too close to—well. When I was a kid, we used to play an old haunted house board game. You could sometimes draw a card that let your future self pass an item to you across a mirror. I always thought, damn, I wish my future self would do that. Most'a my mentors were always so bent on changing what they saw instead of just passing on something useful. So. Here."

She placed something in his palm, and closed his fingers around it. "Oh. Don't do drugs, by the way," she said wryly.

"I'll stick to caffeine," he quipped hoarsely, clenching the gift. It was the weakest grin—an attempt at a joke, at teasing. His face was wet. He sniffed, and coughed. Her gray eyes flickered, watching his, like she was falling asleep. *Please don't.* "I followed your orders, ma'am, and now I'm really mad at you," he said.

"You don't sound mad," she said. "How many did you save?"

He choked. "I don't know."

"At least twenty, right?"

He shook his head. "More."

"Yeah, see? I don't give shit orders," she smiled. "It's math, Kamakura."

"You said you were going to be fine. Liar."

"Yeah, the first thing you need to know about addicts is that addicts lie," she smiled. "I just had some wind turbines to take care of."

"Fuck wind turbines."

"Yeah, I always liked solar better anyway." She closed her eyes, and breathed. "Fuck wind turbines."

It was never completely quiet downrange on Eden Crescent, but Ken—against all of his instincts to fight anyway—was quiet.

As the sun set, he sat hand in hand with Sibila on the hillside at the entrance to the tunnel. Yako rode over on a hoverbike and stopped, floating in front of him.

"You've performed like a true hero young man," he said. "I'm sorry for your loss."

Ken didn't know what to answer; the Yadan was mercifully quick and to the point. "I've heard there's another foreign space-vehicle inbound to Welcome Village in two days. Do you want to catch it, or do you want a mercenary contract?"

"What about him?" Ken asked, nodded to the Sevellans in the distance. He could see Sereno surrounded by his warriors against the setting sun, his stance as controlled and poised as ever—they'd turned the tide of battle when they arrived. The six hours he'd promised would be up soon.

"We're in talks," Yako said. "He kept his word, and I mean to keep mine. I don't know how to manage relocation. But I'm sure he has some ideas. I won't show him my back, though." Yako looked off at the young leader, and back to Ken. "I'll ensure any contact takes into account conflicts of interest. You'd be a medic first and foremost. No combat against Sevella."

Sibila leaned her head against Ken's shoulder. Her forehead just barely nuzzled his chin. "Can we live in my father's house?" she asked.

Ken looked up at Yako. "Instead of paying in credits or dollars," he said.

"No one will want the amphitheater there anymore anyway," Yako nodded. "We'll talk."

With that, he rode off. Ken sighed. His chest hurt. He breathed into his belly, letting his eyes run.

"Will you be alright?" Sibila asked.

"I'll be alright," Ken said. "But first I need to clean my weapon."

The End

ABOUT THE AUTHOR

Jen Finelli is a world-traveling scifi author who's ridden a motorcycle in a monsoon, swum with sharks, crawled under barbed wire in the mud, interviewed everyone from prostitutes to senators, and hiked everywhere from hidden coral deserts and island mountains to steaming underground urban tunnels littered with poetry. In the military, Jen treated sexual assault survivors and found her way through swamp-filled Korean foothills dotted with graveyards on Friday the 13th under a full moon without a flashlight. She now uses fiction to fund her work bringing meds to indigenous communities in the jungles of South America. You're welcome to download some of her stories at byjenfinelli.-com/you-want-heroes-and-fairies, or join her quest to uncover real heroes and villains at becominghero.byjenfinelli.com. Jen's a practicing MD with a fellowship of advanced wilderness medicine—but when she grows up, she wants to be a superhero.

MORE FROM CANNON PUBLISHING

JOIN THE CREW!

Stay up to date! Sign up for our newsletter at https://www.cannonpublishing.us/_for the latest updates on new releases and more.

Follow our authors at their Amazon Pages!

J.F. Holmes
Shane Gries (Dragon Award Finalist)
Lucas Marcum
Al Hagan

James Copley
Jason Kyle
G. Scott Huggins
Michael Morton
Jon LaForce
Jason Weiser
Kal Spriggs
Brian Gifford
Charli Cox
Dan Kemp
Jonathan Shuerger
J.R. Wise
Steven Vickers
David Hensley
M.L. McIntosh

Great Series from Cannon Publishing

The Fae Wars

An ancient enemy invades Earth, returning to claim their home world. The men and women of the US Military find themselves matching technology against magic as cities burn and armies clash.

Volume One: Onslaught
Volume Two: The Fall
Volume Three: Futures Past
Tales From the Occupation: A Fae Wars Anthology
Volume Five: Insurgent
Volume Six: Ghost
Volume Seven: Northwest Front
Volume Eight: Vendetta
Volume Nine: Relics of Empire
Volume Ten: Harley's War
More Tales From the Occupation

Irregular Scout Team One

In July of 2016 a plague swept the world, and the civilization collapsed and fell. For a lone National Guard sergeant, a veteran of the wars overseas who had settled down to a new life, the nightmare began on a hot summer evening at the barricades. Orders and chaos, gunfire and being overrun, his unit dwindles away in the face of the infected.

Volume 1
Volume 2
Volume 3: Civil War
Volume 4: Bad Company

Volume 5: End of Days

The Line

When the world descends into chaos and anarchy with an unbelievably swift plague, turning victims into ravenous maniacs, the soldiers of America's storied 1st Infantry are asked to hold the line. From the brutal streets of urban combat to the bloodied, desperate defense on the plains of Kansas, they fight a war against an unrelenting enemy who used to be their fellow citizens.

As civilization falls, can they hold the line?

The Thin Dead Line
Dead Storm Rising
The Big Dead One

Fallen Empire

Empires rise, but Empires also fall. The Terran Union has spent five centuries under the control of the alien Grausians, like a barbarian tribe under the thumb of Rome. Now, after almost two decades of civil war and succession struggles, the formerly subject races have settled back in their ancient territories to lick their wounds and re-arm, leaving hundreds of settled planets to exist in a political vacuum. Into that space steps the free companies, mercenary units that fight for gold, honor, power and glory. Veterans who can't get the wars out of their souls, new recruits looking for adventure, corporations with their own agenda. Join us in a 27th Century that echoes history.

The Irish Brigade

Overrun
Silent Violence
Doom Company

Dirty Deeds Trilogy

Sandy Decker had a problem. Well, multiple problems. Some good, some bad. Some pretty bad. The good problem is that she was up a whole bunch of credits and the title to an Azelia class yacht called Vagabond King. That was the good problem. The bad problem was that she was in debt to Daresh An-Jaska, Former Princeps in the Golden Legion, Grausian exile, and the biggest gangster in the sector. Not a money debt but a favor debt, one that she paid principle on doing favors in return. Dirty deeds that never seemed to pay enough, of course. That was until yesterday, when she found a line she couldn't cross.

Vagabonds: A Fallen Empire Novel

Athenaeum, Inc

The Professor has problems, and not just what decades of soldiering did to his back and his knees. His boss just died, leaving him as CEO of the extremely discreet intelligence contractor Athenaeum, Incorporated. His old buddy the Operations Director is a highly skilled Army Ranger veteran but his finance chief is slightly unhinged and spends her money on highly inappropriate work outfits. The surviving old men on the Board of Directors are stuck in the 1970s. Running Athenaeum out of an old Cold War bunker and keeping their roster of experts together is expensive, but the government contracts are drying up or going to bigger, flashier corporate players.

Door Number Three
Doubling Down
Triple Play: The Battle of Cell Tower Hill

Off World

When nuclear war erupts on Earth, the American colony in the Alpha Centauri system is left stranded. As the new day dawns, a furious attack by the native inhabitants threatens to overwhelm the colony's defenses. It's left to the thin red line of the US Army's 9th Regiment to stem the tide and ensure humanity's survival in this harsh new world. From two time Dragon Finalist and author of the best selling series "Irregular Scout Team One" and "Invasion" comes a new tale that tells of the struggle for survival on a brutal planet.

Offworld: Ragnarok
Offworld: Expeditions

Valkyrie

Humanity engages in a desperate struggle with an alien species for this side of the Orion Arm. Space ships die in instantaneous bursts of light and turn into vapor, but on the ground Marines scream and lie wounded in the mud and blood, praying for the Valkyries to come save them. They aren't wishing for death and a Nordic goddess to take them to Valhalla, the wounded are praying for the men and women of the '348th Field Hospital MEDEVAC to dive through fire and hell to come save them. Because they know that ...Valkyries never die!

Valkyrie

Valkyrie: Rebellion
Valkyrie: Attrition

High Caliber Awards

The Cannon High Caliber Awards are an annual contest for new writers. In it we ask them to submit a novella length story of Science Fiction, Military or Fantasy genre to challenge their skills.

2024
2025
2026

The Wishkiller Saga

While on patrol Captain Aethal Paaling discovers evidence that an ancient terror has reached the rich soil of his home: the Lotus, a prolific growth whose addictive leaves devour their victims from within turning their hosts into horrible, terrifyingly violent mockeries of humanity. Created at the dawn of history by the twisted power of a godly relic called the Well, the return of the Lotus may be a harbinger of even more horrors to come.

A Cold and Mortal Spring
War of the Shattered Moon

Hexen

When nine out of ten people in the world have died in a brutal plague, what do those who remain do to pick up the pieces? Does the creed, "Duty, Honor, Country" have a place any more if there's no country left? On his way across the devastated remains of Texas, Marine Corps veteran and survivor Eric Marten rescues a young woman from a vicious attack by men who have turned into savages. As Dani slowly learns to trust him, they try to stay alive in the deathlands that America has become, using all their wits to survive a post-apocalyptic nightmare.

90% Death Rate: A Post Apocalyptic Thriller
Angel of Death: A Post Apocalyptic Thriller
The Bloody Princess: A Post Apocalyptic Thriller
The Devil's Pitchfork
Crescent City Shootout

Hell Train

A single train carries what might be the last vestige of civilization through a hellish nightmare.

A few hundred alive out of millions, lights going out all across what was once America as the possessed arose from the dead and murdered the living. A few hundred survivors travel across the country in an armored train, seeking some place to shelter in a fallen world. All that remains is a dystopian nightmare marked by rains of blood, impossible horrors, and portals to Hell opening in the skies.

Hell Train: All Aboard
Hell Train: Green Line

Invasion

More than a decade after the Confederated Earth Forces were defeated, their commanding general, a boyhood protegee, lives in exile and disgrace. His life on an isolated farm is forever changed when two strangers show up at his homestead, and the war comes crashing back down on him. The problem though, remains the same. How do you fight an enemy that is technologically superior and holds the high ground?

Invasion: Resistance
Invasion: Day of Battle
Invasion: Total War

Into the Darkness

A darkening tide of barbarism was washing across Britain's shores and the lights of civilization were slowly flickering out into darkness, only kept burning by the legendary Red Dragons cavalry unit. Led by their Tribune, Arthur, who serves no kingdom but goes where the fight is hardest and most crucial, they wage desperate battles to keep back the tide. The Red Dragons ride the length of Britannia to fight the invading Saxons, Scoti and Picts, wherever they show, from across the seas or down from the Highlands.

Beyond the Wall
The Wolves of Caledonia

Semper Die

The dead rose expecting a feast. What they got was a firefight.

Sergeant Alex Slaughter and the Marines of Alpha Squad

were on a routine training exercise near Quantico when everything went silent. No comms. No command. No clue.

What they find when they return to base is worse than anything they trained for: a bioweapon has unleashed a zombie virus that has shattered civilization, and now they must survive the Collapse.

Lock. Load. Semper Fi. Semper Die.

Semper Die
Espirit De Corpse

More Books from Cannon Publishing

MORE FROM THE FAE WARS

GET THE FULL SERIES!

What would you do if America and the world were invaded tomorrow by a relentless and brutal enemy?In an alternate 2015, a US Army Special Forces Team, part of the legendary black ops unit "Delta", is in midtown Manhattan to take out a Chinese spy and his handlers, sending a message short of outright conflict. All goes smoothly until they find themselves in a full blown shooting war through the canyons of the City. Portals from another world have opened in Central Park, making a way for figures out of historical nightmare to invade. The Fae, creatures banished from Earth thousands of years ago and now only part of our legends, have returned with Dragon fire, spell and sword to conquer and take revenge.

The first volume of The Fae Wars covers Team Three, G squadron, Special Forces Detachment (Delta) as they fight their way off Manhattan and then join the defense of the refugees as the Fae assault the bridges. The fabled 69th Infantry puts up an epic fight against superior weaponry and then the war descends into the asymmetric hell that the Delta Operators know so well. Along the way they find new allies and old powers that come to their aid.

Authors

John Holmes

J.F. Holmes is a retired Army Senior Noncommissioned Officer, having served for 22 years in both the Regular Army and Army National Guard. During that time, he served as everything from an artillery section leader to a member of a Division level planning staff, with tours in Cuba and Iraq, as well as responding to the terrorists attacks in NYC on 9-11.

From 2010 to 2014 he wrote the immensely popular military cartoon strip, "Power Point Ranger", poking fun at military life in the tradition of Beetle Bailey and Willy & Joe.

His books range from Military Sci-Fi to Space Opera to Detective to Fantasy, with a lot in between, and in 2017 two are finalists for the prestigious Dragon Awards.

In 2018, he launched Cannon Publishing, www.cannonpublishing.us specializing in military science fiction, fantasy and thrillers, with an emphasis on works from up and coming authors.

Lucas Marcum

Lucas Marcum is a critical care nurse practitioner and an officer in the US Army Reserve. When he's not working, or performing his reserve duties, he can be found hiking, reading, attempting to perfect his soft pretzel recipe and spending time with his family.

James Copley

James Copley is a former Non-Commissioned Officer of the U.S. Army, having served over twenty-one years in both Active and Reserve/Guard units, variously trained as Infantry, Communications, and Ordnance specialties before finally retiring from the Army National Guard in 2016. During his service, he deployed four separate times, twice to Iraq and twice to Afghanistan.

He is currently working as a software engineer in Central California with his wife, two children, and two dogs. Reading was his number one passion from a very young age, and more recently he decided to try writing his own. Feel free to join him on his writing journey!

Charli Cox

Charli Cox is a best-selling Military Sci-Fi and Horror Comedy author. She also writes Sci-Fi, Alternate History, and Military Fantasy stories.

If you enjoyed Fae Wars: Northwest Front and want to see more stories about Ash and "Gunny," Cannon Publishing has you covered. Burnt Mountain and Sasquatch will be coming to your Kindle later in 2025. Also, please be sure to leave a review!

Representing #teamandmore, Charli's first published short story is in The Phoenix Initiative: First Missions from Chris Kennedy Publishing. She has stories in Bureau 42 and Express Elevator to Hell, also from CKP.

Look for Whistles of the Wendigo, an Alternate History/Military Fantasy novel set in the Joint Task Force 13 universe from Three Ravens Publishing, due to release soon.

An animal lover and #boymom, she lives in SW Oregon with her Leg husband, two sons, an Arabian mare, and two Husky mixes who think they are hooman.

Learn more about Charli and sign up for her newsletter on her website. Hang out with her on Facebook, Instagram, and/or TikTok.

Jason Weiser

Mr. Weiser has been a government contractor for the last eleven years, and before that, a writer working odd jobs trying to get by. He has a BA in History from CUNY Brooklyn. Mr. Weiser released his first novel in 2025, with Cannon Publishing, but before that, released a short story in their 2018 Spring Military Sci Fi Anthology.

Mr. Weiser is also an avid wargamer and has been published quite a bit in the hobby, having most recently run "Military Miniature" magazine as it's editor in chief from 2021-2023. Before that, he wrote for EpochXperience (a division of SJR Research) as a contributing writer for their blog on wargaming and military history topics from 2020 to 2021.

He also wrote two scenario books on Cold War wargaming topics, "Red Star, Burning Streets" and "Red Star, White Lights".

Mr. Weiser encourages all his fans to visit Cannon Publishing at their website

Brian Gifford

A military veteran with more than 25 years of service in the U.S. Air Force and Army (in an order that would surprise you!), Brian is a lifelong science fiction and fantasy nerd of the highest order. A student of the hard sciences and the arcane arts of cybersecurity and IT alike, Brian has spent a lifetime accumulating his unique view of the world, which he now insists on sharing with everyone else. He is a husband in awe of the magnificence that is his wife and the proud father of three awesome sons, and looks forward to retiring from the military in the near future to focus on his family and his writing.

ML McIntosh

ML McIntosh is a part time rock star, part time vengeful essence of femme wrath. She works the always shift in unapologetic science fiction, dream fiction and urban fantasy. Follow her Instagram @ml_mcintosh and stay weird.

www.ingramcontent.com/pod-product-compliance
Lightning Source LLC
LaVergne TN
LVHW010639110826
845149LV00014B/2892

* 9 7 8 1 9 6 9 3 7 4 2 6 5 *